THE INFERNAL DEVICES

· Book One ·

Clockwork Angel

Also by Cassandra Clare

THE MORTAL INSTRUMENTS:

City of Bones

City of Ashes

City of Glass

THE INFERNAL DEVICES

· Book One ·

Clockwork Angel

CASSANDRA CLARE

Margaret K. McElderry Books
NEW YORK LONDON TORONTO SYDNEY

MARGARET K. McELDERRY BOOKS
An imprint of Simon & Schuster Children's Publishing Division
1230 Avenue of the Americas, New York, New York 10020

Also available in a Margaret K. McElderry Books hardcover edition
Book design by Mike Rosamilia
The text for this book is set in Dolly.
Manufactured in the United States of America
First Margaret K. McElderry Books export edition August 2010
2 4 6 8 10 9 7 5 3 1
Library of Congress Cataloging-in-Publication Data
Clare, Cassandra.
Clockwork angel / Cassandra Clare.—1st ed.
p. cm.—(The infernal devices ; bk. 1)
Summary: When sixteen-year-old orphan Tessa Gray's older brother suddenly vanishes, her search for him leads her into Victorian-era London's dangerous supernatural underworld, and when she discovers that she herself is a Downworlder, she must learn to trust the demon-killing Shadowhunters if she ever wants to learn to control her powers and find her brother.
ISBN 978-1-4169-7586-1 (hardcover)
ISBN 978-1-4424-0946-0 (eBook)
[1. Supernatural—Fiction. 2. Demonology—Fiction. 3. Orphans—Fiction. 4. Secret societies—Fiction. 5. London (England)—History—19th century—Fiction. 6. Great Britain—History—Victoria, 1837–1901—Fiction.] I. Title.
PZ7.C5265Cl 2010
[Fic]—dc22
2010008616
ISBN 978-1-4424-1682-6 (export pbk.)

For Jim and Kate

Thames River Song

A note of salt
slips in and the river rises,
darkening to the color of tea,
swelling to meet the green.
Above its banks the cogs and wheels
of monstrous machines
clank and spin, the ghost within
vanishes into its coils,
whispering mysteries.
Each tiny golden cog has teeth,
each great wheel moves
a pair of hands which take
the water from the river,
devour it, convert it into steam,
coerce the great machine to run
on the force of its dissolution.
Gently, the tide is rising,
corrupting the mechanism.
Salt, rust and silt
slowing the gears.
Down at the banks
the iron tanks
sway into their moorings
with the hollow boom
of a gigantic bell,
of drum and cannon
which cry out in a tongue of thunder
and the river rolls under.

—Elka Cloke

THE INFERNAL DEVICES

· Book One ·

Clockwork Angel

Prologue

London, April 1878.

The demon exploded in a shower of ichor and guts.

William Herondale jerked back the dagger he was holding, but it was too late. The viscous acid of the demon's blood had already begun to eat away at the shining blade. He swore and tossed the weapon aside; it landed in a filthy puddle and commenced smoldering like a doused match. The demon itself, of course, had vanished—dispatched back to whatever hellish world it had come from, though not without leaving a mess behind.

"Jem!" Will called, turning around. "Where are you? Did you see that? Killed it with one blow! Not bad, eh?"

But there was no answer to Will's shout; his hunting partner had been standing behind him in the damp and crooked street a few moments before, guarding his back, Will was positive, but now Will was alone in the shadows. He frowned in annoyance—it was much less fun showing off without Jem to show off *to*. He glanced behind him, to where the street narrowed into a passage that gave onto the black, heaving water of the Thames in the distance. Through the gap Will could see the dark outlines of docked ships, a forest of masts like a leafless orchard. No Jem there; perhaps he had gone back to Narrow Street in search of better illumination. With a shrug Will headed back the way he had come.

Narrow Street cut across Limehouse, between the docks beside the river and the cramped slums spreading west toward Whitechapel. It was as narrow as its name suggested, lined with warehouses and lopsided wooden buildings. At the moment it was deserted; even the drunks staggering home from the Grapes up the road had found somewhere to collapse for the night. Will liked Limehouse, liked the feeling of being on the edge of the world, where ships left each day for unimaginably far ports. That the area was a sailor's haunt, and consequently full of gambling hells, opium dens, and brothels, didn't hurt either. It was easy to lose yourself in a place like this. He didn't even mind the smell of it—smoke and rope and tar, foreign spices mixed with the dirty riverwater smell of the Thames.

Looking up and down the empty street, he scrubbed the sleeve of his coat across his face, trying to rub away the ichor that stung and burned his skin. The cloth came away stained green and black. There was a cut on the back of his hand too, a nasty one. He could use a healing rune. One of Charlotte's, preferably. She was particularly good at drawing *iratzes*.

A shape detached itself from the shadows and moved toward Will. He started forward, then paused. It wasn't Jem, but rather a mundane policeman wearing a bell-shaped helmet, a heavy overcoat, and a puzzled expression. He stared at Will, or rather *through* Will. However accustomed Will had become to glamour, it was always strange to be looked through as if he weren't there. Will was seized with the sudden urge to grab the policeman's truncheon and watch while the man flapped around, trying to figure out where it had gone; but Jem had scolded him the few times he'd done that before, and while Will never really could understand Jem's objections to the whole enterprise, it wasn't worth making him upset.

With a shrug and a blink, the policeman moved past Will, shaking his head and muttering something under his breath about swearing off the gin before he truly started seeing things. Will stepped aside to let the man pass, then raised his voice to a shout: "James Carstairs! Jem! Where *are* you, you disloyal bastard?"

This time a faint reply answered him. "Over here. Follow the witchlight."

Will moved toward the sound of Jem's voice. It seemed to be coming from a dark opening between two warehouses; a faint gleam was visible within the shadows, like the darting light of a will-o'-the-wisp. "Did you hear me before? That Shax demon thought it could get me with its bloody great pincers, but I cornered it in an alley—"

"Yes, I heard you." The young man who appeared at the mouth of the alley was pale in the lamplight—paler even than he usually was, which was quite pale indeed. He was bareheaded, which drew the eye immediately to his hair. It was an odd bright silver color, like an untarnished shilling. His eyes were the same silver, and his fine-boned face was angular, the slight curve of his eyes the only clue to his heritage.

There were dark stains across his white shirtfront, and his hands were thickly smeared with red.

Will tensed. "You're bleeding. What happened?"

Jem waved away Will's concern. "It's not my blood." He turned his head back toward the alley behind him. "It's hers."

Will glanced past his friend, into the thicker shadows of the alley. In the far corner of it was a crumpled shape—only a shadow in the darkness, but when Will looked closely, he could make out the shape of a pale hand, and a wisp of fair hair.

"A dead woman?" Will asked. "A mundane?"

"A girl, really. Not more than fourteen."

At that, Will cursed with great volume and expression. Jem waited patiently for him to be done.

"If we'd only happened along a little earlier," Will said finally. "That bloody demon —"

"That's the peculiar thing. I don't think this is the demon's work." Jem frowned. "Shax demons are parasites, brood parasites. It would have wanted to drag its victim back to its lair to lay eggs in her skin while she was still alive. But this girl—she was stabbed, repeatedly. And I don't think it was here, either. There simply isn't enough blood in the alley. I think she was attacked elsewhere, and she dragged herself here to die of her injuries."

"But the Shax demon—"

"I'm telling you, I don't think it *was* the Shax. I think the Shax was pursuing her—hunting her down for something, or someone, else."

"Shaxes have a keen sense of scent," Will allowed. "I've heard of warlocks using them to follow the tracks of the missing. And it did seem to be moving with an odd sort of purpose." He looked past Jem, at the pitiful smallness of the crumpled shape in the alley. "You didn't find the weapon, did you?"

"Here." Jem drew something from inside his jacket—a knife, wrapped in white cloth. "It's a sort of misericord, or hunting dagger. Look how thin the blade is."

Will took it. The blade was indeed thin, ending in a handle made of polished bone. The blade and hilt both were stained with dried blood. With a frown he wiped the flat of the knife across the rough fabric of his sleeve, scraping it clean until a symbol, burned into the blade, became visible. Two serpents, each biting the other's tail, forming a perfect circle.

"Ouroboros," Jem said, leaning in close to stare at the knife. "A double one. Now, what do you think that means?"

"The end of the world," said Will, still looking at the dagger, a small smile playing about his mouth, "and the beginning."

Jem frowned. "I understand the symbology, William. I meant, what do you think its presence on the dagger signifies?"

The wind off the river was ruffling Will's hair; he brushed it out of his eyes with an impatient gesture and went back to studying the knife. "It's an alchemical symbol, not a warlock or Downworlder one. That usually means humans—the foolish mundane sort who think trafficking in magic is the ticket for gaining wealth and fame."

"The sort who usually end up a pile of bloody rags inside some pentagram." Jem sounded grim.

"The sort who like to lurk about the Downworld parts of our fair city." After wrapping the handkerchief around the blade carefully, Will slipped it into his jacket pocket. "D'you think Charlotte will let me handle the investigation?"

"Do *you* think you can be trusted in Downworld? The gambling hells, the dens of magical vice, the women of loose morals . . ."

Will smiled the way Lucifer might have smiled, moments before he fell from Heaven. "Would tomorrow be too early to start looking, do you think?"

Jem sighed. "Do what you like, William. You always do."

Southampton, May.

Tessa could not remember a time when she had not loved the clockwork angel. It had belonged to her mother once, and her mother had been wearing it when she died. After that it had sat in her mother's jewelry box, until her brother, Nathaniel, took it out one day to see if it was still in working order.

The angel was no bigger than Tessa's pinky finger, a tiny statuette made of brass, with folded bronze wings no larger than a cricket's. It had a delicate metal face with shut crescent eyelids, and hands crossed over a sword in front. A thin chain that looped beneath the wings allowed the angel to be worn around the neck like a locket.

Tessa knew the angel was made out of clockwork because if she lifted it to her ear she could hear the sound of its machinery, like the sound of a watch. Nate had exclaimed in surprise that it was still working after so many years, and he had looked in vain for a knob or a screw, or some other method by which the angel might be wound. But there had been nothing to find. With a shrug he'd given the angel to Tessa. From that moment she had never taken it off; even at night the angel lay against her chest as she slept, its constant *ticktock, ticktock* like the beating of a second heart.

She held it now, clutched between her fingers, as the *Main* nosed its way between other massive steamships to find a spot at the Southampton dock. Nate had insisted that she come to Southampton instead of Liverpool, where most transatlantic steamers arrived. He had claimed it was because Southampton was a much pleasanter place to arrive at, so Tessa couldn't help being a little disappointed by this, her first sight of England. It was drearily gray. Rain drummed down onto the spires of a distant church, while black smoke rose from the chimneys of ships and stained the already dull-colored sky. A crowd of people in dark clothes, holding umbrellas, stood on the docks. Tessa strained to see if her brother was among them, but the mist and spray from the ship were too thick for her to make out any individual in great detail.

Tessa shivered. The wind off the sea was chilly. All of Nate's letters had claimed that London was beautiful, the sun shining every day. Well, Tessa thought, hopefully the weather there was better than it was here, because she had no warm clothes with her, nothing more substantial than a woolen shawl that had belonged to Aunt Harriet, and a pair of thin gloves. She had sold most of her clothes to pay for her aunt's funeral, secure in the knowledge that her brother would buy her more when she arrived in London to live with him.

A shout went up. The *Main*, its shining black-painted hull gleaming wet with rain, had anchored, and tugs were plowing their way through the heaving gray water, ready to carry baggage and passengers to the shore. Passengers streamed off the ship, clearly desperate to feel land under their feet. So different from their departure from New York. The sky had been blue then, and a brass band had been playing. Though, with no one there to wish her good-bye, it had not been a merry occasion.

Hunching her shoulders, Tessa joined the disembarking crowd. Drops of rain stung her unprotected head and neck like pinpricks from icy little needles, and her hands, inside their insubstantial gloves, were clammy and wet with rain. Reaching the quay, she looked around eagerly, searching for a sight of Nate. It had been nearly two weeks since she'd spoken to a soul, having kept almost entirely to herself on board the *Main*. It would be wonderful to have her brother to talk to again.

He wasn't there. The wharves were heaped with stacks of luggage and all sorts of boxes and cargo, even mounds of fruit and vegetables wilting and dissolving in the rain. A steamer was departing for Le Havre nearby, and damp-looking sailors swarmed close by Tessa, shouting in French. She tried to move aside, only to be almost trampled by a throng of disembarking passengers hurrying for the shelter of the railway station.

But Nate was nowhere to be seen.

"You are Miss Gray?" The voice was guttural, heavily accented. A man had moved to stand in front of Tessa. He was tall, and was wearing a sweeping black coat and a tall hat, its brim collecting rainwater like a cistern. His eyes were peculiarly bulging, almost protuberant, like a frog's, his skin as rough-looking as scar tissue. Tessa had to fight the urge to cringe away from him. But he knew her name. Who here would know her name except someone who knew Nate, too?

"Yes?"

"Your brother sent me. Come with me."

"Where is he?" Tessa demanded, but the man was already walking away. His stride was uneven, as if he had a limp from an old injury. After a moment Tessa gathered up her skirts and hurried after him.

He wound through the crowd, moving ahead with purposeful speed. People jumped aside, muttering about his rudeness as he shouldered past, with Tessa nearly running to keep up. He turned abruptly around a pile of boxes, and came to a halt in front of a large, gleaming black coach. Gold letters had been painted across its side, but the rain and mist were too thick for Tessa to read them clearly.

The door of the carriage opened and a woman leaned out. She wore an enormous plumed hat that hid her face. "Miss Theresa Gray?"

Tessa nodded. The bulging-eyed man hurried to help the woman out of the carriage—and then another woman, following after her. Each of them immediately opened an umbrella and raised it, sheltering themselves from the rain. Then they fixed their eyes on Tessa.

They were an odd pair, the women. One was very tall and thin, with a bony, pinched face. Colorless hair was scraped back into a chignon at the back of her head. She wore a dress of brilliant violet silk, already spattered here and there with splotches of rain, and matching violet gloves. The other woman was short and plump, with small eyes sunk deep into her head; the bright pink gloves stretched over her large hands made them look like colorful paws.

"Theresa Gray," said the shorter of the two. "What a delight to make your acquaintance at last. I am Mrs. Black, and this is my sister, Mrs. Dark. Your brother sent us to accompany you to London."

Tessa—damp, cold, and baffled—clutched her wet shawl tighter around herself. "I don't understand. Where's Nate? Why didn't he come himself?"

"He was unavoidably detained by business in London. Mortmain's couldn't spare him. He sent ahead a note for you, however." Mrs. Black held out a rolled-up bit of paper, already dampened with rain.

Tessa took it and turned away to read it. It was a short note from her brother apologizing for not being at the docks to meet her, and letting her know that he trusted Mrs. Black and Mrs. Dark—*I call them the Dark Sisters, Tessie, for obvious reasons, and they seem to find the name agreeable!*—to bring her safely to his house in London. They were, his note said, his landladies as well as trusted friends, and they had his highest recommendation.

That decided her. The letter was certainly from Nate. It was in his handwriting, and no one else ever called her Tessie. She swallowed hard and slipped the note into her sleeve, turning back to face the sisters. "Very well," she said, fighting down her lingering sense of disappointment—she had been so looking forward to seeing her brother. "Shall we call a porter to fetch my trunk?"

"No need, no need." Mrs. Dark's cheerful tone was at odds with her pinched gray features. "We've already arranged to have it sent on ahead." She snapped her fingers at the bulging-eyed man, who swung himself up into the driver's seat at the front of the carriage. She placed her hand on Tessa's shoulder. "Come along, child; let's get you out of the rain."

As Tessa moved toward the carriage, propelled by Mrs.

Dark's bony grip, the mist cleared, revealing the gleaming golden image painted on the side of the door. The words "The Pandemonium Club" curled intricately around two snakes biting each other's tails, forming a circle. Tessa frowned. "What does that mean?"

"Nothing you need worry about," said Mrs. Black, who had already climbed inside and had her skirts spread out across one of the comfortable-looking seats. The inside of the carriage was richly decorated with plush purple velvet bench seats facing each other, and gold tasseled curtains hanging in the windows.

Mrs. Dark helped Tessa up into the carriage, then clambered in behind her. As Tessa settled herself on the bench seat, Mrs. Black reached to shut the carriage door behind her sister, closing out the gray sky. When she smiled, her teeth gleamed in the dimness as if they were made out of metal. "Do settle in, Theresa. We've a long ride ahead of us."

Tessa put a hand to the clockwork angel at her throat, taking comfort in its steady ticking, as the carriage lurched forward into the rain.

SIX WEEKS LATER

1

The Dark House

Beyond this place of wrath and tears
Looms but the Horror of the shade
—William Ernest Henley, "Invictus"

"The Sisters would like to see you in their chambers, Miss Gray."

Tessa set the book she had been reading down on the bedside table, and turned to see Miranda standing in the doorway of her small room—just as she did at this time every day, delivering the same message she delivered every day. In a moment Tessa would ask her to wait in the corridor, and Miranda would leave the room. Ten minutes later she'd return and say the same thing again. If Tessa didn't come obediently after a few of these attempts, Miranda would seize her and drag her, kicking and screaming, down the stairs to the hot, stinking room where the Dark Sisters waited.

It had happened every day of the first week that Tessa had been in the Dark House, as she had come to call the place they kept her prisoner, until eventually Tessa had realized that the screaming and kicking didn't do much good and simply wasted her energy. Energy that was probably better saved for other things.

"One moment, Miranda," Tessa said. The maid bobbed an awkward curtsy and went out of the room, shutting the door behind her.

Tessa rose to her feet, glancing around the small room that had been her prison cell for six weeks. It was small, with flowered wallpaper, and sparsely furnished—a plain deal table with a white lace cloth over it where she ate her meals; the narrow brass bed where she slept; the cracked washstand and porcelain jug for her ablutions; the windowsill where she stacked her books, and the small chair where she sat each night and wrote letters to her brother—letters she knew she could never send, letters she kept hidden under her mattress where the Dark Sisters would not find them. It was her way of keeping a diary and of assuring herself, somehow, that she would see Nate again someday and be able to give them to him.

She crossed the room to the mirror that hung against the far wall, and smoothed down her hair. The Dark Sisters, as they in fact seemed to wish to be called, preferred her not to look messy, although they didn't appear to mind her appearance one way or the other past that—which was fortunate, because her reflection made her wince. There was the pale oval of her face dominated by hollow gray eyes—a shadowed face without color in its cheeks or hope in its expression. She wore the unflattering black schoolmarmish dress that the Sisters had given her once she'd arrived; her trunk had never followed her, despite their promises, and this was now the only piece of clothing she owned. She looked away quickly.

She hadn't always flinched from her reflection. Nate, with his fair good looks, was the one in the family generally agreed to have inherited her mother's beauty, but Tessa had always been perfectly content with her own smooth brown hair and steady gray eyes. Jane Eyre had had brown hair, and plenty of other heroines besides. And it wasn't so bad being tall, either—taller than most of the boys her own age, it was true, but Aunt Harriet had always said that as long as a tall woman carried herself well, she would forever look regal.

She didn't look regal now, though. She looked pinched and bedraggled and altogether like a frightened scarecrow. She wondered if Nate would even recognize her if he saw her today.

At that thought her heart seemed to shrink inside her chest. *Nate.* He was the one she was doing all this for, but sometimes she missed him so much it felt like she'd swallowed broken glass. Without him, she was completely alone in the world. There was no one at all for her. No one in the world who cared whether she lived or died. Sometimes the horror of that thought threatened to overwhelm her and plunge her down into a bottomless darkness from which there would be no return. If no one in the entire world cared about you, did you really exist at all?

The click of the lock cut her thoughts off abruptly. The door opened; Miranda stood on the threshold.

"It is time to come with me now," she said. "Mrs. Black and Mrs. Dark are waiting."

Tessa looked at her in distaste. She couldn't guess how old

Miranda was. Nineteen? Twenty-five? There was something ageless about her smooth round face. Her hair was the color of ditch water, pulled back harshly behind her ears. Exactly like the Dark Sisters' coachman, she had eyes that protruded like a frog's and made her look like she was permanently surprised. Tessa thought they must be related.

As they went downstairs together, Miranda marching along with her graceless, clipped gait, Tessa raised her hand to touch the chain around her throat where the clockwork angel hung. It was habit—something she did each time she was forced to see the Dark Sisters. Somehow the feel of the pendant around her neck reassured her. She kept hold of it as they passed landing after landing. There were several levels of corridors to the Dark House, though Tessa had seen nothing of it but the Dark Sisters' chambers, the halls and stairs, and her own room. Finally they reached the shadowed cellar. It was dank down here, the walls clammy with unpleasant moisture, though apparently the Sisters didn't mind. Their office was ahead, through a set of wide double doors. A narrow corridor led away in the other direction, vanishing into darkness; Tessa had no idea what lay down that hallway, but something about the thickness of the shadows made her glad she had never found out.

The doors to the Sisters' office were open. Miranda didn't hesitate, but clomped inside, Tessa following after her with great reluctance. She hated this room more than any other place on earth.

To begin with, it was always hot and wet inside, like a swamp, even when the skies outside were gray and rainy. The walls seemed to seep moisture, and the upholstery on the seats and sofas was always blooming with mold. It smelled strange as well, like the banks of the Hudson on a hot day: water and garbage and silt.

The Sisters were already there, as they always were, seated behind their enormous raised desk. They were their usual colorful selves, Mrs. Black in a dress of vibrant salmon pink and Mrs. Dark in a gown of peacock blue. Above the brilliantly colored satins, their faces were like deflated gray balloons. They both wore gloves despite how hot the room was.

"Leave us now, Miranda," said Mrs. Black, who was spinning the heavy brass globe they kept on the desk with one plump, white-gloved finger. Tessa had many times tried to get a better look at the globe—something about the way the continents were laid out had never looked quite right to her, especially the space in the center of Europe—but the sisters always kept her away from it. "And shut the door behind you."

Expressionless, Miranda did as asked. Tessa tried not to wince as the door shut behind her, closing off what little breeze there was in this airless place.

Mrs. Dark tilted her head to the side. "Come here, Theresa." Of the two women, she was the more kind—more likely to wheedle and persuade than her sister, who liked to convince with slaps and hissed threats. "And take this."

She held something out: a dilapidated bit of pink fabric tied in a bow, the sort that might be used as a girl's hair ribbon.

She was used to being handed things by the Dark Sisters now. Things that had once belonged to people: tie pins and watches, mourning jewelry, and children's toys. Once the laces of a boot; once a single earring, stained with blood.

"Take this," said Mrs. Dark again, a hint of impatience in her voice. "And Change."

Tessa took the bow. It lay in her hand, as light as a moth's wing, and the Dark Sisters stared impassively at her. She remembered books she had read, novels in which characters were on trial, standing quaking in the dock at the Old Bailey and praying for a verdict of not guilty. She often felt she was on trial herself in this room, without knowing of what crime she stood accused.

She turned the bow over in her hand, remembering the first time the Dark Sisters had handed an object to her—a woman's glove, with pearl buttons at the wrist. They had shouted at her to Change, had slapped her and shaken her as she'd told them over and over again with rising hysteria that she had no idea what they were talking about, no idea what they were asking her to do.

She hadn't cried, even though she'd wanted to. Tessa hated to cry, especially in front of people she didn't trust. And of the only two people in the world she trusted, one was dead and the other imprisoned. They had told her that, the Dark Sisters, had told her that they had Nate, and if she didn't do what they said, he would die. They'd showed her his ring, the one that had been her father's—stained with blood now—to prove it. They hadn't let her hold it or touch it, had snatched it back as she'd reached for it, but she'd recognized it. It was Nate's.

After that she had done everything they'd asked. Had drunk the potions they'd given her, done the hours of agonizing exercises, forced herself to think the way they wanted her to. They'd told her to imagine herself as clay, being shaped and molded on the potter's wheel, her form amorphous and changeable. They'd told her to reach down into the objects they'd given her, to imagine them as living things, and to draw out the spirit that animated them.

It had taken weeks, and the first time she had Changed, it had been so blindingly painful that she'd vomited and passed out. When she'd woken, she'd been lying on one of the moldering chaises in the Dark Sisters' rooms, a damp towel being sponged across her face. Mrs. Black had been leaning down over her, her breath as bitter as vinegar, her eyes alight. "You did well today, Theresa," she had said. "Very well."

That evening when Tessa had gone up to her room, there had been gifts for her, two new books on her bedside table. Somehow the Dark Sisters had realized that reading and novels were Tessa's passion. There was a copy of *Great Expectations* and—of all things—*Little Women.* Tessa had hugged the books to herself and, alone and unwatched in her room, had let herself cry.

It had grown easier since then, the Changing. Tessa still didn't understand what happened inside her to make it possible, but she had memorized the series of steps the Dark Sisters had taught her, the way a blind person might memorize the number of paces it takes to walk from their bed to the door of their room. She didn't know what was around her in the strange dark place they asked her to journey to, but she knew the pathway through it.

She drew on those memories now, tightening her grip on the ragged bit of pink fabric she held. She opened her mind and let the darkness come down, let the connection that bound her to the hair ribbon and the spirit inside it—the ghostly echo of the person who had once owned it—unravel like a golden thread leading through the shadows. The room she was in, the oppressive heat, the noisy breathing of the Dark Sisters, all of it fell away as she followed the thread, as the light grew more intense around her and she wrapped herself in it as if she were wrapping herself in a blanket.

Her skin began to tingle and to sting with thousands of tiny shocks. This had been the worst part, once—the part that had convinced her she was dying. Now she was used to it, and bore it stoically as she shuddered all over, from her scalp to her toes. The clockwork angel around her throat seemed to tick faster, as if in rhythm with her speeding heart. The pressure inside her skin built—Tessa gasped—and her eyes, which had been closed, flew open as the sensation built to a crescendo—and then vanished.

It was over.

Tessa blinked dizzily. The first moment after a Change was always like blinking water out of your eyes after submerging yourself in a bath. She looked down at herself. Her new body was slight, almost frail, and the fabric of her dress hung loose, pooling on the floor at her feet. Her hands, clasped in front of her, were pale and thin, with chapped tips and bitten nails. Unfamiliar, alien hands.

"What is your name?" Mrs. Black demanded. She had risen to her feet and was looking down at Tessa with her pale eyes burning. She looked almost hungry.

Tessa didn't have to answer. The girl whose skin she wore answered for her, speaking through her the way spirits were said to speak through their mediums—but Tessa hated to think about it that way; the Change was so much more intimate, so much more frightening, than that. "Emma," the voice that came from Tessa said. "Miss Emma Bayliss, ma'am."

"And who are you, Emma Bayliss?"

The voice replied, words tumbling out of Tessa's mouth,

bringing strong images with them. Born in Cheapside, Emma had been one of six children. Her father was dead, and her mother sold peppermint water from a cart in the East End. Emma had learned to sew to bring in money when she was still a small child. Nights, she spent sitting at the little table in her kitchen, sewing seams by the light of a tallow candle. Sometimes, when the candle burned down and there was no money for another, she would go out into the streets and sit below one of the municipal gas lamps, using its light to sew by. . . .

"Is that what you were doing out on the street the night you died, Emma Bayliss?" asked Mrs. Dark. She was smiling thinly now, running her tongue over her lower lip, as if she could sense what the answer would be.

Tessa saw narrow, shadowy streets, wrapped in thick fog, a silver needle working by faint yellow gaslight. A step, muffled in the fog. Hands that reached out of the shadows and took hold of her shoulders, hands that dragged her, screaming, into the darkness. The needle and thread falling from her hands, the bows ripped from her hair as she struggled. A harsh voice shouting something angry. And then the silver blade of a knife flashing down through the dark, slicing into her skin, drawing out the blood. Pain that was like fire, and terror like nothing else she'd ever known. She kicked out at the man holding her, succeeding in knocking the dagger from his hand; she caught the blade and ran, stumbling as she weakened, the blood draining out of her fast, so fast. She crumpled in an alley, hearing the hissing scream of *something* behind her. She knew it was following her, and she was hoping to die before it reached her—

The Change shattered like glass. With a cry Tessa fell to her knees, the torn little bow falling from her hand. It was *her* hand again—Emma had gone, like a cast-off skin. Tessa was once more alone inside her own mind.

Mrs. Black's voice came from far away. "Theresa? Where is Emma?"

"She's dead," Tessa whispered. "She died in an alley—bled to death."

"Good." Mrs. Dark exhaled, a sound of satisfaction. "Well done, Theresa. That was very good."

Tessa said nothing. The front of her dress was splotched with blood, but there was no pain. She knew it was not her blood; it wasn't the first time this had happened. She closed her eyes, spinning in the darkness, willing herself not to faint.

"We should have had her do this before," said Mrs. Black. "The matter of the Bayliss girl has been bothering me."

Mrs. Dark's reply was curt. "I wasn't sure she was up to it. You remember what happened with the Adams woman."

Tessa knew immediately what they were talking about. Weeks ago she had Changed into a woman who had died of a gunshot wound to the heart; blood had poured down her dress and she had Changed back immediately, screaming in hysterical terror until the Sisters had made her see that she herself was unharmed.

"She's advanced wonderfully since then, don't you think, Sister?" Mrs. Black said. "Given what we had to work with in the beginning—she didn't even know what she *was*."

"Indeed, she was absolutely unformed *clay*," Mrs. Dark agreed. "We have truly worked a miracle here. I can't see how the Magister could fail to be pleased."

Mrs. Black gave a little gasp. "Does that mean—Do you think it's *time*?"

"Oh, absolutely, my dear sister. She's as ready as she'll ever be. It's time for our Theresa to meet her master." There was a gloating note in Mrs. Dark's voice, a sound so unpleasant that it cut through Tessa's blinding dizziness. What were they talking about? Who was the Magister? She watched through lowered eyelashes as Mrs. Dark jerked the silk bellpull that would summon Miranda to come and take Tessa back to her room. It appeared that the lesson was over for today.

"Perhaps tomorrow," Mrs. Black said, "or even tonight. If we told the Magister she was ready, I cannot imagine he would not hurry here without delay."

Mrs. Dark, stepping out from behind the desk, chuckled. "I understand that you're eager to be paid for all our work, dear sister. But Theresa must not be simply *ready*. She must be . . . presentable as well as able. Don't you agree?"

Mrs. Black, following her sister, muttered a response that was cut short as the door opened and Miranda came in. She wore the same dull look as ever. The sight of Tessa crouched and bloody on the floor seemed to occasion no surprise in her. Then again, Tessa thought, she had probably seen far worse in this room.

"Take the girl back up to her room, Miranda." The eagerness was gone from Mrs. Black's voice, and she was all brusqueness again. "Get the things—you know, the ones we showed you—and get her dressed and ready."

"The things . . . you showed me?" Miranda sounded blank.

Mrs. Dark and Mrs. Black exchanged a disgusted look, and approached Miranda, blocking Tessa's view of the girl. Tessa heard them whispering to her, and caught a few words—"dresses" and "wardrobe room" and "do what you can to make her look pretty," and then finally, Tessa heard the rather cruel,

"I'm not sure Miranda is *clever* enough to obey vague instructions of that sort, sister."

Make her look pretty. But what did they care whether she looked pretty or not, when they could force her to look any way they wanted? What did it matter what her true appearance was? And why would the Magister care? Though, it was very clear from the Sisters' behavior that they believed he would.

Mrs. Black swept from the room, her sister following behind her, as she always did. At the door Mrs. Dark paused, and looked back at Tessa. "Do remember, Theresa," she said, "that this day—this very night—is what all of our preparation has been for." She took hold of her skirts in both bony hands. "Do *not* fail us."

She let the door bang shut behind her. Tessa flinched at the noise, but Miranda, as always, seemed utterly unaffected. In all the time that she had passed in the Dark House, Tessa had never been able to startle the other girl, or surprise an unguarded expression out of her.

"Come," Miranda said. "We must go upstairs now."

Tessa rose to her feet, slowly. Her mind was whirling. Her life in the Dark House had been horrible, but she had—she realized now—grown almost used to it. She had known what to expect each day. She had known the Dark Sisters were preparing her for something, but she had not known what that something was. She had believed—naively, perhaps—that they wouldn't kill her. Why waste all this training on her if she was only going to die?

But something in Mrs. Dark's gloating tone gave her pause. Something had changed. They had achieved what they wanted with her. They were going to be "paid." But who was going to do the paying?

"Come," Miranda said again. "We must get you ready for the Magister."

"Miranda," Tessa said. She spoke softly, the way she might have spoken to a nervous cat. Miranda had never answered a question of Tessa's before, but that didn't mean it wasn't worth trying. "Who is the Magister?"

There was a long silence. Miranda stared straight ahead, her doughy face impassive. Then, to Tessa's surprise, she spoke. "The Magister is a very great man," she said. "It will be an honor for you when you are married to him."

"*Married?*" Tessa echoed. The shock was so intense that she could suddenly see the whole room more clearly—Miranda, the blood-splattered rug on the floor, the heavy brass globe on the desk, still tilted in the position Mrs. Black had left it in. "Me? But—who is he?"

"He is a very great man," Miranda said again. "It will be an honor." She moved toward Tessa. "You must come with me now."

"No." Tessa backed away from the other girl, retreating until the small of her back struck painfully against the desk. She looked around desperately. She could run, but she'd never get past Miranda to the door; there were no windows, no doors to other rooms. If she hid behind the desk, Miranda would simply drag her out and haul her to her room. "Miranda, *please*."

"You must come with me now," Miranda repeated; she had almost reached Tessa. Tessa could see herself reflected in the black pupils of the other girl's eyes, could smell the faint, bitter, almost charred smell that clung to Miranda's clothes and skin. "You must —"

With a strength she didn't know she possessed, Tessa seized the base of the brass globe on the desk, lifted it, and swung it with all her might at Miranda's head.

It connected with a sickening sound. Miranda reeled back—and then straightened. Tessa shrieked and dropped the globe, staring—the whole left side of Miranda's face was crushed in, like a paper mask that had been smashed flat on one side. Her cheekbone was flattened, her lip mashed against her teeth. But there was no blood, no blood at all.

"You must come with me now," Miranda said, in the same flat tone she always used.

Tessa gaped.

"You must come—you m-must—you—you—you—yyyyyyyyyyyy—" Miranda's voice shuddered and broke, degenerating into a stream of gibberish. She moved toward Tessa, then jerked to the side, twitching and stumbling. Tessa turned from the desk and began to back away as the injured girl spun, faster and faster. She reeled across the room like a staggering drunk, still shrieking, and crashed into the far wall—which seemed to stun her. She collapsed to the ground and lay still.

Tessa raced to the door and out into the corridor beyond, pausing only once, just outside the room, to look back. It seemed, in that brief moment, as if a thread of black smoke were rising from Miranda's prone body, but there was no time to stare. Tessa darted down the hall, leaving the door hanging open behind her.

She dashed for the stairs and hurtled up them, nearly tripping over her skirts and banging her knee painfully on one of the steps. She cried out and scrambled on, up to the first landing, where she dashed into the corridor. It stretched out ahead of her, long and curving, disappearing into shadows. As she raced down it, she saw that it was lined with doors. She paused and tried one, but it was locked, and so was the next one, and the next after that.

Another set of stairs led down at the end of the hallway. Tessa raced down them and found herself in an entryway. It looked as if it had once been grand—the floor was cracked and stained marble, and high windows on either side were shielded with curtains. A little bit of light spilled through the lace, illuminating an enormous front door. Tessa's heart leaped. She dived for the knob, seized it, and flung the door open.

There was a narrow cobblestoned street beyond, with rows of terraced houses lining either side. The smell of the city hit Tessa like a blow—it had been so long since she'd breathed outside air. It was close to dark, the sky the dimming blue of twilight, obscured by smudges of fog. In the distance she could hear voices, the cries of children playing, the clop of horses' hooves. But here the street was nearly deserted, save for a man leaning against a nearby gas lamp, reading a newspaper by its light.

Tessa dashed down the steps and toward the stranger, catching him by the sleeve. "Please, sir—if you could help me—"

He turned, and looked down at her.

Tessa stifled a scream. His face was as white and waxy as it had been the first time she'd seen him, at the dock in Southampton; his bulging eyes still reminded her of Miranda's, and his teeth gleamed like metal when he grinned.

It was the Dark Sisters' coachman.

Tessa turned to run, but it was already too late.

2

Hell Is Cold

Between two worlds life hovers like a star,
'Twixt night and morn, upon the horizon's verge.
How little do we know that which we are!
How less what we may be!
–Lord Byron, *Don Juan*

"You stupid little girl," Mrs. Black spat as she jerked tight the knots holding Tessa's wrists to her bed frame. "What did you think you were going to accomplish, running away like that? Where did you think you could *possibly* go?"

Tessa said nothing, simply set her chin and looked toward the wall. She refused to let Mrs. Black, or her horrible sister, see how close she was to tears, or how much the ropes binding her ankles and wrists to the bed hurt.

"She is entirely insensible of the honor being done to her," said Mrs. Dark, who was standing by the door as if to make sure

Tessa didn't rip free of her bonds and rush out through it. "It is disgusting to behold."

"We have done what we can for her to make her ready for the Magister," Mrs. Black said, and sighed. "A pity we had such dull clay to work with, despite her talent. She is a deceitful little fool."

"Indeed," agreed her sister. "She does realize, doesn't she, what will happen to her brother if she tries to disobey us again? We might be willing to be lenient this time, but the next . . ." She hissed through her teeth, a sound that made the hairs rise up on the back of Tessa's neck. "Nathaniel will not be so fortunate."

Tessa couldn't stand it anymore; even knowing she shouldn't speak, shouldn't give them the satisfaction, she couldn't hold the words back. "If you told me who the Magister was, or what he wants with me—"

"He wants to marry you, you little fool." Mrs. Black, finished with the knots, stepped back to admire her handiwork. "He wants to give you *everything.*"

"But why?" Tessa whispered. "Why me?"

"Because of your talent," Mrs. Dark said. "Because of what you are and what you can do. What we trained you to do. You should be *grateful* to us."

"But my brother." Tears burned behind Tessa's eyes. *I will not cry, I will not cry, I will not cry,* she told herself. "You told me that if I did everything you said, you'd let him go—"

"Once you marry the Magister, he'll give you whatever you want. If that's your brother, he'll give it to you." There was no remorse or emotion in Mrs. Black's voice.

Mrs. Dark chuckled. "I know what she's thinking. She's

thinking that if she could have whatever she wanted, she'd have us killed."

"Don't waste your energy even imagining the possibility." Mrs. Black chucked Tessa under the chin. "We have an ironclad contract with the Magister. He can never harm us, nor would he want to. He owes us everything, for giving him you." She leaned in closer, dropping her voice to a whisper. "He wants you healthy and intact. If he didn't, I'd have you beaten bloody. If you dare disobey us again, I'll defy his wishes and have you whipped until your skin peels off. Do you understand?"

Tessa turned her face to the wall.

There had been a night on the *Main*, as they'd passed Newfoundland, when Tessa had not been able to sleep. She had gone out on the deck to get a breath of air, and had seen the night sea ablaze with white glittering mountains—icebergs, one of the sailors had told her as he'd passed, broken loose from the ice sheets of the north by the warmer weather. They had drifted slowly on the dark water, like the towers of a drowned white city. Tessa had thought that she'd never seen such a lonely sight.

She had only begun to imagine loneliness, she knew now. Once the Sisters left, Tessa discovered, she no longer felt like she wanted to cry. The pressure at the backs of her eyes was gone, replaced by a dull feeling of hollow despair. Mrs. Dark had been right. If Tessa could have killed them both, she would have.

She pulled experimentally at the ropes tying her legs and arms to the bedposts. They didn't budge. The knots were tight; tight enough to dig into her flesh and make her hands and feet tingle and shiver with pins and needles. She had a few minutes, she estimated, before her extremities went dead entirely.

Part of her—and not a small part—wanted to stop struggling, to lie there limply until the Magister came to take her away. The sky was already darkening outside the small window; it couldn't be much longer now. Perhaps he really did want to marry her. Perhaps he truly wanted to give her everything.

Suddenly she heard Aunt Harriet's voice in her head: *When you find a man you wish to marry, Tessa, remember this: You will know what kind of man he is not by the things he says, but by the things he* does.

Aunt Harriet had been right, of course. No man she would ever want to marry would have arranged to have her treated like a prisoner and a slave, imprisoned her brother, and had her tortured in the name of her "talent." It was a travesty and a joke. Heaven only knew what the Magister wanted to do with her once he had his hands on her. If it was something she could survive, she imagined she would soon enough wish she hadn't.

God, what a useless talent she had! The power to change her appearance? If only she had the power to set things on fire, or shatter metal, or cause knives to grow out of her fingers! Or if she only had the power to make herself invisible, or shrink herself to the size of a mouse—

She went suddenly still, so still that she could hear the ticking of the clockwork angel against her chest. She didn't have to shrink herself down to the size of a mouse, did she? All she had to do was make herself small enough that the ties around her wrists would be loose.

It was possible for her to Change into someone a second

time, without touching something that had belonged to them—as long as she'd done it before. The Sisters had made her memorize how to do it. For the first time, she was glad of something they'd forced her to learn.

She pressed herself back against the hard mattress and made herself remember. The street, the kitchen, the movement of the needle, the glow of the gaslight. She willed it on, willed the Change to come. *What's your name? Emma. Emma Bayliss . . .*

The Change bore down on her like a train, almost knocking the breath out of her—reshaping her skin, reforming her bones. She choked back her screams and arched her back—

And it was done. Blinking, Tessa stared up at the ceiling, then glanced sideways, staring at her wrist, at the rope around it. There were her hands—Emma's hands—thin and frail, the circle of the rope loose around her small wrists. Triumphantly Tessa jerked her hands free and sat up, rubbing at the red marks where the rope had burned her skin.

Her ankles were still tied. She leaned forward, her fingers working quickly at the knots. Mrs. Black, it turned out, could tie knots like a sailor. Tessa's fingers were bloodied and sore by the time the rope fell away and she sprang to her feet.

Emma's hair was so thin and fine that it had slipped free of the clips holding Tessa's own hair back. Tessa pushed her hair back impatiently over her shoulders and shook herself free of Emma, letting the Change wash away from her until her hair slid through her fingers, thick and familiar to the touch. Glancing at the mirror across the room, she saw that little Emma Bayliss was gone and she was herself again.

A noise behind her made her whirl. The knob of the bedroom door was turning, twisting back and forth as if the person on the other side were having difficulty getting it open.

Mrs. Dark, she thought. The woman was back, to whip her until she was bloody. Back, to take her to the Magister. Tessa hurried across the room, seized the porcelain jug from the washstand, and then scuttled to the side of the door, the jug gripped hard in her whitened fist.

The knob turned; the door opened. In the dimness all Tessa could see was shadows as someone stepped into the room. She lunged forward, swinging the jug with all her strength—

The shadowy figure moved, as quick as a whip, but not quite quick enough; the jug slammed into the figure's outstretched arm before flying from Tessa's grasp to crash into the far wall. Broken crockery rained down onto the floor as the stranger yelled.

The yell was undeniably a masculine one. So was the flood of cursing that followed.

She backed away, then dashed for the door—but it had slammed shut, and tug as she would on the knob, it wouldn't budge. Bright light blazed through the room as if the sun had risen. Tessa spun, blinking away the tears in her eyes—and stared.

There was a boy standing in front of her. He couldn't have been much older than she was—seventeen or possibly eighteen. He was dressed in what looked like workman's clothes—a frayed black jacket, trousers, and tough-looking boots. He wore no waistcoat, and thick leather straps crisscrossed his waist and chest. Attached to the straps were weapons—daggers and folding knives and things that looked like blades of ice. In his right hand he held a sort of glowing stone—it was shining, providing the light in the room that had nearly blinded Tessa.

His other hand—slim and long-fingered—was bleeding where she had gashed the back of it with her pitcher.

But that wasn't what made her stare. He had the most beautiful face she had ever seen. Tangled black hair and eyes like blue glass. Elegant cheekbones, a full mouth, and long, thick lashes. Even the curve of his throat was perfect. He looked like every fictional hero she'd ever conjured up in her head. Although she'd never imagined one of them cursing at her while shaking his bleeding hand in an accusing fashion.

He seemed to realize she was staring at him, because the cursing stopped. "You cut me," he said. His voice was pleasant. British. Very ordinary. He looked at his hand with critical interest. "It might be fatal."

Tessa looked at him with wide eyes. "Are you the Magister?"

He tilted his hand to the side. Blood ran down it, spattering the floor. "Dear me, massive blood loss. Death could be imminent."

"Are you the Magister?"

"Magister?" He looked mildly surprised by her vehemence. "That means 'master' in Latin, doesn't it?"

"I . . ." Tessa was feeling increasingly as if she were trapped in a strange dream. "I suppose it does."

"I've mastered many things in my life. Navigating the streets of London, dancing the quadrille, the Japanese art of flower arranging, lying at charades, concealing a highly intoxicated state, delighting young women with my charms . . ."

Tessa stared.

"Alas," he went on, "no one has ever actually referred to me as 'the master,' or 'the magister,' either. More's the pity . . ."

"Are you highly intoxicated at the moment?" Tessa meant

the question in all seriousness, but realized the moment the words were out of her mouth that she must have sounded awfully rude—or worse, flirtatious. He seemed too steady on his feet to really be drunk, anyway. She'd seen Nate intoxicated enough times to know the difference. Perhaps he was merely insane.

"How very direct, but I suppose all you Americans are, aren't you?" The boy looked amused. "Yes, your accent gives you away. What's your name, then?"

Tessa looked at him in disbelief. "What's *my* name?"

"Don't you know it?"

"You—you've come bursting into my room, scared me nearly to death, and now you demand to know my name? What on earth's *your* name? And who are you, anyway?"

"My name is Herondale," the boy said cheerfully. "William Herondale, but everyone calls me Will. Is this really your room? Not very nice, is it?" He wandered toward the window, pausing to examine the stacks of books on her bedside table, and then the bed itself. He waved a hand at the ropes. "Do you often sleep tied to the bed?"

Tessa felt her cheeks flame and was amazed, under the circumstances, that she still had the capacity to be embarrassed. Should she tell him the truth? Was it at all possible that he was the Magister? Though anyone who looked like that wouldn't need to tie girls up and imprison them in order to get them to marry him.

"Here. Hold this." He handed her the glowing stone. Tessa took it, half-expecting it to burn her fingers, but it was cool to the touch. The moment it struck her palm, its light dimmed to a shimmering flicker. She looked toward him in dismay, but he had made his way to the window and was looking out, seemingly unconcerned. "Pity we're on the third floor. I could manage the jump, but it would probably kill you. No, we must go through the door and take our chances in the house."

"Go through the— What?" Tessa, feeling mired in a semi-permanent state of confusion, shook her head. "I don't understand."

"How can you not understand?" He pointed at her books. "You read novels. Obviously, I'm here to rescue you. Don't I *look* like Sir Galahad?" He raised his arms dramatically. "'*My strength is as the strength of ten, Because my heart is pure*—'"

Something echoed, far away inside the house—the sound of a door slamming.

Will said a word Sir Galahad would never have said, and sprang away from the window. He landed with a wince, and glanced ruefully down at his injured hand. "I'll need to take care of this later. Come along . . ." He looked at her pointedly, a question in his eyes.

"Miss Gray," she said faintly. "Miss Theresa Gray."

"Miss Gray," he repeated. "Come along, then, Miss Gray." He sprang past her, moved toward the door, found the knob, turned it, yanked—

Nothing happened.

"It won't work," she said. "The door cannot be opened from the inside."

Will grinned ferociously. "Can't it?" He reached for his belt, for one of the objects that hung on it. He chose what looked like a long, slender twig, picked clean of smaller branches, and made of a whitish-silver material. He placed the end of it against the door and *drew*. Thick black lines spiraled out from the tip of the flexible cylinder, making an audible hissing noise as they spread across the wooden surface like a directed spill of ink.

"You're *drawing*?" Tessa demanded. "I don't really see how that can possibly—"

There was a noise like cracking glass. The doorknob, untouched, spun—fast, then faster, and the door sprang open, a faint puff of smoke rising from the hinges.

"Now you do," Will said, and, pocketing the strange object, gestured for Tessa to follow him. "Let's go."

Inexplicably, she hesitated, looking back toward the room that had been her prison for nearly two months. "My books—"

"I'll get you more books." He urged her into the corridor ahead of him, and pulled the door shut behind them. After catching hold of her wrist, he drew her down the hallway and around a corner. Here were the stairs that she had descended so many times with Miranda. Will took them two at a time, pulling her after him.

From above them Tessa heard a scream. It was unmistakably Mrs. Dark's.

"They've found you missing," Will said. They had reached the first landing, and Tessa slowed her pace—only to be jerked ahead by Will, who seemed disinclined to stop.

"Aren't we going out the front door?" she demanded.

"We can't. The building's surrounded. There's a line of carriages pulled up out front. I appear to have arrived at an unexpectedly exciting time." He started down the stairs again, and Tessa followed. "Do you know what the Dark Sisters had planned for this evening?"

"No."

"But you were expecting someone called the Magister?" They were in the cellar now, where the plaster walls gave way suddenly to damp stone. Without Miranda's lantern it was quite dark. Heat rose to meet them like a wave. "By the Angel, it's like the ninth circle of Hell down here—"

"The ninth circle of Hell is cold," Tessa said automatically.

Will stared at her. "What?"

"In the *Inferno*," she told him. "Hell is cold. It's covered in ice."

He stared at her for another long moment, the corners of his mouth twitching, then held out his hand. "Give me the witchlight." At her blank expression he made an impatient noise. "The stone. Give me the stone."

The moment his hand closed about the stone, light blazed up from it again, raying out through his fingers. For the first time Tessa saw that he had a design on the back of his hand, drawn there as if in black ink. It looked like an open eye. "As for the temperature of Hell, Miss Gray," he said, "let me give you a piece of advice. The handsome young fellow who's trying to rescue you from a hideous fate is *never* wrong. Not even if he says the sky is purple and made of hedgehogs."

He really is *mad,* Tessa thought, but didn't say so; she was too alarmed by the fact that he had started toward the wide double doors of the Dark Sisters' chambers.

"No!" She caught at his arm, pulling him back. "Not that way. There's no way out. It's a dead end."

"Correcting me again, I see." Will turned and strode the other way, toward the shadowy corridor Tessa had always feared. Swallowing hard, she followed him.

The corridor narrowed as they went along it, the walls

pressing in on either side. The heat was even more intense here, making Tessa's hair spring into curls and paste itself to her temples and neck. The air felt thick and was hard to breathe. For a while they walked in silence, until Tessa could stand it no longer. She had to ask, even though she knew the answer would be no.

"Mr. Herondale," she said, "did my brother send you to find me?"

She half-feared he'd make some mad comment in response, but he simply looked at her curiously. "Never heard of your brother," he said, and she felt the dull ache of disappointment gnaw at her heart. She'd known Nate couldn't have sent him—he'd have known her name, then, wouldn't he?—but it still hurt. "And outside of the past ten minutes, Miss Gray, I'd never heard of you, either. I've been following the trail of a dead girl for near on two months. She was murdered, left in an alley to bleed to death. She'd been running from . . . something." The corridor had reached a forking point, and after a pause Will headed to the left. "There was a dagger beside her, covered in her blood. It had a symbol on it. Two snakes, swallowing each other's tails."

Tessa felt a jolt. *Left in an alley to bleed to death. There was a dagger beside her.* Surely the body had been Emma's. "That's the same symbol that's on the side of the Dark Sisters' carriage—That's what I call them, Mrs. Dark and Mrs. Black, I mean—"

"You're not the only one who calls them that; the other Downworlders do the same," said Will. "I discovered that fact while investigating the symbol. I must have carried that knife through a hundred Downworld haunts, searching for someone who might recognize it. I offered a reward for information.

Eventually the name of the Dark Sisters came to my ears."

"Downworld?" Tessa echoed, puzzled. "Is that a place in London?"

"Never mind that," said Will. "I'm boasting of my investigative skills, and I would prefer to do it without interruption. Where was I?"

"The dagger—" Tessa broke off as a voice echoed down the corridor, high and sweet and unmistakable.

"Miss Gray." Mrs. Dark's voice. It seemed to drift between the walls like coiling smoke. *"Oh, Miss Graaaay. Where are you?"*

Tessa froze. "Oh, God, they've caught up with—"

Will seized her wrist again, and they were off running, the witchlight in his other hand throwing a wild pattern of shadows and light against the stone walls as they hurtled down the twisting corridor. The floor sloped down, the stones underfoot growing gradually more slick and damp as the air around them grew hotter and hotter. It was as if they were racing down into Hell itself as the voices of the Dark Sisters echoed off the walls. *"Miss Graaaaaay! We shan't let you run, you know. We shan't let you hide! We'll find you, poppet. You know we will."*

Will and Tessa careened around a corner, and came up short—the corridor ended at a pair of high metal doors. Releasing Tessa, Will flung himself against them. They burst open and he tumbled inside, followed by Tessa, who spun to slam them shut behind her. The weight of them was almost too much for her to manage, and she had to throw her back against them to force them, finally, closed.

The only illumination in the room was Will's glowing stone, its light sunk down now to an ember between his fingers. It lit him in the darkness, like limelight on a stage, as he reached around her to slam the bolt home on the door. The bolt was heavy and flaking with rust, and, standing as close to him as she was, she could feel the tension in his body as he dragged it home and let it fall into place.

"Miss Gray?" He was leaning against her, her back against the closed doors. She could feel the driving rhythm of his heart—or was it her heart? The odd white illumination cast by the stone shimmered against the sharp angle of his cheeks, the faint sheen of sweat on his collarbones. There were marks there, too, she saw, rising from the unbuttoned collar of his shirt—like the mark on his hand, thick and black, as if someone had inked designs onto his skin.

"Where are we?" she whispered. "Are we safe?"

Without answering he drew away, raising his right hand. As he lifted it, the light blazed up higher, illuminating the room.

They were in a sort of cell, though it was very large. The walls, floor, and ceiling were stone, sloping down to a large drain in the middle of the floor. There was only one window, very high up in the wall. There were no doors save the ones they had come through. But none of that was what made Tessa draw in her breath.

The place was a slaughterhouse. There were long wooden tables running the length of the room. Bodies lay on one of them—human bodies, stripped and pale. Each had a black incision in the shape of a *Y* marking its chest, and each head dangled back over the edge of the table, the hair of the women sweeping the floor like brooms. On the center table were piles of bloodstained knives and machinery—copper cogs and brass gears and sharp-toothed silver hacksaws.

Tessa crammed a hand into her mouth, stifling a scream. She tasted blood as she bit down on her own fingers. Will didn't seem to notice; he was white-faced as he looked around, mouthing something under his breath that Tessa couldn't make out.

There was a crashing noise and the metal doors shuddered, as if something heavy had flung itself against them. Tessa lowered her bleeding hand and cried out, "Mr. Herondale!"

He turned, as the doors shuddered again. A voice echoed from the other side of them: "Miss Gray! Come out now, and we won't hurt you!"

"They're lying," Tessa said quickly.

"Oh, do you really think so?" Having packed as much sarcasm into the question as was humanly possible, Will pocketed his glowing witchlight and leaped onto the center table, the one covered in bloodied machinery. He bent down and caught up a heavy-looking brass cog, and weighed it in his hand. With a grunt of effort he hurled it toward the high window; the glass shattered, and Will raised his voice. "Henry! Some assistance, please! Henry!"

"Who's Henry?" Tessa demanded, but at that moment the doors shuddered a third time, and thin cracks appeared in the metal. Clearly, they weren't going to hold much longer. Tessa dashed to the table and seized a weapon, almost at random—this one was a ragged-toothed metal hacksaw, the kind butchers used to cut through bone. She whirled around, clutching it, as the doors burst open.

The Dark Sisters stood in the doorway—Mrs. Dark, as tall and bony as a rake in her shining lime green gown, and Mrs. Black, red-faced, her eyes narrowed to slits. A bright corona of blue sparks surrounded them, like tiny fireworks. Their gazes slid over Will—who, still standing on the table, had drawn one of his icy blades from his belt—and came to rest on Tessa. Mrs. Black's mouth, a red slash in her pale face, stretched into a grin. "Little Miss Gray," she said. "You ought to know better than to run. We told you what would happen if you ran again. . . ."

"Then do it! Whip me bloody. Kill me. I don't care!" Tessa shouted, and was gratified to see that the Dark Sisters looked at least a little taken aback by her outburst; she'd been too terrified to raise her voice to them before. "I won't let you give me to the Magister! I'd rather die!"

"What an unexpectedly sharp tongue you have, Miss Gray, my dear," said Mrs. Black. With great deliberation she reached to draw the glove from her right hand, and for the first time, Tessa saw her bare hand. The skin was gray and thick, like an elephant's hide, her nails long dark talons. They looked as sharp as knives. Mrs. Black gave Tessa a fixed grin. "Perhaps if we cut it out of your head, you'd learn to mind your manners."

She moved toward Tessa—and was blocked by Will leaping down from the table to put himself between them. "*Malik*," he said, and his ice-white blade blazed up like a star.

"Get out of my way, little Nephilim warrior," said Mrs. Black. "And take your seraph blades with you. This is not your battle."

"You're wrong about that." Will narrowed his eyes. "I've heard some things about you, my lady. Whispers that run through Downworld like a river of black poison. I've been told you and your sister will pay handsomely for the bodies of dead humans, and you don't much mind how they get that way."

"Such a fuss over a few mundanes." Mrs. Dark chuckled and moved to stand beside her sister, so that Will, with his blazing sword, was between Tessa and both ladies. "We have no quarrel with you, Shadowhunter, unless you choose to pick one. You have invaded our territory and broken Covenant Law in doing so. We could report you to the Clave—"

"While the Clave disapproves of trespassers, oddly they take an even darker view of beheading and skinning people. They're peculiar that way," Will said.

"People?" Mrs. Dark spat. "*Mundanes.* You care no more about them than we do." She looked toward Tessa then. "Has he told you what he really is? He isn't human—"

"You're one to talk," Tessa said in a trembling voice.

"And has she told *you* what *she* is?" Mrs. Black demanded of Will. "About her talent? What she can do?"

"If I were to venture a guess," Will replied, "I would say it has something to do with the Magister."

Mrs. Dark looked suspicious. "You know of the Magister?" She glanced at Tessa. "Ah, I see. Only what she has told you. The Magister, little boy angel, is more dangerous than you could ever imagine. And he has waited a long time for someone with Tessa's ability. You might even say he is the one who caused her to be born—"

Her words were swallowed up in a colossal crash as the whole east wall of the room suddenly caved in. It was like the walls of Jericho tumbling down in Tessa's old Bible stories picture book. One moment the wall was there, and the next it wasn't; there was a huge gaping rectangular hole instead, steaming with choking swirls of plaster dust.

Mrs. Dark gave a thin scream and seized her skirts with her

bony hands. Clearly she hadn't expected the wall to collapse, any more than Tessa had.

Will caught hold of Tessa's hand and pulled her toward him, blocking her with his body as chunks of stone and plaster rained down on them. As his arms went around her, she could hear Mrs. Black screaming.

Tessa twisted in Will's grip, trying to see what was happening. Mrs. Dark stood, pointing with one gloved, trembling finger toward the dark hole in the wall. The dust was beginning to settle, barely—enough so that the figures moving toward them through the wreckage slowly began to take shape. The shadowy outlines of two human figures became visible; each was holding a blade, and each blade shone with the same blue-white light as Will's. *Angels*, Tessa thought, wondering, but she didn't say it. That light, so bright—what else could they be?

Mrs. Black gave a screech and lunged forward. She threw her hands out, and sparks shot from them like exploding fireworks. Tessa heard someone yell—a very human yell—and Will, releasing Tessa, spun and flung his bright-burning sword at Mrs. Black. It whipped through the air, end over end, and drove into her chest. Screaming and twisting, she staggered backward and fell, crashing down onto one of the horrible tables, which collapsed in a mess of blood and splintering wood.

Will grinned. It wasn't a pleasant sort of grin. He turned to look at Tessa then. For a moment they stared at each other, silently, across the space that separated them—and then his other companions flooded in around him, two men in close-fitting dark coats, brandishing shining weapons, and moving so fast that Tessa's vision blurred.

Tessa backed toward the far wall, trying to avoid the chaos

in the center of the room, where Mrs. Dark, howling imprecations, was holding off her attackers with the burning sparks of energy that flew from her hands like fiery rain. Mrs. Black was writhing on the floor, sheets of black smoke rising from her body as if she were burning from the inside out.

Tessa moved toward the open door that led to the corridor—and strong hands seized her and yanked her backward. Tessa shrieked and twisted, but the hands circling her upper arms were as strong as iron. She turned her head to the side and sank her teeth into the hand gripping her left arm. Someone yelled and let go of her; spinning, she saw a tall man with a shock of untidy ginger hair staring at her with a reproachful expression, his bleeding left hand cradled against his chest. "Will!" he shouted. "Will, she bit me!"

"Did she, Henry?" Will, looking amused as usual, appeared like a summoned spirit from the chaos of smoke and flames. Behind him, Tessa could see the second of his companions, a muscular brown-haired young man, holding a struggling Mrs. Dark. Mrs. Black was a dark humped shape on the ground. Will raised an eyebrow in Tessa's direction. "It's bad form to bite," he informed her. "Rude, you know. Hasn't anyone ever told you that?"

"It's also rude to go about grabbing at ladies you haven't been introduced to," Tessa said stiffly. "Hasn't anyone told you *that?*"

The ginger-haired man whom Will had called Henry shook his bleeding hand with a rueful smile. He had a nice sort of face, Tessa thought; she almost felt guilty for having bitten him.

"Will! Look out!" the brown-haired man shouted. Will

spun as something flew through the air, narrowly missed Henry's head, and crashed into the wall behind Tessa. It was a large brass cog, and it hit the wall with such force that it stuck there like a marble wedged into a bit of pastry. Tessa whirled—and saw Mrs. Black advancing toward them, her eyes burning like coal in her crumpled white face. Black licks of flame sprayed up around the hilt of the sword that protruded from her chest.

"Damn—" Will reached for the hilt of another blade wedged through the belt at his waist. "I thought we'd put that thing down—"

Baring her teeth, Mrs. Black lunged. Will leaped out of the way, but Henry wasn't quite as fast; she struck him and knocked him backward. Clinging on like a tick, she rode him to the ground, snarling, her claws sinking into his shoulders as he yelled. Will whirled, the blade now in his hand; raising it, he shouted "*Uriel!*" and it flared up suddenly in his grip like a blazing torch. Tessa fell back against the wall as he whipped the blade downward. Mrs. Black reared back, her claws out, reaching for him—

And the blade sheared neatly through her throat. Completely severed, her head struck the ground, rolling and bumping, as Henry, yelling in disgust and soaked in blackish blood, shoved the remains of her body off him and scrambled to his feet.

A terrible scream tore through the room. "*Nooooo!*"

The cry had come from Mrs. Dark. The brown-haired man holding her let go with a sudden cry as blue fire shot from her hands and eyes. Yelling in pain, he fell to the side as she tore away from him and advanced on Will and Tessa, Mrs. Dark's eyes flaming like black torches. She was hissing words in a language that Tessa had never heard. It sounded like crackling flames. Raising a hand, the woman flung what looked like a bolt of lightning toward Tessa. With a cry Will sprang in front of her, his glowing blade extended. The lightning ricocheted off the blade and struck one of the stone walls, which glowed with a sudden strange light.

"Henry," Will shouted, without turning, "if you could remove Miss Gray to a place of safety—*soon*—"

Henry's bitten hand came down on Tessa's shoulder, as Mrs. Dark flung another sheet of lightning toward her. *Why is she trying to kill* me? Tessa thought dizzily. *Why not Will?* And then, as Henry pulled her toward him, more light sheared off Will's blade, refracting into a dozen blazing shards of brightness. For a moment Tessa stared, caught by the unlikely beauty of it—and then she heard Henry shout, telling her to drop to the floor, but it was too late. One of the blazing shards had caught her shoulder with incredible force. It was like being struck by a hurtling train. She was knocked free of Henry's grasp, lifted, and flung backward. Her head struck the wall with blinding force. She was conscious only briefly of Mrs. Dark's high screeching laughter, before the world went away.

3

The Institute

Love, hope, fear, faith–these make humanity;
These are its sign and note and character
–Robert Browning, *Paracelsus*

In the dream Tessa lay once again tied to the narrow brass bed in the Dark House. The Sisters leaned over her, clacking pairs of long knitting needles and laughing in shrill high-pitched voices. As Tessa watched, their features changed, their eyes sinking into their heads, their hair falling out, and stitches appearing across their lips, sewing them shut. Tessa shrieked voicelessly, but they did not seem to hear.

The Sisters vanished entirely then, and Aunt Harriet was standing over Tessa, her face flushed with fever as it had been during the terrible illness that had killed her. She looked at Tessa with great sadness. "I tried," she said. "I tried to love you. But it isn't easy to love a child that isn't human in the least. . . ."

"Not human?" said an unfamiliar female voice. "Well, if she isn't human, Enoch, what is she?" The voice sharpened in impatience. "What do you mean, you don't know? Everyone's something. This girl can't be nothing at all. . . ."

Tessa woke with a cry, her eyes flying open, and found herself staring at shadows. Darkness clustered about her thickly. She could barely hear the murmur of voices through her panic, and struggled into a sitting position, kicking away blankets and pillows. Dimly, she recognized that the blanket was thick and heavy, not the thin, braided one that belonged to the Dark House.

She was in a bed, just as she had dreamed, in a great stone room, and there was hardly any light. She heard the rasp of her own breath as she turned, and a scream forced its way out of her throat. The face from her nightmare hovered in the darkness before her—a great white moon of a face, its head shaved bald, smooth as marble. Where the eyes should have been there were only indentations in the flesh—not as if the eyes had been ripped out, but as if they had never grown there at all. The lips were banded with black stitches, the face scrawled with black marks like the ones on Will's skin, though these looked as if they had been cut there with knives.

She screamed again and scrabbled backward, half-falling off the bed. She hit the cold stone floor, and the fabric of the white nightdress she was wearing—someone must have put it on her while she was unconscious—ripped at the hem as she scrambled to her feet.

"Miss Gray." Someone was calling her name, but in her panic, she knew only that the voice was unfamiliar. The speaker was *not* the monster who stood staring at her from the bedside, its scarred face impassive; it had not moved when she did, and though it showed no signs of pursuing her, she began to back away, carefully, feeling behind herself for a door. The room was so dim, she could see only that it was roughly oval, the walls and floor all of stone. The ceiling was high enough to be in black shadow, and there were long windows across the opposite wall, the sort of arched windows that might have belonged in a church. Very little light filtered through them; it looked as if the sky outside was dark. "Theresa Gray—"

She found the door, the metal handle; turning, she seized on it thankfully, and pulled. Nothing happened. A sob rose up in her throat.

"Miss Gray!" the voice said again, and suddenly the room was flooded with light—a sharp, white-silver light that she recognized. "Miss Gray, I am sorry. It was not our intention to frighten you." The voice was a woman's: still unfamiliar, but youthful and concerned. "Miss Gray, please."

Tessa turned slowly and put her back against the door. She could see clearly now. She was in a stone room whose central focus was a large, four-poster bed, its velvet coverlet now rucked and hanging sideways where she had dragged it off the mattress. Tapestry curtains were pulled back, and there was an elegant tapestry rug on the otherwise bare floor. In fact, the room itself was fairly bare. There were no pictures or photographs hanging on the wall, no ornaments cluttering the surfaces of the dark wood furniture. Two chairs stood facing each other near the bed, with a small tea table between them. A Chinese screen in one corner of the room hid what were probably a bathtub and washstand.

Beside the bed stood a tall man who wore robes like a monk's, of a long, coarse, parchment-colored material. Red-brown runes circled the cuffs and hem. He carried a silver staff, its head carved in the shape of an angel and runes decorating its length. The hood of his robe was down, leaving bare his scarred, white, blinded face.

Beside him stood a very small woman, almost child-size, with thick brown hair knotted at the nape of her neck, and a neat, clever little face with bright, dark eyes like a bird's. She wasn't pretty exactly, but there was a calm, kindly look on her face that made the ache of panic in Tessa's stomach ease slightly, though she couldn't have said exactly why. In her hand she held a glowing white stone like the one Will had held at the Dark House. Its light blazed out between her fingers, illuminating the room.

"Miss Gray," she said. "I am Charlotte Branwell, head of the London Institute, and this beside me is Brother Enoch—"

"What kind of monster is he?" Tessa whispered.

Brother Enoch said nothing. He was entirely expressionless.

"I know there are monsters on this earth," said Tessa. "You cannot tell me otherwise. I have seen them."

"I would not want to tell you otherwise," said Mrs. Branwell. "If the world were not full of monsters, there would be no need for Shadowhunters."

Shadowhunter. What the Dark Sisters had called Will Herondale.

Will. "I was—Will was with me," said Tessa, her voice shaking. "In the cellars. Will said—" She broke off and cringed inwardly. She should not have called Will by his Christian name; it implied an intimacy between them that did not exist. "Where is Mr. Herondale?"

"He's here," Mrs. Branwell said calmly. "In the Institute."

"Did he bring me here as well?" Tessa whispered.

"Yes, but there is no need to look betrayed, Miss Gray. You had struck your head quite hard, and Will was concerned about you. Brother Enoch, though his looks might frighten you, is a skilled practitioner of medicine. He has determined that your head injury is slight, and in the main you are suffering from shock and nervous anxiety. In fact, it might be for the best if you sat down now. Hovering barefoot by the door like that will only give you a chill, and do you little good."

"You mean because I can't run," Tessa said, licking her dry lips. "I can't get away."

"If you demand to get away, as you put it, after we have talked, I will let you go," said Mrs. Branwell. "The Nephilim do not trap Downworlders under duress. The Accords forbid it."

"The Accords?"

Mrs. Branwell hesitated, then turned to Brother Enoch and said something to him in a low voice. Much to Tessa's relief, he drew up the hood of his parchment-colored robes, hiding his face. A moment later he was moving toward Tessa; she stepped back hurriedly and he opened the door, pausing only for a moment on the threshold.

In that moment, he spoke to Tessa. Or perhaps "spoke" was not the word for it: She heard his voice inside her head, rather than outside it. *You are Eidolon, Theresa Gray. Shape-changer. But not of a sort that is familiar to me. There is no demon's mark on you.*

Shape-changer. He knew what she was. She stared at him, her heart pounding, as he went through the door and closed it behind him. Tessa knew somehow that if she were to run to the door and try the handle she would once again find it locked, but the urge to escape had left her. Her knees felt as if they had turned to water. She sank down in one of the large chairs by the bed.

"What is it?" Mrs. Branwell asked, moving to sit in the chair opposite Tessa's. Her dress hung so loosely on her small frame, it was impossible to tell if she wore a corset beneath it, and the bones in her small wrists were like a child's. "What did he say to you?"

Tessa shook her head, gripping her hands together in her lap so that Mrs. Branwell could not see her fingers trembling.

Mrs. Branwell looked at her keenly. "First," she said, "please call me Charlotte, Miss Gray. Everyone in the Institute does. We Shadowhunters are not so formal as most."

Tessa nodded, feeling her cheeks flush. It was hard to tell how old Charlotte was; she was so small that she looked quite young indeed, but her air of authority made her seem older, old enough that the idea of calling her by her Christian name seemed very odd. Still, as Aunt Harriet would have said, when in Rome . . .

"Charlotte," Tessa said, experimentally.

With a smile, Mrs. Branwell—Charlotte—leaned back slightly in her chair, and Tessa saw with some surprise that she had dark tattoos. A *woman* with tattoos! Her marks were like the ones Will bore: visible on her wrists below the tight cuffs of her dress, with one like an eye on the back of her left hand. "Second, let me tell you what I already know about you, Theresa Gray." She spoke in the same calm tone she'd had before, but her eyes, though still kind, were sharp as pins. "You're American. You came here from New York City because you were following your brother, who had sent you a steamship ticket. His name is Nathaniel."

Tessa sat frozen. "How do you know all this?"

"I know that Will found you in the Dark Sisters' house," Charlotte said. "I know that you claimed someone named the Magister was coming for you. I know that you have no idea who the Magister is. And I know that in a battle with the Dark Sisters, you were rendered unconscious and brought here."

Charlotte's words were like a key unlocking a door. Suddenly Tessa remembered. Remembered running with Will down the corridor; remembered the metal doors and the room full of blood on the other side; remembered Mrs. Black, her head severed; remembered Will flinging his knife—

"Mrs. Black," she whispered.

"Dead," said Charlotte. "Very." She settled her shoulders against the back of the chair; she was so slight that the chair rose up high above her, as if she were a child sitting in a parent's chair.

"And Mrs. Dark?"

"Gone. We searched the whole house, and the nearby area, but found no trace of her."

"The whole house?" Tessa's voice shook, very slightly. "And there was no one in it? No one else alive, or . . . or dead?"

"We did not find your brother, Miss Gray," Charlotte said. Her tone was gentle. "Not in the house, nor in any of the surrounding buildings."

"You—were looking for him?" Tessa was bewildered.

"We did not find him," Charlotte said again. "But we did find your letters."

"My letters?"

"The letters you wrote to your brother and never sent," said Charlotte. "Folded under your mattress."

"You *read* them?"

"We had to read them," said Charlotte in the same gentle tone. "I apologize for that. It is not often that we bring a Downworlder into the Institute, or anyone who is not a Shadowhunter. It represents a great risk to us. We had to know that you were not a danger."

Tessa turned her head to the side. There was something horribly violating about this stranger having read her inmost thoughts, all the dreams and hopes and fears she'd poured forth, not thinking anyone would ever see them. The backs of her eyes stung; tears were threatening, and she willed them back, furious with herself, with everything.

"You're trying not to cry," Charlotte said. "I know that when I do that myself, it sometimes helps to look at a bright light directly. Try the witchlight."

Tessa moved her gaze to the stone in Charlotte's hand and gazed at it fixedly. The glow of it swelled up in front of her eyes like an expanding sun. "So," she said, fighting past the tightness in her throat, "you have decided I am not a danger, then?"

"Perhaps only to yourself," said Charlotte. "A power such as yours, the power of shape-shifting—it is no wonder the Dark Sisters wanted to get their hands on you. Others will as well."

"Like you do?" Tessa said. "Or are you going to pretend that you've let me into your precious Institute simply out of charity?"

A look of hurt flashed across Charlotte's face. It was brief, but it was real, and it did more to convince Tessa that she might have been wrong about Charlotte than anything the other woman could have said. "It is not charity," she said. "It is my vocation. Our vocation."

Tessa simply looked at her blankly.

"Perhaps," Charlotte said, "it would be better if I explained to you what we are—and what we do."

"*Nephilim*," said Tessa. "That's what the Dark Sisters called Mr. Herondale." She pointed at the dark markings on Charlotte's hand. "You're one as well, aren't you? Is that why you have those—those markings?"

Charlotte nodded. "I am one of the Nephilim—the Shadowhunters. We are . . . a race, if you will, of people, people with special abilities. We are stronger and swifter than most humans. We are able to conceal ourselves with magics called glamours. And we are especially skilled at killing demons."

"Demons. You mean—like Satan?"

"Demons are evil creatures. They travel great distances to come to this world and feed upon it. They would ravage it into ashes and destroy its inhabitants if we did not prevent it." Her voice was intent. "As it is the job of the human police to protect the citizenry of this city from one another, it is our job to protect them from demons and other supernatural dangers. When there are crimes that affect the Shadow World, when the Law of our world is broken, we must investigate. We are bound by the Law, in fact, to make inquiries even into the *rumor* of Covenant Law being contravened. Will told you about the dead girl he found in the alley; she was the only *body*, but there have been other disappearances, dark rumors of mundane boys and girls vanishing off the city's poorer streets. Using magic to murder human beings is against the Law, and therefore a matter for our jurisdiction."

"Mr. Herondale seems awfully young to be a sort of policeman."

"Shadowhunters grow up quickly, and Will did not investigate alone." Charlotte didn't sound as if she wished to elaborate. "That is not all we do. We safeguard the Covenant Law and uphold the Accords—the laws that govern peace among Downworlders."

Will had used that word as well. "Downworld? Is that a place?"

"A Downworlder is a being—a *person*—who is part supernatural in origin. Vampires, werewolves, faeries, warlocks—they are all Downworlders."

Tessa stared. Faeries were a children's tale, and vampires the stuff of penny dreadfuls. "Those creatures exist?"

"*You* are a Downworlder," Charlotte said. "Brother Enoch confirmed it. We simply don't know of what sort. You see, the kind of magic you can do—your ability—it isn't something an ordinary human being could do. Neither is it something one of us, a Shadowhunter, could do. Will thought you were most likely a warlock, which is what I would have guessed myself, but all warlocks have some attribute that marks them as warlocks. Wings, or hooves, or webbed toes, or, as you saw in the case of Mrs. Black, taloned hands. But you, you're completely human in appearance. And it is clear from your letters that you know, or believe, both of your parents to be human."

"*Human?*" Tessa stared. "Why wouldn't they have been human?"

Before Charlotte could answer, the door opened, and a slender, dark-haired girl in a white cap and apron came in, carrying a tea tray, which she set down on the table between them. "Sophie," Charlotte said, sounding relieved to see the girl. "Thank you. This is Miss Gray. She will be a guest of ours this evening."

Sophie straightened, turned to Tessa, and bobbed a curtsy. "Miss," she said, but the novelty of being curtsied to was lost on Tessa as Sophie raised her head and her full face became visible. She ought to have been very pretty—her eyes were a luminous dark hazel, her skin smooth, her lips soft and delicately shaped—but a thick, silvery ridged scar slashed from the left corner of her mouth to her temple, pulling her face sideways and distorting her features into a twisted mask. Tessa tried to hide the shock on her own face, but she could see as Sophie's eyes darkened that it hadn't worked.

"Sophie," Charlotte said, "did you bring in that dark red dress earlier, as I asked? Can you have it brushed and sponged for Tessa?" She turned back to Tessa as the maid nodded and went to the wardrobe. "I took the liberty of having one of our Jessamine's old dresses made over for you. The clothes you were wearing were ruined."

"Much obliged," Tessa said stiffly. She hated having to be grateful. The Sisters had pretended they were doing her favors, and look how that had turned out.

"Miss Gray." Charlotte looked at her earnestly. "Shadowhunters and Downworlders are not enemies. Our accord may be an uneasy one, but it is my belief that Downworlders are to be trusted—that, indeed, they hold the key to our eventual success against the demon realms. Is there something I can do to show you that we do not plan to take advantage of you?"

"I . . ." Tessa took a deep breath. "When the Dark Sisters first told me about my power, I thought they were mad," she said. "I told them such things didn't exist. Then I thought I was trapped in some sort of nightmare where they did. But then Mr. Herondale came, and he knew of magic, and had that glowing stone, and I thought, *Here is someone who might help me.*" She looked up at Charlotte. "But you do not seem to know why I am the way I am, or even *what* I am. And if even you do not . . ."

"It can be . . . difficult to learn how the world truly is, to see it in its true shape and form," Charlotte said. "Most human beings never do. Most could not bear it. But I have read your letters. And I know that you are strong, Miss Gray. You have withstood what might have killed another young girl, Downworlder or not."

"I didn't have a choice. I did it for my brother. They would have murdered him."

"Some people," Charlotte said, "would have let that happen. But I know from reading your own words that you never even considered that." She leaned forward. "Have you any idea where your brother is? Do you think he is most likely dead?"

Tessa sucked in a breath.

"Mrs. Branwell!" Sophie, who had been attending to the hem of a wine-red dress with a brush, looked up and spoke with a reproachful tone that surprised Tessa. It was not the place of servants to correct their employers; the books she'd read had made that very clear.

But Charlotte only looked rueful. "Sophie is my good angel," she said. "I tend to be a little too blunt. I thought there might be something you knew, something that wasn't in your letters, that might give us knowledge of his whereabouts."

Tessa shook her head. "The Dark Sisters told me he was

imprisoned in a safe location. I assume he is still there. But I have no idea how to find him."

"Then you should stay here at the Institute until he can be located."

"I don't want your charity." Tessa said mulishly. "I can find another lodging place."

"It would not be charity. We are bound by our own laws to help and aid Downworlders. To send you away with nowhere to go would break the Accords, which are important rules we must abide by."

"And you wouldn't ask for anything in return?" Tessa's voice was bitter. "You won't ask me to use my—my ability? You won't require me to Change?"

"If," Charlotte said, "you do not wish to use your power, then no, we will not force you to. Though I do believe you yourself might benefit from learning how it might be controlled and used—"

"*No!*" Tessa's cry was so loud that Sophie jumped and dropped her brush. Charlotte glanced over at her and then back at Tessa. She said, "As you wish, Miss Gray. There are other ways you could assist us. I'm sure there is much that you know that was not contained in your letters. And in return, we could help you to search for your brother."

Tessa's head went up. "You would do that?"

"You have my word." Charlotte stood up. Neither of them had touched the tea on its tray. "Sophie, if you could help Miss Gray dress, and then bring her in to dinner?"

"Dinner?" After hearing such a deal about Nephilim, and Downworld, and faeries and vampires and demons, the prospect of dinner was almost shocking in its ordinariness.

"Certainly. It's nearly seven o'clock. You've already met Will; you can meet everyone else. Perhaps you'll see that we're to be trusted."

And with a brisk nod, Charlotte left the room. As the door closed after her, Tessa shook her head mutely. Aunt Harriet had been bossy, but she'd had nothing on Charlotte Branwell.

"She has a strict manner, but she's really very kind," Sophie said, laying out on the bed the dress Tessa was meant to wear. "I've never known anyone with a better heart."

Tessa touched the sleeve of the dress with the tip of her finger. It was dark red satin, as Charlotte had said, with black moiré ribbon trim around the waist and hem. She had never worn anything so nice.

"Would you like me to help you get dressed for dinner, miss?" Sophie asked. Tessa remembered something Aunt Harriet had always said—that you could know a man not by what his friends said about him, but by how he treated his servants. If Sophie thought Charlotte had a good heart, then perhaps she did.

She raised her head. "Much obliged, Sophie. I believe I would."

Tessa had never had anyone assist her in getting dressed before, other than her aunt. Though Tessa was slender, the dress had clearly been made for a smaller girl, and Sophie had to lace Tessa's stays tightly to make it fit. She clucked under her breath while she did it. "Mrs. Branwell doesn't believe in tight lacing," she explained. "She says it causes nervous headaches and weakness, and a Shadowhunter can't afford to be weak. But Miss Jessamine likes the waists of her dresses *very* small, and she does insist."

"Well," said Tessa, a little breathless, "I'm not a Shadowhunter, anyway."

"There is that," Sophie agreed, doing up the back of the dress with a clever little buttonhook. "There. What do you think?"

Tessa looked at herself in the mirror, and was taken aback. The dress was too small on her, and had clearly been designed to be fitted closely to the body as it was. It clung almost shockingly to her figure down to the hips, where it swelled into gathers in the back, draped over a modest bustle. The sleeves were turned back, showing frills of champagne lace at the cuffs. She looked—older, she thought, not the tragic scarecrow she had looked in the Dark House, but not someone entirely familiar to herself either. *What if one of the times I Changed, when I turned back into myself, I didn't do it quite right? What if this isn't even my true face?* The thought sent such a bolt of panic through her that she felt as if she might faint.

"You *are* a little pale," Sophie said, examining Tessa's reflection with a judicious gaze. She didn't appear particularly shocked by the dress's tightness, at least. "You could try pinching your cheeks a bit to bring the color. That's what Miss Jessamine does."

"It was awfully kind of her—Miss Jessamine, I mean—to lend me this dress."

Sophie chuckled low in her throat. "Miss Jessamine's never worn it. Mrs. Branwell gave it to her as a gift, but Miss Jessamine said it made her look sallow and tossed it in the back of her wardrobe. Ungrateful, if you ask me. Now, go on then and pinch your cheeks a bit. You're pale as milk."

Having done so, and having thanked Sophie, Tessa emerged from the bedroom into a long stone corridor. Charlotte was there, waiting for her. She set off immediately, with Tessa behind her, limping slightly—the black silk shoes, which did not quite fit, were not kind to her bruised feet.

Being in the Institute was a bit like being inside a castle—the ceiling disappearing up into gloom, the tapestries hanging on the walls. Or at least it was what Tessa imagined the inside of a castle might look like. The tapestries bore repeating motifs of stars, swords, and the same sort of designs she'd seen inked on Will and Charlotte. There was a single repeating image too, of an angel rising out of a lake, carrying a sword in one hand and a cup in the other. "This place used to be a church," Charlotte said, answering Tessa's unasked question. "The Church of All-Hallows-the-Less. It burned down during the Great Fire of London. We took over the land after that and built the Institute on the ruins of the old church. It's useful for our purposes to remain on consecrated ground."

"Don't people think it's odd, you building on the site of an old church like this?" Tessa asked, hurrying to keep up.

"They don't know about it. Mundanes—that's what we call ordinary people—aren't aware of what we do," Charlotte explained. "To them, from the outside the place looks like an empty patch of land. Beyond that, mundanes aren't really very interested in what doesn't affect them directly." She turned to usher Tessa through a door and into a large brightly lit dining room. "Here we are."

Tessa stood blinking in the sudden illumination. The room was huge, big enough for a table that could have seated twenty people. An immense gasolier hung down from the ceiling, filling the room with a yellowish glow. Over a sideboard loaded with expensive-looking china, a gilt-framed mirror ran the length of the room. A low glass bowl of white flowers decorated the table's center. Everything was tasteful, and very ordinary. There was nothing unusual about the room, nothing that might hint at the nature of the house's occupants.

Though the entire long dining table was draped with white linen, only one end was set, with places for five people. Only two people were already sitting—Will and a fair-haired girl about Tessa's age in a shimmering low-necked gown. They appeared to be studiously ignoring each other; Will looked up in apparent relief when Charlotte and Tessa came in. "Will," Charlotte said. "You remember Miss Gray?"

"My recollection of her," said Will, "is most vivid indeed." He was no longer wearing the odd black clothes he'd been wearing the day before, but an ordinary pair of trousers and a gray jacket with a black velvet collar. The gray made his eyes look bluer than ever. He grinned at Tessa, who felt herself flush and looked quickly away.

"And Jessamine—Jessie, do look up. Jessie, this is Miss Theresa Gray; Miss Gray, this is Miss Jessamine Lovelace."

"So pleased to make your acquaintance," Jessamine murmured. Tessa couldn't help staring at her. She was almost ridiculously pretty, what one of Tessa's novels would have called an English rose—all silvery fair hair, soft brown eyes, and creamy complexion. She wore a very bright blue dress, and rings on almost every one of her fingers. If she had the same black skin markings that Will and Charlotte did, they weren't visible.

Will cast Jessamine a look of plain loathing, and turned to Charlotte. "Where's your benighted husband, then?"

Charlotte, taking a seat, gestured for Tessa to sit opposite her, in the chair beside Will. "Henry is in his workroom. I've sent Thomas to fetch him. He'll be up in a moment."

"And Jem?"

Charlotte's look was warning, but "Jem is unwell" was all she said. "He's having one of his days."

"He's *always* having one of his days." Jessamine sounded disgusted.

Tessa was about to inquire as to who Jem might be, when Sophie entered, followed by a plump woman of middle age whose gray hair was escaping from a bun at the back of her head. The two of them began to serve food from the sideboard. There was roast pork, potatoes, savory soup, and fluffy dinner rolls with creamy yellow butter. Tessa felt suddenly lightheaded; she had forgotten how hungry she was. She bit into a roll, only to check herself when she saw Jessamine staring.

"You know," Jessamine said airily, "I don't believe I've ever seen a warlock eat before. I suppose you needn't ever bant, do you? You can just use magic to make yourself slender."

"We don't know for certain that she's a warlock, Jessie," said Will.

Jessamine ignored him. "Is it dreadful, being so evil? Are you worried you'll go to Hell?" She leaned closer to Tessa. "What do you think the Devil's *like*?"

Tessa set her fork down. "Would you like to meet him? I could summon him up in a trice if you like. Being a warlock, and all."

Will let out a whoop of laughter. Jessamine's eyes narrowed. "There's no call to be rude," she began—then broke off as Charlotte sat bolt upright with an astonished shriek.

"Henry!"

A man was standing in the dining room's arched doorway—a familiar-looking tall man, with a shock of ginger hair and hazel eyes. He wore a torn tweed Norfolk jacket over a shockingly bright striped waistcoat; his trousers were covered in what looked peculiarly like coal dust. But none of that was what had made Charlotte scream; it was the fact that his left arm appeared to be on fire. Little flames licked up his arm from a point above his elbow, releasing tendrils of black smoke.

"Charlotte, darling," Henry said to his wife, who was staring at him in gape-mouthed horror. Jessamine, beside her, was wide eyed. "Sorry I'm late. You know, I think I might nearly have the Sensor working—"

Will interrupted. "Henry," he said, "you're on fire. You do know that, don't you?"

"Oh, yes," Henry said eagerly. The flames were now nearly to his shoulder. "I've been working like a man possessed all day. Charlotte, did you hear what I said about the Sensor?"

Charlotte dropped her hand from her mouth. "Henry!" she shrieked. "Your *arm*!"

Henry glanced down at his arm, and his mouth dropped open. "Bloody *hell*" was all he had time to say before Will, exhibiting a startling presence of mind, stood up, seized the vase of flowers off the table, and hurled the contents over Henry. The flames went out, with a faint protesting sizzle, leaving Henry standing soaking wet in the doorway, one sleeve of his jacket blackened and a dozen damp white flowers strewn at his feet.

Henry beamed and patted the burned sleeve of his jacket with a look of satisfaction. "You know what this means?"

Will set the vase down. "That you set yourself on fire and didn't even notice?"

"That the flame-retardant mixture I developed last week works!" Henry said proudly. "This material must have been burning for a good ten minutes, and it isn't even half burned through!" He squinted down at his arm. "Perhaps I ought to set the other sleeve on fire and see how long—"

"Henry," said Charlotte, who appeared to have recovered from her shock, "if you set yourself on fire deliberately, I will institute divorce proceedings. Now sit down and eat your supper. And say hello to our guest."

Henry sat, glanced across the table at Tessa—and blinked in surprise. "I know you," he said. "You bit me!" He sounded pleased about it, as if recollecting a pleasant memory they'd both shared.

Charlotte shot a despairing look at her husband.

"Have you asked Miss Gray about the Pandemonium Club yet?" Will asked.

The Pandemonium Club. "I know the words. They were written on the side of Mrs. Dark's carriage," Tessa said.

"It's an organization," Charlotte said. "A rather old organization of mundanes who have interested themselves in the magical arts. At their meetings they do spells and try to summon up demons and spirits." She sighed.

Jessamine snorted. "I can't imagine why they bother," she said. "Messing about with spells and wearing hooded robes and setting little fires. It's ridiculous."

"Oh, they do more than that," said Will. "They're more powerful in Downworld than you might think. Many rich and important figures in mundane society are members—"

"That only makes it sillier." Jessamine tossed her hair. "They have money and power. Why are they playing around with magic?"

"A good question," said Charlotte. "Mundanes who involve

themselves in things they know nothing about are likely to meet unpleasant ends."

Will shrugged. "When I was trying to track down the source of the symbol on that knife Jem and I found in the alley, I was directed to the Pandemonium Club. The members of it in turn directed me to the Dark Sisters. It's their symbol—the two serpents. They supervised a set of secret gambling dens frequented by Downworlders. They existed to lure mundanes in and trick them into losing all their money in magical games, then, when the mundanes fell into debt, the Dark Sisters would extort the money back at ruinous rates." Will looked over at Charlotte. "They ran some other businesses as well, most unsavory ones. The house in which they kept Tessa, I had been told, was a Downworlder brothel catering to mundanes with unusual tastes."

"Will, I'm not at all sure—," Charlotte began dubiously.

"Hmph," Jessamine said. "No wonder you were so keen to go there, William."

If she had hoped to annoy Will, it didn't work; she might as well not have spoken, for all the attention he paid her. He was looking at Tessa across the table, his eyebrows arched slightly. "Have I offended you, Miss Gray? I imagined that after all you've seen, you would not be easily shocked."

"I am not offended, Mr. Herondale." Despite her words, Tessa felt her cheeks flame. Well-brought-up young ladies didn't know what a brothel was, and certainly wouldn't say the word in mixed company. Murder was one thing, but this . . . "I, ah, don't see how it could have been a . . . place like that," she said as firmly as she could. "No one ever came or went, and other than the maidservant and the coachman, I never saw anyone else who lived there."

"No, by the time I got there, it was quite deserted," Will agreed. "Clearly they had decided to suspend business, perhaps in the interests of keeping you isolated." He glanced over at Charlotte. "Do you think Miss Gray's brother has the same ability she does? Is that, perhaps, why the Dark Sisters captured him in the first place?"

Tessa interjected, glad for the change of subject. "My brother never showed any sign of such a thing—but, then, neither did I until the Dark Sisters found me."

"What *is* your ability?" Jessamine demanded. "Charlotte won't say."

"Jessamine!" Charlotte scowled at her.

"I don't believe she has one," Jessamine went on. "I think she's simply a little sneak who knows that if we believe she's a Downworlder, we'll have to treat her well because of the Accords."

Tessa set her jaw. She thought of her Aunt Harriet saying *Don't lose your temper, Tessa,* and *Don't fight with your brother simply because he teases you.* But she didn't care. They were all looking at her—Henry with curious hazel eyes, Charlotte with a gaze as sharp as glass, Jessamine with thinly veiled contempt, and Will with cool amusement. What if they all thought what Jessamine thought? What if they all thought she was angling for charity? Aunt Harriet would have hated accepting charity even more than she'd disapproved of Tessa's temper.

It was Will who spoke next, leaning forward to look intently into her face. "You can keep it a secret," he said softly. "But secrets have their own weight, and it can be a very heavy one."

Tessa raised her head. "It needn't be a secret. But it would be easier for me to show you than to tell you."

"Excellent!" Henry looked pleased. "I enjoy being shown things. Is there anything you require, like a spirit lamp, or—"

"It's not a séance, Henry," Charlotte said wearily. She turned to Tessa. "You don't need to do this if you don't want to, Miss Gray."

Tessa ignored her. "Actually, I do require something." She turned to Jessamine. "Something of yours, please. A ring, or a handkerchief—"

Jessamine wrinkled her nose. "Dear me, it sounds to me rather as if your special power is pickpocketing!"

Will looked exasperated. "Give her a ring, Jessie. You're wearing enough of them."

"*You* give her something, then." Jessamine set her chin.

"No." Tessa spoke firmly. "It must be something of yours." *Because of everyone here, you're the closest to me in size and shape. If I transform into tiny Charlotte, this dress will simply fall off me,* Tessa thought. She had considered trying to use the dress itself, but since Jessamine had never worn it, Tessa wasn't sure the Change would work and didn't want to take any chances.

"Oh, very well then." Petulantly Jessamine detached from her smallest finger a ring with a red stone set in it, and passed it across the table to Tessa. "This had better be worth the trouble."

Oh, it will be. Unsmiling, Tessa put the ring in the palm of her left hand and closed her fingers around it. Then she shut her eyes.

It was always the same: nothing at first, then the flicker of something at the back of her mind, like someone lighting a candle in a dark room. She groped her way toward it, as the Dark Sisters had taught her. It was hard to strip away the fear and the shyness, but she had done it enough times now to know what to expect—the reaching forward to touch the light at the center of the darkness; the sense of light and enveloping warmth, as if she were drawing a blanket, something thick and heavy, around herself, covering every layer of her own skin; and then the light blazing up and surrounding her—and she was inside it. Inside someone else's skin. Inside their mind.

Jessamine's mind.

She was only at the edge of it, her thoughts skimming the surface of Jessamine's like fingers skimming the surface of water. Still, it took her breath away. Tessa had a sudden, flashing image of a bright piece of candy with something dark at its center, like a worm at the core of an apple. She felt resentment, bitter hatred, anger—a terrible fierce longing for *something*—

Her eyes flew open. She was still sitting at the table, Jessamine's ring clutched in her hand. Her skin zinged with the sharp pins and needles that always accompanied her transformations. She could feel the oddness that was the different weight of another body, not her own; could feel the brush of Jessamine's light hair against her shoulders. Too thick to be held back by the pins that had clasped Tessa's hair, it had come down around her neck in a pale cascade.

"By the Angel," breathed Charlotte. Tessa looked around the table. They were all staring at her—Charlotte and Henry with their mouths open; Will speechless for once, a glass of water frozen halfway to his lips. And Jessamine—Jessamine was gazing at her in abject horror, like someone who has seen a vision of their own ghost. For a moment Tessa felt a stab of guilt.

It lasted only a moment, though. Slowly Jessamine lowered her hand from her mouth, her face still very pale. "*Goodness*, my nose is enormous," she exclaimed. "Why didn't anyone tell me?"

4

We Are Shadows

Pulvis et umbra sumus.
—Horace, *Odes*

The moment Tessa transformed back to her own shape, she had to suffer a barrage of questions. For people who lived in a shadow world of magic, the assembled Nephilim seemed surprisingly awed by her ability, which only served to underline what Tessa had already begun to suspect—that her shape-changing talent was exceedingly unusual. Even Charlotte, who had known about it before Tessa's demonstration, seemed fascinated.

"So you must be holding something that belongs to the person you're transforming into?" Charlotte asked for the second time. Sophie and the older woman, who Tessa suspected was the cook, had already taken away the dinner plates and had served fancy cake and tea, but none of the diners had touched it yet. "You can't simply *look* at someone and—"

"I explained that already." Tessa's head was beginning to hurt. "I must be holding something that belongs to them, or a bit of hair or an eyelash. Something that's *theirs*. Otherwise nothing happens."

"Do you think a vial of blood would do the trick?" Will asked, in a tone of academic interest.

"Probably—I don't know. I've never tried it." Tessa took a sip of her tea, which had grown cold.

"And you're saying that the Dark Sisters *knew* this was your talent? They knew you had this ability before you did?" Charlotte asked.

"Yes. It's why they wanted me in the first place."

Henry shook his head. "But *how* did they know? I don't quite understand that part."

"I don't *know*," Tessa said, not for the first time. "They never explained it to me. All I know is what I told you—that they seemed to know exactly what it was I could do, and how to train me to do it. They spent hours with me, every day . . ." Tessa swallowed against the bitterness in her mouth. Memories of how it had been rose up in her mind—the hours and hours in the cellar room at the Dark House, the way they had screamed at her that Nate would die if she couldn't Change as they wanted her to, the agony when she finally learned to do it. "It *hurt*, at first," she whispered. "As if my bones were snapping, melting inside my body. They would force me to Change two, three, then a dozen times a day, until I would finally lose consciousness. And then, the next day, they'd start at it again. I was locked in that room, so I couldn't try to leave. . . ." She took a ragged breath. "That last day, they tested me by asking me to Change into a girl who had died. She had memories of being attacked with a dagger, being stabbed. Of some *thing* chasing her into an alley—"

"Perhaps it was the girl Jem and I found." Will sat up straight, his eyes shining. "Jem and I guessed she must have escaped from an attack and run out into the night. I believe they sent the Shax demon after her to bring her back, but I killed it. They must have wondered what happened."

"The girl I changed into was named Emma Bayliss," Tessa said, in a half whisper. "She had very fair hair—tied in little pink bows—and she was only a little thing."

Will nodded as if the description were familiar to him.

"Then they did wonder what had happened to her. That's why they had me Change into her. When I told them she was dead, they seemed relieved."

"The poor soul," Charlotte murmured. "So you can Change into the dead? Not only the living?"

Tessa nodded. "Their voices speak in my mind when I Change too. The difference is that many of them can remember the moment they died."

"Ugh." Jessamine shuddered. "How *morbid*."

Tessa looked over at Will. *Mr. Herondale*, she chided herself silently, but it was hard to think of him that way. She felt somehow as if she knew him better than she really did. But that was foolishness. "You found me because you were looking for the murderer of Emma Bayliss," she said. "But she was only one dead human girl. One dead—what do you call it?—mundane. Why so much time and effort to find out what happened to her?"

For a moment Will's eyes met hers, his own a very dark

blue. Then his expression changed—only a slight change, but she saw it, though she could not have said what the change meant. "Oh, I wouldn't have bothered, but Charlotte insisted. She felt there was something larger at work. And once Jem and I infiltrated the Pandemonium Club, and heard rumors of the other murders, we realized there was more going on than the death of one girl. Whether or not we like mundanes particularly, we can't allow them to be systematically slaughtered. It's the reason we exist."

Charlotte leaned forward across the table. "The Dark Sisters never mentioned what use they intended to make of your abilities, did they?"

"You know about the Magister," Tessa said. "They said they were preparing me for him."

"For him to do what?" Will asked. "Eat you for dinner?"

Tessa shook her head. "To—to marry me, they said."

"To marry you?" Jessamine was openly scornful. "That's ridiculous. They were probably going to blood sacrifice you and didn't want you to panic."

"I don't know about that," Will said. "I looked in several rooms before I found Tessa. I remember one that was done up surprisingly like a wedding chamber. White hangings on an enormous bed. A white dress hanging in the wardrobe. It looked about your size." He eyed Tessa thoughtfully.

"Ceremonial marriage can be a very powerful thing," Charlotte said. "Performed properly, it could allow someone access to your ability, Tessa, even the power to control you." She drummed her fingertips thoughtfully on the tabletop. "As for 'the Magister,' I've researched the term in the archives. It is often used to denote the head of a coven or other group of magicians. The sort of group the Pandemonium Club imagines itself to be. I can't help but feel that the Magister and the Pandemonium Club are connected."

"We've investigated them before and never managed to catch them doing anything dodgy," Henry pointed out. "It isn't against the Law to be an idiot."

"Lucky for you," Jessamine said under her breath.

Henry looked hurt, but said nothing. Charlotte cast Jessamine a freezing look.

"Henry is right," said Will. "It isn't as if Jem and I didn't catch them doing the odd illegal thing—drinking absinthe laced with demon powders, and so forth. As long as they were only hurting themselves, it hardly seemed worth involving ourselves. But if they've graduated to harming others . . ."

"Do you know who any of them are?" Henry asked curiously.

"The mundanes, no," Will said dismissively. "There never seemed a reason to find out, and many of them went masked or disguised at club events. But I recognized quite a few of the Downworlders. Magnus Bane, Lady Belcourt, Ragnor Fell, de Quincey—"

"De Quincey? I hope he wasn't breaking any laws. You know how much trouble we've had finding a head vampire we can see eye to eye with," fretted Charlotte.

Will smiled into his tea. "Whenever I saw him, he was being a perfect angel."

After a hard look at him, Charlotte turned to Tessa. "Did the servant girl you mentioned—Miranda—have your ability? Or what about Emma?"

"I don't think so. If Miranda did, they would have been

training her as well, wouldn't they, and Emma didn't remember anything like that."

"And they never mentioned the Pandemonium Club? Some larger purpose to what they were doing?"

Tessa racked her brain. What was it the Dark Sisters had talked about when they'd thought she wasn't listening? "I don't think they ever said the name of the club, but they would talk sometimes about meetings they were planning on attending, and how the other members would be pleased to see how they were getting on with me. They did say a name once. . . ." Tessa screwed her face up, trying to remember. "Someone else who was in the club. I don't remember, though I recall thinking the name sounded foreign. . . ."

Charlotte leaned forward across the table. "Can you *try*, Tessa? Try to remember?"

Charlotte meant no harm, Tessa knew, and yet her voice called up other voices in Tessa's head—voices urging her to *try*, to reach into herself, to draw out the power. Voices that could turn hard and cold at the slightest provocation. Voices that wheedled and threatened and lied.

Tessa drew herself upright. "First, what about my brother?"

Charlotte blinked. "Your brother?"

"You said that if I gave you information about the Dark Sisters, you'd help me find my brother. Well, I told you what I knew. And I still don't have any idea where Nate is."

"Oh." Charlotte sat back, looking almost startled. "Of course. We'll start investigating his whereabouts tomorrow," she reassured Tessa. "We'll start with his workplace—speak to his employer and find out if he knows anything. We have contacts in all sorts of places, Miss Gray. Downworld runs on gossip like the mundane world does. Eventually we'll turn up someone who knows something about your brother."

The meal ended not long after that, and Tessa excused herself from the table with a feeling of relief, declining Charlotte's offer to guide her back to her room. All she wanted was to be alone with her thoughts.

She made her way down the torchlit corridor, remembering the day she had stepped off the boat at Southampton. She had come to England knowing no one but her brother, and had let the Dark Sisters force her into serving them. Now she had fallen in with the Shadowhunters, and who was to say they would treat her any better? Like the Dark Sisters, they wanted to use her—use her for the information she knew—and now that they were all aware of her power, how long would it be before they wanted to use her for that, too?

Still lost in thought, Tessa nearly walked directly into a wall. She brought herself up short—and looked around, frowning. She had been walking for much longer than it had taken her and Charlotte to reach the dining room, and still she hadn't found the room she remembered. In fact, she wasn't even sure she had found the *corridor* she remembered. She was in a hallway now, lined with torches and hung with tapestries, but was it the same one? Some of the corridors were very bright, some very dim, the torches burning with varying shades of brightness. Sometimes the torches flared up and then faded as she passed, as if responding to some peculiar stimulus she couldn't see. This particular corridor was fairly dim. She picked her way to the end of it carefully, where it branched into two more, each identical to this one.

"Lost?" inquired a voice behind her. A slow, arrogant voice, immediately familiar.

Will.

Tessa turned and saw that he was leaning carelessly against the wall behind her, as if he were lounging in a doorway, his feet in their scuffed boots crossed in front of him. He held something in his hand: his glowing stone. He pocketed it as she looked at him, dousing its light.

"You ought to let me show you around the Institute a bit, Miss Gray," he suggested. "You know, so you don't get lost again."

Tessa narrowed her eyes at him.

"Of course, you can simply continue wandering about on your own if you really wish to," he added. "I ought to warn you, though, that there are at least three or four doors in the Institute that you really shouldn't open. There's the one that leads to the room where we keep trapped demons, for instance. They can get a bit nasty. Then there is the weapons room. Some of the weapons have a mind of their own, and they *are* sharp. Then there are the rooms that open onto empty air. They're meant to confuse intruders, but when you're as high as the top of a church, you don't want to accidentally slip and—"

"I don't believe you," Tessa said. "You're an awful liar, Mr. Herondale. Still—" She bit her lip. "I don't like wandering about. You can show me around if you promise no tricks."

Will promised. And, to Tessa's surprise, he was true to his word. He guided her down a succession of identical-looking corridors, talking as they walked. He told her how many rooms the Institute had (more than you could count), told her how many Shadowhunters could live in it at once (hundreds), and displayed for her the vast ballroom in which was held an annual Christmas party for the Enclave—which, Will explained, was their term for the group of Shadowhunters who lived in London. (In New York, he added, the term was "Conclave." American Shadowhunters, it seemed, had their own lexicon.)

After the ballroom came the kitchen, where the middle-aged woman Tessa had seen in the dining room was introduced as Agatha, the cook. She sat sewing in front of a massive kitchen range and was, to Tessa's intense mystification, also smoking an enormous pipe. She smiled indulgently around it as Will took several chocolate tarts from the plate where they had been left to cool on the table. Will offered one to Tessa.

She shuddered. "Oh, no. I *hate* chocolate."

Will looked horrified. "What kind of monster could possibly hate chocolate?"

"He eats *everything*," Agatha told Tessa with a placid smile. "Since he was twelve, he has. I suppose it's all the training that keeps him from getting fat."

Tessa, amused at the idea of a fat Will, complimented the pipe-puffing Agatha on her mastery of the enormous kitchen. It looked like a place you could cook for hundreds, with row upon row of jarred preserves and soups, spice tins, and a huge haunch of beef roasting on a hook over the open fireplace.

"Well done," Will said after they'd left the kitchen. "Complimenting Agatha like that. Now she'll like you. It's no good if Agatha doesn't like you. She'll put stones in your porridge."

"Oh, dear," Tessa said, but she couldn't hide the fact that she was entertained. They went from the kitchen to the music room, where there were harps and a great old piano, gathering dust. Down a set of stairs was the drawing room, a pleasant place where the walls, instead of being bare stone, were papered with a bright print of leaves and lilies. A fire was going in a large grate, and several comfortable armchairs were pulled up near it. There was a great wooden desk in the room too, which Will explained was the place where Charlotte did much of the work of running the Institute. Tessa couldn't help wondering what it was that Henry Branwell did, and where he did it.

After that there was the weapons room, finer than anything Tessa imagined you might see in a museum. Hundreds of maces, axes, daggers, swords, knives, and even a few pistols hung on the walls, as well as a collection of different kinds of armor, from greaves worn to protect the shins to full suits of chain mail. A solid-looking young man with dark brown hair sat at a high table, polishing a set of short daggers. He grinned when they came in. "Evenin', Master Will."

"Good evening, Thomas. You know Miss Gray." He indicated Tessa.

"You were at the Dark House!" Tessa exclaimed, looking more closely at Thomas. "You came in with Mr. Branwell. I thought—"

"That I was a Shadowhunter?" Thomas grinned. He had a sweet, pleasant, open sort of face, and a lot of curling hair. His shirt was open at the neck, showing a strong throat. Despite his obvious youth, he was extremely tall and muscular, the width of his arms straining against his sleeves. "I'm not, miss—only trained like one."

Will leaned back against the wall. "Did that order of misericord blades come in, Thomas? I've been running into a certain amount of Shax demons lately, and I need something narrow that can pierce armored carapaces."

Thomas started to say something to Will about shipping being delayed due to weather in Idris, but Tessa's attention had been distracted by something else. It was a tall box of golden wood, polished to a high shine, with a pattern burned into the front—a snake, swallowing its own tail.

"Isn't that the Dark Sisters' symbol?" she demanded. "What's it doing here?"

"Not quite," said Will. "The box is a Pyxis. Demons don't have souls; their consciousness comes from a sort of energy, which can sometimes be trapped and stored. The Pyxis contains them safely—oh, and the design is an *ouroboros*—the 'tail devourer.' It's an ancient alchemical symbol meant to represent the different dimensions—our world, inside the serpent, and the rest of existence, outside." He shrugged. "The Sisters' symbol is the first time I've seen anyone draw an *ouroboros* with two snakes— Oh, no you don't," he added as Tessa reached for the box. He deftly stepped in front of her. "The Pyxis can't be touched by anyone who isn't a Shadowhunter. Nasty things will happen. Now let's go. We've taken up enough of Thomas's time."

"I don't mind," Thomas protested, but Will was already on his way out. Tessa glanced back at Thomas from the doorway. He'd gone back to polishing the weaponry, but there was something about the set of his shoulders that made Tessa think he seemed a little bit lonely.

"I didn't realize you let mundanes fight with you," she said to Will after they'd left the weapons room behind. "Is Thomas a servant, or—"

"Thomas has been with the Institute for almost his entire life," Will said, guiding Tessa around a sharp turn in the corridor. "There are families who have the Sight in their veins, families who have always served Shadowhunters. Thomas's parents served Charlotte's parents in the Institute, and now Thomas serves Charlotte and Henry. And his children will serve theirs. Thomas does everything—drives, cares for Balios and Xanthos—those are our horses—and helps with the weapons. Sophie and Agatha manage the rest, though Thomas assists them on occasion. I suspect he's sweet on Sophie and doesn't like to see her work too hard."

Tessa was glad to hear it. She'd felt awful about her reaction to Sophie's scar, and the thought that Sophie had a male admirer—and a handsome one at that—eased her conscience slightly. "Perhaps he's in love with Agatha," she said.

"I hope not. I intend to marry Agatha myself. She may be a thousand years old, but she makes an incomparable jam tart. Beauty fades, but cooking is eternal." He paused in front of a door—big and oak, with thick brass hinges. "Here we are, now," he said, and the door swung open at his touch.

The room they entered was bigger even than the ballroom she had seen before. It was longer than it was wide, with rectangular oak tables set down the middle of it, vanishing up to the far wall, which was painted with an image of an angel. Each table was illuminated by a glass lamp that flickered white. Halfway up the walls was an interior gallery with a wooden railing running around it that could be reached by means of spiral staircases on either side of the room. Rows upon rows of bookshelves stood at intervals, like sentries forming alcoves on either side of the room. There were more bookshelves upstairs as well; the books inside were hidden behind screens of fretted metal, each screen stamped with a pattern of four *C*s. Huge, outward-curving stained-glass windows, lined with worn stone benches, were set at intervals between the shelves.

A vast tome had been left out on a stand, its pages open and inviting; Tessa moved toward it, thinking it must be a dictionary, only to find that its pages were scrawled with illegible, illuminated script and etched with unfamiliar-looking maps.

"This is the Great Library," said Will. "Every Institute has a library, but this one is the largest of them all—the largest in the West, at any rate." He leaned against the door, his arms crossed over his chest. "I said I would get you more books, didn't I?"

Tessa was so startled that he remembered what he had said, that it took her several seconds to respond. "But the books are all behind bars!" she said. "Like a literary sort of prison!"

Will grinned. "Some of these books are dangerous," he said. "It's wise to be careful."

"One must always be careful of books," said Tessa, "and what is inside them, for words have the power to change us."

"I'm not sure a book has ever changed me," said Will. "Well, there is one volume that promises to teach one how to turn oneself into an entire flock of sheep—"

"Only the very weak-minded refuse to be influenced by literature and poetry," said Tessa, determined not to let him run wildly off with the conversation.

"Of course, why one would want to be an entire flock of sheep is another matter entirely," Will finished. "Is there something you want to read here, Miss Gray, or is there not? Name it, and I shall attempt to free it from its prison for you."

"Do you think the library has *The Wide, Wide World?* Or *Little Women?*"

"Never heard of either of them," said Will. "We haven't many novels."

"Well, I want novels," said Tessa. "Or poetry. Books are for reading, not for turning oneself into livestock."

Will's eyes glittered. "I think we may have a copy of *Alice's Adventures in Wonderland* about somewhere."

Tessa wrinkled her nose. "Oh, that's for little children, isn't it?" she said. "I never liked it much—seemed like so much nonsense."

Will's eyes were very blue. "There's plenty of sense in non-sense sometimes, if you wish to look for it."

But Tessa had already spied a familiar volume on a shelf and went over to greet it like an old friend. "*Oliver Twist!*" she cried. "Have you any other of Mr. Dickens's novels?" She clasped her hands together. "Oh! Do you have *A Tale of Two Cities?*"

"That silly thing? Men going around getting their heads chopped off for love? Ridiculous." Will unpeeled himself from the door and made his way toward Tessa where she stood by the bookshelves. He gestured expansively at the vast number of volumes all around him. "No, here you'll find all sorts of advice about how to chop off someone's *else's* head if you need to; much more useful."

"I don't!" Tessa protested. "Need to chop off anyone's head, that is. And what's the point of a lot of books no one actually wants to *read?* Haven't you really any other novels?"

"Not unless *Lady Audley's Secret* is that she slays demons in her spare time." Will bounded up onto one of the ladders and yanked a book off the shelf. "I'll find you something else to read. Catch." He let it fall without looking, and Tessa had to dart forward to seize it before it hit the floor.

It was a large squarish volume bound in dark blue velvet. There was a pattern cut into the velvet, a swirling symbol reminiscent of the marks that decorated Will's skin. The title was stamped on the front in silver: *The Shadowhunter's Codex.* Tessa glanced up at Will. "What is this?"

"I assumed you'd have questions about Shadowhunters, given that you're currently inhabiting our sanctum sanctorum, so to speak. That book ought to tell you anything you want to know—about us, about our history, even about Downworlders like you." Will's face turned grave. "Be careful with it, though. It's six hundred years old and the only copy of its kind. Losing or damaging it is punishable by death under the Law."

Tessa thrust the book away from her as if it were on fire. "You can't be serious."

"You're right. I'm not." Will leaped down from the ladder and landed lightly in front of her. "You do believe everything I say, though, don't you? Do I seem unusually trustworthy to you, or are you just a naïve sort?"

Instead of replying, Tessa scowled at him and stalked across the room toward one of the stone benches inside a window alcove. Throwing herself down onto the seat, she opened the *Codex* and began to read, studiously ignoring Will even as he moved to sit beside her. She could feel the weight of his gaze on her as she read.

The first page of the Nephilim book showed the same image she'd grown used to seeing on the tapestries in the corridors: the angel rising out of the lake, holding a sword in one hand

and a cup in the other. Underneath the illustration was a note: *The Angel Raziel and the Mortal Instruments.*

"That's how it all began," Will said cheerfully, as if oblivious to the fact that she was ignoring him. "A summoning spell here, a bit of angel blood there, and you've a recipe for indestructible human warriors. You'll never understand us from reading a book, mind you, but it's a start."

"Hardly human—more like avenging angels," Tessa said softly, turning the pages. There were dozens of pictures of angels—tumbling out of the sky, shedding feathers as a star might shed sparks as it fell. There were more images of the Angel Raziel, holding open a book on whose pages runes burned like fire, and there were men kneeling around him, men on whose skin Marks could be seen. Images of men like the one she'd seen in her nightmare, with missing eyes and sewed-shut lips; images of Shadowhunters brandishing flaming swords, like warrior angels out of Heaven. She looked up at Will. "You are, then, aren't you? Part angel?"

Will didn't answer. He was looking out the window, through a clear lower pane. Tessa followed his gaze; the window gave out onto what had to be the front of the Institute, for there was a rounded courtyard below them, surrounded by walls. Through the bars of a high iron gate surmounted by a curved arch, she could glimpse a bit of the street beyond, lit by dim yellow gaslight. There were iron letters worked into the wrought arch atop the gate; when looked at from this direction, they were backward, and Tessa squinted to decipher them.

"*Pulvis et umbra sumus.* It's a line from Horace. '*We are dust and shadows.*' Appropriate, don't you think?" Will said. "It's not a long life, killing demons; one tends to die young, and then they burn your body—dust to dust, in the literal sense. And then we vanish into the shadows of history, nary a mark on the page of a mundane book to remind the world that once we existed at all."

Tessa looked at him. He was wearing that look she found so odd and compelling—that amusement that didn't seem to pass beyond the surface of his features, as if he found everything in the world both infinitely funny and infinitely tragic all at the same time. She wondered what had made him this way, how he had come to find darkness amusing, for it was a quality he didn't appear to share with any of the other Shadowhunters she had met, however briefly. Perhaps it was something he had learned from his parents—but what parents?

"Don't you ever worry?" she said softly. "That what's out there—might come in here?"

"Demons and other unpleasantness, you mean?" Will asked, though Tessa wasn't sure if that was what she had meant, or if she had been speaking of the evils of the world in general. He placed a hand against the wall. "The mortar that made these stones was mixed with the blood of Shadowhunters. Every beam is carved of rowan wood. Every nail used to hammer the beams together is made of silver, iron, or electrum. The place is built on hallowed ground surrounded by wards. The front door can be opened only by one possessing Shadowhunter blood; otherwise it remains locked forever. This place is a fortress. So no, I am *not* worried."

"But why live in a fortress?" At his surprised look she elaborated. "You clearly aren't related to Charlotte and Henry, they're hardly old enough to have adopted you, and not all

Shadowhunter children must live here or there would be more than you and Jessamine—"

"And Jem," Will reminded her.

"Yes, but—you see what I mean. Why don't you live with your family?"

"None of us *have* parents. Jessamine's died in a fire, Jem's—well Jem came from quite a distance away to live here, after his parents were murdered by demons. Under Covenant Law, the Clave is responsible for parentless Shadowhunter children under the age of eighteen."

"So you are one another's family."

"If you must romanticize it, I suppose we are—all brothers and sisters under the Institute's roof. You as well, Miss Gray, however temporarily."

"In that case," Tessa said, feeling hot blood rise to her face, "I think I would prefer it if you called me by my Christian name, as you do with Miss Lovelace."

Will looked at her, slow and hard, and then smiled. His blue eyes lit when he smiled. "Then you must do the same for me," he said. "Tessa."

She had never thought about her name much before, but when he said it, it was as if she were hearing it for the first time—the hard *T*, the caress of the double *S*, the way it seemed to end on a breath. Her own breath was very short when she said, softly, "Will."

"Yes?" Amusement glittered in his eyes.

With a sort of horror Tessa realized that she had simply said his name for the sake of saying it; she hadn't actually had a question. Hastily she said, "How do you learn—to fight like you do? To draw those magical symbols, and the rest of it?"

Will smiled. "We had a tutor who provided our schooling and physical training—though he's left for Idris, and Charlotte's looking for a replacement—along with Charlotte, who takes care of teaching us history and ancient languages."

"So she's your governess?"

A look of dark mirth passed across Will's features. "You could say that. But I wouldn't call Charlotte a governess if I were you, not if you want to preserve your limbs intact. You wouldn't think it to look at her, but she's quite skilled with a variety of weapons, our Charlotte."

Tessa blinked in surprise. "You don't mean—Charlotte doesn't *fight*, does she? Not the way you and Henry do."

"Certainly she does. Why wouldn't she?"

"Because she's a woman," Tessa said.

"So was Boadicea."

"Who?"

"'*So the Queen Boadicea, standing loftily charioted,/Brandishing in her hand a dart and rolling glances lioness-like*—'" Will broke off at Tessa's look of incomprehension, and grinned. "Nothing? If you were English, you'd know. Remind me to find a book about her for you. Regardless, she was a powerful warrior queen. When she was finally defeated, she took poison rather than let herself be captured by the Romans. She was braver than any man. I like to think Charlotte is much in the same mold, if somewhat smaller."

"But she can't be any good at it, can she? I mean, women don't have those sort of feelings."

"What kind of feelings are those?"

"Bloodlust, I suppose," Tessa said after a moment. "Fierceness. Warrior feelings."

"I saw you waving that hacksaw at the Dark Sisters," Will pointed out. "And if I recall correctly, Lady Audley's secret was, in fact, that she was a murderer."

"So you've read it!" Tessa couldn't hide her delight.

He looked amused. "I prefer *The Trail of the Serpent.* More adventure, less domestic drama. Neither is as good as *The Moonstone*, though. Have you read Collins?"

"I *adore* Wilkie Collins," Tessa cried. "Oh—*Armadale*! And *The Woman in White* . . . Are you laughing at me?"

"Not *at* you," said Will, grinning, "more *because* of you. I've never seen anyone get so excited over books before. You'd think they were diamonds."

"Well, they are, aren't they? Isn't there anything *you* love like that? And don't say 'spats' or 'lawn tennis' or something silly."

"Good Lord," he said with mock horror, "it's like she knows me already."

"Everyone has something they can't live without. I'll find out what it is for you, never you fear." She meant to speak lightly, but at the look on his face, her voice trailed off into uncertainty. He was looking at her with an odd steadiness; his eyes were the same dark blue as the velvet binding of the book she held. His gaze passed over her face, down her throat, to her waist, before rising back up to her face, where it lingered on her mouth. Tessa's heart was pounding as if she had been running up stairs. Something in her chest ached, as if she were hungry or thirsty. There was something she *wanted*, but she didn't know what—

"It's late," Will said abruptly, looking away from her. "I should show you back to your room."

"I—" Tessa wanted to protest, but there was no reason to do

so. He was right. It *was* late, the pinprick light of stars visible through the clear panes of the window. She rose to her feet, cradling the book to her chest, and went with Will out into the corridor.

"There are a few tricks to learning your way around the Institute that I ought to teach you," he said, still not looking at her. There was something oddly diffident in his attitude now that hadn't been there moments before, as if Tessa had done something to offend him. But what could she have done? "Ways to identify the different doors and turn—"

He broke off, and Tessa saw that someone was coming down the corridor toward them. It was Sophie, a basket of laundry tucked under one of her arms. Seeing Will and Tessa, she paused, her expression growing more guarded.

"Sophie!" Will's diffidence turned to mischief. "Have you finished putting my room in order yet?"

"It's done." Sophie didn't return his smile. "It was filthy. I hope that in future you can refrain from tracking bits of dead demon through the house."

Tessa's mouth fell open. How could Sophie talk to Will like that? She was a servant, and he—even if he *was* younger than she was—was a gentleman.

And yet Will seemed to take it in stride. "All part of the job, young Sophie."

"Mr. Branwell and Mr. Carstairs seem to have no problem cleaning their boots," Sophie said, looking darkly from Will to Tessa. "Perhaps you could learn from their example."

"Perhaps," said Will. "But I doubt it."

Sophie scowled, and started off along the corridor again, her shoulders tightly set with indignation.

Tessa looked at Will in amazement. "What was that?"

Will shrugged lazily. "Sophie enjoys pretending she doesn't like me."

"Doesn't like you? She *hates* you!" Under other circumstances, she might have asked if Will and Sophie had had a falling out, but one didn't fall out with *servants*. If they were unsatisfactory, one ceased to employ them. "Did—did something happen between you?"

"Tessa," Will said with exaggerated patience. "Enough. There are things you can't hope to understand."

If there was one thing Tessa hated, it was being told that there were things she couldn't understand. Because she was young, because she was a girl—for any of a thousand reasons that never seemed to make any real sense. She set her chin stubbornly. "Well, not if you won't tell me. But then I'd have to say that it looks a great deal like she hates you because you did something awful to her."

Will's expression darkened. "You can think what you like. It's not as if you know anything about me."

"I know you don't like giving straightforward answers to questions. I know you're probably around seventeen. I know you like Tennyson—you quoted him at the Dark House, and again just now. I know you're an orphan, as I am—"

"I *never* said I was an orphan." Will spoke with unexpected savagery. "And I loathe poetry. So, as it happens, you really don't know anything about me at all, do you?"

And with that, he spun on his heel and walked away.

5

The Shadowhunter's Codex

Dreams are true while they last, and do we not live in dreams?
—Alfred, Lord Tennyson, "The Higher Pantheism"

It took an age of wandering glumly from corridor to identical corridor before Tessa, by lucky chance, recognized a rip in yet another of the endless tapestries and realized that the door to her bedroom must be one of the ones lining that particular hallway. A few minutes of trial and error later, and she was gratefully shutting the correct door behind her and sliding the bolt home in the lock.

The moment she was back in her nightgown and had slipped under the covers, she opened *The Shadowhunter's Codex* and began to read. *You'll never understand us from reading a book*, Will had said, but that wasn't the point really. He didn't know what books meant to her, that books were symbols of truth and meaning, that this one acknowledged that she existed and that there were others like her in the world. Holding it in her hands made Tessa feel that everything that had happened to her in the past six weeks was real—more real even than living through it had been.

Tessa learned from the *Codex* that all Shadowhunters descended from an archangel named Raziel, who had given the first of them a volume called the Gray Book, filled with "the language of Heaven"—the black runic Marks that covered the skin of trained Shadowhunters such as Charlotte and Will. The Marks were cut into their skin with a styluslike tool called a stele—the odd penlike object she'd seen Will use to draw on the door at the Dark House. The Marks provided Nephilim with all sorts of protection: healing, superhuman strength and speed, night vision, and even allowed them to hide themselves from mundane eyes with runes called glamours. But they were not a gift anyone could use. Cutting Marks into the skin of a Downworlder or human—or even a Shadowhunter who was too young or improperly trained—would be torturously painful and result in madness or death.

The Marks were not the only way they protected themselves—they wore tough, enchanted leather garments called gear when they went into battle. There were sketches of men in the gear of different countries. To Tessa's surprise, there were also sketches of women in long shirts and trousers—not bloomers, such as the sort she'd seen ridiculed in newspapers, but real men's trousers. Turning the page, she shook her head, wondering if Charlotte and Jessamine really wore such outlandish getups.

The next pages were devoted to the other gifts Raziel had

given the first Shadowhunters—powerful magical objects called the Mortal Instruments—and a home country: a tiny piece of land sliced out of what was then the Holy Roman Empire, surrounded with wardings so that mundanes could not enter it. It was called Idris.

The lamp flickered low as Tessa read, her eyelids slipping lower and lower. Downworlders, she read, were supernatural creatures such as faeries, werewolves, vampires, and warlocks. In the case of vampires and werewolves, they were humans infected with demon disease. Faeries, on the other hand, were half-demon and half-angel, and therefore possessed both great beauty and an evil nature. But warlocks—warlocks were the direct offspring of humans and demons. No wonder Charlotte had asked if both her parents were human. *But they were,* she thought, *so I can't possibly be a warlock, thank God.* She stared down at an illustration showing a tall man with shaggy hair, standing in the center of a pentagram chalked onto a stone floor. He looked completely normal, save for the fact that he had eyes with slit pupils like a cat's. Candles burned at each of the star's five points. The flames seemed to slide together, blurring as Tessa's own vision blurred in exhaustion. She closed her eyes—and was instantly dreaming.

In the dream she danced through whirling smoke down a corridor lined with mirrors, and each mirror she passed showed her a different face. She could hear lovely, haunting music. It seemed to come from some distance away, and yet was all around. There was a man walking ahead of her—a boy, really, slender and beardless—but though she felt that she knew him, she could neither see his face nor recognize him. He might have been her brother, or Will, or someone else entirely. She followed, calling to him, but he receded down the corridor as if the smoke carried him with it. The music rose and rose to a crescendo—

And Tessa woke, breathing hard, the book sliding off her lap as she sat up. The dream was gone, but the music remained, high and haunting and sweet. She made her way to the door and peered out into the hallway.

The music was louder in the corridor. In fact, it was coming from the room across the hall. The door was ajar slightly, and notes seemed to pour through the opening like water through the narrow neck of a vase.

A dressing gown hung on a hook by the door; Tessa drew it down and slipped it on over her nightclothes, stepping out into the hallway. As if in a dream, she crossed the corridor and put her hand gently to the door; it swung open under her touch. The room within was dark, lit only by moonlight. She saw that it was not unlike her own bedroom across the hall, the same large four-poster bed, the same dark heavy furniture. The curtains had been pulled back from one tall window, and pale silver light poured into the room like a rain of needles. In the square patch of moonlight before the window, someone was standing. A boy—he seemed too slight to be a grown man—with a violin propped against his shoulder. His cheek rested against the instrument, and the bow sawed back and forth over the strings, wringing notes out of it, notes as fine and perfect as anything Tessa had ever heard.

His eyes were closed. "Will?" he said, without opening his eyes or ceasing to play. "Will, is that you?"

Tessa said nothing. She could not bear to speak, to interrupt the music—but in a moment the boy broke it off himself, lowering his bow and opening his eyes with a frown.

"Will—," he started, and then, seeing Tessa, his lips parted in surprise. "You're not Will." He sounded curious, but not at all annoyed, despite the fact that Tessa had barged into his bedroom in the middle of the night and surprised him playing the violin in his nightclothes, or what Tessa assumed were his nightclothes. He wore a light loose-fitting set of trousers and a collarless shirt, with a black silk dressing gown tied loosely over them. She had been right. He was young, probably the same age as Will, and the impression of youth was heightened by his slightness. He was tall but very slender, and disappearing below the collar of his shirt, she could see the curling edges of the black designs that she had earlier seen on Will's skin, and on Charlotte's.

She knew what they were called now. Marks. And she knew what they made him. Nephilim. The descendant of men and angels. No wonder that in the moonlight his pale skin seemed to shine like Will's witchlight. His hair was pale silver as well, as were his angular eyes.

"I'm so sorry," she said, clearing her throat. The noise sounded terribly harsh to her, and loud in the silence of the room; she wanted to cringe. "I—I didn't mean to come in here like this. It's— My room is across the hall, and . . ."

"That's all right." He lowered the violin from his shoulder. "You're Miss Gray, aren't you? The shape-changer girl. Will told me a bit about you."

"Oh," Tessa said.

"Oh?" The boy's eyebrows rose. "You don't sound terribly pleased that I know who you are."

"It's that I think Will is angry with me," Tessa explained. "So whatever he told you—"

He laughed. "Will is angry with everyone," he said. "I don't let it color my judgment."

Moonlight spilled off the polished surface of the boy's violin as he turned to lay it down on top of the wardrobe, the bow beside it. When he turned back to her, he was smiling. "I should have introduced myself earlier," he said. "I'm James Carstairs. Please call me Jem—everyone does."

"Oh, you're Jem. You weren't at dinner," Tessa recalled. "Charlotte said you were ill. Are you feeling better?"

He shrugged. "I was tired, that's all."

"Well, I imagine it must be tiring, doing what you all do." Having just read the *Codex*, Tessa felt herself burning up with questions about Shadowhunters. "Will said you came from a long way away to live here—were you in Idris?

He raised his eyebrows. "You know of Idris?"

"Or did you come from another Institute? They're in all the big cities, aren't they? And why to London—"

He interrupted her, bemused. "You ask a lot of questions, don't you?"

"My brother always says curiosity is my besetting sin."

"As sins go, it isn't the worst one." He sat down on the steamer trunk at the foot of the bed, and regarded her with a curious gravity. "So go ahead; ask me whatever you want. I can't sleep anyway, and distractions are welcome."

Immediately Will's voice rose up in the back of Tessa's head. Jem's parents had been killed by demons. *But I can't ask him about that,* Tessa thought. Instead she said, "Will told me you came from very far away. Where did you live before?"

"Shanghai," Jem said. "You know where that is?"

"China," said Tessa with some indignation. "Doesn't everyone know that?"

Jem grinned. "You'd be surprised."

"What were you doing in China?" Tessa asked, with honest interest. She couldn't quite picture the place Jem was from. When she thought of China, all that came to mind was Marco Polo and tea. She had the sense that it was very, very far, as if Jem had come from the ends of the earth—east of the sun and west of the moon, Aunt Harriet would have said. "I thought no one went there but missionaries and sailors."

"Shadowhunters live all over the world. My mother was Chinese; my father was British. They met in London and moved to Shanghai when he was offered the position of running the Institute there."

Tessa was startled. If Jem's mother had been Chinese, then so was he, wasn't he? She knew there were Chinese immigrants in New York—they mostly worked in laundries or sold hand-rolled cigars from stands on the street. She had never seen one of them who looked anything like Jem, with his odd silvery hair and eyes. Perhaps it had something to do with him being a Shadowhunter? But she couldn't think of a way to ask that didn't seem horrendously rude.

Fortunately, Jem didn't seem to be waiting for her to continue the conversation. "I apologize for asking, but—your parents are dead, aren't they?"

"Did Will tell you that?"

"He didn't need to. We orphans learn to recognize one another. If I might ask—were you very young when it happened?"

"I was three when they died in a carriage accident. I hardly remember them at all." *Only in tiny flashes—the scent of tobacco smoke, or the pale lilac of my mother's dress.* "My aunt raised me. And my brother, Nathaniel. My aunt, though—" At this, to her surprise, her throat began to tighten. A vivid picture of Aunt Harriet came to her mind, lying in the narrow brass bed in her bedroom, her eyes bright with fever. Not recognizing Tessa at the end and calling her by her mother's name, Elizabeth. Aunt Harriet had been the only mother Tessa had really ever known. Tessa had held her thin hand while she'd died, there in the room with the priest. She remembered thinking that now she truly was alone. "She died recently. She took a fever unexpectedly. She never had been very strong."

"I'm sorry to hear that," Jem said, and he genuinely did sound sorry.

"It was terrible because my brother was already gone by then. He'd left for England a month before. He'd even sent us back presents—tea from Fortnum and Mason, and chocolates. And then Aunt took sick and died, and I wrote to him over and over, but my letters came back. I was in despair. And then the ticket arrived. A ticket for a steamship to Southampton, and a note from Nate saying he'd meet me at the docks, that I must come live with him in London now that Aunt was gone. Except now I don't think he ever wrote that note at all—" Tessa broke off, her eyes stinging. "I'm sorry. I'm maundering on. You don't need to hear all this."

"What sort of man is your brother? What is he like?"

Tessa looked at Jem with a little surprise. The others had asked her what he might have done to get himself into his current situation, if she knew where the Dark Sisters might be keeping him, if he had the same power she did. But no one had ever asked what he was *like*.

"Aunt used to say he was a dreamer," she said. "He always lived in his head. He never cared about how things were, only how they would be, someday, when he had everything he wanted. When *we* had everything *we* wanted," she corrected herself. "He used to gamble, I think because he couldn't imagine losing—it wasn't part of his dreams."

"Dreams can be dangerous things."

"No—no." She shook her head. "I'm not saying it right. He was a wonderful brother. He . . ." Charlotte was right; it was easier to fight back tears if she found something, some object, to fix her gaze on. She stared at Jem's hands. They were slender and long, and he had the same design on the back of his hand that Will did, the open eye. She pointed at it. "What's that meant to do?"

Jem seemed not to notice she had changed the subject. "It's a Mark. You know what those are?" He held his hand out to her, palm down. "This one is the Voyance. It clears our Sight. Helps us to see Downworld." He turned his hand over, and drew up the sleeve of his shirt. All along the pale inside of his wrist and inner arm were more of the Marks, very black against his white skin. They seemed to thread with the pattern of his veins, as if his blood ran through the Marks, too. "For swiftness, night vision, angelic power, to heal quickly," he read out loud. "Though their names are more complex than that, and not in English."

"Do they hurt?"

"They hurt when I received them. They don't hurt at all now." He drew his sleeve down and smiled at her. "Now, don't tell me that's all the questions you have."

Oh, I have more than you think. "Why can't you sleep?"

She saw that she had caught him off guard; a look of hesitancy flashed across his face before he spoke. *But why hesitate?* she thought. He could always lie, or simply deflect, as Will would have. But Jem, she sensed instinctively, wouldn't lie. "I have bad dreams."

"I was dreaming too," she said. "I dreamed about your music."

He grinned. "A nightmare, then?"

"No. It was lovely. The loveliest thing I've heard since I came to this horrible city."

"London isn't horrible," Jem said equably. "You simply have to get to know it. You must come with me out into London someday. I can show you the parts of it that are beautiful—that I love."

"Singing the praises of our fair city?" a light voice inquired. Tessa whirled, and saw Will, leaning against the frame of the doorway. The light from the corridor behind him outlined his damp-looking hair with gold. The hem of his dark overcoat and his black boots were edged with mud, as if he had just come from outdoors, and his cheeks were flushed. He was bareheaded as always. "We treat you well here, don't we, James? I doubt I'd have that kind of luck in Shanghai. What do you call us there, again?"

"*Yang guizi,*" said Jem, who appeared unsurprised by Will's sudden appearance. "'Foreign devils.'"

"Hear that, Tessa? I'm a devil. So are you." Will unhitched himself from the doorway and sauntered into the room. He flung himself down onto the edge of the bed, unbuttoning his coat. It had a shoulder cape attached to it, very elegant, lined in blue silk.

"Your hair's wet," Jem said. "Where have you been?"

"Here, there, and everywhere." Will grinned. Despite his usual grace, there was something about the way he moved—the flush on his cheeks and the glitter in his eyes—

"Boiled as an owl, are you?" Jem said, not without affection.

Ah, Tessa thought. *He's drunk.* She'd seen her own brother under the influence of alcohol enough times to recognize the symptoms. Somehow, she felt obscurely disappointed.

Jem grinned. "Where have you been? The Blue Dragon? The Mermaid?"

"The Devil Tavern, if you must know." Will sighed and leaned against one of the posts of the bed. "I had such plans for this evening. The pursuit of blind drunkenness and wayward women was my goal. But alas, it was not to be. No sooner had I consumed my third drink in the Devil than I was accosted by a delightful small flower-selling child who asked me for two-pence for a daisy. The price seemed steep, so I refused. When I told the girl as much, she proceeded to rob me."

"A little girl robbed you?" Tessa said.

"Actually, she wasn't a little girl at all, as it turns out, but a midget in a dress with a penchant for violence, who goes by the name of Six-Fingered Nigel."

"Easy mistake to make," Jem said.

"I caught him in the act of slipping his hand into my pocket," Will said, gesturing animatedly with his scarred, slender hands. "I couldn't let that stand, of course. A fight broke out almost immediately. I had the upper hand until Nigel leaped onto the bar and struck me from behind with a pitcher of gin."

"Ah," said Jem. "That does explain why your hair's wet."

"It was a fair fight," Will said. "But the proprietor of the Devil didn't see it that way. Threw me out. I can't go back for a fortnight."

"Best thing for you," Jem said unsympathetically. "Glad to hear it's business as usual, then. I was worried for a moment there that you'd come home early to see if I was feeling better."

"You seem to be doing perfectly well without me. In fact, I see you've met our resident shape-shifting mystery woman," Will said, glancing toward Tessa. It was the first time he'd acknowledged her presence since he'd appeared in the doorway. "Do you normally turn up in gentlemen's bedrooms in the middle of the night? If I'd known that, I would have campaigned harder to make sure Charlotte let you stay."

"I don't see how what I do is your concern," Tessa replied. "Especially since you abandoned me in the corridor and left me to find my own way back to my room."

"And you found your way to Jem's room instead?"

"It was the violin," Jem explained. "She heard me practicing."

"Ghastly wailing noise, isn't it?" Will asked Tessa. "I don't know how all the cats in the neighborhood don't come running every time he plays."

"I thought it was pretty."

"That's because it was," Jem agreed.

Will pointed a finger accusingly in their direction. "You're ganging up on me. Is this how it's going to be from now on? I'll be odd man out? Dear God, I'll have to befriend Jessamine."

"Jessamine can't stand you," Jem pointed out.

"Henry, then."

"Henry will set you on fire."

"Thomas," Will suggested.

"Thomas," Jem began—and doubled up, suddenly racked with an explosive fit of coughing so violent that he slid from the steamer trunk to crouch on his knees. Too shocked to move, Tessa could only stare as Will—his expansive drunkenness seeming to vanish in a split second—sprang off the bed and knelt down by Jem, placing a hand on his shoulder.

"James," he said quietly. "Where is it?"

Jem held up a hand to ward him off. Racking gasps shook his thin frame. "I don't need it—I'm all right—"

He coughed again, and a fine spray of red splattered the floor in front of him. Blood.

Will's hand tightened on his friend's shoulder; Tessa saw the knuckles whiten. "Where is it? Where did you put it?"

Jem waved his hand feebly toward the bed. "On—," he gasped. "On the mantel—in the box—the silver one—"

"I'll get it, then." It was as gently as Tessa had ever heard Will say anything. "Stay here."

"As if I'd go anywhere." Jem scrubbed the back of his hand across his mouth; it came away with red streaking the open-eye Mark.

Standing up, Will turned—and saw Tessa. For a moment he looked purely startled, as if he'd forgotten she was there at all.

"Will—," she whispered. "Is there anything—"

"Come with me." Catching her by the arm, Will marched her, gently, toward the open door. He thrust her out into the corridor, moving to block her view of the room. "Good night, Tessa."

"But he's coughing blood," Tessa protested in a low voice. "Perhaps I should get Charlotte—"

"No." Will glanced over his shoulder, then back at Tessa. He leaned toward her, his hand on her shoulder. She could feel every one of his fingers pressing into the flesh. They were close enough that she could smell the night air on his skin, the scent of metal and smoke and fog. Something about the way he smelled was strange, but she couldn't place exactly what it was.

Will spoke in a low voice. "He has medicine. I'll get it for him. There's no need for Charlotte to know about this."

"But if he's ill—"

"Please, Tessa." There was a pleading urgency in Will's blue eyes. "It would be better if you said nothing about it."

Somehow Tessa found she could not say no. "I—all right."

"Thank you." Will released her shoulder, and raised his hand to touch her cheek—so lightly she thought she might almost have imagined it. Too startled to say anything, she stood in silence as he closed the door between them. As she heard the lock slide home, she realized why she had thought something was odd when Will had leaned toward her.

Though Will had said he'd been out all night drinking—though he'd even claimed to have had a pitcher of gin smashed over his head—there had been no smell of alcohol on him at all.

It was a long time before Tessa could sleep again. She lay awake, the *Codex* open at her side, the clockwork angel ticking at her chest, and she watched the lamplight trace patterns across the ceiling.

Tessa stood looking at herself in the mirror over the vanity table as Sophie did up the buttons on the back of her dress. In the morning light that streamed through the high windows, she looked very pale, the gray shadows under her eyes standing out in splotches.

She had never been one to stare in mirrors. A quick glance to see that her hair was all right and that there were no spots on her clothes. Now she could not stop looking at that thin, pale face in the glass. It seemed to ripple as she looked at it, like a reflection seen in water, like the vibration that took her just before the Change. Now that she had worn other faces, seen through other eyes, how could she ever say any face was really her own, even if it was the face she had been given at birth? When she Changed back to herself, how was she to know there wasn't some slight shift in her very self, something that made her not who she was anymore? Or did it matter what she looked like at all? Was her face nothing but a mask of flesh, irrelevant to her true self?

She could see Sophie reflected in the mirror as well; her face was turned so that her scarred cheek was to the mirror. It looked even more awful in daylight. It was like seeing a lovely painting slashed to ribbons with a knife. Tessa itched to ask her what had happened, but knew she shouldn't. Instead she said, "I'm much obliged to you for helping me with the dress."

"Pleased to be of service, miss." Sophie's tone was flat.

"I only wanted to ask," Tessa began. Sophie stiffened. *She thinks I'm going to ask her about her face,* Tessa thought. Out loud she said, "The way you talked to Will in the corridor last night—"

Sophie laughed. It was a short laugh, but a real one. "I am permitted to speak to Mr. Herondale however I like, whenever I like. It's one of the conditions of my employment."

"Charlotte lets you make your own conditions?"

"It's not simply anyone who can work at the Institute," Sophie explained. "You need to have a touch of the Sight. Agatha has it, and so does Thomas. Mrs. Branwell wanted me right away when she knew I had it, said she'd been looking for a maid for Miss Jessamine for simply ages. She warned me about Mr. Herondale, though, said he'd likely be rude to me, and familiar. She said I could be rude right back, that nobody would mind."

"Someone ought to be rude to him. He's rude enough to everyone else."

"I'd warrant that's what Mrs. Branwell thought." Sophie shared a grin with Tessa in the mirror; she was absolutely lovely when she smiled, Tessa thought, scar or no scar.

"You like Charlotte, don't you?" she said. "She does seem awfully kind."

Sophie shrugged. "In the old house I was in service in, Mrs. Atkins—that was the housekeeper—she would keep track of every candle we used, every bit of soap we had. We had to use the soap down to a sliver before she'd give us a new bit. But Mrs. Branwell gives me new soap whenever I want it." She said this as if it were a firm testament to Charlotte's character.

"I suppose they have a lot of money here at the Institute." Tessa thought of the gorgeous furnishings and the grandeur of the place.

"Perhaps. But I've made over enough dresses for Mrs. Branwell to know she doesn't buy them new."

Tessa thought of the blue gown Jessamine had worn to dinner the night before. "What about Miss Lovelace?"

"She has her own money," said Sophie darkly. She stepped back from Tessa. "There. You're fit to be seen now."

Tessa smiled. "Thank you, Sophie."

***

When Tessa came into the dining room, the others were already midway through breakfast—Charlotte in a plain gray dress, spreading jam onto a piece of toast; Henry half-hidden behind a newspaper; and Jessamine picking daintily at a bowl of porridge. Will had a pile of eggs and bacon on his plate and was digging into them industriously, which Tessa couldn't help noting was unusual for someone who claimed to have been out drinking all night.

"We were just talking about you," Jessamine said as Tessa found a seat. She pushed a silver toast rack across the table toward Tessa. "Toast?"

Tessa, picking up her fork, looked around the table anxiously. "What about me?"

"What to do with you, of course. Downworlders can't live in the Institute forever," said Will. "I say we sell her to the Gypsies on Hampstead Heath," he added, turning to Charlotte. "I hear they purchase spare women as well as horses."

"Will, stop it." Charlotte glanced up from her breakfast. "That's ridiculous."

Will leaned back in his chair. "You're right. They'd never buy her. Too scrawny."

"That's enough," Charlotte said. "Miss Gray shall remain. If for no other reason than because we're in the middle of an investigation that requires her assistance. I've already dispatched a message to the Clave telling them that we're keeping her here until this Pandemonium Club matter is cleared up and her brother is found. Isn't that right, Henry?"

"Quite," Henry said, setting the newspaper down. "The Pandemonium thingie is a top priority. Absolutely."

"You'd better tell Benedict Lightwood, too," said Will. "You know how he is."

Charlotte blanched slightly, and Tessa wondered who Benedict Lightwood might be. "Will, today I'd like you to revisit the site of the Dark Sisters' house; it's abandoned now, but it's still worth a final search. And I want you to take Jem with you—"

At that, the amusement left Will's expression. "Is he well enough?"

"He is quite well enough." The voice wasn't Charlotte's. It was Jem's. He had come into the room quietly and was standing by the sideboard, his arms folded across his chest. He was much less pale than he had been the previous night, and the red waistcoat he wore brought a slight tinge of color to his cheeks. "In fact, he's ready when you are."

"You should have some breakfast first," Charlotte fretted, pushing the plate of bacon toward him. Jem sat, and smiled at Tessa across the table. "Oh, Jem—this is Miss Gray. She's—"

"We've met," Jem said quietly, and Tessa felt a rush of heat in her face. She couldn't help staring at him as he picked up a piece of bread and applied butter to it. It seemed hard to imagine that anyone quite so ethereal-looking could possibly eat toast.

Charlotte looked puzzled. "You have?"

"I encountered Tessa in the corridor last night and introduced myself. I think I may have given her something of a fright." His silver eyes met Tessa's across the table, sparkling with amusement.

Charlotte shrugged. "Very well, then. I'd like you to go with Will. In the meantime, today, Miss Gray—"

"Call me Tessa," Tessa said. "I would prefer it if everyone did."

"Very well, Tessa," said Charlotte with a little smile. "Henry and I will be paying a call on Mr. Axel Mortmain, your brother's employer, to see if he, or any of his employees, might have any information as to your brother's whereabouts."

"Thank you." Tessa was surprised. They had said they were going to look for her brother, and they were actually doing it. She hadn't expected that they would.

"I've heard of Axel Mortmain," said Jem. "He was a taipan, one of the big business heads in Shanghai. His company had offices on the Bund."

"Yes," said Charlotte, "the newspapers say he made his fortune in imports of silk and tea."

"Bah." Jem spoke lightly, but there was an edge to his voice. "He made his fortune in opium. All of them did. Buying opium in India, sailing it to Canton, trading it for goods."

"He wasn't breaking the law, James." Charlotte pushed the newspaper across the table toward Jessamine. "Meanwhile, Jessie, perhaps you and Tessa can go through the paper and make note of anything that might pertain to the investigation, or be worth a second look—"

Jessamine recoiled from the paper as if it were a snake. "A lady does not read the newspaper. The society pages, perhaps, or the theater news. Not this filth."

"But you are not a lady, Jessamine—," Charlotte began.

"Dear me," said Will. "Such harsh truths so early in the morning cannot be good for the digestion."

"What I mean," Charlotte said, correcting herself, "is that you are a Shadowhunter first, and a lady second."

"Speak for yourself," Jessamine said, pushing her chair back. Her cheeks had turned an alarming shade of red. "You know," she said, "I wouldn't have expected you to notice, but it seems clear that the only thing Tessa has to put on her back is that awful old red dress of mine, and it doesn't fit her. It doesn't even fit me anymore, and she's taller than I am."

"Can't Sophie . . . ," Charlotte began vaguely.

"You can take a dress in. It's another thing to make it twice as big as it was to start with. Really, Charlotte." Jessamine blew out her cheeks in exasperation. "I think you ought to let me take poor Tessa into town to get some new clothes. Otherwise, the first time she takes a deep breath, that dress will fall right off her."

Will looked interested. "I think she should try that out now and see what happens."

"Oh," Tessa said, thoroughly confused. Why was Jessamine being so kind to her suddenly when she'd been so unpleasant only the day before? "No, really it's not necessary—"

"It is," Jessamine said firmly.

Charlotte was shaking her head. "Jessamine, as long as you live in the Institute, you are one of us, and you have to contribute—"

"You're the one who insists we have to take in Downworlders who are in trouble, and feed and shelter them," Jessamine said. "I'm quite sure that includes clothing them as well. You see, I will be contributing—to Tessa's upkeep."

Henry leaned across the table toward his wife. "You'd better let her do it," he advised. "Remember the last time you tried to get her to sort the daggers in the weapons room, and she used them to cut up all the linens?"

"We needed new linens," said Jessamine, unabashed.

"Oh, all right," Charlotte snapped. "Honestly, sometimes I despair of the lot of you."

"What've I done?" Jem inquired. "I only just arrived."

Charlotte put her face into her hands. As Henry began to pat her shoulders and make soothing noises, Will leaned across Tessa toward Jem, ignoring her completely as he did so. "Should we leave now?"

"I need to finish my tea first," Jem said. "Anyway, I don't see what you're so fired up about. You said the place hadn't been used as a brothel in ages?"

"I want to be back before dark," Will said. He was leaning nearly across Tessa's lap, and she could smell that faint boy-smell of leather and metal that seemed to cling to his hair and skin. "I have an assignation in Soho this evening with a certain attractive someone."

"Goodness," Tessa said to the back of his head. "If you keep seeing Six-Fingered Nigel like this, he'll expect you to declare your intentions."

Jem choked on his tea.

Spending the day with Jessamine began as badly as Tessa had feared. The traffic was dreadful. However crowded New York might have been, Tessa had never seen anything like the snarling mess of the Strand at midday. Carriages rolled side by side with costermongers' carts piled high with fruit and vegetables; women shawled and carrying shallow baskets full of flowers dived madly in and out of traffic as they tried to interest the occupants of various carriages in their wares; and cabs came to a full stop in the midst of traffic so that the cabdrivers could scream at one another out their windows. This noise added to the already awesome din—ice cream peddlers shouting "Hokey-pokey, penny a lump," newspaper boys hawking the day's latest headline, and someone somewhere playing a barrel organ. Tessa wondered how everyone living and working in London wasn't deaf.

As she stared out the window, an old woman carrying a large metal cage full of fluttering colorful birds stepped out alongside their coach. The old woman turned her head, and Tessa saw that her skin was as green as a parrot's feathers, her eyes wide and all black like a bird's, her hair a shock of multicolored feathers. Tessa started, and Jessamine, following her gaze, frowned. "Close the curtains," she said. "It keeps out the dust." And, reaching past Tessa, Jessamine did just that.

Tessa looked at her. Jessamine's small mouth was set in a thin line. "Did you see—?" Tessa began.

"No," Jessamine said, shooting Tessa what she had often seen referred to in novels as a "killing" look. Tessa glanced hastily away.

Things did not improve when they finally reached the fashionable West End. Leaving Thomas patiently waiting with the horses, Jessamine dragged Tessa in and out of various dressmakers' salons, looking at design after design, standing by while the prettiest shop assistant was chosen to model a sample. (No real lady would let a dress that might have been worn by a stranger touch her skin.) In each establishment she gave a different false name and a different story; in each establishment the owners seemed enchanted by her looks and obvious wealth and couldn't help her fast enough. Tessa, mostly ignored, lurked on the sidelines, half-dead from boredom.

In one salon, posing as a young widow, Jessamine even examined the design for a black mourning dress of crepe and lace. Tessa had to admit it would have set off her blond pallor well.

"You would look absolutely beautiful in this, and could not possibly fail to make an advantageous remarriage." The dressmaker winked in a conspiratorial fashion. "In fact, do you know what we call this design? 'The Trap Rebaited.'"

Jessamine giggled, the dressmaker smiled limpidly, and Tessa considered racing out into the street and ending it all by throwing herself under a hansom cab. As if conscious of her annoyance, Jessamine glanced toward her with a condescending smile. "I'm also looking for a few dresses for my cousin from America," she said. "The clothes there are simply horrible. She's as plain as a pin, which doesn't help, but I'm sure you can do something with her."

The dressmaker blinked as if this were the first time she'd noticed Tessa, and perhaps it was. "Would you like to choose a design, ma'am?"

The following whirlwind of activity was something of a revelation for Tessa. In New York her clothes had been bought by her aunt—ready-made pieces that had had to be altered to fit, and always cheap material in drab shades of dark gray or navy. She had never before learned, as she did now, that blue was a color that suited her and brought out her gray-blue eyes, or that she should wear rose pink to put color in her cheeks. As her measurements were taken amidst a blur of discussion of princess sheaths, cuirass bodices, and someone named Mr. Charles Worth, Tessa stood and stared at her face in the mirror, half-waiting for the features to begin to slip and change, to reform themselves. But she remained herself, and at the end of it all she had four new dresses on order to be delivered later in the week—one pink, one yellow, one striped blue and white with bone buttons, and a gold and black silk—as well as two smart jackets, one with darling beaded tulle adorning the cuffs.

"I suspect you may actually look pretty in that last outfit," Jessamine said as they climbed back up into the carriage. "It's amazing what fashion can do."

Tessa counted silently to ten before she replied. "I'm awfully obliged to you for everything, Jessamine. Shall we return to the Institute now?"

At that, the brightness went out of Jessamine's face. *She truly hates it there,* Tessa thought, puzzled more than anything else. What was so dreadful about the Institute? Of course its whole reason for existing was peculiar enough, certainly, but Jessamine had to be used to that by now. She was a Shadow-hunter like the rest.

"It's such a lovely day," Jessamine said, "and you've hardly seen anything of London. I think a walk in Hyde Park is in order. And after that, we could go to Gunter's and have Thomas get ices for us!"

Tessa glanced out the window. The sky was hazy and gray, shot through with lines of blue where the clouds briefly drifted apart from one another. In no way would this be considered a lovely day in New York, but London seemed to have different standards for weather. Besides, she owed Jessamine something now, and the last thing in the world the other girl wanted to do, clearly, was go home.

"I adore parks," said Tessa.

Jessamine almost smiled.

* * *

"You didn't tell Miss Gray about the cogs," Henry said.

Charlotte looked up from her notes and sighed. It had always been a sore point for her that, however often she had requested a second, the Clave only allowed the Institute one carriage. It was a fine one—a town coach—and Thomas was an excellent driver. But it did mean that when the Institute's Shadowhunters went their separate ways, as they were doing today, Charlotte was forced to borrow a carriage from Benedict Lightwood, who was far from her favorite person. And the only carriage he was willing to lend her was small and uncomfortable. Poor Henry, who was so very tall, was bumping his head against the low roof.

"No," she said. "The poor girl, she seemed so dazed already. I couldn't tell her that the mechanical devices we found in the cellar had been manufactured by the company that employed her brother. She's so worried about him. It seemed more than she'd be able to bear."

"It might not mean anything, darling," Henry reminded her. "Mortmain and Company manufactures most of the machine tools used in England. Mortmain is really something of a genius. His patented system for producing ball bearings—"

"Yes, yes." Charlotte tried to keep the impatience out of her voice. "And perhaps we should have told her. But I thought it best that we speak to Mr. Mortmain first and gather what impressions we can. You're correct. He may know nothing at all, and there may be little connection. But it would be quite a coincidence, Henry. And I am very wary of coincidence."

She glanced back down at the notes she'd made about Axel Mortmain. He was the only (and likely, though the notes did not specify, illegitimate) son of Dr. Hollingworth Mortmain, who in a matter of years had risen from the humble position of ship's surgeon on a trading vessel bound for China to wealthy private trader, buying and selling spices and sugar, silk and tea, and—it wasn't stated, but Charlotte was in agreement with Jem on the matter—probably opium. When Dr. Mortmain had died, his son, Axel, at barely twenty years of age, had inherited his fortune, which he'd promptly invested in building a fleet of ships faster and sleeker than any others plying the seas. Within a decade the younger Mortmain had doubled, then quadrupled, his father's riches.

In more recent years he had retired from Shanghai to London, had sold his trading ships, and had used the money to buy a large company that produced the mechanical devices needed to make timepieces, everything from pocket watches to grandfather clocks. He was a very wealthy man.

The carriage drew up in front of one of a row of white terraced houses, each with tall windows looking out over the square. Henry leaned out of the carriage and read the number off a brass plaque affixed to a front gatepost. "This must be it." He reached for the carriage door.

"Henry," said Charlotte, placing a hand on his arm. "Henry, do keep in mind what we talked about this morning, won't you?"

He smiled ruefully. "I will do my best not to embarrass you or trip up the investigation. Honestly, sometimes I wonder why you bring me along on these things. You know I'm a bumbler when it comes to people."

"You're not a bumbler, Henry," Charlotte said gently. She longed to reach out and stroke his face, push his hair back and reassure him. But she held herself back. She knew—she had been advised enough times—not to force on Henry affection he probably did not want.

Leaving the carriage with the Lightwoods' driver, they mounted the stairs and rang the bell; the door was opened by a footman wearing dark blue livery and a dour expression. "Good morning," he said brusquely. "Might I inquire as to your business here?"

Charlotte glanced sideways at Henry, who was staring past the footman with a dreamy sort of expression. Lord knew what his mind was on—cogs, gears, and gadgets, no doubt—but it certainly wasn't on their present situation. With an inward sigh she said, "I am Mrs. Gray, and this is my husband, Mr. Henry Gray. We're seeking a cousin of ours—a young man named Nathaniel Gray. We haven't heard from him in nearly six weeks. He is, or was, one of Mr. Mortmain's employees—"

For a moment—it might have been her imagination—she thought she saw something, a flicker of uneasiness, in the footman's eyes. "Mr. Mortmain owns quite a large company. You can't expect him to know the whereabouts of everyone who works for him. That would be impossible. Perhaps you should inquire with the police."

Charlotte narrowed her eyes. Before they had left the Institute, she had traced the insides of her arms with persuasion runes. It was the rare mundane who was totally unsusceptible to their influence. "We have, but they don't seem to have progressed at all with the case. It's so dreadful, and we're so concerned about Nate, you see. If we could see Mr. Mortmain for a moment . . ."

She relaxed as the footman nodded slowly. "I'll inform Mr.

Mortmain of your visit," he said, stepping back to allow them inside. "Please wait in the vestibule." He looked startled, as if surprised at his own acquiescence.

He swung the door wide, and Charlotte followed him in, Henry behind her. Though the footman failed to offer Charlotte a seat—a failure of politesse she attributed to the confusion brought on by the persuasion runes—he did take Henry's coat and hat, and Charlotte's wrap, before leaving the two of them to stare curiously around the entryway.

The room was high ceilinged but not ornate. It was also absent the expected pastoral landscapes and family portraits. Instead, hanging from the ceiling were long silk banners painted with the Chinese characters for good luck; an Indian platter of hammered silver propped in one corner; and pen-and-ink sketches of famous landmarks lining the walls. Charlotte recognized Mount Kilimanjaro, the Egyptian pyramids, the Taj Mahal, and a section of China's Great Wall. Mortmain clearly was a man who traveled a great deal and was proud of the fact.

Charlotte turned to look at Henry to see if he was observing what she was, but he was staring vaguely off toward the stairs, lost in his own mind again; before she could say anything, the footman rematerialized, a pleasant smile on his face. "Please come this way."

Henry and Charlotte followed the footman to the end of the corridor, where he opened a polished oak door and ushered them before him.

They found themselves in a grand study, with wide windows looking out onto the square. Dark green curtains were pulled back to let in the light, and through the windowpanes

Charlotte could see their borrowed carriage waiting for them at the curb, the horse with its head dipped into a nose-bag, the driver reading a newspaper on his high seat. The green branches of trees moved on the other side of the street, an emerald canopy, but it was noiseless. The windows blocked all sound, and there was nothing audible in this room at all save the faint ticking of a wall clock with MORTMAIN AND COMPANY engraved on the face in gold.

The furniture was dark, a heavy black-grained wood, and the walls were lined with animal heads—a tiger, an antelope, and a leopard—and more foreign landscapes. There was a great mahogany desk in the center of the room, neatly arranged with stacks of paper, each pile weighted down with a heavy copper gear. A brass-bound globe bearing the legend WYLD'S GLOBE OF THE EARTH, WITH THE LATEST DISCOVERIES! anchored one corner of the desk, the lands under the rule of the British empire picked out in pinkish red. Charlotte always found the experience of examining mundane globes a strange one. Their world was not the same shape as the one she knew.

Behind the desk sat a man, who rose to his feet as they entered. He was a small energetic-looking figure, a middle-aged man with hair graying suitably at the sideburns. His skin looked windburned, as if he had often been outside in rough weather. His eyes were a very, very light gray, his expression pleasant; despite his elegant, expensive-looking clothes, it was easy to imagine him on the deck of a ship, peering keenly into the distance. "Good afternoon," he said. "Walker gave me to understand that you are looking for Mr. Nathaniel Gray?"

"Yes," Henry said, to Charlotte's surprise. Henry rarely, if ever, took the lead in conversations with strangers. She wondered if it had anything to do with the intricate-looking blueprint on the desk. Henry was looking at it as yearningly as if it were food. "We're his cousins, you know."

"We do appreciate you taking this time to talk to us, Mr. Mortmain," Charlotte added hastily. "We know he was only an employee of yours, one of dozens—"

"Hundreds," said Mr. Mortmain. He had a pleasant baritone voice, which at the moment sounded very amused. "It is true I can't keep track of them all. But I do remember Mr. Gray. Though I must say, if he ever mentioned that he had cousins who were Shadowhunters, I can't say I recall it."

6

Strange Earth

We must not look at goblin men,
We must not buy their fruits:
Who knows upon what soil they fed
Their hungry thirsty roots?
–Christina Rossetti, "Goblin Market"

"You know," said Jem, "this isn't at all what I thought a brothel would look like."

The two boys stood at the entrance to what Tessa called the Dark House, off Whitechapel High Street. It looked dingier and darker than Will remembered, as if someone had swabbed it with a coating of extra dirt. "What were you imagining exactly, James? Ladies of the night waving from the balconies? Nude statues adorning the entranceway?"

"I suppose," Jem said mildly, "I was expecting something that looked a bit less drab."

Will had thought rather the same thing the first time he had been there. The overwhelming sensation one had inside the Dark House was that it was a place no one had ever really thought of as a home. The latched windows looked greasy, the drawn curtains dingy and unwashed.

Will rolled up his sleeves. "We'll probably have to knock down the door—"

"Or," said Jem, reaching out and giving the knob a twist, "not."

The door swung open onto a rectangle of darkness.

"Now, that's simply laziness," said Will. Taking a hunting dagger from his belt, he stepped cautiously inside, and Jem followed, keeping tight hold of his jade-headed walking stick. They tended to take turns going first into dangerous situations, though Jem preferred to be rear guard much of the time—Will always forgot to look behind him.

The door swung shut behind them, prisoning them in the half-lit gloom. The entryway looked almost the same as it had the first time Will had been there—the same wooden staircase leading up, the same cracked but still elegant marble flooring, the same air thick with dust.

Jem raised his hand, and his witchlight flared into life, frightening a group of blackbeetles. They scurried across the floor, causing Will to grimace. "Nice place to live, isn't it? Let's hope they left something behind other than filth. Forwarding addresses, a few severed limbs, a prostitute or two . . ."

"Indeed. Perhaps, if we're fortunate, we can still catch syphilis."

"Or demon pox," Will suggested cheerfully, trying the door under the stairs. It swung open, unlocked as the front door had been. "There's always demon pox."

"Demon pox does not exist."

"Oh ye of little faith," said Will, disappearing into the darkness under the stairs.

Together they searched the cellar and the ground-floor rooms meticulously, finding little but rubbish and dust. Everything had been stripped from the room where Tessa and Will had fought off the Dark Sisters; after a long search Will discovered something on the wall that looked like a smear of blood, but there seemed no source for it, and Jem pointed out it could just as well be paint.

Abandoning the cellar, they moved upstairs, and found a long corridor lined with doors that was familiar to Will. He had raced down it with Tessa behind him. He ducked into the first room on the right, which had been the room he'd found her in. No sign lingered of the wild-eyed girl who'd hit him with a flowered pitcher. The room was empty, the furniture having been taken away to be searched inside the Silent City. Four dark indentations on the floor indicated where a bed had once stood.

The other rooms were much the same. Will was trying the window in one when he heard Jem shout that he should come quickly; he was in the last room on the left. Will made haste and found Jem standing in the center of a large square room, his witchlight shining in his hand. He was not alone. There was one piece of furniture remaining here—an upholstered armchair, and seated in it was a woman.

She was young—probably no older than Jessamine—and wore a cheap-looking printed dress, her hair gathered up at the nape of her neck. It was dull-brown mousy hair, and her hands were bare and red. Her eyes were wide open and staring.

"Gah," said Will, too surprised to say anything else. "Is she—"

"She's dead," said Jem.

"Are you certain?" Will could not take his eyes off the woman's face. She was pale, but not with a corpse's pallor, and her hands lay folded in her lap, the fingers softly curved, not stiff with the rigor of death. He moved closer to her and placed a hand on her arm. It was rigid and cold beneath his fingers. "Well, she's not responding to my advances," he observed more brightly than he felt, "so she *must* be dead."

"Or she's a woman of good taste and sense." Jem knelt down and looked up into the woman's face. Her eyes were pale blue and protuberant; they stared past him, as dead-looking as painted eyes. "Miss," he said, and reached for her wrist, meaning to take a pulse.

She moved, jerking under his hand, and let out a low inhuman moan.

Jem stood up hastily. "What in—"

The woman raised her head. Her eyes were still blank, unfocused, but her lips moved with a grinding sound. "Beware!" she cried. Her voice echoed around the room, and Will, with a yell, jumped back.

The woman's voice sounded like gears grating against one another. "Beware, Nephilim. As you slay others, so shall you be slain. Your angel cannot protect you against that which neither God nor the devil has made, an army born neither of Heaven nor Hell. Beware the hand of man. Beware." Her voice rose to a high, grinding shriek, and she jerked back and forth in the chair like a puppet being yanked on invisible strings. "BEWARE BEWAREBEWAREBEWARE—"

"Good God," muttered Jem.

"BEWARE!" the woman shrieked one last time, and toppled

forward to sprawl on the ground, abruptly silenced. Will stared, openmouthed.

"Is she . . . ?" he began.

"Yes," Jem said. "I think she's *quite* dead this time."

But Will was shaking his head. "Dead. You know, I don't *think* so."

"What do you think, then?"

Instead of answering, Will went and knelt down by the body. He put two fingers to the side of the woman's cheek and turned her head gently until she faced them. Her mouth was wide, her right eye staring at the ceiling. The left dangled halfway down her cheek, attached to its socket by a coil of copper wire.

"She's not alive," said Will, "but not dead, either. She may be . . . like one of Henry's gadgets, I think." He touched her face. "Who could have done this?"

"I can hardly guess. But she called us Nephilim. She knew what we are."

"Or someone did," said Will. "I don't imagine she *knows* anything. I think she's a machine, like a clock. And she has run down." He stood up. "Regardless, we had best get her back to the Institute. Henry will want to have a look at her."

Jem did not reply; he was looking down at the woman on the floor. Her feet were bare beneath the hem of her dress, and dirty. Her mouth was open and he could see the gleam of metal inside her throat. Her eye dangled eerily on its bit of copper wire as somewhere outside the windows a church clock chimed the midday hour.

Once inside the park, Tessa found herself beginning to relax. She hadn't been in a green, quiet place since she'd come to

London, and she found herself almost reluctantly delighted by the sight of grass and trees, though she thought the park nowhere near as fine as Central Park in New York. The air was not as hazy here as it was over the rest of the city, and the sky overhead had achieved a color that was almost blue.

Thomas waited with the carriage while the girls made their promenade. As Tessa walked beside Jessamine, the other girl kept up a constant stream of chatter. They were making their way down a broad thoroughfare that, Jessamine informed her, was inexplicably called Rotten Row. Despite the inauspicious name, it was apparently *the* place to see and be seen. Down the center of it paraded men and women on horseback, exquisitely attired, the women with their veils flying, their laughter echoing in the summer air. Along the sides of the avenue walked other pedestrians. Chairs and benches were set up under the trees, and women sat twirling colorful parasols and sipping peppermint water; beside them bewhiskered gentlemen smoked, filling the air with the smell of tobacco mixed with cut grass and horses.

Though no one stopped to talk to them, Jessamine seemed to know who everyone was—who was getting married, who was seeking a husband, who was having an affair with so-and-so's wife and everyone knew all about it. It was a bit dizzying, and Tessa was glad when they stepped off the row and onto a narrower path leading into the park.

Jessamine slid her arm through Tessa's and gave her hand a companionable squeeze. "You don't know what a relief it is to finally have another girl around," she said cheerfully. "I mean, Charlotte's all right, but she's boring and married."

"There's Sophie."

Jessamine snorted. "Sophie's a servant."

"I've known girls who were quite companionable with their ladies' maids," Tessa protested. This was not precisely true. She had read about such girls, though she had never known one. Still, according to novels, the main function of a ladies' maid was to listen to you as you poured your heart out about your tragic love life, and occasionally to dress in your clothes and pretend to be you so you could avoid being captured by a villain. Not that Tessa could picture Sophie participating in anything like that on Jessamine's behalf.

"*You've* seen what her face looks like. Being hideous has made her bitter. A ladies' maid is meant to be pretty, and speak French, and Sophie can't manage either. I told Charlotte as much when she brought the girl home. Charlotte didn't listen to me. She never does."

"I can't imagine why," said Tessa. They had turned onto a narrow path that wound between trees. The glint of the river was visible through them, and the branches above knotted together into a canopy, blocking the brightness of the sun.

"I know! Neither can I!" Jessamine raised her face, letting what sun broke through the canopy dance across her skin. "Charlotte never listens to anyone. She's always henpecking poor Henry. I don't know why he married her at all."

"I assume because he loved her?"

Jessamine snorted. "No one thinks that. Henry wanted access to the Institute so he could work on his little experiments in the cellar and not have to fight. And I don't think he *minded* marrying Charlotte—I don't think there was anyone else he wanted to marry—but if someone else had been running the Institute, he would have married them instead."

She sniffed. "And then there's the boys—Will and Jem. Jem's pleasant enough, but you know how foreigners are. Not really trustworthy and basically selfish and lazy. He's always in his room, pretending to be ill, refusing to do anything to help out," Jessamine went on blithely, apparently forgetting the fact that Jem and Will were off searching the Dark House right now, while she promenaded in the park with Tessa. "And *Will.* Handsome enough, but behaves like a lunatic half the time; it's as if he were brought up by savages. He has no respect for anyone or anything, no concept of the way a gentleman is supposed to behave. I suppose it's because he's Welsh."

Tessa was baffled. "Welsh?" *Is that a bad thing to be?* she was about to add, but Jessamine, thinking that Tessa was doubting Will's origins, went on with relish.

"Oh, yes. With that black hair of his, you can absolutely tell. His mother was a Welshwoman. His father fell in love with her, and that was that. He left the Nephilim. Maybe she cast a spell on him." Jessamine laughed. "They have all kinds of odd magic and things in Wales, you know."

Tessa did not know. "Do you know what happened to Will's parents? Are they dead?"

"I suppose they must be, mustn't they, or they would have come looking for him?" Jessamine furrowed her brow. "Ugh. Anyway. I don't want to talk about the Institute anymore." She swung around to look at Tessa. "You must be wondering why I've been being so nice to you."

"Er . . ." Tessa had been wondering, rather. In novels girls like herself, girls whose families had once had money but who had fallen on hard times, were often taken in by kindly wealthy protectors and were furnished with new clothes and a good education. (Not, Tessa thought, that there had been anything wrong with her education. Aunt Harriet had been as learned as any governess.) Of course, Jessamine did not in any way resemble the saintly older ladies of such tales, whose acts of generosity were totally selfless. "Jessamine, have you ever read *The Lamplighter?*"

"Certainly not. Girls shouldn't read novels," said Jessamine, in the tone of someone reciting something she'd heard somewhere else. "Regardless, Miss Gray, I have a proposition to put to you."

"Tessa," Tessa corrected automatically.

"Of course, for we are already the best of friends," Jessamine said, "and shall soon be even more so."

Tessa regarded the other girl with bafflement. "What do you mean?"

"As I am sure horrid Will has told you, my parents, my dear papa and mama, are dead. But they left me a not inconsiderable sum of money. It was put aside in trust for me until my eighteenth birthday, which is only in a matter of months. You see the problem, of course."

Tessa, who did not see the problem, said, "I do?"

"I am not a Shadowhunter, Tessa. I despise everything about the Nephilim. I have never wanted to be one, and my dearest wish is to leave the Institute and never speak to a single soul who resides there ever again."

"But I thought that your parents were Shadowhunters. . . ."

"One does not have to be a Shadowhunter if one does not wish to," Jessamine snapped. "My parents did not. They left the Clave when they were young. Mama was always perfectly clear. She never wanted the Shadowhunters near me. She said she would never wish that life on a girl. She wanted other things for me. That I would make my debut, meet the Queen, find a good husband, and have darling little babies. An *ordinary life.*" She said the words with a savage sort of hunger. "There are other girls in this city right now, Tessa, other girls my age, who aren't as pretty as me, who are dancing and flirting and laughing and catching husbands. They get lessons in French. I get lessons in horrid demon languages. It's not *fair.*"

"You can still get married." Tessa was puzzled. "Any man would—"

"I could marry a *Shadowhunter.*" Jessamine spat out the word. "And live like Charlotte, having to dress like a man and fight like a man. It's disgusting. Women aren't meant to behave like that. We are meant to graciously preside over lovely homes. To decorate them in a manner that is pleasing to our husbands. To uplift and comfort them with our gentle and angelic presence."

Jessamine sounded neither gentle nor angelic, but Tessa forbore mentioning this. "I don't see how I . . ."

Jessamine caught Tessa's arm fiercely. "Don't you? I can leave the Institute, Tessa, but I cannot live alone. It wouldn't be respectable. Perhaps if I were a widow, but I am only a girl. It just isn't done. But if I had a companion—a sister—"

"You wish me to pretend to be your *sister*?" Tessa squeaked.

"Why not?" Jessamine said, as if this were the most reasonable suggestion in the world. "Or you could be my cousin from America. Yes, that would work. You do see," she added, more practically, "that it isn't as if you have anywhere else to go, is it? I'm quite positive we would catch husbands in no time at all."

Tessa, whose head had begun to ache, wished Jessamine would cease to speak of "catching" husbands the way one might catch a cold, or a runaway cat.

"I could introduce you to all the best people," Jessamine continued. "There would be balls, and dinner parties—" She broke off, looking around in sudden confusion. "But—where are we?"

Tessa glanced around. The path had narrowed. It was now a dark trail leading between high twisted trees. Tessa could no longer see the sky, nor hear the sound of voices. Beside her, Jessamine had come to a halt. Her face creased with sudden fear. "We've wandered off the path," she whispered.

"Well, we can find our way back, can't we?" Tessa spun around, looking for a break in the trees, a patch of sunlight. "I think we came from that way—"

Jessamine caught suddenly at Tessa's arm, her fingers claw-like. Something—no, someone—had appeared before them on the path.

The figure was small, so small that for a moment Tessa thought they were facing a child. But as the form stepped forward into the light, she saw that it was a man—a hunched, wizened-looking man, dressed like a peddler, in ragged clothes, a battered hat pushed back on his head. His face was wrinkled and white, like a mold-covered old apple, and his eyes were gleaming black between thick folds of skin.

He grinned, showing teeth as sharp as razors. "Pretty girls."

Tessa glanced at Jessamine; the other girl was rigid and

staring, her mouth a white line. "We ought to go," Tessa whispered, and pulled at Jessamine's arm. Slowly, as if she were in a dream, Jessamine allowed Tessa to turn her so they faced back the way they had come—

And the man was before them once again, blocking the way back to the park. Far, far in the distance, Tessa thought she could see the park, a sort of clearing, full of light. It looked impossibly far away.

"You wandered off the path," said the stranger. His voice was singsong, rhythmic. "Pretty girls, you wandered off the path. You know what happens to girls like you."

He took a step forward.

Jessamine, still rigid, was clutching her parasol as though it were a lifeline. "Goblin," she said, "hobgoblin, whatever you are—we have no quarrel with any of the Fair Folk. But if you touch us—"

"You wandered from the path," sang the little man, coming closer, and as he did, Tessa saw that his shining shoes were not shoes after all but gleaming hooves. "Foolish Nephilim, to come to this place un-Marked. Here is land more ancient than any Accords. Here there is strange earth. If your angel blood should fall upon it, golden vines will grow from the spot, with diamonds at their tips. And I claim it. I claim your blood."

Tessa tugged at Jessamine's arm. "Jessamine, we should—"

"Tessa, be *quiet*." Shaking her arm free, Jessamine pointed her parasol at the goblin. "You don't want to do this. You don't want—"

The creature sprang. As he hurtled toward them, his mouth seemed to peel wide, his skin splitting, and Tessa saw the face beneath—fanged and vicious. She screamed and stumbled backward, her shoe catching on a tree root. She thumped to the ground as Jessamine raised her parasol, and with a flick of Jessamine's wrist, the parasol burst open like a flower.

The goblin screamed. He screamed and fell back and rolled on the ground, still screaming. Blood streamed from a wound in his cheek, staining his ragged gray jacket.

"I told you," Jessamine said. She was breathing hard, her chest rising and falling as if she had been racing through the park. "I told you to leave us alone, you filthy creature—" She struck at the goblin again, and now Tessa could see that the edges of Jessamine's parasol gleamed an odd gold-white, and were as sharp as razors. Blood was splattered across the flowered material.

The goblin howled, throwing up his arms to protect himself. He looked like a little old hunched man now, and though Tessa knew it was an illusion, she couldn't help feeling a pang of pity. "Mercy, mistress, mercy—"

"Mercy?" Jessamine spat. "You wanted to grow flowers out of my blood! Filthy goblin! Disgusting creature!" She slashed at him again with the parasol, and again, and the goblin screamed and thrashed. Tessa sat up, shaking the dirt out of her hair, and staggered to her feet. Jessamine was still screaming, the parasol flying, the creature on the ground spasming with each blow. "I hate you!" Jessamine shrieked, her voice thin and trembling. "I hate you, and everything like you—Downworlders—disgusting, *disgusting*—"

"Jessamine!" Tessa ran to the other girl and threw her arms around her, pinning Jessamine's arms against her body. For a moment Jessamine struggled, and Tessa realized there was no way she could hold her. She was *strong*, the muscles under her soft feminine skin coiled and as tense as a whip. And then Jessamine went suddenly limp, sagging back against Tessa, her breath hitching as the parasol drooped in her hand. "No," she wailed. "No. I didn't want to. I didn't mean to. *No*—"

Tessa glanced down. The goblin's body was humped and motionless at their feet. Blood spread across the ground from the place where he lay, running across the earth like dark vines. Holding Jessamine as she sobbed, Tessa could not help but wonder what would grow there now.

It was, unsurprisingly, Charlotte who recovered from her astonishment first. "Mr. Mortmain, I'm not sure what you could possibly mean—"

"Of course you are." He was smiling, his lean face split from ear to ear by an impish grin. "Shadowhunters. The Nephilim. That's what you call yourselves, isn't it? The by-blows of men and angels. Strange, since the Nephilim in the Bible were hideous monsters, weren't they?"

"You know, that's not necessarily true," Henry said, unable to restrain his inner pedant. "There's an issue of translation from the original Aramaic—"

"Henry," Charlotte said warningly.

"Do you really trap the souls of the demons you kill in a gigantic crystal?" Mortmain went on, wide eyed. "How magnificent!"

"D'you mean the Pyxis?" Henry looked baffled. "It's not a crystal, more like a wooden box. And they aren't so much souls—demons don't *have* souls. They have energy—"

"Be *quiet*, Henry," Charlotte snapped.

"Mrs. Branwell," Mortmain said. He sounded dreadfully

cheerful. "Please do not concern yourself. I already know everything about your kind, you see. You're Charlotte Branwell, aren't you? And this is your husband, Henry Branwell. You run the London Institute from the site of what was once the church of All-Hallows-the-Less. Did you honestly think I wouldn't know who you were? *Especially* once you tried to glamour my footman? He can't bear being glamoured, you know. Gives him a rash."

Charlotte narrowed her eyes. "And how have you come by all this information?"

Mortmain leaned forward eagerly, templing his hands. "I am a student of the occult. Since my time in India as a young man, when I first learned of them, I have been fascinated with the shadow realms. For a man in my position, with sufficient funds and more than sufficient time, many doors are open. There are books one may purchase, information that can be paid for. Your knowledge is not as secret as you might think."

"Perhaps," said Henry, looking deeply unhappy, "but— It is *dangerous*, you know. Killing demons—it's not like shooting tigers. They can hunt you as well as you can hunt them."

Mortmain chuckled. "My boy, I have no intention of racing out to fight demons bare-handed. Of course this sort of information is dangerous in the hands of the flighty and the hotheaded, but mine is a careful and sensible mind. I seek only an expansion of my knowledge of the world, nothing more." He looked about the room. "I must say, I've never had the honor of talking to Nephilim before. Of course, mention of you is frequent in the literature, but to read about something and to truly experience it are two very different things, I'm sure you'll agree. There is so very much you could teach me—"

"That," Charlotte said in a freezing tone, "will be quite enough of that."

Mortmain looked at her, puzzled. "Pardon me?"

"Since you seem to know so much about Nephilim, Mr. Mortmain, might I ask if you know what our mandate is?"

Mortmain looked smug. "To destroy demons. To protect humans—mundanes, as I understand you call us."

"Yes," said Charlotte, "and a great deal of the time what we are protecting humans from is their own very foolish selves. I see that you are no exception to this rule."

At that, Mortmain looked actually astonished. His glance went to Henry. Charlotte knew that look. It was a look only exchanged between men, a look that said, *Can you not control your wife, sir?* A look, she knew, that was quite wasted on Henry, who seemed to be trying to read the upside-down blueprints on Mortmain's desk and was paying very little attention to the conversation.

"You think the occult knowledge you have acquired makes you very clever," said Charlotte. "But I have seen my share of dead mundanes, Mr. Mortmain. I cannot count the times we have attended to the remains of some human who fancied himself expert in magical practices. I remember, when I was a girl, being summoned to the home of a barrister. He belonged to some silly circle of men who believed themselves to be magicians. They spent their time chanting and wearing robes and drawing pentagrams on the ground. One evening he determined that his skill was sufficient to attempt the raising of a demon."

"And was it?"

"It was," Charlotte said. "He raised the demon Marax. It

proceeded to slaughter him, and all of his family." Her tone was matter-of-fact. "We found most of them hanging headless, upside down in the carriage house. The youngest of his children was roasting on a spit over the fire. We never did find Marax."

Mortmain had paled, but retained his composure. "There are always those who overreach their abilities," he said. "But I—"

"But you would never be so foolish," Charlotte said. "Save that you are, at this very moment, being that foolish. You look at Henry and myself and you are not afraid of us. You are amused! A fairy tale come to life!" She slammed her hand down hard on the edge of his desk, making him jump. "The might of the Clave stands behind us," she said, in as cold a tone as she could muster. "Our mandate is to protect humans. Such as Nathaniel Gray. He has vanished, and something occult is clearly behind that vanishing. And here we find his erstwhile employer, clearly steeped in matters of the occult. It beggars belief that the two facts are not connected."

"I—He—Mr. Gray has vanished?" Mortmain stammered.

"He has. His sister came to us, searching for him; she had been informed by a pair of warlocks that he was in grave danger. While you, sir, are amusing yourself, he may be dying. And the Clave does not look kindly on those who stand in the way of its mandate."

Mortmain passed a hand over his face. When he emerged from behind it, he looked gray. "I shall, of course," he said, "tell you whatever you want to know."

"Excellent." Charlotte's heart was beating fast, but her voice betrayed no anxiety.

"I used to know his father. Nathaniel's father. I employed him almost twenty years ago when Mortmain's was mainly a shipping concern. I had offices in Hong Kong, Shanghai, Tianjin—" He broke off as Charlotte tapped her fingers impatiently on the desk. "Richard Gray worked for me here in London. He was my head clerk, a kind and clever man. I was sorry to lose him when he moved his family to America. When Nathaniel wrote to me and told me who he was, I offered him a job on the spot."

"Mr. Mortmain." Charlotte's voice was steely. "This is not germane—"

"Oh, but it is," the small man insisted. "You see, my knowledge of the occult has always been of assistance to me in business matters. Some years ago, for instance, a well-known Lombard Street bank collapsed—destroyed dozens of large companies. My acquaintance with a warlock helped me avoid disaster. I was able to withdraw my funds before the bank dissolved, and that saved my company. But it raised Richard's suspicions. He must have investigated, for eventually he confronted me with his knowledge of the Pandemonium Club."

"You are a member, then," Charlotte murmured. "Of course."

"I offered Richard membership in the club—even took him to a meeting or two—but he was uninterested. Shortly after that he moved his family to America." Mortmain spread his hands wide. "The Pandemonium Club is not for everyone. Traveling widely as I have, I heard stories of similar organizations in many cities, groups of men who know of the Shadow World and wish to share their knowledge and advantages, but one pays the heavy price of secrecy for membership."

"One pays a heavier price than that."

"It isn't an evil organization," Mortmain said. He sounded almost wounded. "There were many great advancements, many great inventions. I saw a warlock create a silver ring that could transport the wearer to another location whenever he twisted one around his finger. Or a doorway that could bring you anywhere in the world you wanted to go. I've seen men brought back from the brink of death—"

"I'm aware of magic and what it can do, Mr. Mortmain." Charlotte glanced at Henry, who was examining a blueprint for some sort of mechanical gadget, mounted on a wall. "There is one question that concerns me. The warlocks who appear to have kidnapped Mr. Gray are somehow associated with the club. I have always heard it called a club for mundanes. Why would there be Downworlders in it?"

Mortmain's forehead creased. "Downworlders? You mean the supernatural folk—warlocks and lycanthropes and the like? There are levels and levels of membership, Mrs. Branwell. A mundane such as myself can become a member of the club. But the chairmen—those who run the enterprise—they are Downworlders. Warlocks, lycanthropes, and vampires. The Fair Folk shun us, though. Too many captains of industry—railroads, factories, and the like—for them. They hate such things." He shook his head. "Lovely creatures, faeries, but I do fear progress will be the death of them."

Charlotte was uninterested in Mortmain's thoughts on faeries; her mind was whirling. "Let me guess. You introduced Nathaniel Gray to the club, exactly as you had introduced his father."

Mortmain, who had seemed to be regaining a bit of his old confidence, wilted again. "Nathaniel had worked in my office in London for only a few days before he confronted me. I gathered he had learned of his father's experience at the club, and it had given him a fierce desire to know more. I couldn't refuse. I brought him to a meeting and thought that would be the end of it. But it wasn't." He shook his head. "Nathaniel took to the club like a duck to water. A few weeks after that first meeting, he was gone from his lodging house. He sent a letter for me, terminating his employment and saying he was going to work for another Pandemonium Club member, someone who apparently was willing to pay him enough to sustain his gambling habits." He sighed. "Needless to say, he left no forwarding address."

"And that's all?" Charlotte's voice rose in disbelief. "You didn't try to look for him? Find out where he had gone? Who his new employer was?"

"A man can take employment where he likes," Mortmain said, blustering. "There was no reason to think—"

"And you haven't seen him since?"

"No. I told you—"

Charlotte cut him off. "You say he took to the Pandemonium Club like a duck to water, yet you haven't seen him at a single meeting since he left your employment?"

A look of panic flickered in Mortmain's eyes. "I . . . I have not been to a meeting since then myself. Work has kept me extremely busy."

Charlotte looked hard at Axel Mortmain across his massive desk. She was a good judge of character, she had always thought. It wasn't as if she hadn't come across men like Mortmain before. Bluff, genial, confident men, men who believed that their success in business or some other worldly pursuit meant that they would have the same success should they choose to pursue the magical arts. She thought of the barrister again, the walls of his Knightsbridge house painted scarlet with the blood of his family. She thought what his terror might have been like, in those last moments of his life. She could see the beginnings of a similar fear in Axel Mortmain's eyes.

"Mr. Mortmain," she said, "I am not a fool. I know there is something you are concealing from me." She took from her reticule one of the cogs that Will had retrieved from the Dark Sisters' house, and set it on the desk. "This looks like something your factories might produce."

With a distracted look Mortmain glanced down at the small piece of metal on his desk. "Yes—yes, that's one of my cogs. What of it?"

"Two warlocks calling themselves the Dark Sisters—both members of the Pandemonium Club—they've been murdering humans. Young girls. Barely more than children. And we found this in the cellar of their home."

"I've nothing to do with any murders!" Mortmain exclaimed. "I never—I thought—" He had begun to sweat.

"What did you think?" Charlotte's voice was soft.

Mortmain picked up the cog in shaking fingers. "You can't imagine . . ." His voice trailed off. "A few months ago one of the club's board members—a Downworlder, and very old and powerful—came to me and asked me to sell him some mechanical equipment cheaply. Cogs and cams and the like. I didn't ask what it was for—why would I? There seemed nothing remarkable about the request."

"By any chance," Charlotte said, "was this the same man whose employment Nathaniel joined after he left yours?"

Mortmain dropped the cog. As it rolled across the table,

he slammed his hand down on top of it, halting its progress. Though he said nothing, Charlotte could tell by the flicker of fear in his eyes that her guess was correct. A tingle of triumph ran through her nerves.

"His name," she said. "Tell me his name."

Mortmain was staring at the desk. "It would be worth my life to tell you."

"What about Nathaniel Gray's life?" said Charlotte.

Without meeting her eyes Mortmain shook his head. "You've no idea how powerful this man is. How dangerous."

Charlotte straightened up. "Henry," she said. "Henry, bring me the Summoner."

Henry turned away from the wall and blinked at her in confusion. "But, darling—"

"Bring me the device!" Charlotte snapped. She loathed snapping at Henry; it was like kicking a puppy. But sometimes it had to be done.

The look of confusion didn't leave Henry's face as he joined his wife before Mortmain's desk, and drew something from his jacket pocket. It was a dark metal oblong, with a series of peculiar-looking dials across the face of it. Charlotte took it and brandished it at Mortmain.

"This is a Summoner," she told him. "It will allow me to summon the Clave. Inside of three minutes they will surround your house. Nephilim will drag you from this room, screaming and kicking. They will perform upon you the most exquisite tortures until you are forced to speak. Do you know what happens to a man when demon blood is dripped into his eyes?"

Mortmain gave her a ghastly look, but said nothing.

"Please don't test me, Mr. Mortmain." The device in

Charlotte's hand was slippery with sweat, but her voice was even. "I would hate to watch you die."

"Good Lord, man, tell her!" Henry burst out. "Really, there's no need for this, Mr. Mortmain. You're only making it harder on yourself."

Mortmain covered his face with his hands. He had always wanted to meet real Shadowhunters, Charlotte thought, looking at him. And now he had.

"De Quincey," he said. "I don't know his first name. Just de Quincey."

By the Angel. Charlotte exhaled slowly, lowering the device to her side. "De Quincey? It can't be . . ."

"You know who he is?" Mortmain's voice was dull. "Well, I suppose you would."

"He's the head of a powerful London vampire clan," Charlotte said almost reluctantly, "a very influential Downworlder, and an ally of the Clave. I can't imagine that he would—"

"He's the head of the club," said Mortmain. He looked exhausted, and a little gray. "Everyone else answers to him."

"The head of the club. Has he a title?"

Mortmain looked faintly surprised to be asked. "The Magister."

With a hand that shook only slightly, Charlotte slipped the device she had been holding into her sleeve. "Thank you, Mr. Mortmain. You've been most helpful."

Mortmain looked at her with a sort of drained resentment. "De Quincey will find out that I've told you. He'll have me killed."

"The Clave will see that he does not. And we will keep your name out of this. He shall never know you spoke to us."

"You would do that?" Mortmain said softly. "For what was it—a foolish mundane?"

"I have hopes for you, Mr. Mortmain. You seem to have realized your own folly. The Clave will be watching you—not only for your own protection, but to see that you stay away from the Pandemonium Club and organizations like it. For your own sake, I hope you will regard our meeting as a warning."

Mortmain nodded. Charlotte moved to the door, Henry behind her; she already had it open and was standing on the threshold when Mortmain spoke again. "They were only cogs," he said softly. "Only gears. Harmless."

It was Henry, to Charlotte's surprise, who replied, without turning, "Inanimate objects are harmless indeed, Mr. Mortmain. But one cannot always say the same of the men who use them."

Mortmain was silent as the two Shadowhunters left the room. A few moments later they were out in the square, breathing fresh air—as fresh as the air of London ever was. It might be thick with coal smoke and dust, Charlotte thought, but at least it was free of the fear and desperation that had hung like a haze in Mortmain's study.

Drawing the device from her sleeve, Charlotte offered it to her husband. "I suppose I ought to ask you," she said as he received it with a grave expression, "what *is* that object, Henry?"

"Something I've been working on." Henry looked at it fondly. "A device that can sense demon energies. I was going to call it a Sensor. I haven't got it working yet, but when I do!"

"I'm sure it will be splendid."

Henry transferred his fond expression from the device

to his wife, a rare occurrence. "What pure genius, Charlotte. Pretending you could summon the Clave on the spot, just to frighten that man! But how did you know I'd have a device you could put to your uses?"

"Well, you did, darling," said Charlotte. "Didn't you?"

Henry looked sheepish. "You are as terrifying as you are wonderful, my dear."

"Thank you, Henry."

The ride back to the Institute was a silent one; Jessamine stared out the window of the cab at the snarling London traffic and refused to say a word. She held her parasol across her lap, seemingly indifferent to the fact that the blood on its edges was staining her taffeta jacket. When they reached the churchyard, she let Thomas help her down from the carriage before reaching to grip Tessa's hand.

Surprised at the contact, Tessa could only stare. Jessamine's fingers in hers were icy. "Come *along*," Jessamine snapped impatiently, and pulled her companion toward the Institute doors, leaving Thomas staring after them.

Tessa let the other girl draw her up the stairs, into the Institute proper, and down a long corridor, this one almost identical to the one outside Tessa's bedroom. Jessamine located a door, pushed Tessa through it, and followed, shutting the door behind them. "I want to show you something," she said.

Tessa looked around. It was another of the large bedrooms of which the Institute seemed to have an infinite number. Jessamine's, though, had been decorated somewhat to her taste. Above the wooden wainscoting the walls were papered in rose silk, and the coverlet on the bed was printed with flowers. There was a white vanity table too, its surface covered with an expensive-looking dressing table set: a ring stand, a bottle of flower water, and a silver-backed hairbrush and mirror.

"Your room is lovely," Tessa said, more in hopes of calming Jessamine's evident hysteria than because she meant it.

"It's much too small," Jessamine said. "But come—over here." And flinging the bloodied parasol down onto her bed, she marched across the room to a corner by the window. Tessa followed with some puzzlement. There was nothing in the corner but a high table, and on the table was a dollhouse. Not the sort of two-room cardboard Dolly's Playhouse that Tessa had had as a child. This was a beautiful miniature reproduction of a real London town house, and when Jessamine touched it, Tessa saw that the front of it swung open on tiny hinges.

Tessa caught her breath. There were beautiful tiny rooms perfectly decorated with miniature furniture, everything built to scale, from the little wooden chairs with needlepoint cushions to the cast-iron stove in the kitchen. There were small dolls, too, with china heads, and real little oil paintings on the walls.

"This was my house." Jessamine knelt down, bringing herself to eye level with the dollhouse rooms, and gestured for Tessa to do the same.

Awkwardly, Tessa did, trying not to kneel on Jessamine's skirts. "You mean this was the dollhouse you had when you were a little girl?"

"No." Jessamine sounded irritated. "This was my *house*. My father had this made for me when I was six. It's modeled exactly on the house we lived in, on Curzon Street. This was the wallpaper we had in the dining room"—she pointed—"and those are exactly the chairs in my father's study. You see?"

She looked at Tessa intently, so intently that Tessa felt sure she was supposed to be seeing something here, something beyond an extremely expensive toy that Jessamine should have long ago grown out of. She simply didn't know what that could be. "It's very pretty," she said finally.

"See, here in the parlor is Mama," said Jessamine, touching one of the tiny dolls with her finger. The doll wobbled in its plush armchair. "And here in the study, reading a book, is Papa." Her hand glided over the little porcelain figure. "And upstairs in the nursery is Baby Jessie." Inside the little crib there was indeed another doll, only its head visible above tiny coverlets. "Later they'll have dinner here, in the dining room. And then Mama and Papa will sit in the drawing room by the fire. Some nights they go to the theater, or to a ball or a dinner." Her voice had grown hushed, as if she were reciting a well-remembered litany. "And then Mama will kiss Papa good night, and they will go to their rooms, and they will sleep *all night long.* There will be no calls from the Clave that drive them out in the middle of the night to fight demons in the dark. There will be no one tracking blood into the house. No one will lose an arm or an eye to a werewolf, or have to choke down holy water because a vampire attacked them."

Dear God, Tessa thought.

As if Jessamine could read Tessa's mind, her face twisted. "When our house burned, I had nowhere else to go. It wasn't as if there were relations that could take me in; all of Mama and Papa's relations were Shadowhunters and hadn't spoken to them since they'd broken with the Clave. Henry is the one who made me that parasol. Did you know that? I thought it was quite pretty until he told me that the fabric is edged with electrum, as sharp as a razor. It was always meant to be a weapon."

"You saved us," Tessa said. "In the park today. I can't fight at all. If you hadn't done what you did—"

"I shouldn't have done it." Jessamine stared into the dollhouse with empty eyes. "I will not have this life, Tessa. I *will not have it*. I don't care what I have to do. I won't live like this. I'd rather die."

Alarmed, Tessa was about to tell her not to talk like that, when the door opened behind them. It was Sophie, in her white cap and neat dark dress. Her eyes, when they rested on Jessamine, were wary. She said, "Miss Tessa, Mr. Branwell very much wants to see you in his study. He says it's important."

Tessa turned to Jessamine to ask her if she would be all right, but Jessamine's face had closed like a door. The vulnerability and anger were gone; the cold mask was back. "Go along, then, if Henry wants you," she said. "I'm quite tired of you already, and I think I'm getting a headache. Sophie, when you return, I'll need you to massage my temples with eau de cologne."

Sophie's eyes met Tessa's across the room with something like amusement. "As you like, Miss Jessamine."

7

The Clockwork Girl

But helpless Pieces of the Game He plays
Upon this chequer-board of Nights and Days
Hither and thither moves, and checks and slays.
—"The Rubaiyat of Omar Khayyam,"
translated by Edward FitzGerald, 1859

It had grown dark outside the Institute, and Sophie's lantern cast strange dancing shadows on the walls as she led Tessa down one flight of stone stairs after another. The steps were old, concave in the centers, where generations of feet had worn them down. The walls were roughly textured stone, the tiny windows set into them at intervals giving way eventually to blankness that seemed to indicate that they had passed belowground.

"Sophie," Tessa said finally, her nerves rubbed raw by the darkness and silence, "are we going down into the church *crypt*, by any chance?"

Sophie chuckled, and the lights of the lantern flickered on the walls. "It used to be the crypt, before Mr. Branwell had it fixed up into a laboratory for himself. He's always down there, tinkering with his toys and his experiments. It doesn't half drive Mrs. Branwell wild."

"What's he making?" Tessa nearly tripped over an uneven stair, and had to grab for the wall to right herself. Sophie didn't appear to notice.

"All sorts of things," Sophie said, her voice echoing strangely off the walls. "Inventing new weapons, protective gear for the Shadowhunters. He loves clockwork and mechanisms and that sort of thing. Mrs. Branwell sometimes says she thinks he'd love her better if she ticked like a clock." She laughed.

"It sounds," Tessa said, "as if you're fond of them. Mr. and Mrs. Branwell, I mean."

Sophie said nothing, but the already proud set of her back seemed to harden slightly.

"Fonder of them than you are of Will, anyway," Tessa said, hoping to soften the other girl's mood with humor.

"*Him.*" The disgust was plain in Sophie's voice. "He's—Well, he's a bad sort, isn't he? Reminds me of the son of my last employer. He was proud just like Mr. Herondale. And whatever he wanted, he got, from the day he was born. And if he didn't get it, well . . ." She reached up then, almost unconsciously, and touched the side of her face, where the scar ran from mouth to temple.

"Then what?"

But Sophie's brusque manner was back. "Then he'd be like to pitch a fit, that's all." Transferring her glowing lantern from one hand to the other, she peered down into the shadowy darkness. "Be careful here, miss. The stairs can get awfully damp and slippery toward the bottom."

Tessa moved closer to the wall. The stone was cold against her bare hand. "Do you think it's simply because Will's a Shadowhunter?" she inquired. "And they— Well, they rather think they're superior, don't they? Jessamine, too—"

"But Mr. Carstairs is *not* like that. He isn't at all like the others. And neither are Mr. and Mrs. Branwell."

Before Tessa could say anything else, they came to an abrupt stop at the foot of the stairs. There was a heavy oak door there with a barred grille set into it; Tessa could see nothing through the grille but shadows. Sophie reached for the wide iron bar across the door and pushed it down, hard.

The door swung open onto an enormous brightly lit space. Tessa moved into the room with wide eyes; this had clearly been the crypt of the church that had originally stood on this spot. Squat pillars held up a roof that disappeared into darkness. The floor was made up of great stone slabs darkened with age; some were carved with words, and Tessa guessed that she stood on the gravestones—and the bones—of those who had been buried in the crypt. There were no windows, but the bright white illumination that Tessa had come to know as witchlight shone down from brass fixtures fastened to the pillars.

In the center of the room were a number of large wooden tables, their surfaces covered with all manner of mechanical objects—gears and cogs made of dully shining brass and iron; long strings of copper wire; glass beakers filled with liquids of different colors, some of them giving off wisps of smoke or bitter odors. The air smelled metallic and sharp, like the air before a storm. One table was entirely covered with a scatter of weapons, the blades shining under the witchlight. There was a half-finished suit of what looked like thinly scaled metal armor, hanging on a wire frame by a great stone table whose surface was concealed by a lumpy cluster of thick woolen blankets.

Behind the table stood Henry, and beside him, Charlotte. Henry was showing his wife something he held in his hand—a copper wheel, perhaps a gear—and was speaking to her in a low voice. He wore a loose canvas shirt over his clothes, like a fisherman's smock, and it was smeared with dirt and dark fluid. Still, what struck Tessa most about him was the assurance with which he spoke to Charlotte. There was none of his usual diffidence. He sounded confident and direct, and his hazel eyes, when he raised them to look at Tessa, were clear and steady.

"Miss Gray! So Sophie showed you the way down here, did she? Very good of her."

"Why, yes, she—," Tessa began, glancing behind her, but Sophie was not there. She must have turned at the door and gone soundlessly back up the stairs. Tessa felt foolish for not having noticed. "She did," she finished. "She said that you wanted to see me?"

"Indeed," Henry said. "We could use your help with something. Could you come over here for a moment?"

He gestured for her to join him and Charlotte by the table. As Tessa approached, she saw that Charlotte's face was white and pinched, her brown eyes shadowed. She looked at Tessa, bit her lip, and glanced down toward the table, where the heaped fabric—*moved.*

Tessa blinked. Had she imagined it? But no, there had been a flicker of movement—and now that she was closer, she saw that what was on the table was not so much a pile of fabric as fabric *covering* something—something approximately the size and shape of a human body. She stopped in her tracks, as Henry reached out, took hold of a corner of the fabric, and drew it away, revealing what lay beneath.

Tessa, feeling suddenly dizzy, reached to grasp the edge of the table. "*Miranda.*"

The dead girl lay on her back on the table, her arms flung out to either side, her dull brown hair straggling down around her shoulders. The eyes that had so unnerved Tessa were gone. Now there were hollow black sockets in her white face. Her cheap dress had been cut open down the front, baring her chest. Tessa winced, looked away—and then looked back quickly, in disbelief. For there was no naked flesh, and no blood, despite the fact that Miranda's chest had been sliced open down the front, her skin peeled back on either side like the skin of an orange. Beneath the grotesque mutilation gleamed the brightness of—metal?

Tessa moved forward until she was standing across from Henry at the table where Miranda lay. Where there should have been blood, torn flesh, and mutilation, there were only the two sheets of white skin folded back, and beneath them a carapace of metal. Sheets of copper, intricately fitted together, made up her chest, flowing smoothly down into a jointed cage of copper and flexible brass that was Miranda's waist. A square of copper, about the size of Tessa's palm, was missing from the center of the dead girl's chest, revealing a hollow space.

"Tessa." Charlotte's voice was soft but insistent. "Will and

Jem found this—this body in the house where you were kept. The house was completely empty except for her; she'd been left in a room, alone."

Tessa, still staring in fascination, nodded. "Miranda. The Sisters' maidservant."

"Do you know anything about her? Who she might be? Her history?"

"No. No. I thought . . . I mean, she hardly ever spoke, and then she only repeated things the Sisters had said."

Henry hooked a finger into Miranda's lower lip and pulled her mouth open. "She has a rudimentary metal tongue, but her mouth was never really constructed for speech, or for consuming food. She has no gullet, and I would guess no stomach. Her mouth ends in a sheet of metal behind her teeth." He turned her head from side to side, his eyes narrowing.

"But what *is* she?" Tessa asked. "A sort of Downworlder, or demon?"

"No." Henry let go of Miranda's jaw. "She is not precisely a *living* creature at all. She is an automaton. A mechanical creature, made to move and appear as a human being moves and appears. Leonardo da Vinci designed one. You can find it in his drawings—a mechanical creature that could sit up, walk, and turn its head. He was the first to suggest that human beings are only complex machines, that our insides are like cogs and pistons and cams made of muscle and flesh. So why could they not be replaced with copper and iron? Why couldn't you *build* a person? But *this*. Jaquet Droz and Maillardet could never have dreamed of this. A true biomechanical automaton, self-moving, self-directing, wrapped in human flesh." His eyes shone. "It's beautiful."

"Henry." Charlotte's voice was tight. "That flesh you're admiring. It came from *somewhere.*"

Henry passed the back of his hand across his forehead, the light dying out of his eyes. "Yes—those bodies in the cellar."

"The Silent Brothers have examined them. Most are missing organs—hearts, livers. Some are missing bones and cartilage, even hair. We cannot but assume the Dark Sisters were harvesting these bodies for parts to create their mechanical creatures. Creatures like Miranda."

"And the coachman," Tessa said. "I think he was one as well. But why would anyone do such a thing?"

"There is more," Charlotte said. "The mechanical tools in the Dark Sisters' cellar were manufactured by Mortmain and Company. The company your brother worked for."

"Mortmain!" Tessa tore her gaze from the girl on the table. "You went to see him, didn't you? What did he say about Nate?"

For a moment Charlotte hesitated, glancing at Henry. Tessa knew that glance. It was the sort of glance people gave each other when they were preparing to engage in a joint falsehood. The sort of look she and Nathaniel had given each other, once, when they'd been concealing something from Aunt Harriet.

"You're hiding something from me," she said. "Where's my brother? What does Mortmain know?"

Charlotte sighed. "Mortmain is deeply involved in the occult underworld. He's a member of the Pandemonium Club, which seems to be run by Downworlders."

"But what has that to do with my brother?"

"Your brother found out about the club and was fascinated by it. He went to work for a vampire named de Quincey. A very influential Downworlder. De Quincey is in fact the head of the

Pandemonium Club." Charlotte sounded bitterly disgusted. "There is a title to go with the job, it seems."

Feeling suddenly dizzy, Tessa braced her hand against the edge of the table. "The Magister?"

Charlotte looked at Henry, who had his hand inside the creature's chest panel. He reached in and drew something out—a human heart, red and fleshy, but hard and shiny-looking as if it had been lacquered. It had been bound around with copper and silver wires. Every few moments it would give a listless thump. Somehow it was still beating. "Would you like to hold it?" he asked Tessa. "You'd have to be careful. These copper tubes wind throughout the creature's body, carrying oil and other flammable liquids. I have yet to identify them all."

Tessa shook her head.

"Very well." Henry looked disappointed. "There was something I wished you to see. If you'll simply look here—" He turned the heart carefully in his long fingers, revealing a flat metal panel on the opposite side of it. The panel had been etched with a seal—a large *Q*, a small *D* inside it.

"De Quincey's mark," said Charlotte. She looked bleak. "I've seen it before, on correspondence from him. He's always been an ally of the Clave, or so I thought. He was there at the Accords when they were signed. He's a powerful man. He controls all the Night Children in the western part of the city. Mortmain says that de Quincey bought mechanical parts from him, and this would seem to bear that out. It looks as if you weren't the only thing in the Dark Sisters' house that was being prepared for the Magister's use. These clockwork creatures were as well."

"If this vampire is the Magister," Tessa said slowly, "then he is the one who had the Dark Sisters capture me, and he is the one who forced Nate to write me that letter. He must know where my brother is."

Charlotte almost smiled. "You *are* single-minded, aren't you."

Tessa's voice was hard. "Don't imagine that I don't want to know what the Magister wants with me. Why he had me captured and trained. How on earth he knew I had my—my ability. And don't think I wouldn't want revenge if I could have it." She took a shuddering breath. "But my brother is all I have. I must find him."

"*We* will find him, Tessa," Charlotte said. "Somehow all of this—the Dark Sisters, your brother, your own ability, and de Quincey's involvement—fits together like a puzzle. We simply haven't found all the missing bits of it yet."

"I must say, I hope we find them soon," Henry said, casting a sad glance at the body on the table. "What could a vampire want with a lot of half-mechanical people? None of this makes any sense."

"Not yet," said Charlotte, and she set her small chin. "But it will."

Henry remained in his laboratory even after Charlotte had announced that it was past time for them to return upstairs for supper. Insisting that he would be along in five minutes, he waved them off absently as Charlotte shook her head.

"Henry's laboratory—I've never seen anything like it," Tessa said to Charlotte when they were halfway up the stairs. She was already out of breath, though Charlotte was moving with a steady, purposeful gait and looked as if she would never tire.

"Yes," Charlotte replied a little sadly. "Henry would spend all day and all night there if I allowed it."

If I allowed it. The words surprised Tessa. It was the husband, wasn't it, who decided what was and was not allowed, and how his home should be run? The wife's duty was simply to carry out his wishes, and to provide him with a calm and stable refuge from the chaos of the world. A place he might retreat. But the Institute was hardly that. It was part home, part boarding school, and part battle station. And whoever might be in charge of it, it clearly wasn't Henry.

With an exclamation of surprise, Charlotte stopped short on the step above Tessa. "Jessamine! What on earth's the matter?"

Tessa looked up. Jessamine stood at the head of the stairs, framed in the open doorway. She still wore her day clothes, though her hair, now in elaborate ringlets, had clearly been arranged for evening, no doubt by the ever-patient Sophie. There was an immense scowl on her face.

"It's Will," she said. "He's being absolutely ridiculous in the dining room."

Charlotte looked puzzled. "How is this different from his being totally ridiculous in the library or the weapons room or any of the other places he's usually ridiculous?"

"Because," Jessamine said, as if this should be obvious, "we have to *eat* in the dining room." She turned and flounced off down the hallway, glancing back over her shoulder to make sure that Tessa and Charlotte were following her.

Tessa couldn't help but smile. "It is a bit like they're your children, isn't it?"

Charlotte sighed. "Yes," she said. "Except for the part where they're required to love me, I suppose."

Tessa could think of nothing to say in reply to that.

***

Since Charlotte insisted that there was something she had to do in the drawing room before supper, Tessa made her way to the dining room by herself. Once she had arrived there—quite proud of herself for not having lost her way—she found that Will was standing on one of the sideboards, tinkering with something attached to the ceiling.

Jem was seated in a chair, looking up at Will with a dubious expression. "It serves you right if you break it," he said, and inclined his head as he caught sight of Tessa. "Good evening, Tessa." Following her stare, he grinned. "I was hanging the gasolier crookedly, and Will is endeavoring to straighten it."

Tessa could see nothing wrong with the gasolier, but before she could say so, Jessamine stalked into the room and shot a glare at Will. "Really! Can't you get Thomas to do that? A gentleman needn't—"

"Is that blood on your sleeve, Jessie?" Will inquired, glancing down.

Jessamine's face tightened. Without another word she turned on her heel and stalked to the far end of the table, where she set herself down in a chair and stared stonily ahead.

"Did something happen while you and Jessamine were out?" It was Jem, looking genuinely worried. As he turned his head to look at Tessa, she saw something green gleam against the base of his throat.

Jessamine looked over at Tessa, a look of near panic on her face. "No," Tessa began. "It was nothing—"

"I've done it!" Henry entered the room triumphantly, brandishing something in his hand. It looked like a copper tube with a black button on one side. "I'll wager you didn't think I could, did you?"

Will abandoned his efforts with the gasolier to glare at Henry. "None of us have the slightest idea what you're on about. You do know that?"

"I've gotten my Phosphor to work at last." Henry proudly brandished the object. "It functions on the principle of witch-light but is five times more powerful. Merely press a button, and you will see a blaze of light the like of which you have never imagined."

There was a silence. "So," said Will finally, "it's a very, very bright witchlight, then?"

"Exactly," Henry said.

"Is that useful, precisely?" Jem inquired. "After all, witch-light is just for illumination. It's not as if it's dangerous. . . ."

"Wait till you see it!" Henry replied. He held up the object. "Watch."

Will moved to object, but it was too late; Henry had already pressed the button. There was a blinding flare of light and a whooshing sound, and the room was plunged into blackness. Tessa gave a yelp of surprise, and Jem laughed softly.

"Am I blind?" Will's voice floated out of the darkness, tinged with annoyance. "I'm not going to be at all pleased if you've blinded me, Henry."

"No." Henry sounded worried. "No, the Phosphor seems to— Well, it seems to have turned all the lights in the room *off*."

"It's not supposed to do that?" Jem sounded mild, as always.

"Er," said Henry, "no."

Will muttered something under his breath. Tessa couldn't quite hear him, but was fairly sure she'd caught the words "Henry" and "fatheaded." A moment later there was an enormous crash.

"Will!' someone cried out in alarm. Bright light filled the room, sending Tessa into a fit of blinking. Charlotte was standing in the doorway, holding a witchlight lamp aloft in one hand, and Will was lying on the floor at her feet in a welter of broken crockery from the sideboard. "What on earth . . ."

"I was trying to straighten the gasolier," Will said crossly, sitting up and brushing crockery bits off his shirt.

"Thomas could have done that. And now you've gone and wrecked half the plates."

"And much obliged to your idiot husband for that." Will looked down at himself. "I think I've broken something. The pain is quite agonizing."

"You seem quite intact to me." Charlotte was remorseless. "Get up. I suppose we'll be eating by witchlight tonight."

Jessamine, down at the end of the table, sniffed. It was the first noise she'd made since Will had asked her about the blood on her jacket. "I *hate* witchlight. It makes my complexion look absolutely green."

Despite Jessamine's greenness, Tessa found she rather liked the witchlight. It laid a diffuse white glow over everything and made even the peas and onions look romantic and mysterious. As she buttered a dinner roll with a heavy silver knife, she couldn't help but think of the small apartment in Manhattan where she, her brother, and her aunt had eaten their meager suppers around a plain deal table by the light of a few candles. Aunt Harriet had always been careful to keep everything so scrupulously clean, from the white lace curtains at the front windows to the shining copper kettle on the stove. She had always said that the less you had, the more careful you had to be about everything you *did* have. Tessa wondered if the Shadowhunters were careful about everything they had.

Charlotte and Henry were recounting what they had learned from Mortmain; Jem and Will listened attentively while Jessamine gazed in boredom at the window. Jem seemed especially interested in the description of Mortmain's house, with its artifacts from all over the globe. "I told you," he said. "Taipan. They all think of themselves as very important men. Above the law."

"Yes," Charlotte said. "He had that manner about him, as if he were used to being listened to. Men like that are often easy marks for those who want to draw them into the Shadow World. They are used to having power and expect to be able to get more power easily and with little cost to themselves. They have no idea how high the price for power in Downworld is." She turned, frowning, to Will and Jessamine, who seemed to be quarreling about something in snappish tones. "What is the matter with you two?"

Tessa took the opportunity to turn to Jem, who was sitting on her right side. "Shanghai," she said in a low voice. "It sounds so fascinating. I wish I could travel there. I've always wanted to travel."

As Jem smiled at her, she saw that gleam again at his throat. It was a pendant carved out of dull green stone. "And now you have. You're here, aren't you?"

"I've only ever traveled before in books. I know that sounds silly, but—"

Jessamine interrupted them by slamming her fork down onto the table. "Charlotte," she demanded shrilly, "make Will let me *alone*."

Will was leaning back in his chair, his blue eyes glittering. "If she'd say why she has blood on her clothes, I *would* leave her alone. Let me guess, Jessie. You ran across some poor woman in the park who had the misfortune of wearing a gown that clashed with yours, so you slit her throat with that clever little parasol of yours. Do I have it right?"

Jessamine bared her teeth at him. "You're being ridiculous."

"You are, you know," Charlotte told him.

"I mean, I'm wearing blue. Blue goes with *everything*," Jessamine went on. "Which, really, you ought to know. You're vain enough about your own clothes."

"Blue does not go with everything," Will told her. "It does not go with red, for instance."

"I have a red and blue striped waistcoat," Henry interjected, reaching for the peas.

"And if *that* isn't proof that those two colors should never be seen together under Heaven, I don't know what is."

"Will," Charlotte said sharply. "Don't speak to Henry like that. Henry—"

Henry raised his head. "Yes?"

Charlotte sighed. "That's Jessamine's plate you're spooning peas onto, not yours. Do pay attention, darling."

As Henry looked down in surprise, the dining room door opened and Sophie came in. Her head was down, her dark hair shining. As she bent to speak softly to Charlotte, the witchlight cast its harsh glow over her face, making her scar gleam like silver against her skin.

A look of relief spread over Charlotte's face. A moment later she had risen to her feet and hurried out of the room, pausing only to touch Henry lightly on the shoulder as she went.

Jessamine's brown eyes widened. "Where's she going?"

Will looked at Sophie, his gaze sliding over her in that way that Tessa knew was like fingertips stroking over your skin. "Indeed, Sophie, my dear. Where *did* she go?"

Sophie shot him a venomous look. "If Mrs. Branwell had wanted you to know, I'm sure she would have told you," she snapped, and hurried out of the room after her mistress.

Henry, having set down the peas, attempted a genial smile. "Well, then," he said. "What was it we were discussing?"

"None of that," Will said. "We want to know where Charlotte's gone. Did something happen?"

"No," Henry said. "I mean, I don't *think* so—" He glanced around the room, saw four pairs of eyes fixed on him, and sighed. "Charlotte doesn't always tell me what she's doing. You know that." He smiled a little painfully. "Can't blame her, really. Can't count on me to be sensible."

Tessa wished she could say something to comfort Henry. Something about him made her think of Nate when he was younger, gawkish and awkward and easily hurt. Reflexively she put up her hand to touch the angel at her throat, seeking reassurance in its steady ticking.

Henry looked over at her. "That clockwork object you wear around your neck—might I see it for a moment?"

Tessa hesitated, then nodded. It was only Henry, after all. She unhooked the clasp of the chain, drew off the necklace, and handed it to him.

"This is a clever little object," he said, turning it over in his hands. "Where did you get it?"

"It was my mother's."

"Like a sort of talisman." He glanced up. "Would you mind if I examined it in the laboratory?"

"Oh." Tessa couldn't hide her anxiety. "If you're very careful with it. It's all I have of my mother's. If it were broken . . ."

"Henry won't break or damage it," Jem reassured her. "He's really very good with this sort of thing."

"It's true," said Henry, so modest and matter-of-fact about it that there seemed nothing conceited about the statement. "I'll return it to you in pristine condition."

"Well . . ." Tessa hesitated.

"I don't see what the fuss is," said Jessamine, who had looked bored throughout this exchange. "It's not like it has diamonds in it."

"Some people value sentiment over diamonds, Jessamine." It was Charlotte, standing in the doorway. She looked troubled. "There is someone here who wants to speak with you, Tessa."

"With *me*?" Tessa demanded, the clockwork angel forgotten for the moment.

"Well, who *is* it?" Will said. "Must you keep us all in suspense?"

Charlotte sighed. "It's Lady Belcourt. She's downstairs. In the Sanctuary Room."

"Now?" Will frowned. "Did something happen?"

"I contacted her," said Charlotte. "About de Quincey. Just before supper. I hoped she would have some information, and she does, but she insists on seeing Tessa first. It seems that despite all our precautions, rumors about Tessa have leaked into Downworld, and Lady Belcourt is . . . interested."

Tessa set her fork down with a clatter. "Interested in what?"

She looked around the table, realizing that four pairs of eyes were now fixed on *her*. "Who is Lady Belcourt?" When no one replied, she turned to Jem as the likeliest to give her an answer. "Is she a Shadowhunter?"

"She's a vampire," Jem said. "A vampire *informant*, actually. She gives information to Charlotte and keeps us apprised of what's going on in the Night community."

"You needn't speak to her if you don't want to, Tessa," Charlotte said. "I can send her away."

"No." Tessa pushed her plate away. "If she's well informed about de Quincey, perhaps she knows something about Nate as well. I can't risk her being sent off if she might have information. I'll go."

"Don't you even want to know what she wants from you?" Will asked.

Tessa looked at him measuredly. The witchlight made his skin paler, his eyes more intently blue. They were the color of the water of the North Atlantic, where the ice drifted on its blue-black surface like snow clinging to the dark glass pane of a window. "Aside from the Dark Sisters, I've never really met another Downworlder," she said. "I think—that I would like to."

"Tessa—," Jem began, but she was already on her feet. Not looking back at anyone at the table, she hurried out of the room after Charlotte.

8

Camille

Fruits fail and love dies and time ranges;
Thou art fed with perpetual breath,
And alive after infinite changes,
And fresh from the kisses of death;
Of langours rekindled and rallied,
Of barren delights and unclean,
Things monstrous and fruitless, a pallid
And poisonous queen.
–Algernon Charles Swinburne, "Dolores"

Tessa was only halfway down the corridor when they caught up to her—Will and Jem, walking on either side of her. "You didn't *really* think we weren't going to come along, did you?" Will asked, raising his hand and letting the witchlight flare up between his fingers, lighting the corridor to daylight brightness. Charlotte, hurrying along ahead of them, turned and frowned, but said nothing.

"I know *you* can't leave anything well enough alone," Tessa replied, looking straight ahead. "But I thought better of Jem."

"Where Will goes, I go," Jem said good-naturedly. "And besides, I'm as curious as he is."

"That hardly seems a subject for boasting. Where *are* we going?" Tessa added, startled, as they reached the end of the corridor and turned left. The next hall stretched away behind them into unprepossessing shadow. "Have we turned the wrong way?"

"Patience is a virtue, Miss Gray," said Will. They had reached a long corridor that sloped precipitously downward. The walls were bare of tapestries or torches, and the dimness made Tessa realize why Will had carried his witchlight stone.

"This corridor leads to our Sanctuary," said Charlotte. "It is the only part of the Institute that is not on hallowed ground. It is where we meet with those who, for whatever reason, cannot enter hallowed ground: those who are cursed, vampires, and the like. It is also often a place we choose to shelter Downworlders who are in danger from demons or other denizens of the Shadow World. For that reason, there are many protections placed on the doors, and it is difficult to enter or exit the room without possessing either a stele or the key."

"Is it a curse? Being a vampire?" Tessa asked.

Charlotte shook her head. "No. We think it is a sort of demon disease. Most diseases that affect demons are not transmissible to human beings, but in some cases, usually through a bite or a scratch, the disease can be passed on. Vampirism. Lycanthropy—"

"Demon pox," said Will.

"Will, there's no such thing as demon pox, and you know it," Charlotte said. "Now, where was I?"

"Being a vampire isn't a curse. It's a disease," Tessa filled in. "But they still can't enter hallowed ground, then? Does that mean they're damned?"

"That depends on what you believe," said Jem. "And whether you even believe in damnation at all."

"But you hunt demons. You must believe in damnation!"

"I believe in good and evil," said Jem. "And I believe the soul is eternal. But I don't believe in the fiery pit, the pitchforks, or endless torment. I do not believe you can threaten people into goodness."

Tessa looked at Will. "What about you? What do you believe?"

"Pulvis et umbra sumus," said Will, not looking at her as he spoke. "I believe we are dust and shadows. What else is there?"

"Whatever you believe, please don't suggest to Lady Belcourt that you think she's damned," said Charlotte. She had come to a halt where the corridor ended in a set of high iron doors, each carved with a curious symbol that looked like two pairs of back-to-back *C*s. She turned and looked at her three companions. "She has very kindly offered to help us, and there's no purpose in offering her such insults. That applies to you especially, Will. If you can't be polite, I'll send you out of the Sanctuary. Jem, I trust you to be your charming self. Tessa . . ." Charlotte turned her grave, kind eyes on Tessa. "Try not to be frightened."

She drew an iron key from a pocket of her dress, and slid it into the lock of the door. The head of the key was in the shape of an angel with outspread wings; the wings gleamed out once, briefly, as Charlotte turned the key, and the door swung open.

The room beyond was like the vault of a treasure-house. There were no windows, and no doors save the one they had entered through. Enormous stone pillars held up a shadowed roof, illuminated by the light of a row of burning candelabras. The pillars were carved all around with loops and scrolls of runes, forming intricate patterns that teased the eye. Huge tapestries hung down from the walls, each one slashed with the figure of a single rune. There was a great gilt-framed mirror, too, making the place seem twice as large. A massive stone fountain rose in the middle of the room. It had a circular base, and in the center was the statue of an angel with folded wings. Rivers of tears poured from its eyes and plashed into the fountain below.

Beside the fountain, between two of the massive pillars, stood a group of chairs upholstered in black velvet. The woman who sat in the tallest of the chairs was slender and stately. A hat was tipped forward on her head, balancing a massive black plume at its top. Her dress was of rich red velvet, her icy white skin swelling gently over the fitted bodice, though her chest never rose or fell with a breath. A rope of rubies wound her throat like a scar. Her hair was thick and pale blond, clustered in delicate icy curls around her nape; her eyes were a luminous green that shone like a cat's.

Tessa caught her breath. So Downworlders could be beautiful.

"Douse your witchlight, Will," Charlotte said under her breath, before hurrying forward to greet her guest. "So good of you to wait for us, Baroness. I trust you have found the Sanctuary comfortable enough for your tastes?"

"As always, Charlotte." Lady Belcourt sounded bored; she had a faint accent that Tessa couldn't identify.

"Lady Belcourt. Please let me introduce you to Miss Theresa Gray." Charlotte indicated Tessa, who, not knowing what else to do, inclined her head politely. She was trying to remember how one addressed baronesses. She rather thought it had something to do with whether they were married to barons or not, but she couldn't exactly recall. "Beside her is Mr. James Carstairs, one of our young Shadowhunters, and with him is—"

But Lady Belcourt's green eyes were already resting on Will. "William Herondale," she said, and smiled. Tessa tensed, but the vampire's teeth seemed absolutely normal; no sign of sharpened incisors. "Fancy you coming to greet me."

"You *know* each other?" Charlotte looked astonished.

"William won twenty pounds from me at faro," said Lady Belcourt, her green gaze lingering on Will in a way that made Tessa's neck prickle. "A few weeks ago, in a Downworld gambling house run by the Pandemonium Club."

"He did?" Charlotte looked at Will, who shrugged.

"It was part of the investigation. I was disguised as a foolish mundane who had come to the place to partake in vice," explained Will. "It would have aroused suspicion had I refused to gamble."

Charlotte set her chin. "Nevertheless, Will, that money you won was evidence. You should have given it to the Clave."

"I spent it on gin."

"Will."

Will shrugged. "The spoils of vice are a burdensome responsibility."

"Yet one you seem strangely able to bear," observed Jem, with an amused flash of his silvery eyes.

Charlotte threw up her hands. "I will deal with you later, William. Lady Belcourt, am I to understand that you also are a member of the Pandemonium Club?"

Lady Belcourt made a dreadful face. "Certainly not. I was at the gambling house that night because a warlock friend of mine was hoping to win a little easy money at cards. The club's events are open to most Downworlders. The members like us to appear there; it impresses the mundanes and opens their pocketbooks. I know there are Downworlders running the enterprise, but I would never become one of them. The entire business seems so déclassé."

"De Quincey is a member," said Charlotte, and behind her large brown eyes, Tessa could see the light of her fierce intelligence. "I have been told he is the head of the organization, in fact. Did you know that?"

Lady Belcourt shook her head, clearly uninterested in this piece of information. "De Quincey and I were close years ago, but no longer, and I have been direct with him about my lack of interest in the club. I suppose he could be the head of the club; it's a ridiculous organization, if you ask me, but doubtless very lucrative." She leaned forward, folding her slim gloved hands in her lap. There was something oddly fascinating about her movements, even the smallest ones. They had a strange animal grace. It was like watching a cat as it slunk through the shadows. "The first thing you must understand about de Quincey," she said, "is that he is the most dangerous vampire in London. He has made his way to the top of the city's most powerful clan. Any vampire living within London is subject to his whim." Her scarlet lips thinned. "The second thing you must understand is that de Quincey is old—old even for one of the Night Children. He lived most of his life before the Accords, and he loathes them, and loathes living beneath the yoke of the Law. And most of all, he hates the Nephilim."

Tessa saw Jem lean in and whisper something to Will, whose mouth quirked up at the corner in a smile. "Indeed," Will said. "How could anyone despise us when we are so charming?"

"I am sure you know that you are not loved by most Downworlders."

"But we thought de Quincey was an ally." Charlotte rested her thin nervous hands on the back of one of the velvet chairs. "He has always cooperated with the Clave."

"Pretense. It is in his interest to cooperate with you, so he does. But he would happily see you all sunk fathoms below the sea."

Charlotte had gone pale, but rallied. "And you know nothing of his involvement with two women called the Dark Sisters? Nothing of his interest in automatons—mechanical creatures?"

"Ugh, the Dark Sisters." Lady Belcourt shuddered. "Such ugly, unpleasant creatures. Warlocks, I believe. I avoided them. They were known to provide for the members of the club who might have less . . . savory interests. Demon drugs, Downworld prostitutes, that sort of thing."

"And the automatons?"

Lady Belcourt fluttered her delicate hands in a bored fashion. "If de Quincey has some fascination with watch parts, I know nothing of it. In fact, when you first contacted me about de Quincey, Charlotte, I had no intention of coming forward with *any* information at all. It is one thing to share a few Downworld secrets with the Clave, another thing entirely to betray the most powerful vampire in London. That was, until I heard about your little shape-shifter." Her green eyes came to rest on Tessa. The red lips smiled. "I can see the family resemblance."

Tessa stared. "The resemblance to whom?"

"Why, to Nathaniel, of course. To your brother."

Tessa felt as if ice water had been dumped down the back of her neck, shocking her to full alertness. "You've seen my brother?"

Lady Belcourt smiled, the smile of a woman who knows she holds a room in the palm of her hand. "I saw him a few times at various Pandemonium Club occasions," she said. "He had that hapless look about him, poor creature, of a mundane under a spell. Probably gambled away everything he had. They always do. Charlotte told me the Dark Sisters took him; that doesn't surprise me. They love to drive a mundane into the ground with debt and then collect in the most shocking ways. . . ."

"But he's alive?" Tessa said. "You've seen him alive?"

"It was some time ago, but yes." Lady Belcourt gave a wave of her hand. Her gloves were scarlet, and her hands looked as if they had been dipped in blood. "To return to the matter at hand," she said. "We were speaking of de Quincey. Tell me, Charlotte, did you know he holds parties at his town house in Carleton Square?"

Charlotte took her hands off the chair back. "I've heard it mentioned."

"Unfortunately," said Will, "it seems he neglected to invite us. Perhaps our invitations went astray in the post."

"At these parties," Lady Belcourt went on, "humans are

tortured and killed. I believe their bodies are dumped into the Thames for the mudlarks to pick over. Now, did you know *that?*"

Even Will looked taken aback. Charlotte said, "But the murder of humans by the Night Children is forbidden under the Law—"

"And de Quincey despises the Law. He does this as much to mock the Nephilim as because he enjoys the killing. Though he does enjoy that, make no mistake about it."

Charlotte's lips were bloodless. "How long has this been going on, Camille?"

So that was her name, Tessa thought. *Camille.* It was a French-sounding name; perhaps that explained her accent.

"At least a year. Perhaps longer." The vampire's tone was cool, indifferent.

"And you are telling me this only now because . . ." Charlotte sounded hurt.

"The price for revealing the secrets of the Lord of London is death," Camille said, her green eyes darkening. "And it would have done you no good, even if I had told you. De Quincey is one of your allies. You have no reason and no excuse to burst into his home as if he were a common criminal. Not with no evidence of wrongdoing on his part. My understanding is that, under these new Accords, a vampire must actually be observed harming a human before the Nephilim can take action?"

"Yes," said Charlotte reluctantly, "but if we had been able to attend one of the parties—"

Camille let out a short laugh. "De Quincey would never let that happen! At the first sight of a Shadowhunter, he would have locked the place up tightly. You would never have been permitted to enter."

"But *you* could," Charlotte said. "You could have brought one of us with you—"

The plume on Camille's hat trembled as she tossed her head. "And risk my own life?"

"Well, you're not precisely *alive*, are you?" said Will.

"I value my existence as much as you do, Shadowhunter," said Lady Belcourt, narrowing her eyes. "A lesson you would do well to learn. It could hardly hurt the Nephilim to cease thinking that all those who do not live exactly as they do must therefore not truly *live* at all."

It was Jem who spoke then, for what seemed like the first time since they had entered the room. "Lady Belcourt—if you'll pardon my asking—what is it exactly that you want from Tessa?"

Camille looked directly at Tessa then, her green eyes as brilliant as jewels. "You can disguise yourself as anyone, is that correct? A perfect disguise—appearance, voice, and manner? That's what I have heard." Her lip curled. "I have my sources."

"Yes," Tessa said hesitantly. "That is, I have been told the disguise is identical."

Camille looked at her narrowly. "It would have to be perfect. If you were to disguise yourself as me—"

"As *you*?" Charlotte said. "Lady Belcourt, I don't see—"

"I see," said Will immediately. "If Tessa were disguised as Lady Belcourt, she could make her way into one of de Quincey's parties. She could observe him breaking the Law. Then the Clave could attack, without shattering the Accords."

"Quite the little strategist, you are." Camille smiled, revealing her white teeth once again.

"And it would also provide a perfect opportunity to search de Quincey's residence," said Jem. "See what we can discover about his interest in these automatons. If he really has been murdering mundanes, there's no reason to think that it wasn't for more purposes than mere sport." He gave Charlotte a meaningful look, and Tessa knew that he was thinking, as she was, of the bodies in the cellar of the Dark House.

"We would have to figure out some way to signal the Clave from inside de Quincey's," Will mused, his blue eyes already alight. "Perhaps Henry could devise something. It would be invaluable to have a blueprint of the house's construction—"

"*Will,*" Tessa protested. "I don't—"

"And of course you wouldn't be going alone," Will said impatiently. "I would go with you. I wouldn't let anything happen to you."

"Will, no," Charlotte said. "You and Tessa alone, in a house full of vampires? I forbid it."

"Then who would you send in with her, if not me?" Will demanded. "You know I can protect her, and you know I'm the right choice—"

"*I* could go. Or Henry—"

Camille, who had been watching all this with a look of mixed boredom and amusement, said, "I'm afraid I agree with William. The only individuals admitted to these parties are de Quincey's close friends, vampires, and the human subjugates of vampires. De Quincey has seen Will before, passing as a mundane fascinated by the occult; he won't be surprised to find that he's graduated to vampiric servitude."

Human subjugate. Tessa had read of them in the *Codex*: Subjugates, or darklings, were mundanes who had sworn themselves to the service of a vampire. For the vampire, they provided companionship and food, and in return received small transfusions of vampire blood at intervals. This blood kept them bound to their vampire master, and also ensured that when they died, they would become vampires as well.

"But Will is only seventeen," Charlotte protested.

"Most human subjugates *are* young," said Will. "Vampires like to acquire their subjugates when they're youthful—prettier to look at, and less chance of diseased blood. And they'll live a bit longer, though not much." He looked pleased with himself. "Most of the rest of the Enclave wouldn't be able to pass convincingly as a handsome young human subjugate—"

"Because the rest of us all are hideous, are we?" Jem inquired, looking amused. "Is that why I can't do it?"

"No," Will said. "You know why it can't be you." He said it without any inflection, and Jem, after looking at him for a moment, shrugged and looked away.

"I'm truly not sure about this," Charlotte said. "When is the next of these events set to happen, Camille?"

"Saturday night."

Charlotte took a deep breath. "I'll have to speak to the Enclave, before I can agree. And Tessa would have to agree as well."

Everyone looked at Tessa.

She licked her dry lips nervously. "You believe," she said to Lady Belcourt, "that there's a chance my brother might be there?"

"I cannot promise he will be there. He might. But *someone* there will likely know what has happened to him. The Dark Sisters were regulars at de Quincey's parties; doubtless they or their cohorts, if captured and interrogated, will yield you some answers."

Tessa's stomach churned. "I'll do it," she said. "But I want to be promised that *if* Nate is there, we'll get him out, and if he isn't, we'll find out where he is. I want to make sure it's not all about catching de Quincey. It must be about saving Nate, too."

"Of course," Charlotte said. "But I don't know, Tessa. It will be very dangerous—"

"Have you ever Changed yourself into a Downworlder?" Will inquired. "Do you even know if it's something that would be possible?"

Tessa shook her head. "I've never done anything like that. But . . . I could try." She turned to Lady Belcourt. "Could I have something of yours? A ring, or a handkerchief perhaps."

Camille reached her hands behind her head, brushing aside the thick coils of silver-blond hair that lay against her neck, and unclasped her necklace. Letting it dangle from her slender fingers, she held it out to Tessa. "Here. Take this."

With a frown Jem stepped forward to take the necklace, and then held it out to Tessa. She felt the weight of it as she took it from him. It was heavy, and the square ruby pendant the size of a bird's egg felt cold to the touch, as cold as if it had been lying in snow. Closing her hand around it was like closing her fingers around a shard of ice. She took a sharp breath, and closed her eyes.

It was strange, different this time as the transformation took hold. The darkness rose quickly, wrapping itself around her, and the light she saw in the distance was a cold silver glow. The chill that flowed from the light was scalding. Tessa drew the light toward her, surrounding herself with its icy burning light, pushing herself through to the core of it. The light rose in shimmering white walls around her—

She felt a sharp pain then, in the center of her chest, and for a moment her vision went red—deep scarlet, the color of blood. Everything was blood-colored, and she began to panic, fighting her way free, her eyelids flying open—

And she was there again, in the Sanctuary Room, with all the others staring at her. Camille was smiling slightly; the others looked startled, if not as thunderstruck as they had when she had transformed into Jessamine.

But something was terribly wrong. There was a great hollow emptiness inside her—not pain, but a cavernous sense of something *missing*. Tessa choked, and a searing shock went through her. She sank down into an armchair, her hands pressed against her chest. She was trembling all over.

"Tessa?" Jem sank down onto his heels beside the chair, taking one of her hands. She could see herself in the mirror that hung on the opposite wall—or more accurately, she could see the image of Camille. Camille's shimmering pale hair, unpinned, rained down over her shoulders, and her white skin swelled and spilled over the bodice of Tessa's now too-tight dress in a way that would have made Tessa flush—if she could have flushed. But blushing required blood actually running in one's veins, and she remembered, with a dawning terror, that vampires did not breathe, did not get hot or cold, and did not have hearts that beat in their chests.

So *that* was the hollowness, the strangeness that she felt. Her heart was still, in her chest like a dead thing. She took another sobbing breath. It hurt, and she realized that while she *could* breathe, her new body did not want or need to.

"Oh, God," she said in a soft whisper to Jem. "I—my heart's not beating. I feel as if I've died. Jem—"

He stroked her hand, carefully, soothingly, and looked up at her with his silver eyes. The expression in them had not changed with the change in her; he looked at her as he had before, as if she were still Tessa Gray. "You're alive," he said, in a voice so soft only she could hear it. "You're wearing a different skin, but you're Tessa, and you're alive. Do you know how I know that?"

She shook her head.

"Because you said the word 'God' just now to me. No vampire could say that." He squeezed her hand. "Your soul is still the same."

She closed her eyes and sat still for a moment, concentrating on the pressure of his hand on hers, his warm skin against hers that was icy cold. Slowly the trembling that shook her body began to fade; she opened her eyes, and gave Jem a faint, shaky smile.

"Tessa," said Charlotte. "Are you— Is everything all right?"

Tessa drew her eyes away from Jem's face and looked at Charlotte, who was watching her with an anxious gaze. Will, beside Charlotte, wore an unreadable expression.

"You will have to practice a bit, moving and holding yourself, if you wish to convince de Quincey that you are me," Lady Belcourt said. "I would never slump in a chair like that." She tilted her head to the side. "Still, overall, an impressive showing. Someone trained you well."

Tessa thought of the Dark Sisters. Had they trained her well? Had they done her a favor, unlocking this dormant power inside her, despite how much she had hated them and it? Or would it have been better if she had never known that she was different?

Slowly she let go, let the Camille skin slip away from her. It felt as if she were rising up out of icy water. Her hand tightened on Jem's as the chill ran through her, head to toe, a freezing cascade. Something leaped inside her chest then. Like a bird that has lain stunned and motionless after flying into a window, only to gather its strength and leap from the ground to soar into the air, her heart began suddenly to beat again. Air filled her lungs, and she released Jem, her hands flying to her chest, her fingers pressed against the skin to feel the soft rhythm beneath.

She looked in the mirror across the room. She was herself again: Tessa Gray, not a miraculously beautiful vampire. She felt an overwhelming relief.

"My necklace?" Lady Belcourt said coolly, and held out her slender hand. Jem took the ruby pendant from Tessa to bring it to the vampire; as he lifted it, Tessa saw that there were words etched on the silver frame of the pendant: *AMOR VERUS NUMQUAM MORITUR*.

She looked across the room at Will, she wasn't sure why, only to find that he was looking back at her. They both glanced hastily away. "Lady Belcourt," Will said, "since none of us have ever been in de Quincey's home, do you think it would be possible for you to provide a floor plan, or even a sketch of the grounds and rooms?"

"I shall provide you with something better." Lady Belcourt raised her arms to clasp the necklace around her throat. "Magnus Bane."

"The warlock?" Charlotte's eyebrows rose.

"Indeed," said Lady Belcourt. "He knows the town house as well as I do and is often invited to de Quincey's social events.

Though, like me, he has formerly eschewed the parties at which murder is committed."

"Noble of him," muttered Will.

"He will meet you there, and guide you through the house. No one there will be surprised to see us together. Magnus Bane is my lover, you see."

Tessa's mouth opened slightly. This was not the sort of thing ladies said in polite company, or any company. But perhaps it was different for vampires? Everyone else looked as stunned as she did, except Will, who as usual looked as if he were trying not to laugh.

"How nice," Charlotte said at last, after a pause.

"Indeed it is," Camille said, and rose to her feet. "And now, if someone will escort me out. It grows late, and I have not yet fed."

Charlotte, who was regarding Tessa with concern, said, "Will, Jem, if you'll go?"

Tessa watched as the two boys flanked Camille like soldiers—which, she supposed, was what they were—and followed her from the room. Last through the door, the vampire paused and looked back over her shoulder. Her pale blond curls brushed her cheeks as she smiled; she was so beautiful that Tessa felt a sort of pang, looking at her, overriding her instinctive feeling of aversion.

"If you do this," said Camille, "and you succeed—whether or not you find your brother—I can promise you, little shapeshifter, that you won't regret it."

Tessa frowned, but Camille was already gone. She moved so fast that it was as though she had vanished between one breath and the next. Tessa turned toward Charlotte. "What do you think she meant by that? That I won't regret it?"

Charlotte shook her head. "I don't know." She sighed. "I'd like to think that she meant that the knowledge of a good deed done would console you, but it's Camille, so . . ."

"Are all vampires like that?" Tessa asked. "Cold like that?"

"Many of them have been alive a long time," Charlotte said diplomatically. "They don't see things the way we do."

Tessa put her fingers to her aching temples. "Indeed, they don't."

Of all the things that bothered Will about vampires—the way they moved soundlessly, the low and inhuman timbre of their voices—it was the way they smelled that bothered him most. Or rather, the way they didn't smell. All human beings smelled like *something*—sweat, soap, perfume—but vampires had no scent, like wax mannequins.

Ahead of him, Jem was holding the last of the doors that led from the Sanctuary to the outer foyer of the Institute. All these spaces had been deconsecrated so that vampires and others of their ilk could use them, but Camille could never come any farther into the Institute than that. Escorting her out was more than a courtesy. They were making sure she didn't accidentally wander onto consecrated ground, which would be dangerous for everyone involved.

Camille brushed by Jem, hardly looking at him, and Will followed, pausing only long enough to mutter "She doesn't smell like anything" to Jem under his breath.

Jem looked alarmed. "You've been *smelling* her?"

Camille, who was waiting by the next doorway for them, turned her head at this and smiled. "I can hear everything you say, you know," she said. "It is true, vampires have no scent. It makes us better predators."

"That, and excellent hearing," Jem said, and let the door swing shut behind Will. They were standing in the small square entryway with Camille now, her hand on the knob of the front door as if she meant to hurry out, but there was nothing hurried in her expression as she looked them over.

"Look at you both," she said, "all black and silver. You could be a vampire," she said to Jem, "with your pallor, and your looks. And you," she said to Will, "well, I don't think anyone at de Quincey's will doubt that you could be my human subjugate."

Jem was looking at Camille, with that look that Will always thought could cut glass. He said:

"Why are you doing this, Lady Belcourt? This plan of yours, de Quincey, all of it—why?"

Camille smiled. She was beautiful, Will had to admit—but then, a lot of vampires were beautiful. Their beauty had always seemed to him like the beauty of pressed flowers—lovely, but dead. "Because the knowledge of what he was doing weighed on my conscience."

Jem shook his head. "Perhaps you are the sort who would sacrifice yourself on the altar of principle, but I doubt it. Most of us do things for reasons that are more purely personal. For love, or for hate."

"Or for revenge," Will said. "After all, you've known about what was going on for a year now, and you only just came to us."

"That was because of Miss Gray."

"Yes, but that's not all it is, is it?" Jem said. "Tessa is your opportunity, but your reason, your motive, is something else."

He cocked his head to the side. "Why do you hate de Quincey so much?"

"I don't see what business it is of yours, little silver Shadowhunter," Camille said, and her lips had drawn back from her teeth, leaving her fangs visible, like bits of ivory against the red of her lips. Will knew that vampires could show their fangs at will, but it was still unnerving. "Why does it matter what my motives are?"

Will filled in the answer for Jem, already knowing what the other boy had been thinking. "Because otherwise we can't trust you. Perhaps you're sending us into a trap. Charlotte wouldn't want to believe it, but that doesn't make it not possible."

"Lead you into a trap?" Camille's tone was mocking. "And incur the terrifying wrath of the Clave? Hardly likely!"

"Lady Belcourt," said Jem, "whatever Charlotte might have promised you, if you want our help, you will answer the question."

"Very well," she said. "I can see you will not be satisfied unless I give you an explanation. You," she said, nodding toward Will, "are correct. And you seem to know a curious amount about love and revenge for one so young; we must discuss them someday, together." She smiled again, but the smile did not reach her eyes. "I had a lover, you see," she said. "He was a shape-changer, a lycanthrope. It is forbidden for the Night Children to love or to lie with the Moon's Children. We were careful, but de Quincey found us out. Found us out and murdered him, in much the way he will be murdering some poor mundane prisoner at his next party." Her eyes shone like green lamps as she looked at them both. "I loved him, and de

Quincey murdered him, and the others of my kind helped and abetted him. I will not forgive them for it. Kill them all."

> *The Accords, now ten years old, marked a historic moment for both Nephilim and Downworlders. No longer would the two groups strive to destroy each other. They would be united against a common foe, the demon. There were fifty men at the signing of the Accords in Idris: ten of the Night Children; ten of Lilith's Children, known as warlocks; ten of the Fair Folk; ten of the Moon's Children; and ten of Raziel's blood—*

Tessa jerked awake at the sound of a knock on her door; she had been half-drowsing on the pillow, her finger still keeping a place in *The Shadowhunter's Codex*. After setting the book down, she barely had time to sit up and draw the covers about herself before the door opened.

In came lamplight, and Charlotte with it. Tessa felt an odd twinge, almost disappointment—but who else had she been expecting? Despite the late hour, Charlotte was dressed as if she planned to go out. Her face was very serious, and there were lines of tiredness below her dark eyes. "You're awake?"

Tessa nodded, and lifted the book she had been reading. "Reading."

Charlotte said nothing, but crossed the room and sat down at the foot of Tessa's bed. She held out her hand. Something gleamed in her palm; it was Tessa's angel pendant. "You left this with Henry."

Tessa set her book down and took the pendant. She slipped the chain over her head, and felt reassured as the familiar weight settled against the hollow of her throat. "Did he learn anything from it?"

"I'm not sure. He said it was all clogged up on the inside with years of rust, that it was a wonder it was working at all. He cleaned out the mechanism, though it doesn't seem to have resulted in much of a change. Perhaps it ticks more regularly now?"

"Perhaps." Tessa didn't care; she was just happy to have the angel, the symbol of her mother and her life in New York, back in her possession.

Charlotte folded her hands in her lap. "Tessa, there is something I haven't told you."

Tessa's heart began to beat faster. "What is it?"

"Mortmain . . ." Charlotte hesitated. "When I said that Mortmain introduced your brother to the Pandemonium Club, that was true, but not the whole truth. Your brother already knew about the Shadow World, before Mortmain ever told him. It seems he learned about it from your father."

Stunned, Tessa was silent.

"How old were you when your parents died?" Charlotte asked.

"It was an accident," Tessa said, a little dazed. "I was three. Nate was six."

Charlotte frowned. "So young for your father to confide in your brother, but . . . I suppose it's possible."

"No," Tessa said. "No, you don't understand. I had the most ordinary, the most human, upbringing imaginable. Aunt Harriet, she was the most practical woman in the world. And she would have known, wouldn't she? She was mother's younger sister; they brought her with them from London when they came to America."

"People keep secrets, Tessa, sometimes even from the ones they love." Charlotte brushed her fingers across the cover of the *Codex*, with its embossed seal. "And you must admit, it does make sense."

"Sense? It doesn't make any kind of sense!"

"Tessa . . ." Charlotte sighed. "We don't know why you have the ability that you do. But if one of your parents was connected in some way to the magical world, doesn't it make sense that that connection might have something to do with it? If your father was a member of the Pandemonium Club, isn't that how de Quincey might have known about you?"

"I suppose." Tessa spoke grudgingly. "It's only . . . I believed so strongly when I first came to London that everything that was happening to me was a dream. That my life before had been real and this was a dreadful nightmare. I thought that if only I could find Nate, we could go back to the life we had before." She raised her eyes to Charlotte's. "But now I cannot help but wonder if perhaps the life I had before was the dream and all this was the truth. If my parents knew of the Pandemonium Club—if they were part of the Shadow World too—then there is no world I can go back to that will be clean of all this."

Charlotte, her hands still folded in her lap, looked at Tessa steadily. "Have you ever wondered why Sophie's face is scarred?"

Caught off guard, Tessa could only stammer. "I—I wondered, but I—didn't like to ask."

"Nor should you," said Charlotte. Her voice was cool and firm. "When I first saw Sophie, she was crouched in a doorway, filthy, with a bloody rag clutched to her cheek. She *saw* me as I went by, even though I was glamoured at the time. That's what drew my attention to her. She has a touch of the Sight, as do Thomas and Agatha. I offered her money, but she wouldn't take it. I wheedled her into accompanying me to a tea shop, and she told me what had happened to her. She had been a parlor maid, in a fine house in St. John's Wood. Parlor maids, of course, are chosen for their looks, and Sophie was beautiful—which turned out to be both a great advantage and a great disadvantage for her. As you might imagine, the son of the house took an interest in seducing her. She turned him away repeatedly. In a rage, he took a knife and cut open her face, saying that if he couldn't have her, he'd make sure no one ever wanted her again."

"How awful," Tessa whispered.

"She went to her mistress, the boy's mother, but he claimed that she'd tried to seduce *him*, and he'd taken up the knife to fight her off and protect *his* virtue. Of course, they threw her out on the street. By the time I found her, her cheek was badly infected. I brought her here and had the Silent Brothers see to her, but while they cured the infection, they couldn't heal the scar."

Tessa put her hand to her own face in a gesture of unconscious sympathy. "Poor Sophie."

Charlotte cocked her head to the side and looked at Tessa out of her bright brown eyes. She had such a strong presence, Tessa thought, that it was hard to remember sometimes how physically small she was, how birdlike and tiny. "Sophie has a gift," she said. "She has the Sight. She can see what others do not. In her old life she often wondered if she was mad. Now she knows that she is not mad but special. There, she was only a parlor maid, who would likely have lost her position once her looks had faded. Now she is a valued member of our household, a gifted girl with much to contribute." Charlotte leaned forward. "You look back on the life you had, Tessa, and it seems safe to you in comparison to this one. But you and your aunt were very poor, if I am not mistaken. If you had not come to London, where would you have gone once she died? What would you have done? Would you have found yourself weeping in an alley like our Sophie?" Charlotte shook her head. "You have a power of incalculable value. You need ask nothing of anyone. You need depend on no one. You are free, and that freedom is a gift."

"It is hard to think of something as a gift when you have been tormented and imprisoned for it."

Charlotte shook her head. "Sophie said to me once that she was glad she had been scarred. She said that whoever loved her now would love her true self, and not her pretty face. This is your true self, Tessa. This power is who you are. Whoever loves you now—and you must also love yourself—will love the truth of you."

Tessa picked up the *Codex* and hugged it against her chest. "So you are saying I am right. This is what is real, and the life I had before was the dream."

"That is correct." Gently Charlotte patted Tessa's shoulder; Tessa almost jumped at the contact. It had been a long time, she thought, since anyone had touched her in such a motherly fashion; she thought of Aunt Harriet, and her throat hurt. "And now it is time to wake up."

9

The Enclave

May make my heart as a millstone, set my face as a flint,
Cheat and be cheated, and die: who knows? we are ashes and dust.
—Alfred, Lord Tennyson, "Maud"

"Try it again," Will suggested. "Simply walk from one end of the room to the other. We'll tell you if you look convincing."

Tessa sighed. Her head throbbed, as did the backs of her eyes. It was exhausting learning how to pretend to be a vampire.

It had been two days since Lady Belcourt's visit, and Tessa had spent almost every moment since then attempting to convincingly transform herself into the vampire woman, without enormous success. She still felt as if she were sliding around on the surface of Camille's mind, unable to reach through and grasp hold of thoughts or personality. It made it difficult to know how to walk, how to talk, and what sort of expressions she ought to be wearing when she met the vampires at de Quincey's party—whom, no doubt, Camille knew very well, and whom Tessa would be expected to know too.

She was in the library now, and had spent the last few hours since lunch practicing walking with Camille's odd gliding walk, and speaking with her careful drawling voice. Pinned at her shoulder was a jeweled brooch that one of Camille's human subjugates, a wrinkled little creature called Archer, had brought over in a trunk. There had been a dress, too, for Tessa to wear to de Quincey's, but it was much too heavy and elaborate for daytime. Tessa made do with her own new blue and white dress, which was bothersomely too tight in the bosom and too loose in the waist whenever she changed into Camille.

Jem and Will had set up camp on one of the long tables in the back of the library, ostensibly to help and advise her, but more likely, it seemed, to mock and be amused by her consternation. "You point your feet out too much when you walk," Will went on. He was busy polishing an apple on his shirtfront, and appeared not to notice Tessa glaring at him. "Camille walks delicately. Like a faun in the woods. Not like a duck."

"I do not walk like a duck."

"I like ducks," Jem observed diplomatically. "Especially the ones in Hyde Park." He glanced sideways at Will; both boys were sitting on the edge of the high table, their legs dangling over the side. "Remember when you tried to convince me to feed a poultry pie to the mallards in the park to see if you could breed a race of cannibal ducks?"

"They ate it too," Will reminisced. "Bloodthirsty little beasts. Never trust a duck."

"Do you mind?" Tessa demanded. "If you're not going to help me, you might as well both leave. I didn't let you stay here so that I could listen to you nattering on about ducks."

"Your impatience," said Will, "is most unladylike." He grinned at her around the apple. "Perhaps Camille's vampire nature is asserting itself?"

His tone was playful. It was so odd, Tessa thought. Only a few days ago he had snarled at her about his parents, and later had begged her to help him hide Jem's bloody coughing, his face burning with intensity as he did so. And now he was teasing her as if she were a friend's little sister, someone whom he knew casually, perhaps thought of with affection, but for whom he had no complex feelings at all.

Tessa bit her lip—and winced at the unexpected sharp pain. Camille's vampire teeth—*her* teeth—were ruled by an instinct she couldn't understand. They seemed to slide forward without warning or prompting, alerting her to their presence only by sudden bursts of pain as they punctured the fragile skin of her lip. She tasted blood in her mouth—her own blood, salty and hot. She pressed her fingertips to her mouth; when she drew her hand away, her fingers were spotted with red.

"Leave it alone," said Will, setting down his apple and rising to his feet. "You'll find you heal very quickly."

Tessa poked at her left incisor with her tongue. It was flat again, an ordinary tooth. "I don't understand what makes them come out like that!"

"Hunger," said Jem. "Were you thinking about blood?"

"No."

"Were you thinking about eating me?" Will inquired.

"No!"

"No one would blame you," said Jem. "He's very annoying."

Tessa sighed. "Camille is so *difficult*. I don't understand the first thing about her, much less *being* her."

Jem looked at her closely. "Are you able to touch her thoughts? The way you said you could touch the thoughts of those you transformed into?"

"Not yet. I've been trying, but all I get are occasional flashes, images. Her thoughts seem very well protected."

"Well, hopefully you can break through that protection before tomorrow night," said Will. "Or I wouldn't say much about our chances."

"Will," Jem chided. "Don't say that."

"You're right," Will said. "I shouldn't underestimate my own skills. Should Tessa make a mess of things, I'm sure I'll be able to fight our way through the slavering vampire masses to freedom."

Jem—as was his habit, Tessa was starting to realize—simply ignored this. "Perhaps," he said, "you can only touch the thoughts of the dead, Tessa? Perhaps most of the objects given to you by the Dark Sisters were taken from people they had murdered."

"No. I touched Jessamine's thoughts when I Changed into her. So that can't be it, thankfully. What a morbid talent that would be."

Jem was looking at her with thoughtful silver eyes; something about the intensity of his gaze made her feel almost uncomfortable. "How clearly can you see the thoughts of the dead? For instance, if I gave you an item that had once belonged to my father, would you know what he was thinking when he died?"

It was Will's turn to look alarmed. "James, I don't think—," he began, but broke off as the door to the library opened and Charlotte entered the room. She wasn't alone. There were at least a dozen men following her, strangers whom Tessa had never seen before.

"The Enclave," Will whispered, and gestured for Jem and Tessa to duck behind one of the ten-foot bookcases. They observed from their hiding place as the room filled with Shadowhunters—most of them men. But Tessa saw, as they filed into the room, that among them were two women.

She could not help staring at them, remembering what Will had said about Boadicea, that women could be warriors as well. The taller of the women—and she must have been nearly six feet in height—had powder white hair wound into a crown at the back of her head. She looked as if she were well into her sixties, and her presence was regal. The second of the women was younger, with dark hair, catlike eyes, and a secretive demeanor.

The men were a more mixed group. The eldest was a tall man dressed all in gray. His hair and skin were gray as well, his face bony and aquiline, with a strong, thin nose and a sharp chin. There were hard lines at the corners of his eyes and dark hollows under his cheekbones. His eyes were rimmed with red. Beside him stood the youngest of the group, a boy probably no more than a year older than Jem or Will. He was handsome in an angular sort of way, with sharp but regular features, tousled brown hair, and a watchful expression.

Jem made a noise of surprise and displeasure. "Gabriel Lightwood," he muttered to Will under his breath. "What's he doing here? I thought he was in school in Idris."

Will hadn't moved. He was staring at the brown-haired boy with his eyebrows raised, a faint smile playing about his lips.

"Just don't get into a fight with him, Will," Jem added hastily. "Not here. That's all I ask."

"Rather a lot to ask, don't you think?" Will said without looking at Jem. Will had leaned out from behind the bookcase, and was watching Charlotte as she ushered everyone toward the large table at the front of the room. She seemed to be urging everyone to settle themselves into seats around it.

"Frederick Ashdown and George Penhallow, here, if you please," Charlotte said. "Lilian Highsmith, if you'd sit over there by the map—"

"And where is Henry?" asked the gray-haired man with an air of brusque politeness. "Your husband? As one of the heads of the Institute, he really ought to be here."

Charlotte hesitated for only a fraction of a second before plastering a smile onto her face. "He's on his way, Mr. Lightwood," she said, and Tessa realized two things—one, that the gray-haired man was most likely the father of Gabriel Lightwood, and two, that Charlotte was lying.

"He'd better be," Mr. Lightwood muttered. "An Enclave meeting without the head of the Institute present—most irregular." He turned then, and though Will moved to duck back behind the tall bookcase, it was too late. The man's eyes narrowed. "And who's back there, then? Come out and show yourself!"

Will glanced toward Jem, who shrugged eloquently. "No point hiding till they drag us out, is there?"

"Speak for yourself," Tessa hissed. "I don't need Charlotte angry at me if we're not supposed to be in here."

"Don't work yourself into a state. There's no reason you'd have had any idea about the Enclave meeting, and Charlotte's perfectly well aware of that," Will said. "She always knows exactly who to blame." He grinned. "I'd turn yourself back into yourself, though, if you take my meaning. No need to give too much of a shock to their hoary old constitutions."

"Oh!" For a moment Tessa had nearly forgotten she was still disguised as Camille. Hastily she went to work stripping away the transformation, and by the time the three of them stepped out from behind the bookshelves, she was her own self again.

"Will." Charlotte sighed on seeing him, and shook her head at Tessa and Jem. "I told you the Enclave would be meeting here at four o'clock."

"Did you?" Will said. "I must have forgotten that. Dreadful." His eyes slid sideways, and he grinned. "'Lo there, Gabriel."

The brown-haired boy returned Will's look with a furious glare. He had very bright green eyes, and his mouth, as he stared at Will, was hard with disgust. "William," he said finally, and with some effort. He turned his gaze on Jem. "And James. Aren't you both a little young to be lurking around Enclave meetings?"

"Aren't you?" Jem said.

"I turned eighteen in June," Gabriel said, leaning so far back in his chair that the front legs came off the ground. "I have every right to participate in Enclave activities now."

"How fascinating for you," said the white-haired woman Tessa had thought looked regal. "So is this her, Lottie? The warlock girl you were telling us about?" The question was directed at Charlotte, but the woman's gaze rested on Tessa. "She doesn't look like much."

"Neither did Magnus Bane the first time I saw him," said Mr. Lightwood, bending a curious eye on Tessa. "Let's have it then. Show us what you can do."

"I'm not a warlock," Tessa protested angrily.

"Well, you're certainly something, my girl," said the older woman. "If not a warlock, then what?"

"That will do." Charlotte drew herself up. "Miss Gray has already proved her bona fides to me and Mr. Branwell. That will have to be good enough for now—at least until the Enclave makes the decision that they wish to utilize her talents."

"Of course they do," said Will. "We haven't a hope of succeeding in this plan without her—"

Gabriel brought his chair forward with such force that the front legs slammed into the stone floor with a cracking noise. "Mrs. Branwell," he said furiously, "is William, or is he not, too young to be participating in an Enclave meeting?"

Charlotte's gaze went from Gabriel's flushed face to Will's expressionless one. She sighed. "Yes, he is. Will, Jem, if you'll please wait outside in the corridor with Tessa."

Will's expression tightened, but Jem bent a warning look on him, and he remained silent. Gabriel Lightwood looked triumphant. "I will show you out," he announced, springing to his feet. He ushered the three of them out of the library, then swung out into the corridor after them. "You," he spat at Will, pitching his voice low so that those in the library couldn't overhear him. "You disgrace the name of Shadowhunters everywhere."

Will leaned against the corridor wall and regarded Gabriel with cool blue eyes. "I didn't realize there was much of a name left to disgrace, after your father—"

"I will thank you *not* to speak of my family," Gabriel snarled, reaching behind himself to pull the library door shut.

"How unfortunate that the prospect of your gratitude is not a tempting one," Will said.

Gabriel stared at him, his hair disarrayed, his green eyes brilliant with rage. He reminded Tessa of someone in that moment, though she could not have said who. "What?" Gabriel growled.

"He means," Jem clarified, "that he doesn't care for your thanks."

Gabriel's cheeks darkened to a dull scarlet. "If you weren't underage, Herondale, it would be *monomachia* for us. Just you and me, to the death. I'd chop you into bloody carpet rags—"

"Stop it, Gabriel," Jem interrupted, before Will could reply. "Goading Will into single combat—that's like punishing a dog after you've tormented it into biting you. You know how he is."

"Much obliged, James," Will said, without taking his eyes off Gabriel. "I appreciate the testament to my character."

Jem shrugged. "It is the truth."

Gabriel shot Jem a dark glare. "Stay out of this, Carstairs. This doesn't concern you."

Jem moved closer to the door, and to Will, who was standing perfectly still, matching Gabriel's cold stare with one of his own. The hairs on the back of Tessa's neck had begun to prickle. "If it concerns Will, it concerns me," Jem said.

Gabriel shook his head. "You're a decent Shadowhunter, James," he said, "and a gentleman. You have your—disability, but no one blames you for that. But this—" He curled his lip, jabbing a finger in Will's direction. "This filth will only drag you down. Find someone else to be your *parabatai*. No one expects Will Herondale to live past nineteen, and no one will be sorry to see him go, either—"

That was too much for Tessa. Without thinking about it she burst out indignantly, "What a thing to say!"

Gabriel, interrupted midrant, looked as shocked as if one of the tapestries had suddenly started talking. "Pardon me?"

"You heard me. Telling someone you wouldn't be sorry if they died! It's inexcusable!" She took hold of Will by the sleeve. "Come along, Will. This—this person—obviously isn't worth wasting your time on."

Will looked hugely entertained. "So true."

"You—you—" Gabriel, stammering slightly, looked at Tessa in an alarmed sort of way. "You haven't the slightest idea of the things he's done—"

"And I don't care, either. You're all Nephilim, aren't you? Well, aren't you? You're supposed to be on the same side." Tessa frowned at Gabriel. "I think you owe Will an apology."

"I," said Gabriel, "would rather have my entrails yanked out and tied in a knot in front of my own eyes than apologize to such a worm."

"Gracious," said Jem mildly. "You can't mean that. Not the Will being a worm part, of course. The bit about the entrails. That sounds dreadful."

"I do mean it," said Gabriel, warming to his subject. "I would rather be dropped into a vat of Malphas venom and left to dissolve slowly until only my bones were left."

"Really," said Will. "Because I happen to know a chap who could sell us a vat of—"

The door of the library opened. Mr. Lightwood stood on the threshold. "Gabriel," he said in a freezing tone. "Do you plan to attend the meeting—your first Enclave meeting, if I must remind you—or would you rather play out here in the corridor with the rest of the children?"

No one looked particularly pleased by that comment, especially Gabriel, who swallowed hard, nodded, shot one last glare at Will, and followed his father back into the library, slamming the door shut behind them.

"Well," said Jem after the door had closed behind Gabriel. "That was about as bad as I had expected it would be. Is this the first time you've seen him since last year's Christmas party?" he asked, addressing the question to Will.

"Yes," said Will. "Do you think I should have told him I missed him?"

"No," said Jem.

"Is he always like that?" Tessa asked. "So awful?"

"You should see his older brother," said Jem. "Makes Gabriel look sweeter than gingerbread. Hates Will even more than Gabriel, too, if that's possible."

Will grinned at that, then turned and began making his way down the corridor, whistling as he went. After a moment's hesitation, Jem went after him, gesturing for Tessa to follow.

"Why would Gabriel Lightwood hate you, Will?" Tessa asked as they went. "What did you do to him?"

"It wasn't anything I did to him," Will said, stalking along at a rapid pace. "It was something I did to his sister."

Tessa looked sideways at Jem, who shrugged. "Where there's our Will, there's a half-dozen angry girls claiming he's compromised their virtue."

"Did you?" Tessa asked, hurrying to keep up with the boys. There was simply only so fast you could walk in heavy skirts that swished around your ankles as you went. The delivery of dresses from Bond Street had come the day before, and she was only just beginning to get used to wearing such expensive stuff. She remembered the light dresses she'd worn as a little girl, when she'd been able to run up to her brother, kick him in the ankle, and dart away without him being able to catch her. She wondered briefly what would happen if she tried to do that to Will. She doubted it would work out to her advantage, though the thought had a certain appeal. "Compromise her virtue, I mean."

"You have a lot of questions," Will said, veering sharply to the left and up a set of narrow stairs. "Don't you?"

"I do," Tessa said, the heels of her boots clicking loudly on the stone steps as she followed Will upward. "What's *parabatai?* And what did you mean about Gabriel's father being a disgrace to Shadowhunters?"

"*Parabatai* in Greek is just a term for a soldier paired with a chariot driver," said Jem, "but when Nephilim say it, we mean a matched team of warriors—two men who swear to protect each other and guard each other's backs."

"Men?" said Tessa. "There couldn't be a team of women, or a woman and a man?"

"I thought you said women didn't have bloodlust," Will said without turning around. "And as for Gabriel's father, let's say that he has something of a reputation for liking demons and Downworlders more than he should. I would be surprised if some of the elder Lightwood's nocturnal visits to certain houses in Shadwell haven't left him with a nasty case of demon pox."

"Demon pox?" Tessa was horrified and fascinated at the same time.

"He's made that up," Jem hastily reassured her. "Really, Will. How many times do we have to tell you there's no such thing as demon pox?"

Will had stopped in front of a narrow door at a bend in the staircase. "I think this is it," he said, half to himself, and jiggled the knob. When nothing happened, he took his stele out of his jacket and scrawled a black Mark on the door. It swung open, with a puff of dust. "This ought to be a storeroom."

Jem followed him inside, and after a moment so did Tessa. She found herself in a small room whose only illumination was from an arched window set high in the wall above. Watery light poured through, showing a square space filled with trunks and boxes. It could have been any spare storage room anywhere, if it hadn't been for what looked like piles of old weapons stacked in the corners—heavy rusty-looking iron things with broad blades and chains connected to spiked chunks of metal.

Will took hold of one of the trunks and moved it sideways to create a clear square of space on the floor. More dust puffed up. Jem coughed and shot him a reproachful look. "One would think you brought us here to murder us," he said, "if it weren't that your motivations for doing so seem cloudy at best."

"Not murder," Will said. "Hold on. I need to move one more trunk."

As he pushed the heavy thing toward the wall, Tessa cast a sidelong look at Jem. "What did Gabriel mean," she asked, pitching her voice too low for Will to hear, "'your disability'?"

Jem's silvery eyes widened fractionally, before he said, "My ill health. That's all."

He was lying, Tessa knew. He had the same sort of look Nate did when he lied—a little too clear-eyed a gaze to be a truthful one. But before she could say anything else, Will straightened up and announced, "There we are. Come sit down."

He then proceeded to seat himself on the dusty stained floor; Jem went to sit beside him, but Tessa hung back for a moment, hesitant. Will, who had his stele out, looked up at her with a crooked smile. "Not going to join us, Tessa? I suppose you don't want to ruin the pretty dress Jessamine bought you."

It was the truth, actually. Tessa had no desire to wreck the nicest item of clothing she had ever owned. But Will's mocking tone was more annoying than the thought of destroying the dress. Setting her jaw, she went and sat down opposite the boys, so that they formed a triangle between them.

Will placed the tip of the stele against the dirty floor, and began to move it. Broad dark lines flowed from the tip, and Tessa watched in fascination. There was something particular and beautiful about the way the stele scrawled—not like ink flowing from a pen, but more as if the lines had always been there, and Will was uncovering them.

He was halfway through when Jem made a noise of realization, clearly recognizing the Mark that his friend was drawing. "What do you—," he began, but Will held up the hand he wasn't drawing with, shaking his head.

"Don't," Will said. "If I make a mess of this, we could well fall through the floor."

Jem rolled his eyes, but it didn't seem to matter: Will was already finished, and was lifting the stele away from the design he had drawn. Tessa gave a little cry as the warped floorboards between them seemed to shimmer—and then became as transparent as a window. Scooting forward, forgetting entirely about her dress, she found herself staring through it as if through a pane of glass.

She was looking down into what she realized was the library. She could see the large round table and the Enclave seated at it, Charlotte between Benedict Lightwood and the elegant white-haired woman. Charlotte was easily recognizable, even from above, by the neat knotting of her brown hair and the quick movements of her small hands as she spoke.

"Why up here?" Jem asked Will in a low voice. "Why not the weapons room? It's next to the library."

"Sound radiates," said Will. "Just as easy to listen from up here. Besides which, who's to say one of them wouldn't decide to pay a visit to the weapons room halfway through the meeting to see what we've in stock? It's happened before."

Tessa, staring down in fascination, realized that indeed she could hear the murmur of voices. "Can they hear us?"

Will shook his head. "The enchantment is strictly one-way." He frowned, leaning forward. "What are they talking about?"

The three of them fell silent, and in the quiet the sound of Benedict Lightwood's voice rose clearly to their ears. "I don't know about this, Charlotte," he said. "This whole plan seems very risky."

"But we cannot simply let de Quincey go on as he has," Charlotte argued. "He's the head vampire of the London clans. The rest of the Night Children look to him for guidance. If we allow him to cavalierly break the Law, what message does that send to Downworld? That the Nephilim have grown lax in their guardianship?"

"Just so I understand," Lightwood said, "you're willing to take Lady Belcourt's word that de Quincey, a longtime ally of the Clave, is actually murdering mundanes in his own house?"

"I don't know why you're surprised, Benedict." There was an edge to Charlotte's voice. "Is it your suggestion that we *ignore* her report, despite the fact that she has given us nothing but reliable information in the past? And despite the fact that if she is once again telling the truth, the blood of everyone that de Quincey murders from this point onward will be on our hands?"

"And despite the fact that we are bound by the Law to investigate any report of the Covenant being broken," said a slender dark-haired man at the far end of the table. "You know that as well as the rest of us, Benedict; you're simply being stubborn."

Charlotte exhaled as Lightwood's face darkened. "Thank you, George. I appreciate that," she said.

The tall woman who had earlier called Charlotte Lottie gave a low, rumbling laugh. "Don't be so dramatic, Charlotte," she said. "You must admit, the whole business is bizarre. A shape-changing girl who may or may not be a warlock, brothels full of dead bodies, and an informant who swears he sold de Quincey some machine tools—a fact that you seem to regard as a piece of the most consummate evidence, despite refusing to tell us your informant's name."

"I swore I wouldn't involve him," Charlotte protested. "He fears de Quincey."

"Is he a Shadowhunter?" Lightwood demanded. "Because if not, he isn't reliable."

"Really, Benedict, your views are most antiquated," said the woman with the catlike eyes. "One might believe, talking to you, that the Accords had never happened."

"Lilian is correct; you're being ridiculous, Benedict," said George Penhallow. "Looking for an entirely reliable informant is like looking for a chaste mistress. If they were virtuous, they would be little use to you in the first place. An informant merely provides information; it is our job to *verify* that information, which is what Charlotte is suggesting that we do."

"I would simply hate to see the powers of the Enclave misused in this instance," Lightwood said in a silky tone. It was very odd, Tessa thought, hearing this group of elegant adults addressing one another without honorifics, simply by their first names. But it seemed to be Shadowhunter custom. "If, for instance, there were a vampire who had a grudge against the head of her clan, and perhaps wanted to see him removed from power, what better way than to get the Clave to do her dirty work for her?"

"Hell," Will muttered, exchanging a glance with Jem. "How does he know about that?"

Jem shook his head, as if to say *I don't know.*

"Know about what?" Tessa whispered, but her voice was drowned out by Charlotte and the white-haired woman both talking at once.

"Camille would *never* do that!" Charlotte protested. "She isn't a fool, for one thing. She knows what the punishment for lying to us would be!"

"Benedict has a point," said the older woman. "It would be better if a Shadowhunter had seen de Quincey breaking the Law—"

"But that's the point of this whole enterprise," Charlotte said. There was a tinge to her voice—of nervousness, a strained desire to prove herself. Tessa felt a flicker of sympathy for her. "To observe de Quincey breaking the Law, Aunt Callida."

Tessa made a startled noise.

Jem looked up. "Yes, she's Charlotte's aunt," he said. "It was her brother—Charlotte's father—who used to run the Institute. She likes to tell people what to do. Although, of course *she* always does whatever she wants."

"She does at that," Will agreed. "Did you know she propositioned me once?"

Jem did not look as if he believed this even slightly. "She did not."

"She did," Will insisted. "It was all very scandalous. I might have acceded to her demands too, if she didn't frighten me so much."

Jem simply shook his head and turned his attention back to the scene unfolding in the library. "There is also the matter of de Quincey's seal," Charlotte was saying, "which we found inside the body of the clockwork girl. There is simply too much evidence linking him to these events, too much evidence not to investigate."

"I agree," said Lilian. "I for one am concerned about this matter of the clockwork creatures. Making clockwork girls is one thing, but what if he's making a clockwork army?"

"That's pure speculation, Lilian," said Frederick Ashdown.

Lilian dismissed this with a wave of her hand. "An automaton is neither seraph nor demon in its alliance; it is not one of the children of God or of the Devil. Would it be vulnerable to our weapons?"

"I think you're imagining a problem that does not exist,"

said Benedict Lightwood. "There have been automatons for years now; mundanes are fascinated with the creatures. None has posed a threat to us."

"None has been made using magic before," said Charlotte.

"That you know of." Lightwood looked impatient.

Charlotte straightened her back; only Tessa and the others, looking down upon her, could see that her hands were knotted tightly together in her lap. "Your concern, Benedict, seems to be that we will unfairly punish de Quincey for a crime he has not committed, and in doing so jeopardize the relationship between the Night Children and the Nephilim. Am I correct?"

Benedict Lightwood nodded.

"But all that Will's plan calls for is for us to *observe* de Quincey. If we do not see him breaking the Law, we will not act against him, and the relationship will not be threatened. If we do see him breaking the Law, then the relationship is a lie. We cannot allow abuse of Covenant Law, however . . . convenient it might be for us to ignore."

"I agree with Charlotte," said Gabriel Lightwood, speaking up for the first time, and much to Tessa's surprise. "I think her plan is a sound one. Except in one part—sending the shape-shifter girl in there with Will Herondale. He isn't even old enough to be at this meeting. How can he be trusted with a mission of this gravity?"

"Smarmy little prig," Will snarled, leaning farther forward, as if he longed to reach through the magical portal and strangle Gabriel. "When I get him alone . . ."

"I ought to go in with her instead," Gabriel went on. "I can look out for her a bit more. Instead of simply looking out for myself."

"Hanging's too good for him," agreed Jem, who looked as if he were trying not to laugh.

"Tessa knows Will," protested Charlotte. "She *trusts* Will."

"I wouldn't go that far," muttered Tessa.

"Besides," Charlotte said, "it's Will who devised this plan, Will who de Quincey will recognize from the Pandemonium Club. It's Will who knows what to search for inside de Quincey's town house to tie him to the clockwork creatures and the murdered mundanes. Will's an excellent investigator, Gabriel, and a good Shadowhunter. You have to give him that."

Gabriel sat back in his chair, crossing his arms over his chest. "I don't have to give him anything."

"So Will and your warlock girl enter the house, endure de Quincey's party until they observe some contravention of the Law, and then signal to the rest of us—how?" inquired Lilian.

"With Henry's invention," Charlotte said. There was a slight—only very slight—tremble to her voice as she said it. "The Phosphor. It will send up a flare of extremely bright witchlight, illuminating all the windows in de Quincey's house, just for a moment. That will be the signal."

"Oh, good Lord, not one of Henry's inventions again," said George.

"There were some complications with the Phosphor at first, but Henry demonstrated it for me last night," Charlotte protested. "It works perfectly."

Frederick snorted. "Remember the last time Henry offered us the use of one of his inventions? We were all cleaning fish guts off our gear for days."

"But it wasn't supposed to be used near water—," Charlotte began, still in the same quavering voice, but the others had already begun talking over her, chattering excitedly about Henry's failed inventions and the dreadful consequences thereof, while Charlotte lapsed into silence. *Poor Charlotte,* Tessa thought. Charlotte, whose sense of her own authority was so important, and so dearly bought.

"Bastards, talking over her like that," muttered Will. Tessa looked at him in astonishment. He was staring intently down at the scene before him, his fists tight at his sides. So he was fond of Charlotte, she thought, and she was surprised how pleased she was to realize it. Perhaps it meant Will actually did have feelings after all.

Not that it had anything to do with her, whether he did or not, of course. She looked hastily away from Will, at Jem, who seemed equally out of countenance. He was biting his lip. "Where is Henry? Shouldn't he have arrived by now?"

As if in answer, the door to the storage room banged open with a crash, and the three of them spun around to see Henry standing wild-eyed and wild-haired in the doorway. He was clutching something in his hand—the copper tube with the black button on the side that had nearly caused Will to break his arm falling off the sideboard in the dining room.

Will eyed it fearfully. "Get that blasted object away from me."

Henry, who was red-faced and sweating, stared at them all in horror. "Hell," he said. "I was looking for the library. The Enclave—"

"Is meeting," said Jem. "Yes, we know. It's a flight down from here, Henry. Third door on the right. And you'd better go. Charlotte's waiting for you."

"I know," Henry wailed. "Blast, blast, blast. I was just trying to get the Phosphor right, is all."

"Henry," Jem said, "Charlotte *needs* you."

"Right." Henry turned as if to dart out of the room, then swung around and stared at them, a look of confusion passing over his freckled face, as if he had only now had cause to wonder why Will, Tessa, and Jem might be crouching together in a mostly disused storage room. "What are you three doing in here, anyway?"

Will tilted his head to the side and smiled at Henry. "Charades," he said. "Massive game."

"Ah. Right, then," said Henry, and dashed out the door, letting it swing shut behind him.

"Charades." Jem snorted in disgust, then leaned forward again, elbows on his knees, as Callida's voice drifted up from below. "Honestly, Charlotte," she was saying, "when will you admit that Henry hasn't anything to do with running this place, and that you're doing it all by yourself? Perhaps with help from James Carstairs and Will Herondale, but neither of them is any older than seventeen. How much help can they be?"

Charlotte made a murmured noise of deprecation.

"It's too much for one person, especially someone your age," said Benedict. "You're only twenty-three years old. If you'd like to step down—"

Only twenty-three! Tessa was astonished. She'd thought Charlotte was much older, probably because she exuded such an air of competence.

"Consul Wayland assigned the running of the Institute to me and my husband five years ago," Charlotte replied sharply, apparently having found her voice again. "If you have some issue with his choice, you should take it up with him. In the meantime I shall direct the Institute as I see fit."

"I hope that means that plans such as the one you're suggesting are still up for a vote?" said Benedict Lightwood. "Or are you governing by fiat now?"

"Don't be ridiculous, Lightwood, of course it's up for a vote," said Lilian crossly, without giving Charlotte a chance to answer. "All in favor of moving on de Quincey, say aye."

To Tessa's surprise, there was a chorus of ayes, and not a single nay. The discussion had been contentious enough that she'd been certain at least one of the Shadowhunters would try to back out. Jem caught her startled look and smiled. "They're always like this," he murmured. "They like to jockey for power, but none of them would vote no on an issue like this. They'd be branded a coward for doing so."

"Very well," said Benedict. "Tomorrow night it is, then. Is everyone sufficiently prepared? Are there—"

The door to the library banged open, and Henry charged in—looking, if possible, even more wild-eyed and wild-haired than before. "I'm here!" he announced. "Not too late, am I?"

Charlotte covered her face with her hands.

"Henry," said Benedict Lightwood dryly. "How pleasant to see you. Your wife was just briefing us on your newest invention. The Phosphor, is it?"

"Yes!" Henry held the Phosphor up proudly. "This is it. And I can promise it works as advertised. See?"

"Now, there's no need for a demonstration," Benedict began hastily, but it was too late. Henry had already pressed the button. There was a bright flash, and the lights in the library winked out suddenly, leaving Tessa staring at an unlit black square in the floor. Gasps rose up from below. There was a shriek, and something crashed to the ground and shattered. Rising above it all was the sound of Benedict Lightwood, swearing fluently.

Will looked up and grinned. "Bit awkward for Henry, of course," he remarked cheerfully, "and yet, somehow quite satisfying, don't you think?"

Tessa couldn't help but agree, on both counts.

10

Pale Kings and Princes

I saw pale kings and princes too,
Pale warriors, death-pale were they all
–John Keats, "La Belle Dame Sans Merci"

As the coach rattled along the Strand, Will raised a black-gloved hand and drew one of the velvet curtains back from the window, letting a splash of yellow gaslight find its way into the carriage's dark interior. "It rather looks," he said, "as if we might be in for rain tonight."

Tessa followed his gaze; out the window the sky was a cloudy steel gray—the usual for London, she thought. Men in hats and long dark coats hurried along the pavement on either side of the street, their shoulders hunched against a brisk wind that carried coal dust, horse manure, and all sorts of eye-stinging rubbish in its wake. Once again Tessa thought she could smell the river.

"Is that a *church* directly in the middle of the street?" she wondered aloud.

"It's St. Mary le Strand," said Will, "and there's a long story about it, but I'm not going to tell it to you now. Have you been listening to anything I've been saying?"

"I was," Tessa said, "until you started on about rain. Who cares about rain? We're on our way to some sort of—vampire society event, and I've no idea how I'm supposed to behave, and so far you haven't helped me much at all."

The corner of Will's mouth twitched upward. "Just be careful. When we arrive at the house, you can't look to me for help or instruction. Remember, I am your human subjugate. You keep me about you for blood—blood whenever you want it—and nothing else."

"So you're not going to speak tonight," Tessa said. "At all."

"Not unless you instruct me to," said Will.

"This evening sounds as if it might be better than I thought."

Will seemed not to have heard her. With his right hand he was tightening one of the metal knife-bearing cuffs on his left wrist. He was staring off toward the window, as if seeing something that wasn't visible to her. "You might be thinking of vampires as feral monsters, but these vampires are not like that. They are as cultured as they are cruel. Sharpened knives to humanity's dull blade." The line of his jaw was set hard in the dim light. "You will have to try to keep up. And for God's sake, if you can't, don't say anything at all. They have a tortuous and opaque sense of etiquette. A serious social gaffe could mean instant death."

Tessa's hands tightened on each other in her lap. They were cold. She could feel the cold of Camille's skin, even through her gloves. "Are you joking? The way you were in the library, about dropping that book?"

"No." His voice was remote.

"Will, you're frightening me." The words came out of Tessa's mouth before she could stop them; she tensed, expecting mockery.

Will drew his gaze away from the window and looked at her as if some realization had dawned on him. "Tess," he said, and Tessa felt a momentary jolt; no one had ever called her Tess. Sometimes her brother had called her Tessie, but that was all. "You know you don't have to do this if you don't want to."

She took a breath, one she didn't need. "And then what? We would turn the carriage around and go home?"

He put his hands out, and took hers. Camille's hands were so small that Will's capable dark-gloved ones seemed to swallow them up. "One for all, and all for one," he said.

She smiled at that, weakly. "*The Three Musketeers*?"

His steady gaze held hers. His blue eyes were very dark, uniquely so. She had known people before with blue eyes, but they had always been light blue. Will's were the color of the sky just on the edge of night. His long lashes veiled them as he said, "Sometimes, when I have to do something I don't want to do, I pretend I'm a character from a book. It's easier to know what *they* would do."

"Really? Who do you pretend you are? D'Artagnan?" Tessa asked, naming the only one of the Three Musketeers that she could remember.

"'*It is a far, far better thing that I do, than I have ever done*,'" Will quoted. "'*It is a far, far better rest that I go to than I have ever known*.'"

"Sydney Carton? But you said you hated *A Tale of Two Cities*!"

"I don't really." Will seemed unabashed by his lie.

"And Sydney Carton was a dissipated alcoholic."

"Exactly. There was a man who was worthless, and knew he was worthless, and yet however far down he tried to sink his soul, there was always some part of him capable of great action." Will lowered his voice. "What is it he says to Lucie Manette? That though he is weak, he can still burn?"

Tessa, who had read *A Tale of Two Cities* more times than she could count, whispered, "'*And yet I have had the weakness, and have still the weakness, to wish you to know with what a sudden mastery you kindled me, heap of ashes that I am, into fire.*'" She hesitated. "But that was because he loved her."

"Yes," said Will. "He loved her enough to know she was better off without him." His hands were still on hers, the heat of them burning through her gloves. The wind was brisk outside, and had ruffled his ink black hair as they had crossed the Institute courtyard to the carriage. It made him look younger, and more vulnerable—and his eyes, too, were vulnerable, open like a door. The way he was looking at her, she would not have thought Will could, or would, look at anyone like that. If she could blush, she thought, how she would be blushing now.

And then she wished she had not thought of that. For that thought led, inevitably and unpleasantly, to another: Was he looking at her now, or at Camille, who was, indeed, exquisitely beautiful? Was that the reason for his change in expression? Could he see Tessa through the disguise, or only the shell of her?

She drew back, taking her hands from his, though his were closed tightly around hers. It took her a moment to disengage them.

"Tessa—," he began, but before he could say more, the carriage came to a jerking stop that set the velvet curtains swaying. Thomas called, "We're here!" from the driver's seat. Will, after taking a deep breath, swung the door open and leaped down to the pavement, lifting his hand to help her down after him.

Tessa bent her head as she exited the carriage to avoid crushing any of the roses on Camille's hat. Though Will wore gloves, as she did, she could almost imagine she felt the pulsing of blood under his skin, even through the double layer of fabric that separated them. He was flushed, the color high in his cheeks, and she wondered if it was the cold whipping the blood into his face, or something else.

They were standing in front of a tall white house with a white-pillared entrance. It was surrounded by similar houses on either side, like rows of pale dominoes. Up a row of white steps was a pair of double doors painted black. They were ajar, and Tessa could see the glimmer of candlelight from within, shimmering like a curtain.

Tessa turned to look at Will. Behind him Thomas was seated at the front of the carriage, his hat tipped forward to hide his face. The silver-handled pistol tucked into his waistcoat pocket was entirely hidden from view.

Somewhere in the back of her head, she felt Camille laugh, and she knew, without knowing how she knew, that she was sensing the vampire woman's amusement at her admiration of Will. *There you are,* Tessa thought, relieved despite her annoyance. She had begun to fear that Camille's inner voice would never come to her.

She drew away from Will, lifting her chin. The haughty pose wasn't natural to her—but it was to Camille. "You will address me not as Tessa but as a servant would," she said, her lip curling. "Now come." She jerked her head imperiously toward the steps, and started off without looking back to see if he followed.

An elegantly dressed footman awaited her at the top of the steps. "Your Ladyship," he murmured, and as he bowed, Tessa saw the two fang punctures in his neck, just above the collar. She turned her head to see Will behind her, and was about to introduce him to the footman when Camille's voice whispered in the back of her head, *We do not introduce our human pets to each other. They are our nameless property, unless we choose to give them names.*

Ugh, Tessa thought. In her disgust, she hardly noticed as the footman guided her down a long corridor and into a large marble-floored room. He bowed again and departed; Will moved to her side, and for a moment they both stood staring.

The space was lit only by candles. Dozens of gold candelabras dotted the room, fat white candles blazing in the holders. Hands carved of marble reached from the walls, each gripping a scarlet candle, drips of red wax blooming like roses along the sides of the carved marble.

And among the candelabras moved vampires, their faces as white as clouds, their movements graceful and liquid and strange. Tessa could see their similarities to Camille, the features they shared—the poreless skin, the jewel-colored eyes, the pale cheeks splotched with artificial rouge. Some looked more human than others; many were dressed in the fashions of bygone ages—knee breeches and cravats, skirts as full as Marie Antoinette's or gathered into trains at the back, lace cuffs and linen frills. Tessa's gaze scanned the room frantically, searching for a familiar fair-haired figure, but Nathaniel was nowhere to be seen. Instead she found herself trying not to stare at a tall skeletal woman, dressed in the heavily wigged and powdered fashion of a hundred years ago. Her face was stark and dreadful, whiter than the white powder dusting her hair. Her name was Lady Delilah, Camille's voice whispered in Tessa's mind. Lady Delilah held a slight figure by the hand, and Tessa's mind recoiled—a child, in this place?—but when the figure turned, she saw that it was a vampire as well, sunken dark eyes like pits in its rounded childish face. It smiled at Tessa, showing bared fangs.

"We must look for Magnus Bane," Will said under his breath. "He is meant to guide us through this mess. I shall point him out if I see him."

She was about to tell Will that Camille would recognize Magnus for her, when she caught sight of a slender man with a shock of fair hair, wearing a black swallowtail coat. Tessa felt her heart leap—and then fall in bitter disappointment as he turned. It was not Nathaniel. This man was a vampire, with a pale, angular face. His hair was not yellow like Nate's but was almost colorless under the candlelight. He dropped Tessa a wink and began to move toward her, pushing through the crowd. There were not only vampires among them, Tessa saw, but human subjugates as well. They carried gleaming serving trays, and on the trays were sets of empty glasses. Beside the glasses lay an array of silver utensils, all sharp-pointed. Knives, of course, and thin tools like the awls shoemakers used to punch holes in leather.

As Tessa stared in confusion, one of the subjugates was stopped by the woman in the white powdered wig. She snapped her fingers imperiously, and the darkling—a pale boy in a gray jacket and trousers—turned his head to the side obediently. After plucking a thin awl from the tray with her skinny fingers, the vampire drew the sharp tip across the skin of the boy's throat, just below his jaw. The glasses rattled on the tray as his hand shook, but he didn't drop the tray, not even when the woman lifted a glass and pressed it against his throat so that the blood ran down into it in a thin stream.

Tessa's stomach tightened with a sudden mixture of revulsion—and hunger; she could not deny the hunger, even though it belonged to Camille and not her. Stronger than the thirst, though, was her horror. She watched as the vampire woman lifted the glass to her lips, the human boy beside her standing gray-faced and trembling as she drank.

She wanted to reach for Will's hand, but a vampire baroness would never hold the hand of her human subjugate. She straightened her spine, and beckoned Will to her side with a quick snap of her fingers. He looked up in surprise, then moved to join her, clearly fighting to hide his annoyance. But hide it he must. "Now, don't go wandering off, William," she said with a meaningful glance. "I don't want to lose you in the crowd."

Will's jaw set. "I'm getting the oddest feeling that you're enjoying this," he said under his breath.

"Nothing odd about it." Feeling unbelievably bold, Tessa chucked him under the chin with the tip of her lace fan. "Simply behave yourself."

"They are *so* hard to train, aren't they?" The man with the colorless hair emerged out of the crowd, inclining his head toward Tessa. "Human subjugates, that is," he added, mistaking her startled expression for confusion. "And then once you have them properly trained, they die of something or other. Delicate creatures, humans. All the longevity of butterflies."

He smiled. The smile showed teeth. His skin had the bluish paleness of hardened ice. His hair was nearly white and hung arrow-straight to his shoulders, just brushing the collar of his elegant dark coat. His waistcoat was gray silk, figured with a pattern of twisting silver symbols. He looked like a Russian prince out of a book. "It's good to see you, Lady Belcourt," he said, and there was an accent to his voice too, not French—more Slavic. "Did I catch a glimpse of a new carriage through the window?"

This is de Quincey, Camille's voice breathed in Tessa's mind. Images rose up suddenly in her brain, like a fountain turned on, pouring fourth visions instead of water. She saw herself dancing with de Quincey, her hands on his shoulders; she stood by a black stream under the white sky of a northern night, watching as he fed on something pale and sprawled in the grass; she sat motionless at a long table of other vampires, de Quincey at the head of it, as he shouted and screamed at her and brought his fist down so hard that the marble top of the table shivered into cracks. He was shouting at her, something about a werewolf and a relationship she would live to regret. Then she was sitting alone in a room, in the dark, and weeping, and de Quincey came in and knelt by her chair and took her hand, wanting to comfort her, though he had been the one to cause her pain. *Vampires can weep?* Tessa thought first, and then, *They have known each other a long time, Alexei de Quincey and Camille Belcourt. They were friends once, and he thinks they are friends still.*

"Indeed, Alexei," she said, and as she said it, she knew this was the name she had been trying to recall at the dinner table the other night—the foreign name the Dark Sisters had spoken. *Alexei.* "I wanted something a bit . . . roomier."She held her hand out, and stood still while he kissed it, his lips cold on her skin.

De Quincey's eyes slid past Tessa to Will, and he licked his lips. "And a new subjugate as well, I see. This one is quite fetching." He reached out a thin pale hand, and drew his forefinger down the side of Will's cheek to his jaw. "Such unusual coloring," he mused. "And these eyes."

"Thank you," said Tessa, in the manner of one being complimented on an especially tasteful choice of wallpaper. She watched nervously as de Quincey moved even closer to Will, who looked pale and strained. She wondered if he was having trouble holding himself back when surely every one of his nerves was screaming *Enemy! Enemy!*

De Quincey trailed his finger from Will's jaw to his throat, to the point at his collarbone where his pulse beat. "There," he said, and this time when he smiled, his white fangs were visible. They were sharp and fine at the points, like needles. His eyelids drooped, languorous and heavy, and his voice when he spoke was thick. "You wouldn't mind, Camille, would you, if I just had a little bite. . . ."

Tessa's vision went white. She saw de Quincey again, the front of his white shirt scarlet with blood—and she saw a body hanging upside down from a tree at the dark stream's edge, pale fingers dangling in the black water. . . .

Her hand whipped out, faster than she'd ever imagined she could have moved, and caught de Quincey's wrist. "My darling, no," she said, a wheedling tone in her voice. "I'd so like to keep him to myself for just a little while. You know how your appetite runs away with you sometimes." She lowered her eyelids.

De Quincey chuckled. "For you, Camille, I will exercise my restraint." He drew his wrist away, and for a moment, under the flirtatious poise, Tessa thought she saw a flash of anger in his eyes, quickly masked. "In honor of our long acquaintance."

"Thank you, Alexei."

"Have you given any further thought, my dear," he said, "to my offer of a membership in the Pandemonium Club? I know the mundanes bore you, but they are a source of funds, nothing more. Those of us on the board are on the verge of some very . . . exciting discoveries. Power beyond your wildest dreams, Camille."

Tessa waited, but Camille's inner voice was silent. Why? She fought down panic and managed to smile at de Quincey. "My dreams," she said, and hoped he would think the hoarseness in her voice was from amusement and not fear, "may be more wild already than you imagine."

Beside her, she could tell that Will had shot her a surprised look; he quickly schooled his features to blandness, though, and glanced away. De Quincey, his eyes gleaming, only smiled.

"I ask only that you consider my offer, Camille. And now I must attend to my other guests. I trust I will see you at the ceremony?"

Dazed, she simply nodded. "Of course."

De Quincey bowed, turned, and vanished into the crowd. Tessa let her breath out. She hadn't realized she'd been holding it.

"Don't," said Will softly at her side. "Vampires don't need to breathe, remember."

"My God, Will." Tessa realized she was shaking. "He would have bitten you."

Will's eyes were dark with rage. "I would have killed him first."

A voice spoke at Tessa's elbow. "And then you would both be dead."

She whirled and saw that a tall man had appeared just behind her, as soundlessly as if he had drifted there like smoke. He wore an elaborate brocade jacket, like something out of the previous century, with a riot of white lace at his collar and cuffs. Below the long jacket Tessa glimpsed knee breeches, and high buckled shoes. His hair was like rough black silk, so dark it had a bluish sheen to it; his skin was brown, the cast of his features like Jem's. She wondered if perhaps, like Jem, he was of foreign extraction. In one ear he sported a silver loop from which dangled a diamond pendant the size of a finger, which sparkled brilliantly under the lights, and there were diamonds set into the head of his silver walking stick. He seemed to gleam all over, like witchlight. Tessa stared; she had never seen anyone dressed in such a mad fashion.

"*This* is Magnus," said Will quietly, sounding relieved. "Magnus Bane."

"My darling Camille," Magnus said, bending to kiss her gloved hand. "We have been parted too long."

The moment he touched her, Camille's memories came rushing up in a flood—memories of Magnus holding her, kissing her, touching her in a distinctly intimate and personal manner. Tessa jerked her hand back with a squeak.

And now *you reappear,* she thought resentfully in Camille's direction.

"I see," he murmured, straightening. His eyes, when he raised them to Tessa's, nearly made her lose her composure: They were gold-green with slit pupils, the eyes of a cat set in a distinctly human face. They were full of shimmering amusement. Unlike Will, whose eyes held a trace of sadness even when he was amused, Magnus's eyes were full of a surprising joy. They darted sideways, and he jerked his chin toward the far side of the room, indicating that Tessa should follow him. "Come along, then. There's a private room where we can talk."

In a daze Tessa followed him, Will at her side. Was she imagining it, or did the white faces of the vampires turn to follow her as she passed? A redheaded female vampire in an elaborate blue dress glared at her as she went; Camille's voice whispered that the woman was jealous of de Quincey's regard for her. Tessa was grateful when Magnus finally reached a door—so cleverly set into the paneled wall that she didn't realize it was a door until the warlock had produced a key. He slid the door open with a soft click. Will and Tessa followed him inside.

The room was a library, obviously rarely used; though volumes lined the walls, they were grimed with dust, as were the velvet curtains that hung across the windows. When the door shut behind them, the light in the room dimmed; before Tessa could say anything, Magnus snapped his fingers and twin fires leaped up in the fireplaces on either side of the room. The flames of the fire were blue, and the fire itself had a strong scent, like burning joss sticks.

"Oh!" Tessa could not stop a small exclamation of surprise from passing her lips.

With a grin Magnus flung himself onto the great marble-topped table in the center of the room, and lay down on his side, his head propped on his hand. "Have you never seen a warlock do magic before?"

Will gave an exaggerated sigh. "Please refrain from teasing her, Magnus. I expect Camille told you she knows very little of the Shadow World."

"Indeed," Magnus said unrepentantly, "but it's hard to believe, considering what she can do." His eyes were on Tessa. "I saw your face when I kissed your hand. You knew who I was immediately, didn't you? You know what Camille knows. There are some warlocks and demons who can shift—take on any shape. But I have never heard of one who could do what you do."

"It cannot be said for certain that I'm a warlock," Tessa said. "Charlotte says I'm not marked like a warlock would be marked."

"Oh, you're a warlock. Depend on it. Just because you don't have bat ears . . ." Magnus saw Tessa frown, and raised his eyebrows. "Oh, you don't *want* to be a warlock, do you? You despise the idea."

"I just never thought . . . ," Tessa said in a whisper. "That I was anything other than human."

Magnus's tone was not unsympathetic. "Poor thing. Now that you know the truth, you can never go back."

"Leave her alone, Magnus." Will's tone was sharp. "I must search the room. If you won't help, at least try not to torment Tessa while I do it." He moved toward the big oak desk in the corner of the room and began rummaging among the papers atop it.

Magnus glanced toward Tessa and winked. "I think he's jealous," he said in a conspiratorial whisper.

Tessa shook her head and moved toward the nearest bookshelf. There was a book propped open on the middle shelf as if to display it. The pages were covered with bright, intricate figures, some parts of the illustrations gleaming as if they had been painted onto the parchment with gold. Tessa exclaimed in surprise. "It's a Bible."

"Does that astonish you?" Magnus inquired.

"I thought vampires couldn't touch holy things."

"It depends on the vampire—how long they've been alive, what kind of faith they have. De Quincey actually collects old Bibles. He says there's hardly another book out there with so much blood on the pages."

Tessa glanced toward the closed door. The faint swell of voices on the other side was audible. "Won't we excite some sort of comment, hiding in here like this? The others—the vampires—I'm sure they were staring at us as we came in."

"They were staring at Will." In some ways Magnus's smile was as unnerving as a vampire's, even though he didn't have fangs. "Will looks wrong."

Tessa glanced over at Will, who was rummaging through the desk drawers with gloved hands. "I find that hard to credit coming from someone dressed as you are," Will said.

Magnus ignored this. "Will doesn't behave like the other human subjugates. He doesn't stare at his mistress with blind adoration, for instance."

"It's that monstrous hat of hers," said Will. "Puts me off."

"Human subjugates are never 'put off,'" said Magnus. "They adore their vampire masters, whatever they wear. Of course, the guests were also staring because they know of my relationship with Camille, and are wondering what we might be doing here in the library . . . alone." He wiggled his eyebrows at Tessa.

Tessa thought back to her visions. "De Quincey . . . He said something to Camille about regretting her relationship with a werewolf. He made it sound as if it were a crime she committed."

Magnus, who was now lying on his back and twirling his walking stick over his head, shrugged. "To him it would be. Vampires and werewolves despise each other. They claim it has something to do with the fact that the two races of demons that spawned them were involved in a blood feud, but if you ask me, it's simply that they're both predators, and predators always resent incursions into their territory. Not that vampires are all that fond of the fey, or my kind either, but de Quincey rather likes me. He thinks we're friends. In fact, I suspect he'd like to be more than friends." Magnus grinned, to Tessa's confusion. "But I despise him, though he doesn't know it."

"Then, why spend time with him at all?" asked Will, who had moved to a tall secretary between two of the windows and was examining its contents. "Why come to his house?"

"Politics," said Magnus with another shrug. "He is the head of the clan; for Camille not to come to his parties when invited would be construed as an insult. And for me to allow her to go alone would be . . . careless. De Quincey is dangerous, and no less to those of his own kind. Especially those who have displeased him in the past."

"Then you should—," Will began, and broke off, his voice altering. "I've found something." He paused. "Perhaps you should have a look at this, Magnus." Will came over to the table and set down on it what looked like a long sheet of rolled paper. He gestured for Tessa to join him, and unrolled the paper across the table's surface. "There was little of interest in the desk," he said, "but I did find this, hidden in a false drawer in the cabinet. Magnus, what do you think?"

Tessa, who had moved to stand beside Will at the table, gazed down at the paper. It was covered with a rough blueprint drawing of a human skeleton made up of pistons, cogs, and plates of hammered metal. The skull had a hinged jaw, open sockets for eyes, and a mouth that ended just behind the teeth. There was a panel in the chest too, just like Miranda's. All along the left side of the page were scrawled what looked like notes, in a language Tessa could not decipher. The letters were utterly unfamiliar.

"Blueprint for an automaton," said Magnus, cocking his head to the side. "An artificial human being. Humans have always been fascinated by the creatures—I suppose because they are humanoid but cannot die or be hurt. Have you ever read *The Book of Knowledge of Ingenious Mechanical Devices?*"

"I've never even heard of it," said Will. "Are there any bleak moors in it, shrouded in mysterious mists? Ghostly brides wandering the halls of ruined castles? A handsome fellow rushing to the rescue of a beauteous yet penniless maiden?"

"No," said Magnus. "There's a rather racy bit about cogs halfway through, but really most of it is rather dry."

"Then Tessa won't have read it, either," said Will.

Tessa glared at him, but said nothing; she *hadn't* read it, and she wasn't in the mood to let Will get to her.

"Well, then," said Magnus. "It was written by an Arab scholar, two centuries before Leonardo da Vinci, and described how machines could be built that would mimic the actions of human beings. Now, there is nothing alarming about that in and of itself. But it is this"—Magnus's long finger brushed gently across the writing on the left side of the page—"that concerns me."

Will leaned closer. His sleeve brushed Tessa's arm. "Yes, that was what I wanted to ask you about. Is it a spell?"

Magnus nodded. "A binding spell. Meant to infuse demonic energy into an inanimate object, thus giving that object a sort of life. I've seen the spell used. Before the Accords vampires liked to amuse themselves by creating little demonic mechanisms like music boxes that would play only at night, mechanical horses that could ride only after sundown, that sort of silliness." He tapped thoughtfully on the head of his walking stick. "One of the great problems of creating convincing automatons, of course, has always been their appearance. No other material quite gives the semblance of human flesh."

"But what if one were to use it—human flesh, I mean?" Tessa asked.

Magnus paused delicately. "The problem there, for human designers, is, ah, obvious. Preserving the flesh destroys its appearance. One would have to use magic. And then magic again, to bind the demon energy to the mechanical body."

"And what would that achieve?" Will asked, an edge to his voice.

"Automatons have been built that can write poems, draw landscapes—but only those they are directed to create. They have no individual creativity or imagination. Animated by a demon energy, however, an automaton would have a measure of thought and will. But any bound spirit is enslaved. It would inevitably be entirely obedient to whoever had done the binding."

"A clockwork army," Will said, and there was a sort of bitter humor in his voice. "Born of neither Heaven nor Hell."

"I wouldn't go that far," Magnus said. "Demon energies are hardly an easy item to come by. One must summon demons up, then bind them, and you know what a difficult process that is. Obtaining enough demon energies to create an army would be well-nigh impossible and extraordinarily risky. Even for an evil-minded bastard like de Quincey."

"I see." And with that, Will rolled up the paper and slipped it into his jacket. "Much obliged for your help, Magnus."

Magnus looked faintly puzzled, but his response was courteous: "Of course."

"I gather you wouldn't be sorry to see de Quincey gone and another vampire in his place," said Will. "Have you actually observed him breaking the Law?"

"Once. I was invited here to witness one of his 'ceremonies.' As it turned out—" Magnus looked uncharacteristically grim. "Well, let me show you."

He turned and moved toward the bookshelf that Tessa had been examining earlier, gesturing for them to join him. Will followed, Tessa beside him. Magnus snapped his fingers again, and as blue sparks flew, the illustrated Bible slid to the side, revealing a small hole that had been cut into the wood at the back of the shelf. As Tessa leaned forward in surprise, she saw that it offered a view into an elegant music room. At least, that was what she thought at first, seeing the chairs set up in rows facing the back of the room; it made a sort of theater. Rows of lit candelabras were set up for illumination. Red satin floor-length curtains blocked off the back walls, and the floor was slightly raised, creating a sort of makeshift stage. There was nothing on it but a single chair with a high wooden back.

Steel manacles were attached to the arms of the chair, glittering like insect carapaces in the candlelight. The wood of the chair was blotched, here and there, with dark red stains. The legs of the chair, Tessa saw, were nailed to the floor.

"This is where they have their little . . . performances," said Magnus, an undertone of distaste in his voice. "They bring out the human and lock him—or her—to the chair. Then they take turns draining their victim slowly, while the crowd watches and applauds."

"And they enjoy that?" Will said. The disgust in his voice was more than an undertone. "The mundanes' pain? Their fear?"

"Not all the Night Children are like this," Magnus said quietly. "These are the worst of them."

"And the victims," said Will, "where do they find them?"

"Criminals, mostly," said Magnus. "Drunkards, addicts, whores. The forgotten and lost. Those who will not be missed." He looked squarely at Will. "Would you like to elaborate on your plan?"

"We begin when we see the Law being broken," said Will. "The moment a vampire moves to harm a human, I will signal the Enclave. They'll attack."

"Really," Magnus said. "How will they get in?"

"Don't worry about that." Will was unfazed. "Your job is to take Tessa at that point and get her safely out of here. Thomas is waiting outside with the carriage. Bundle yourselves into it and he'll take you back to the Institute."

"Seems a waste of my talents, assigning me to look after one moderately sized girl," Magnus observed. "Surely you could use me—"

"This is a Shadowhunter affair," said Will. "We make the Law, and we uphold the Law. The assistance you've given us so far has been invaluable, but we require no more from you."

Magnus met Tessa's eyes over Will's shoulder; his look was wry. "The proud isolation of the Nephilim. They have use for you when they have use for you, but they cannot bring themselves to share a victory with Downworlders."

Tessa turned to Will. "You're sending me away as well, before the fighting starts?"

"I must," said Will. "It would be best for Camille not to be seen to be cooperating with Shadowhunters."

"That's nonsense," said Tessa. "De Quincey will know I—she—brought you here. He'll know she lied about where she found you. Does she think that after this, the rest of the clan won't know she's a traitor?"

Somewhere in the back of her head, Camille's soft laughter purred. She did not sound afraid.

Will and Magnus exchanged a look. "She does not expect," said Magnus, "that a single vampire who is here tonight will survive the evening to accuse her."

"The dead can tell no tales," said Will softly. The flickering light in the room painted his face in alternating shades of black and gold; the line of his jaw was hard. He looked toward the peephole, eyes narrowing. "Look."

The three of them jostled to get close to the peephole, through which they saw the pocket doors at one end of the music room slide open. Through them was the large candlelit drawing room; vampires began to stream through the doors, taking their places in the seats before the "stage."

"It's time," Magnus said softly, and slid the peephole closed.

***

The music room was nearly full. Tessa, arm in arm with Magnus, watched as Will threaded his way through the crowd, looking for three seats together. He was keeping his head bowed, his eyes on the floor, but even so—

"They're still looking at him," she said to Magnus under her breath. "At Will, I mean."

"Of course they are," said Magnus. His eyes reflected light like a cat's as they surveyed the room. "Look at him. The face of a bad angel and eyes like the night sky in Hell. He's very pretty, and vampires like that. I can't say I mind either." Magnus grinned. "Black hair and blue eyes are my favorite combination."

Tessa reached up to pat Camille's pale blond curls.

Magnus shrugged. "Nobody's perfect."

Tessa was spared answering; Will had found a set of chairs together, and was beckoning them over with a gloved hand. She tried not to pay attention to the way the vampires were looking at him as she let Magnus lead her toward the seats. It was true that he was beautiful, but what did they care? Will was just food to them, wasn't he?

She sat down with Magnus on one side of her and Will on the other, her silk taffeta skirts rustling like leaves in a stiff wind. The room was cool, not like a room crowded with human beings, who would have been giving off body heat. Will's sleeve slid up his arm as he reached to pat the pocket of his waistcoat, and she saw that his arm was dotted with goose bumps. She wondered if the human companions of vampires were always cold.

A rustle of whispers went through the room, and Tessa tore

her eyes from Will. The light of the candelabras did not reach the far recesses of the room; portions of the "stage"—the back of the room—were blotched with shadows, and even Tessa's vampire eyes could not discern what was moving within the darkness until de Quincey appeared suddenly from the shadows.

The audience was silent. Then de Quincey grinned. It was a manic grin, showing fangs, and it transformed his face. He looked wild and savage now, wolflike. A murmur of hushed appreciation went through the room, the way a human audience might show appreciation for an actor with a particularly good stage presence.

"Good evening," said de Quincey. "Welcome, friends. Those of you who have joined me here"—and he smiled directly at Tessa, who was too nervous to do anything but stare back—"are proud sons and daughters of the Night Children. We do not bend our necks beneath the oppressive yoke called the Law. We do not answer to Nephilim. Nor shall we abandon our ancient customs at their whim."

It was impossible not to notice the effect de Quincey's speech was having on Will. He was as taut as a bow, his hands clenched in his lap, the veins standing out in his neck.

"We have a prisoner," de Quincey went on. "His crime is betraying the Night Children." He swept his gaze across the audience of waiting vampires. "And what is the punishment for such treason?"

"It is death!" cried a voice, the vampire woman Delilah. She was straining forward in her seat, a terrible eagerness on her face.

The other vampires took up her cry. "Death! Death!"

More shadowy forms slipped between the curtains that

formed the makeshift stage. Two male vampires, holding between them the struggling form of a human man. A black hood concealed the man's features. All Tessa could see was that he was slender, probably young—and filthy, his fine clothes torn and ragged. His bare feet left bloody smears on the boards as the men dragged him forward and flung him into the chair. A faint gasp of sympathy escaped Tessa's throat; she felt Will tense beside her.

The man continued to thrash feebly, like an insect on the end of a pin, as the vampires strapped his wrists and ankles to the chair, and then stepped back. De Quincey grinned; his fangs were out. They shone like ivory pins as he surveyed the crowd. Tessa could sense the vampires' restlessness—and more than their restlessness, their hunger. No longer did they resemble a well-bred audience of human theatergoers. They were as avid as lions scenting prey, lurching forward in their chairs, theirs eyes wide and glowing, their mouths open.

"When can you summon the Enclave?" Tessa said to Will in an urgent whisper.

Will's voice was tight. "When he draws blood. We must *see* him do it."

"Will—"

"Tessa." He whispered her real name, his fingers gripping hers. "Be *quiet*."

Reluctantly Tessa returned her attention to the stage, where de Quincey was approaching the shackled prisoner. He paused by the chair—reached out—and his thin pale fingers brushed the man's shoulder, as light as a spider's touch. The prisoner convulsed, jerking in desperate terror as the vampire's hand slid from his shoulder to his neck. De Quincey laid two white fingers to the man's pulse point, as if he were a doctor checking a patient's heartbeat.

De Quincey wore a silver ring on one finger, Tessa saw, one side of which sharpened to a needle point that protruded when he tightened his hand into a fist. There was a flash of silver, and the prisoner screamed—the first sound he had made. There was something familiar about the sound.

A thin line of red appeared on the prisoner's throat, like a loop of red wire. Blood welled and spilled down into the hollow of his collarbone. The prisoner thrashed and struggled as de Quincey, his face now a rictus mask of hunger, reached to touch two fingers to the red liquid. He lifted the stained fingertips to his mouth. The crowd was hissing and moaning, barely able to stay in their seats. Tessa glanced toward the woman in the white-plumed hat. Her mouth was open, her chin wet with drool.

"Will," Tessa murmured. "Will, *please*."

Will glanced past her, at Magnus. "Magnus. Take her out of here."

Something in Tessa rebelled at the idea of being sent away. "Will, no, I'm all right here—"

Will's voice was quiet, but his eyes blazed. "We've been over this. Go, or I won't summon the Enclave. Go, or that man will die."

"Come." It was Magnus, his hand on her elbow, guiding her to stand. Reluctantly she allowed the warlock to draw her to her feet, and then toward the doors. Tessa glanced around anxiously to see if anyone noticed their departure, but no one was looking at them. All attention was riveted on de Quincey and the prisoner, and many vampires were already on their feet, hissing and cheering and making inhuman hungry sounds.

Among the seething crowd, Will was still seated, leaning forward like a hunting dog yearning to be released from the leash. His left hand slid into his waistcoat pocket, and emerged with something copper held between his fingers.

The Phosphor.

Magnus swung the door open behind them. "Hurry."

Tessa hesitated, looking back at the stage. De Quincey was standing behind the prisoner now. His grinning mouth was smeared with blood. He reached out and took hold of the prisoner's hood.

Will rose to his feet, the Phosphor held aloft. Magnus swore and pulled at Tessa's arm. She half-turned as if to go with him, then froze as de Quincey whipped off the black hood to reveal the prisoner beneath.

His face was swollen and bruised with beatings. One of his eyes was black and swelled shut. His blond hair was pasted to his skull with blood and sweat. But none of that mattered; Tessa would have known him anyway, anywhere. She knew now why his cry of pain had sounded so familiar to her.

It was Nathaniel.

11

Few Are Angels

We all are men,
In our own natures frail, and capable
Of our flesh; few are angels
–Shakespeare, *King Henry VIII*

Tessa screamed.

Not a human scream but a vampire scream. She barely recognized the sound that came from her own throat—it sounded like shattering glass. Only later did she even realize that she was screaming words. She would have thought she'd cry her brother's name, but she didn't.

"Will!" she screamed. "Will, now! Do it now!"

A gasp ran through the room. Dozens of white faces swung toward Tessa. Her scream had broken through their bloodlust. De Quincey was motionless on the stage; even Nathaniel was looking at her, dazed and staring, as if wondering if her screams were a dream born out of his agony.

Will, his finger on the button of the Phosphor, hesitated. His eyes met Tessa's across the room. It was only for a split second, but de Quincey saw their glance. As if he could read it, the look on his face changed, and he swung his hand up to point directly at Will.

"The boy," he spat. "Stop him!"

Will tore his gaze from Tessa's. The vampires were already rising to their feet, moving toward him, their eyes glittering with rage and hunger. Will looked past them, at de Quincey, who was staring at Will with fury. There was no fear on Will's face as his gaze met the vampire's—no hesitation, and no surprise.

"I am not a boy," he said. "I am Nephilim."

And he pressed the button.

Tessa braced herself for a flare of white witchlight. Instead there was a great *whoosh* of sound as the flames of the candelabras shot toward the ceiling. Sparks flew, scattering the floor with glowing embers, catching in the curtains, in the skirts of women's dresses. Suddenly the room was full of billowing black smoke and screams—high-pitched and horrible.

Tessa could no longer see Will. She tried to dart forward, but Magnus—she had nearly forgotten he was there—caught her firmly by the wrist. "Miss Gray, no," he said, and when she responded by pulling away harder, he added, "Miss Gray! You're a vampire now! If you catch fire, you'll go up like kindling wood—"

As if to illustrate his point, at that moment a stray spark landed atop Lady Delilah's white wig. It burst into flames. With a cry she tried to rip it from her head, but as her hands came in contact with the flames, they, too, caught fire as if they were made of paper instead of skin. In less than a second both her arms were burning like torches. Howling, she raced toward the door, but the fire was faster than she was. Within seconds a bonfire raged where she had stood. Tessa could just see the outline of a blackened screaming creature writhing inside it.

"Do you see what I mean?" Magnus shouted in Tessa's ear, struggling to make himself heard over the howls of the vampires, who were diving this way and that, trying to avoid the flames.

"Let me go!" Tessa shrieked. De Quincey had leaped into the melee; Nathaniel was slumped alone onstage, apparently unconscious, only his manacles holding him to the chair. "That's my brother up there. My *brother*!"

Magnus stared at her. Taking advantage of his confusion, Tessa jerked her arm free and began to run toward the stage. The room was chaos: vampires rushing to and fro, many of them stampeding toward the doorway. The vampires who had reached the door were pushing and shoving to get through it first; others had turned course and were streaming toward the French doors that looked out over the garden.

Tessa veered to avoid a fallen chair, and nearly ran headlong into the redheaded vampire in the blue dress who had glared at her earlier. She looked terrified now. She plunged toward Tessa—then seemed to stumble. Her mouth opened in a scream, and blood poured from it like a fountain. Her face crumpled, folding in on itself, the skin resolving into dust and raining down from the bones of her skull. Her red hair shriveled and turned gray; the skin of her arms melted and turned to powder, and with a last despairing shriek the vampire woman collapsed into a stringy heap of bones and dust lying atop an empty satin dress.

Tessa gagged, tore her eyes away from the remains, and saw Will. He stood directly in front of her, holding a long silver knife; the blade was smeared with scarlet blood. His face was bloody too, his eyes wild. "What the *hell* are you still doing here?" he shouted at Tessa. "You *unbelievably* stupid—"

Tessa heard the noise before Will did, a thin whining sound, like a piece of broken machinery. The fair-haired boy in the gray jacket—the human servant Lady Delilah had drunk from earlier—was rushing at Will, a high-pitched wailing sound coming from his throat, his face smeared with tears and blood. He was carrying a torn-off chair leg in one hand; the end of it was ragged and sharp.

"Will, look *out*!" Tessa shouted, and Will spun. He moved *fast*, Tessa saw, like a dark blur, and the knife in his hand was a flash of silver in the smoky dimness. When he stopped moving, the boy was lying on the ground, the blade protruding from his chest. Blood welled around it, thicker and darker than vampire blood.

Will, staring down, was ashen. "I thought . . ."

"He would have killed you if he could," Tessa said.

"You know nothing of it," Will said. He shook his head, once, as if clearing it of her voice, or of the sight of the boy on the ground. The subjugate looked very young, his twisted face softer in death. "I told you to go—"

"That's my brother," Tessa said, pointing toward the back of the room. Nathaniel was still unconscious, limp in his manacles. If it weren't for the blood still flowing from the wound in his neck, she would have thought he was dead. "Nathaniel. In the chair."

Will's eyes widened in astonishment. "But how—?" he began. He didn't get a chance to finish his question. At that moment the sound of shattering glass filled the room. The French windows burst inward, and the room was suddenly flooded with Shadowhunters in their dark fighting gear. They were driving before them in a screaming, ragged group the vampires who had fled into the garden. As Tessa stared, more Shadowhunters began flooding in from the other doors as well, herding more vampires in front of them, like dogs herding sheep into a pen. De Quincey staggered before the other vampires, his pale face smeared with black ash, his teeth bared.

Tessa saw Henry among the Nephilim, easily recognizable by his ginger hair. Charlotte was there too, dressed like a man all in dark fighting gear, like the women pictured in Tessa's Shadowhunter book. She looked small and determined and surprisingly fierce. And then there was Jem. His gear made him appear all the more startlingly pale, and the black Marks on his skin stood out like ink on paper. In the crowd she recognized Gabriel Lightwood; his father, Benedict; slim black-haired Mrs. Highsmith; and behind them all strode Magnus, blue sparks flying from his hands as he gestured.

Will exhaled, some of the color returning to his face. "I wasn't sure they'd come," he muttered, "not with the Phosphor malfunctioning." He tore his eyes away from his friends and looked at Tessa. "Go attend to your brother," he said. "That'll get you out of the worst of it. I hope."

He turned and walked away from her without a backward glance. The Nephilim had herded the remaining vampires, those who had not been killed by the fire—or by Will—into the center of a makeshift circle of Shadowhunters. De Quincey towered among the group, his pale face twisted in rage; his shirt was stained with blood—his own or someone else's, she couldn't tell. The other vampires huddled behind him like children behind a parent, looking both fierce and wretched at the same time.

"The Law," de Quincey growled, as Benedict Lightwood advanced on him, a shining blade in his right hand, its surface scored with black runes. "The Law protects us. We surrender to you. The Law—"

"You have broken the Law," snarled Benedict. "Therefore its protection no longer extends to you. The sentence is death."

"One mundane," said de Quincey, sparing a glance toward Nathaniel. "One mundane who has *also* broken Covenant Law—"

"The Law does not extend to mundanes. They cannot be expected to follow the laws of a world they know nothing of."

"He is worthless," de Quincey said. "You do not know how worthless. Do you really desire to shatter our alliance over one worthless mundane?"

"It is more than just one mundane!" Charlotte cried, and from her jacket she drew the paper Will had taken from the library. Tessa had not seen Will pass it to Charlotte, but he must have. "What of these spells? Did you think we would not discover them? This—this black sorcery is absolutely forbidden by the Covenant!"

De Quincey's still face betrayed only a hint of his surprise. "Where did you find that?"

Charlotte's mouth was a hard thin line. "That doesn't matter."

"Whatever it is you think you know—," de Quincey began.

"We know enough!" Charlotte's voice was full of passion. "We know you hate and despise us! We know your alliance with us has been a sham!"

"And have you made it against Covenant Law now to dislike Shadowhunters?" de Quincey said, but the sneer was gone from his voice. He sounded ragged.

"Do not play your games with us," spat Benedict. "After all we've done for you, after we passed the Accords into Law— Why? We've tried to make you equal to ourselves—"

De Quincey's face twisted. "*Equal?* You don't know what the word means. You cannot let go of your own conviction, let go of your belief in your inherent superiority, for long enough to even *consider* what that would mean. Where are our seats on the Council? Where is our embassy in Idris?"

"But that—that's ridiculous," Charlotte said, though she had blanched.

Benedict shot Charlotte an impatient look. "And irrelevant. None of this excuses your behavior, de Quincey. While you sat in council with us, pretending you were interested in peace, behind our backs you broke the Law and mocked our power. Surrender yourself, tell us what we want to know, and we might let your clan survive. Otherwise, there will be no mercy."

Another vampire spoke. It was one of the men who had strapped Nathaniel to his chair, a big flame-haired man with an angry face. "If we needed any further proof that the Nephilim have never meant their promises of peace, here it is. Dare to attack us, Shadowhunters, and you'll have a war on your hands!"

Benedict only grinned. "Then let the war begin here," he

said, and flung the blade at de Quincey. It whipped through the air—and plunged hilt-deep into the chest of the redheaded vampire, who had flung himself in front of his clan leader. He exploded in a shower of blood as the other vampires shrieked. With a howl de Quincey rushed Benedict. The other vampires seemed to awaken from their panicked stupor, and swiftly followed suit. Within seconds the room was a melee of screams and chaos.

The sudden chaos unfroze Tessa as well. Catching up her skirts, she ran for the stage, and dropped to her knees next to Nathaniel's chair. His head lolled to the side, his eyes closed. The blood from the wound in his neck had flowed to a slow trickle. Tessa caught at his sleeve. "Nate," she whispered. "Nate, it's me."

He moaned, but made no other reply. Biting her lip, Tessa went to work on the manacles that fastened his wrists to the chair. They were hard iron, fastened to the sturdy chair arms with rows of nails—clearly designed to withstand even vampire strength. She pulled at them until her fingers bled, but they didn't budge. If only she had one of Will's knives.

She glanced out over the room. It was still dark with smoke. In among the swirls of blackness, she could see the bright flashes of weapons, the Shadowhunters brandishing the brilliant white daggers Tessa knew now were called seraph blades, each one brought into shimmering life by the name of an angel. Vampire blood flew from the blades' edges, as bright as a scatter of rubies. She realized—with a shock of surprise, for the vampires at first had terrified her—that the vampires were clearly overmatched here. Though the Night Children were vicious and fast, the Shadowhunters were nearly as fast, and had weapons and training on their side. Vampire after vampire fell under the onslaught of the seraph blades. Blood ran in sheets across the floor, soaking the edges of the Persian rugs.

The smoke cleared in a spot, and Tessa saw Charlotte dispatching a burly vampire in a gray morning jacket. She slashed the blade of her knife across his throat, and blood sprayed across the wall behind them. He sank, snarling, to his knees, and Charlotte finished him with a thrust of her blade to his chest.

A blur of motion exploded behind Charlotte; it was Will, followed by a wild-eyed vampire brandishing a silver pistol. He pointed it at Will, aimed, and fired. Will dived out of the way and skidded across the bloody floor. He rolled to his feet, and bounded up onto a velvet-seated chair. Ducking another shot, he leaped again, and Tessa watched with amazement as he ran lightly along the *backs* of a row of chairs, leaping down from the last of them. He whirled to face the vampire, now a distance from him across the room. Somehow a short-bladed knife gleamed in his hand, though Tessa had not seen him draw it. He threw it. The vampire ducked aside, but was not quite fast enough; the knife sank into his shoulder. He roared in pain and was reaching for the knife when a slim, dark shadow reared up out of nowhere. There was a flash of silver, and the vampire blew apart in a shower of blood and dust. As the mess cleared, Tessa saw Jem, a long blade still raised in his fist. He was grinning, but not at her; he kicked the silver pistol—now lying abandoned among the vampire's remains—hard, and it skidded across the floor, fetching up at Will's feet. Will nodded toward Jem with a return of his grin, swept the pistol off the floor, and shoved it through his belt.

"Will!" Tessa called to him, though she wasn't sure if he could hear her over the din. "Will—"

Something seized her by the back of her dress and hauled her up and backward. It was like being caught in the talons of an enormous bird. Tessa screamed once, and found herself flung forward, skidding across the floor. She hit the stack of chairs. They crashed to the floor in a deafening mass, and Tessa, sprawled among the mess, looked up with a shout of pain.

De Quincey stood over her. His black eyes were wild, rimmed with red; his white hair straggled over his face in matted clumps, and his shirt was slashed open across the front, the edges of the tear soaked with blood. He must have been cut, though not deeply enough to kill him, and had healed. The skin under the torn shirt looked unmarked now. "*Bitch*," he snarled at Tessa. "Lying traitorous bitch. You brought that boy in here, Camille. That Nephilim."

Tessa scrambled backward; her back hit the wall of fallen chairs.

"I welcomed you back to the clan, even after your disgusting little—interlude—with the lycanthrope. I tolerate that ridiculous warlock of yours. And this is how you repay me. Repay *us*." He held his hands out to her; they were streaked with black ash. "You see this," he said. "The dust of our dead people. Dead *vampires*. And you betrayed them for *Nephilim*." He spat the word as if it were poison.

Something bubbled up out of Tessa's throat. Laughter. Not her laughter; Camille's. "'*Disgusting interlude*'?" The words came out of Tessa's mouth before she could stop them. It was as if she had no control over what she was saying. "I loved him—like you never loved me—like you've never loved anything.

And you killed him just to show the clan that you could. I want you to know what it is like to lose everything that matters to you. I want you to know, as your home burns and your clan is brought to ashes and your own miserable life ends, that *I am the one who is doing this to you.*"

And Camille's voice was gone just as quickly as it had come, leaving Tessa feeling drained and shocked. That didn't stop her, though, from using her hands, behind her, to scrabble among the smashed chairs. Surely there had to be *something*, some broken-off piece that she could use as a weapon. De Quincey was staring at her in shock, his mouth open. Tessa imagined that no one had ever talked to him like that. Certainly not another vampire.

"Perhaps," he said. "Perhaps I underestimated you. Perhaps you will destroy me." He advanced on her, his hands out, reaching. "But I will bring you with me—"

Tessa's fingers closed around the leg of a chair; without even thinking about it, she swung the chair up and over and brought it crashing down on de Quincey's back. She felt elated as he yelled and staggered back. She scrambled to her feet as the vampire straightened up, and she swung the chair at him again. This time a jagged bit of broken chair arm caught him across the face, opening up a long red cut. His lips curled back from his teeth in a silent snarl, and he *sprang*—there was no other word for it. It was like the silent spring of a cat. He struck Tessa to the ground, landing on top of her and knocking the chair from her hand. He lunged at her throat, teeth bared, and she raked her clawed hand across his face. His blood, where it dripped on her, seemed to burn, like acid. She screamed and struck out at him harder, but he only laughed; his pupils had disappeared into the black of his eyes, and he looked entirely inhuman, like some sort of monstrous predatory serpent.

He caught her wrists in his grasp and forced them down on either side of her, hard against the floor. "Camille," he said, leaning down over her, his voice thick. "Be still, little Camille. It will be over in moments—"

He threw his head back like a striking cobra. Terrified, Tessa struggled to free her trapped legs, meaning to kick him, kick him as hard as she could—

He yelled. Yelled and writhed, and Tessa saw that there was a hand caught in his hair, yanking his head up and back, dragging him to his feet. A hand inked all over with swirling black Marks.

Will's hand.

De Quincey was hauled screaming to his feet, his hands clamped to his head. Tessa struggled upright, staring, as Will flung the howling vampire contemptuously away from him. Will wasn't smiling anymore, but his eyes were glittering, and Tessa could see why Magnus had described their color as the sky in Hell.

"*Nephilim.*" De Quincey staggered, righted himself, and spat at Will's feet.

Will drew the pistol from his belt and aimed it at de Quincey. "One of the Devil's own abominations, aren't you? You don't even deserve to live in this world with the rest of us, and yet when we let you do so out of pity, you throw our gift back in our faces."

"As if we need your pity," de Quincey replied. "As if we could ever be less than you. You Nephilim, thinking you are—" He stopped abruptly. He was so smeared with filth that it was hard to tell, but it looked as if the cut on his face had already healed.

"Are what?" Will cocked the pistol; the click was loud even above the noise of the battle. "Say it."

The vampire's eyes burned. "Say what?"

"'God,'" said Will. "You were going to tell me that we Nephilim play at God, weren't you? Except you can't even say the word. Mock the Bible all you want with your little collection, you still can't say it." His finger was white on the trigger of the gun. "Say it. Say it, and I'll let you live."

The vampire bared his teeth. "You cannot kill me with that—that stupid human toy."

"If the bullet passes through your heart," Will said, his aim unwavering, "you'll die. And I am a very good shot."

Tessa stood, frozen, staring at the tableau before her. She wanted to step backward, to go to Nathaniel, but she was afraid to move.

De Quincey raised his head. He opened his mouth. A thin rattle came out as he tried to speak, tried to shape a word his soul would not let him say. He gasped again, choked, and put a hand to his throat. Will began to laugh—

And the vampire sprang. His face twisted in a mask of rage and pain, he launched himself at Will with a howl. There was a blur of movement. Then the gun went off and there was a spray of blood. Will hit the floor, the pistol skidding from his grip, the vampire on top of him. Tessa scrambled to retrieve the pistol, caught it, and turned to see that de Quincey had seized Will from the back, his forearm jammed against Will's throat.

She raised the pistol, her hand shaking—but she had never used a pistol before, had never shot anything, and how to shoot the vampire without injuring Will? Will was clearly choking, his face suffused with blood. De Quincey snarled something and tightened his grip—

And Will, ducking his head, sank his teeth into the vampire's forearm. De Quincey yelled and jerked his arm away; Will flung himself to the side, retching, and rolled to his knees to spit blood onto the stage. When he looked up, glittering red blood was smeared across the lower half of his face. His teeth shone red too when he—Tessa couldn't believe it—*grinned*, actually grinned, and looking at de Quincey, said, "How do *you* like it, vampire? You were going to bite that mundane earlier. Now you know what it's like, don't you?"

De Quincey, on his knees, stared from Will to the ugly red hole in his own arm, which was already beginning to close up, though dark blood still trickled from it thinly. "For that," he said, "you will die, Nephilim."

Will spread his arms wide. On his knees, grinning like a demon, blood dripping from his mouth, he barely looked human himself. "Come and get me."

De Quincey gathered himself to spring—and Tessa pulled the trigger. The gun kicked back, hard, into her hand, and the vampire fell sideways, blood streaming from his shoulder. She had missed the heart. *Damn it.*

Howling, de Quincey began to pull himself to his feet. Tessa raised her arm, pulled the trigger on the pistol again—nothing. A soft click let her know the gun was empty.

De Quincey laughed. He was still clutching his shoulder, though the blood flow had already slowed to a trickle. "*Camille,*" he spat at Tessa. "I will be back for you. I will make you sorry you were ever reborn."

Tessa felt a chill at the pit of her stomach—not just *her* fear. Camille's. De Quincey bared his teeth one last time and whirled with incredible speed. He raced across the room and flung himself into a high glass window. It shattered outward in an explosion of glass, carrying him forward as if his body were being carried on a wave, vanishing into the night.

Will swore. "We can't lose him—," he began, and started forward. Then he spun as Tessa screamed. A ragged-looking male vampire had risen up behind her like a ghost appearing out of the air, and had snatched her by the shoulders. She tried to pull free, but his grip was too strong. She could hear him murmuring in her ear, horrible words about how she was a traitor to the Night Children, and how he would tear her open with his teeth.

"Tessa," Will shouted, and she wasn't sure if he sounded angry, or something else. He reached for the gleaming weapons at his belt. His hand closed around the hilt of a seraph blade, just as the vampire spun Tessa around. She caught sight of his leering white face, the blood-tipped fangs out, ready to tear. The vampire lunged forward—

And exploded in a shower of dust and blood. He dissolved, the flesh melting away from his face and hands, and Tessa caught sight for a moment of the blackened skeleton beneath before it, too, crumbled, leaving an empty pile of clothes behind. Clothes, and a gleaming silver blade.

She looked up. Jem stood a few feet away, looking very pale. He held the blade in his left hand; his right was empty. There was a long cut along one of his cheeks, but he seemed otherwise uninjured. His hair and eyes gleamed a brutal silver in the light of the dying flames. "I think," he said, "that that was the last of them."

Surprised, Tessa glanced around the room. The chaos had subsided. Shadowhunters moved here and there in the wreckage—some were seated on chairs, being attended to by stele-wielding healers—but she could not see a single vampire. The smoke of the burning had subsided as well, though white ash from the torched curtains still floated down over the room like unexpected snow.

Will, blood still dripping from his chin, looked at Jem with his eyebrows raised. "Nice throw," he said.

Jem shook his head. "You bit de Quincey," he said. "You fool. He's a *vampire*. You know what it means to bite a vampire."

"I had no choice," said Will. "He was choking me."

"I know," Jem said. "But really, Will. *Again?*"

It was Henry, in the end, who freed Nathaniel from the torture chair by the simple expedient of smashing it apart with the flat side of a sword until the manacles came free. Nathaniel slid to the floor, where he lay moaning, Tessa cradling him. Charlotte fussed a bit, bringing wet cloths to clean Nate's face, and a ragged bit of curtain to throw over him, before she raced off to engage Benedict Lightwood in an energetic conversation—during which she alternated between pointing back at Tessa and Nathaniel and waving her hands in a dramatic manner. Tessa, utterly dazed and exhausted, wondered what on earth Charlotte could be doing.

It hardly mattered, really. Everything seemed to be going on in a dream. She sat on the floor with Nathaniel as the Shadowhunters moved around her, drawing on one another with their steles. It was incredible to watch their injuries vanishing as the healing Marks went onto their skin. They all seemed equally able to draw the Marks. She watched as Jem, wincing, unbuttoned his shirt to show a long cut along one pale shoulder; he looked away, his mouth tight, as Will drew a careful Mark below the injury.

It wasn't until Will, having finished with Jem, came sauntering over to her that she realized why she was so tired.

"Back to yourself, I see," he said. He had a damp towel in one hand but hadn't yet bothered to clean the blood off his face and neck.

Tessa glanced down at herself. It was true. At some point she had lost Camille and become herself again. She must have been dazed indeed, she thought, not to have noticed the return of her own heartbeat. It pulsed inside her chest like a drum.

"I didn't know you knew how to use a pistol," Will added.

"I don't," Tessa said. "I think Camille must have. It was—instinctive." She bit her lip. "Not that it matters, since it didn't work."

"We rarely use them. Etching runes into the metal of a gun or bullet prevents the gunpowder from igniting; no one knows why. Henry has tried to address the problem, of course, but not with any success. Since you can't kill a demon without a runed weapon or a seraph blade, guns aren't much use to us. Vampires die if you shoot them through the heart, admittedly, and werewolves can be injured if you have a silver bullet, but if you miss the vitals, they'll just come at you angrier than ever. Runed blades simply work better for our purposes. Get a vampire with a runed blade and it's much harder for them to recover and heal."

Tessa looked at him, her gaze steady. "Isn't it hard?"

Will tossed the damp cloth aside. It was scarlet with blood. "Isn't *what* hard?"

"Killing vampires," she said. "They may not be people, but they *look* like people. They feel as people do. They scream and bleed. Isn't it hard to slaughter them?"

Will's jaw tightened. "No," he said. "And if you really knew anything about them—"

"Camille feels," she said. "She loves and hates."

"And *she* is still alive. Everyone has choices, Tessa. Those vampires would not have been here tonight if they hadn't made theirs." He glanced down at Nathaniel, limp in Tessa's lap. "Nor, I imagine, would your brother have been."

"I don't know why de Quincey wanted him dead," Tessa said softly. "I don't know what he could have done to incur the wrath of vampires."

"Tessa!" It was Charlotte, darting up to Tessa and Will like a hummingbird. She still seemed so tiny, and so harmless, Tessa thought—despite the fighting gear she wore and the black Marks that laced her skin like curling snakes. "We've been given permission to bring your brother back to the Institute with us," she announced, gesturing at Nathaniel with a small hand. "The vampires may well have drugged him. He's certainly been bitten, and who knows what else? He could turn darkling—or worse, if we don't prevent it. In any case, I doubt they'll be able to help him in a mundane hospital. With us, at least the Silent Brothers can see to him, poor thing."

"Poor thing?" echoed Will rather rudely. "He rather got himself into this, didn't he? No one told him to run off and get himself involved with a bunch of Downworlders."

"Really, Will." Charlotte eyed him coldly. "Can't you have a little empathy?"

"Dear God," said Will, looking from Charlotte to Nate and

back again. "Is there anything that makes women sillier than the sight of a wounded young man?"

Tessa slitted her eyes at him. "You might want to clean the rest of the blood off your face before you continue arguing in *that* vein."

Will threw his arms up into the air and stalked off. Charlotte looked at Tessa, a half smile curving the side of her mouth. "I must say, I rather like the way you manage Will."

Tessa shook her head. "No one manages Will."

It was quickly decided that Tessa and Nathaniel would go with Henry and Charlotte in the town coach; Will and Jem would ride home in a smaller carriage borrowed from Charlotte's aunt, with Thomas as their driver. The Lightwoods and the rest of the Enclave would stay behind to search de Quincey's house, leaving no evidence of their battle for the mundanes to find in the morning. Will had wanted to stay and take part in the search, but Charlotte had been firm. He had ingested vampire blood and needed to return to the Institute as soon as possible to begin the cure.

Thomas, however, would not allow Will into the carriage as covered in blood as he was. After announcing that he would return in "half a tick," Thomas had gone off to find a damp piece of cloth. Will leaned against the side of the carriage, watching as the Enclave rushed in and out of de Quincey's house like ants, salvaging papers and furniture from the remains of the fire.

Returning with a soapy rag, Thomas handed it over to Will, and leaned his big frame against the side of the carriage. It rocked under his weight. Charlotte had always encouraged

Thomas to join Jem and Will for the physical parts of their training, and as the years had gone by, Thomas had grown from a scrawny child to a man so large and muscular that tailors despaired over his measurements. Will might have been the better fighter—his blood made him that—but Thomas's commanding physical presence was not easy to ignore.

Sometimes Will could not help remembering Thomas as he had first come to the Institute. He belonged to a family that had served the Nephilim for years, but he had been born so frail they'd thought he wouldn't live. When he'd reached twelve years of age, he'd been sent to the Institute; at that time he'd still been so small that he'd looked barely nine. Will had made fun of Charlotte for wanting to employ him, but had secretly hoped he would stay so that there might be another boy his own age in the house. And they had been friends of a sort, the Shadowhunter and the servant boy—until Jem had come and Will had forgotten Thomas almost completely. Thomas had never seemed to hold it against him, treating Will always with the same friendliness with which he treated everyone else.

"Always rum to see this sort of thing goin' on, and none of the neighbors out for so much as a gander," Thomas said now, glancing up and down the street. Charlotte had always demanded that the Institute servants speak "proper" English within its walls, and Thomas's East End accent tended to come and go depending on whether he remembered.

"There are heavy glamours at work here." Will scrubbed at his face and neck. "And I would imagine there are quite a few on this street who are not mundanes, who know to mind their own business when Shadowhunters are involved."

"Well, you are a terrifying lot, that's true," Thomas said, so equably that Will suspected he was being made fun of. Thomas pointed at Will's face. "You'll have a stunner of a mouse tomorrow, if you don't get an *iratze* on there."

"Maybe I *want* a black eye," said Will peevishly. "Did you think of that?"

Thomas just grinned and swung himself up into the driver's box at the front of the carriage. Will went back to scrubbing dried vampire blood off his hands and arms. The task was absorbing enough that he was able to almost completely ignore Gabriel Lightwood when the other boy appeared out of the shadows and sauntered over to Will, a superior smile plastered on his face.

"Nice work in there, Herondale, setting the place on fire," Gabriel observed. "Good thing we were there to clean up after you, or the whole plan would have gone down in flames, along with the shreds of your reputation."

"Are you implying that shreds of my reputation remain intact?" Will demanded with mock horror. "Clearly I have been doing something wrong. Or *not* doing something wrong, as the case may be." He banged on the side of the carriage. "Thomas! We must away at once to the nearest brothel! I seek scandal and low companionship."

Thomas snorted and muttered something that sounded like "bosh," which Will ignored.

Gabriel's face darkened. "Is there *anything* that isn't a joke to you?"

"Nothing that comes to mind."

"You know," Gabriel said, "there was a time I thought we could be friends, Will."

"There was a time I thought I was a ferret," Will said, "but that turned out to be the opium haze. Did you know it had that effect? Because I didn't."

"I think," Gabriel said, "that perhaps you might consider whether jokes about opium are either amusing or tasteful, given the . . . situation of your friend Carstairs."

Will froze. Still in the same tone of voice, he said, "You mean his disability?"

Gabriel blinked. "What?"

"That's what you called it. Back at the Institute. His 'disability.'" Will tossed the bloody cloth aside. "And you wonder why we aren't friends."

"I just wondered," Gabriel said, in a more subdued voice, "if perhaps you have ever had enough."

"Enough of what?"

"Enough of behaving as you do."

Will crossed his arms over his chest. His eyes glinted dangerously. "Oh, I can never get enough," he said. "Which, incidentally, is what your sister said to me when—"

The carriage door flew open. A hand shot out, grabbed Will by the back of the shirt, and hauled him inside. The door banged shut after him, and Thomas, sitting bolt upright, seized the reins of the horses. A moment later the carriage had lurched forth into the night, leaving Gabriel staring, infuriated, after it.

"What were you thinking?" Jem, having deposited Will onto the carriage seat opposite him, shook his head, his silvery eyes shining in the dimness. He held his cane between his knees, his hand resting lightly atop the dragon's-head carving. The cane had belonged to Jem's father, Will knew, and had been designed for him by a Shadowhunter weapons maker in

Beijing. "Baiting Gabriel Lightwood like that—why do you do it? What's the point?"

"You heard what he said about you—"

"I don't care what he says about me. It's what everyone thinks. He just has the nerve to say it." Jem leaned forward, resting his chin on his hand. "You know, I cannot function as your missing sense of self-preservation forever. Eventually you will have to learn to manage without me."

Will, as he always did, ignored this. "Gabriel Lightwood is hardly much of a threat."

"Then forget Gabriel. Is there a particular reason you keep biting vampires?"

Will touched the dried blood on his wrists, and smiled. "They don't expect it."

"Of course they don't. They know what happens when one of us consumes vampire blood. *They* probably expect you to have more sense."

"That expectation never seems to serve them very well, does it?"

"It hardly serves you, either." Jem looked at Will thoughtfully. He was the only one who never fell out of temper with Will. Whatever Will did, the most extreme reaction he seemed to be able to provoke in Jem was mild exasperation. "What happened in there? We were waiting for the signal—"

"Henry's bloody Phosphor didn't work. Instead of sending up a flare of light, it set the curtains on fire."

Jem made a choked noise.

Will glared at him. "It's not funny. I didn't know whether the rest of you were going to show up or not."

"Did you really think we wouldn't come after you when the

whole place went up like a torch?" Jem asked reasonably. "They could have been roasting you over a spit, for all we knew."

"And Tessa, the silly creature, was supposed to be out the door with Magnus, but she wouldn't leave—"

"Her brother *was* manacled to a chair in the room," Jem pointed out. "I'm not sure I would have left either."

"I see you're determined to miss my point."

"If your point is that there was a pretty girl in the room and it was distracting you, then I think I've taken your point handily."

"You think she's pretty?" Will was surprised; Jem rarely opined on this sort of thing.

"Yes, and you do too."

"I hadn't noticed, really."

"Yes, you have, and I've noticed you noticing." Jem was smiling. Despite the stress of the battle, he looked healthy tonight. There was color in his cheeks, and his eyes were a dark and steady silver. There were times, when the illness was at its worst, when all the color drained even from his eyes, leaving them horribly pale, nearly white, with that black speck of pupil in the center like a speck of black ash on snow. It was times like that when he also became delirious. Will had held Jem down while he'd thrashed about and cried out in another language and his eyes had rolled back into his head, and every time it happened, Will thought that this was it, and Jem was really going to die this time. He sometimes then thought about what he would do afterward, but he couldn't imagine it, any more than he could look back and remember his life before he had come to the Institute. Neither bore thinking about for very long.

But then there were other times, like this, when he looked at Jem and saw no mark of illness on him, and wondered what it would be like in a world where Jem was not dying. And that did not bear thinking about either. It was a terrible black place in himself that the fear came from, a dark voice he could only silence with anger, risk, and pain.

"Will." Jem's voice cut into Will's unpleasant reverie. "Have you heard a single word I've said in the past five minutes?"

"Not really."

"We needn't talk about Tessa if you don't want to, you know."

"It's not Tessa." This was true. Will hadn't been thinking about Tessa. He was getting good at not thinking about her, really; all it took was determination and practice. "One of the vampires had a human servant who rushed me. I killed him," said Will. "Without even thinking about it. He was just a stupid human boy, and I killed him."

"He was a darkling," said Jem. "He was Turning. It would have been a matter of time."

"He was just a boy," Will said again. He turned his face toward the window, though the brightness of the witchlight in the carriage meant that all he could see was his own face, reflected back at him. "I'm going to get drunk when we get home," he added. "I think I'm going to have to."

"No, you won't," said Jem. "You know exactly what will happen when we get home."

Because he was right, Will scowled.

Ahead of Will and Jem, in the first carriage, Tessa sat on the velvet bench seat across from Henry and Charlotte; they were talking in murmurs about the night and how it had gone.

Tessa let the words wash over her, barely caring. Only two Shadowhunters had been killed, but de Quincey's escape was a disaster, and Charlotte was worried that the Enclave would be angry with her. Henry made soothing noises, but Charlotte seemed inconsolable. Tessa would have felt bad for her, if she'd had the energy to feel much at all.

Nathaniel lay across Tessa, his head in her lap. She bent over him, stroking his filthy matted hair with her gloved fingers. "Nate," she said, so softly that she hoped Charlotte couldn't hear her. "It's all right now. Everything's all right."

Nathaniel's lashes fluttered and his eyes opened. His hand came up—the fingernails broken, his joints swollen and twisted—and he took tight hold of her hand, lacing his fingers through hers. "Don't go," he said thickly. His eyes fluttered shut again; he was clearly drifting in and out of consciousness, if he was really conscious at all. "Tessie—stay."

No one else ever called her that; she shut her eyes, willing the tears back. She did not want Charlotte—or any Shadowhunter—to see her cry.

12

Blood and Water

I dare not always touch her, lest the kiss
Leave my lips charred. Yea, Lord, a little bliss,
Brief bitter bliss, one hath for a great sin;
Nathless thou knowest how sweet a thing it is.
–Algernon Charles Swinburne, "Laus Veneris"

When they reached the Institute, Sophie and Agatha were waiting at the open doors with lanterns. Tessa stumbled with tiredness as she left the carriage, and was surprised—and grateful—when Sophie came to help her up the steps. Charlotte and Henry half-carried Nathaniel. Behind them the carriage with Will and Jem in it rattled through the gates, Thomas's voice carrying on the cool night air as he called out a greeting.

Jessamine, not to Tessa's surprise, was nowhere to be seen.

They installed Nathaniel in a bedroom much like Tessa's—

the same dark heavy wood furniture, the same grand bed and wardrobe. As Charlotte and Agatha settled Nathaniel into the bed, Tessa sank into the chair beside it, half-feverish with worry and exhaustion. Voices—soft sickroom voices—swirled around her. She heard Charlotte say something about the Silent Brothers, and Henry answered in a subdued voice. At some point Sophie appeared at her elbow and urged her to drink something hot and sweet-sour that brought energy slowly flooding back into her veins. Soon enough she was able to sit up and look around her a bit, and she realized to her surprise that except for herself and her brother, the room was empty. Everyone had gone.

She glanced down at Nathaniel. He lay corpse-still, his face lividly bruised, his matted hair tangled against the pillows. Tessa could not help but recall with a pang the beautifully dressed brother of her memories, his fair hair always so carefully brushed and arranged, shoes and cuffs spotless. This Nathaniel did not look like someone who had ever spun his sister around the living room in a dance, humming to himself under his breath for the sheer joy of being alive.

She leaned forward, meaning to look more closely at his face, and saw a flicker of movement out of the corner of her eye. Turning her head, she saw it was only herself, reflected in the mirror on the far wall. In Camille's dress, she looked to her own eyes like a child playing dress-up. She was too slight for the sophisticated style of it. She looked like a child—a silly child. No wonder Will had—

"Tessie?" Nathaniel's voice, weak and frail, broke her instantly out of her thoughts of Will. "Tessie, don't leave me. I think I'm ill."

"Nate." She reached for his hand, seized it between her gloved palms. "You're all right. You'll be all right. They've sent for doctors. . . ."

"Who are 'they'?" His voice was a thin cry. "Where are we? I don't know this place."

"This is the Institute. You'll be safe here."

Nathaniel blinked. There were dark rings, almost black, around each of his eyes, and his lips were crusted with what looked like dried blood. His eyes wandered from side to side, not fixing on anything. "Shadowhunters." He sighed the word on an exhale of breath. "I didn't think they really existed. . . . The Magister," Nathaniel whispered suddenly, and Tessa's nerves jumped. "He said they were the Law. He said they were to be feared. But there is no law in this world. There is no punishment—just killing or being killed." His voice rose. "Tessie, I'm so sorry—about everything—"

"The Magister. Do you mean de Quincey?" Tessa demanded, but Nate made a choking sound then, and stared behind her with a look of terrible fear. Releasing his hand, Tessa turned to see what he was staring at.

Charlotte had come into the room almost noiselessly. She was still wearing her men's clothes, though she had thrown an old-fashioned long cloak on over them, with a double clasp at the throat. She looked very small, in part because Brother Enoch stood beside her, casting a vast shadow across the floor. He wore the same parchment robes he had before, though now his staff was black, its head carved in the shape of dark wings. His hood was up, casting his face in shadow.

"Tessa," Charlotte said. "You remember Brother Enoch. He is here to help Nathaniel."

With an animal howl of terror, Nate caught at Tessa's wrist. She looked down at him in bewilderment. "Nathaniel? What's wrong?"

"De Quincey told me about them," Nathaniel gasped. "The Gregori—the Silent Brothers. They can kill a man with a thought." He shuddered. "Tessa." His voice was a whisper. "Look at his *face*."

Tessa looked. While she had been talking to her brother, Brother Enoch had soundlessly drawn back his hood. The smooth pits of his eyes reflected the witchlight, the glare unforgiving on the red, scarred stitching around his mouth.

Charlotte took a step forward. "If Brother Enoch might examine Mr. Gray—"

"No!" Tessa cried. Wrenching her arm from Nate's grasp, she put herself between her brother and the other two occupants of the room. "Don't touch him."

Charlotte paused, looking troubled. "The Silent Brothers are our best healers. Without Brother Enoch, Nathaniel . . ." Her voice trailed off. "Well, there isn't much we can do for him."

Miss Gray.

It took her a moment to realize that the word, her name, hadn't been spoken out loud. Instead, like a snatch of a half-forgotten song, it had echoed inside her own head—but not in the voice of her own thoughts. This thought was alien, inimical—*other*. Brother Enoch's voice. It was the way he had spoken to her as he had left the room on her first day at the Institute.

It is interesting, Miss Gray, Brother Enoch went on, *that you are a Downworlder, and yet your brother is not. How did such a thing come to pass?*

Tessa went still. "You—you can tell that just by looking at him?"

"Tessie!" Nathaniel pushed himself upright against the pillows, his pale face flushed. "What are you doing, talking to the Gregori? He's dangerous!"

"It's all right, Nate," Tessa said, not taking her eyes off Brother Enoch. She knew she ought to be frightened, but what she really felt was a stab of disappointment. "You mean there's nothing unusual about Nate?" she asked, in a low voice. "Nothing supernatural?"

Nothing at all, said the Silent Brother.

Tessa hadn't realized how much she was half-hoping that her brother was like her until this moment. Disappointment sharpened her voice. "I don't suppose, since you know so much, that you know what I am? Am I a warlock?"

I cannot tell you. There is that about you that marks you as one of Lilith's Children. Yet there is no demon's sign on you.

"I did notice that," Charlotte said, and Tessa realized that she could hear Brother Enoch's voice as well. "I thought perhaps she wasn't a warlock. Some humans are born with some slight power, like the Sight. Or she could have faerie blood—"

She isn't human. She is something else. I will study on it. Perhaps there is something in the archives to guide me. Eyeless as he was, Brother Enoch seemed to be searching Tessa's face with his gaze. *There is a power I sense you have. A power no other warlock does.*

"The Changing, you mean," said Tessa.

No. I do not mean that.

"Then what?" Tessa was astonished. "What could I—?" She broke off at a noise from Nathaniel. Turning, she saw that he had fought free of his blankets and was lying half-off the bed, as if he'd attempted to get up; his face was sweaty and deathly white. Guilt stabbed at her. She'd been caught up in what Brother Enoch had been saying and had forgotten her brother.

She darted to the bed, and with Charlotte's assistance she wrestled Nate back onto the pillows, pulling the blanket up around him. He seemed much worse than he had been moments before. As Tessa tucked the blanket around him, he caught at her wrist again, his eyes wild. "Does he know?" he demanded. "Does he know where I am?"

"Who do you mean? De Quincey?"

"Tessie." He squeezed her wrist tightly, pulling her down to hiss a whisper into her ear. "You must forgive me. He told me you would be the queen of them all. He said they were going to kill me. I don't want to die, Tessie. I don't *want* to die."

"Of course not," she soothed, but he didn't seem to hear her. His eyes, fixed on her face, went suddenly wide, and he screamed.

"Keep it away from me! Keep it away from me!" he howled. He pushed at her, thrashing his head back and forth on the pillows. "Dear God, don't let it touch me!"

Frightened, Tessa snatched her hand back, turning to Charlotte—but Charlotte had moved away from the bed, and Brother Enoch stood in her place, his eyeless face immobile. *You must let me help your brother. Or he will likely die*, he said.

"What is he raving about?" Tessa demanded wretchedly. "What's wrong with him?"

The vampires gave him a drug, to keep him calm while they fed. If he is not cured, the drug will drive him mad and then kill him. Already he has begun to hallucinate.

"It's not my fault!" Nathaniel shrieked. "I had no choice! It's not my fault!" He turned his face toward Tessa; she saw to her horror that his eyes had gone entirely black, like an insect's eyes. She gasped, backing away.

"Help him. Please help him." She caught at Brother Enoch's sleeve, and immediately regretted it; the arm beneath the sleeve was as hard as marble, and freezing to the touch. She dropped her hand in horror, but the Silent Brother did not seem to even notice her presence. He had stepped past her, and now put his scarred fingers against Nathaniel's forehead. Nathaniel sank back against the pillows, his eyes closing.

You must leave. Brother Enoch spoke without turning from the bed. *Your presence will only slow his healing.*

"But Nate asked me to stay—"

Go. The voice in Tessa's mind was icy.

Tessa looked at her brother; he was still against the pillows, his face gone slack. She turned toward Charlotte, meaning to protest, but Charlotte met her glance with a small shake of the head. Her eyes were sympathetic, but unyielding. "As soon as your brother's condition changes, I will find you. I promise."

Tessa looked at Brother Enoch. He had opened the pouch at his waist and was setting objects down on the bedside table, slowly and methodically. Glass vials of powder and liquid, bunches of dried plants, sticks of some black substance like soft coal. "If anything happens to Nate," Tessa said, "I shall never forgive you. Never."

It was like speaking to a statue. Brother Enoch did not respond to her with so much as a twitch.

Tessa fled from the room.

After the dimness of Nate's sickroom, the brightness of the sconces in the corridor stung Tessa's eyes. She leaned against the wall by the door, willing her tears back. It was the second time that evening she had nearly cried, and she was annoyed with herself. Clenching her right hand into a fist, she slammed it against the wall behind her, hard, sending a shock wave of pain up her arm. *That* cleared the tears, and her head.

"That looked like it hurt."

Tessa turned. Jem had come up behind her in the corridor, as silent as a cat. He had changed out of his gear. He wore loose dark trousers tied at the waist, and a white shirt only a few shades lighter than his skin. His fine bright hair was damp, curling against his temples and the nape of his neck.

"It did." Tessa cradled her hand against her chest. The glove she wore had softened the blow, but her knuckles still ached.

"Your brother," Jem said. "Is he going to be all right?"

"I don't know. He's in there with one of those—those monk creatures."

"Brother Enoch." Jem regarded her with sympathetic eyes. "I know how the Silent Brothers look, but they're really very good doctors. They set great store by healing and medicinal arts. They live a long time, and know a great deal."

"It hardly seems worth living a long time if you're going to look like *that*."

The corner of Jem's mouth twitched. "I suppose it depends on what you're living for." He looked at her more closely. There was something about the *way* Jem looked at her, she thought. Like he could see into and through her. But nothing inside her, nothing he saw or heard, could bother or upset or disappoint him.

"Brother Enoch," she said suddenly. "Do you know what he

said? He told me that Nate isn't like me. He's fully human. No special powers at all."

"And that upsets you?"

"I don't know. On the one hand I wouldn't wish this—this *thing* I am—on him, or anyone. But if he isn't like me, then it means he isn't completely my brother. He's my parents' son. But whose daughter am I?"

"You can't concern yourself with that. Certainly it would be wonderful if we all knew exactly who we were. But that knowledge doesn't come from outside, but from inside. '*Know thyself*,' as the oracle says." Jem grinned. "My apologies if that sounds like sophistry. I'm only telling you what I've learned from my own experience."

"But I *don't* know myself." Tessa shook her head. "I'm sorry. After the way you fought at de Quincey's, you must think I'm a terrible coward, crying because my brother *isn't* a monster and I don't have the courage to be a monster all by myself."

"You're not a monster," said Jem. "Or a coward. On the contrary, I was quite impressed by the way you shot at de Quincey. You would almost certainly have killed him if there'd been any more bullets in the gun."

"Yes, I think I would have. I *wanted* to kill them all."

"That's what Camille asked us to do, you know. *Kill them all.* Perhaps it was her emotions you were feeling?"

"But Camille has no reason to care about Nate, or what happens to him, and that was when I felt most murderous. When I saw Nate there, when I realized what they were planning to do—" She took a shuddering breath. "I don't know how much of that was me and how much was Camille. And I don't even know if it's right to have those sort of feelings—"

"You mean," asked Jem, "for a girl to have those feelings?"

"For anyone to have them, maybe—I don't know. Maybe I mean for a girl to have them."

Jem seemed to look through her then, as if he were seeing something beyond her, beyond the corridor, beyond the Institute itself. "Whatever you are physically," he said, "male or female, strong or weak, ill or healthy—all those things matter less than what your heart contains. If you have the soul of a warrior, you are a warrior. Whatever the color, the shape, the design of the shade that conceals it, the flame inside the lamp remains the same. *You* are that flame." He smiled then, seeming to have come back to himself, slightly embarrassed. "That's what I believe."

Before Tessa could reply, Nate's door opened, and Charlotte came out. She responded to Tessa's questioning look with an exhausted-looking nod. "Brother Enoch has helped your brother a great deal," she said, "but there is much left to be done, and it will be morning before we know more. I suggest you go to sleep, Tessa. Exhausting yourself won't help Nathaniel."

With an effort of will Tessa forced herself simply to nod, and not to fling herself at Charlotte with a barrage of questions she knew she wouldn't get answers to.

"And Jem." Charlotte turned to him. "If I could talk to you for a few moments? Will you walk with me to the library?"

Jem nodded. "Of course." He smiled at Tessa, inclining his head. "Tomorrow, then," he said, and followed Charlotte down the corridor.

The moment they vanished around the corner, Tessa tried the door of Nate's room. It was locked. With a sigh she turned and headed the other way down the corridor. Perhaps Charlotte was right. Perhaps she ought to get some sleep.

Halfway down the corridor she heard a commotion. Sophie, a metal pail in each of her hands, suddenly appeared in the hallway, banging a door shut behind her. She looked livid. "His Highness is in a particularly fine temper this evening," she announced as Tessa approached. "He threw a pail at my head, he did."

"Who?" Tessa asked, and then realized. "Oh, you mean Will. Is he all right?"

"Well enough to throw pails," Sophie said crossly. "And to call me a nasty name. I don't know what it meant. I think it was in French, and that usually means someone's calling you a whore." She tightened her lips. "I'd best run and get Mrs. Branwell. Maybe *she* can get him to take the cure, if I can't."

"The cure?"

"He must drink this." Sophie thrust a pail toward Tessa; Tessa couldn't quite see what was in it, but it looked like ordinary water. "He *has* to. Or I wouldn't like to say as what'll happen."

A mad impulse took hold of Tessa. "*I'll* get him to do it. Where is he?"

"Upstairs, in the attic." Sophie's eyes were large. "But I wouldn't if I was you, miss. He's downright nasty when he's like this."

"I don't care," Tessa said, reaching for the pail. Sophie handed it to her with a look of relief and apprehension. It was surprisingly heavy, filled to the brim with water and slopping over. "Will Herondale needs to learn to take his medicine like a man," Tessa added, and pushed open the door to the attic,

Sophie looking after her with an expression that clearly said she thought Tessa had gone out of her head.

Beyond the door was a narrow flight of stairs going up. She held the pail in front of her as she went; it slopped water onto the bodice of her dress, raising goose bumps on her skin. By the time she had reached the top of the steps, she was damp and breathless.

There was no door at the head of the stairs; they ended abruptly at the attic, a huge room whose roof was so steeply gabled that it gave the impression of being low-ceilinged. Rafters just above Tessa's head ran the length of the room, and there were very low square windows set at intervals in the walls, through which Tessa could see the gray dawn light. The floor was bare polished boards. There was no furniture at all, and no light beyond the pale illumination that came from the windows. A set of even narrower stairs led to a closed trapdoor in the ceiling.

In the center of the room lay Will, barefoot, flat on his back on the floor. A number of pails surrounded him—and the floor around him, Tessa saw as she approached, was soaked with water. Water ran in rivulets down the boards and pooled in the uneven hollows of the floor. Some of the water was tinged reddish, as if it had been mixed with blood.

Will had an arm thrown over his face, hiding his eyes. He was not lying still, but moving restlessly, as if he were in some pain. As Tessa neared, he said something in a low voice, something that sounded like a name. *Cecily*, Tessa thought. Yes, it sounded very much as if he had said the name Cecily.

"Will?" she said. "Who are you talking to?"

"Back, are you, Sophie?" Will replied without raising his

head. "I told you if you brought me another one of those infernal pails, I'd—"

"It's not Sophie," Tessa said. "It's me. Tessa."

For a moment Will was silent—and motionless, save for the rise and fall of his chest as he breathed. He wore only a pair of dark trousers and a white shirt, and like the floor around him, he was soaking wet. The fabric of his clothes clung to him, and his black hair was pasted to his head like wet cloth. He must have been freezing cold.

"They sent *you*?" he said finally. He sounded incredulous, and something else, too.

"Yes," answered Tessa, though this was not strictly true.

Will opened his eyes and turned his head toward her. Even in the dimness she could see the intensity of his eye color. "Very well, then. Leave the water and go."

Tessa glanced down at the pail. For some reason her hands did not seem to want to let go of the metal handle. "What is it, then? I mean to say—what am I bringing you, exactly?"

"They didn't tell you?" He blinked at her in surprise. "It's holy water. To burn out what's in me."

It was Tessa's turn to blink. "You mean—"

"I keep forgetting everything you don't know," Will said. "Do you recall earlier this evening when I bit de Quincey? Well, I swallowed some of his blood. Not much, but it doesn't take much to do it."

"To do what?"

"To turn you into a vampire."

At that, Tessa nearly did drop the pail. "You're turning into a *vampire?*"

Will grinned at that, propping himself up on one elbow.

"Don't alarm yourself unduly. It requires days for the transformation to occur, and even then, I would have to die before it took hold. What the blood *would* do is make me irresistibly drawn to vampires—drawn to them in the hopes that they'd make me one of them. Like their human subjugates."

"And the holy water . . ."

"Counteracts the effects of the blood. I must keep drinking it. It makes me sick, of course—makes me cough up the blood and everything else in me."

"Good Lord." Tessa thrust the pail toward him with a grimace. "I suppose I had better give it to you, then."

"I suppose you had." Will sat up, and put his hands out to take the pail from her. He scowled down at the contents, then held it up and tipped it toward his mouth. After swallowing a few mouthfuls, he grimaced and dumped the rest unceremoniously over his head. Finished, he tossed the bucket aside.

"Does that help?" Tessa asked with honest curiosity. "Pouring it over your head like that?"

Will made a strangled noise that was only somewhat of a laugh. "The questions you ask . . ." He shook his head, flinging droplets of water from his hair onto Tessa's clothes. Water soaked the collar and front of his white shirt, turning it transparent. The way it clung to him, showing the lines of him underneath—the ridges of hard muscle, the sharp line of collarbone, the Marks burning through like black fire—it made Tessa think of the way one might lay thin paper down over a brass engraving, brushing charcoal over it to bring the shape through. She swallowed, hard. "The blood makes me feverish, makes my skin burn," Will said. "I can't get cool. But, yes, the water helps."

Tessa just stared at him. When he had come into her room at the Dark House, she had thought he was the most beautiful boy she'd ever seen, but just now, looking at him—she had never looked at a boy like that, not in this way that brought blood hot to her face, and tightened her chest. More than anything else she wanted to touch him, to touch his wet hair, to see if his arms, corded with muscle, were as hard as they looked, or if his callused palms were rough. To put her cheek against his, and feel his eyelashes brush her skin. Such long lashes . . .

"Will," she said, and her voice sounded thin to her own ears. "Will, I want to ask you . . ."

He looked up at her. The water made his lashes cling to one another, so that they formed starlike sharp points. "What?"

"You act like you don't care about anything," she said on an exhale of breath. She felt as if she had been running, and had crested a hill and was racing down the other side, and there was no stopping now. Gravity was taking her where she had to go. "But—everyone cares about *something*. Don't they?"

"Do they?" Will said softly. When she didn't answer, he leaned back on his hands. "Tess," he said. "Come over here and sit by me."

She did. It was cold and damp on the floor, but she sat, gathering her skirts up around her so only the tips of her boots showed. She looked at Will; they were very close together, facing each other. His profile in the gray light was cold and clean; only his mouth had any softness.

"You never laugh," she said. "You behave as if everything is funny to you, but you never laugh. Sometimes you smile when you think no one is paying attention."

For a moment he was silent. Then, "You," he said, half-reluctantly. "You make me laugh. From the moment you hit me with that bottle."

"It was a jug," she said automatically.

His lips quirked up at the corners. "Not to mention the way that you always correct me. With that funny look on your face when you do it. And the way you shouted at Gabriel Lightwood. And even the way you talked back to de Quincey. You make me . . ." He broke off, looking at her, and she wondered if she looked the way she felt—stunned and breathless. "Let me see your hands," he said suddenly. "Tessa?"

She gave them to him, palms up, hardly looking at them herself. She could not look away from his face.

"There's still blood," he told her. "On your gloves." And, looking down, she saw it was true. She had not taken off Camille's white leather gloves, and they were streaked with blood and dirt, shredded near the fingertips where she had pried at Nate's manacles.

"Oh," she said, and began to draw her hands back, meaning to take the gloves off, but Will let go of only her left hand. He continued to hold the right one, lightly, by the wrist. There was a heavy silver ring on his right index finger, she saw, carved with a delicate design of birds in flight. His head was bent, his damp black hair falling forward; she couldn't see his face. He brushed his fingers lightly over the surface of the glove. There were four pearl buttons fastening it closed at the wrist, and as he ran his fingertips over them, they sprang open and the pad of his thumb brushed against the bare skin of her inner wrist, where the blue veins pulsed.

She nearly jumped out of her skin. "*Will.*"

"Tessa," he said. "What do you want from me?"

He was still stroking the inside of her wrist, his touch doing odd delicious things to her skin and nerves. Her voice shook when she spoke. "I—I want to understand you."

He looked up at her, through his lashes. "Is that really necessary?"

"I don't know," Tessa said. "I'm not sure anyone *does* understand you, except possibly Jem."

"Jem doesn't understand me," Will said. "He cares for me—like a brother might. It's not the same thing."

"Don't you *want* him to understand you?"

"Dear God, no," he said. "Why should he need to know my reasons for living my life as I do?"

"Maybe," Tessa said, "he simply wants to know that there *is* a reason."

"Does it matter?" Will asked softly, and with a swift motion he slipped her glove entirely off her hand. The chilly air of the room struck the bare skin of her fingers with a shock, and a shiver passed over Tessa's entire body, as if she had found herself suddenly naked in the cold. "Do reasons matter when there's nothing that can be done to change things?"

Tessa reached for an answer, and found none. She was shivering, almost too hard to speak.

"Are you cold?" Lacing his fingers with hers, Will took her hand and pressed it to his cheek. She was startled by the feverish heat of his skin. "Tess," he said, his voice thick and soft with desire, and she leaned toward him, swaying like a tree whose branches were weighted by snow. Her whole body ached; *she* ached, as if there were a terrible hollow emptiness inside her. She was more conscious of Will than she had ever been of anything or anyone else in her life, of the faint shine of blue beneath his half-closed lids, of the shadow of light stubble across his jaw where he hadn't shaved, of faint white scars that dotted the skin of his shoulders and throat—and more than anything else of his mouth, the crescent shape of it, the slight dent in the center of his bottom lip. When he leaned toward her and brushed his lips across hers, she reached for him as if she would otherwise drown.

For a moment their mouths pressed hotly together, Will's free hand tangling in her hair. Tessa gasped when his arms went around her, her skirts snagging on the floor as he pulled her hard against him. She put her hands lightly around his neck; his skin was burning hot to the touch. Through the thin wet material of his shirt, she could feel the muscles of his shoulders, hard and smooth. His fingers found her jeweled hair clasp and pulled at it, and her hair spilled down around her shoulders, the comb rattling to the floor, and Tessa gave a little cry of surprise against his mouth. And then, without warning, he ripped his hands from her and pushed hard against her shoulders, shoving her away from him with such force that she nearly fell backward, and only stopped herself awkwardly, her hands braced on the floor behind her.

She sat with her hair hanging down around her like a tangled curtain, staring at him in amazement. Will was on his knees, his chest hitching up and down as if he had been running incredibly fast and far. He was pale, except for two fever splotches of red across his cheeks. "God in Heaven," he whispered. "What was that?"

Tessa felt her cheeks turn scarlet. Wasn't Will the one who

was supposed to know exactly what *that* was, and wasn't she the one who was supposed to have pushed him away?

"I *can't*." His hands were fists at his sides; she could see them trembling. "Tessa, I think you had better go."

"*Go?*" Her mind whirled; she felt as if she had been in a warm, safe place and without warning had been cast out into a freezing, empty darkness. "I . . . I should not have been so forward. I'm sorry—"

A look of intense pain flashed across his face. "God. Tessa." The words seemed dragged out of him. "Please. Just leave. I can't have you here. It's—not possible."

"Will, please—"

"*No.*" He jerked his gaze away from hers, averting his face, his eyes fixed on the floor. "I'll tell you anything you want to know tomorrow. Anything. Just leave me alone now." His voice broke unevenly. "Tessa. I'm begging you. Do you understand? I'm *begging you*. Please, *please* leave."

"Very well," Tessa said, and saw with a mixture of amazement and pain that the lines of tension went out of his shoulders. Was it that much of a horror having her there, and that much of a relief that she was leaving? She rose to her feet, her dress damp and cold and heavy, her feet nearly slipping on the wet floor. Will didn't move or look up, but stayed where he was on his knees, staring at the ground as Tessa made her way across the room and down the stairs, without looking back.

Some time later, her room half-lit with the wan glow of the London sunrise, Tessa lay on the bed, too exhausted to change out of Camille's clothes—too exhausted, even, to sleep. It had been a day of firsts. The first time she had used her power at her own wish and discretion, and had felt good about it. The first time she had fired a pistol. And—the only first she had ever dreamed of, for years—her first kiss.

Tessa rolled over, burying her face in the pillow. For so many years she had wondered what her first kiss would be like—if he would be handsome, if he would love her, if he would be kind. She had never imagined that the kiss would be so brief and desperate and wild. Or that it would taste of holy water. Holy water and blood.

13

SOMETHING DARK

Sometimes we are less unhappy in being deceived by those we love, than in being undeceived by them.
—François La Rochefoucauld, *Maxims*

Tessa woke the next day to Sophie lighting the lamp by her bedside. With a moan Tessa made a move to cover her aching eyes.

"Now, then, miss." Sophie addressed Tessa with her usual briskness. "You've gone and slept the day away. It's past eight o'clock in the evening, and Charlotte said to wake you."

"Past eight? At *night*?" Tessa threw back her blankets, only to realize, to her surprise, that she was still wearing Camille's gown, now crushed and crumpled, not to mention stained. She must have collapsed into bed still entirely dressed. Memories of the night before began to flood into her mind—the white faces of vampires, the fire eating its way up the curtains, Magnus Bane laughing, de Quincey, Nathaniel, and Will. *Oh, God,* she thought. *Will.*

She pushed the thought of him from her mind and sat up, looking anxiously at Sophie. "My brother," she said. "Is he . . ."

Sophie's smile wavered. "No worse, really, but no better, either." Seeing Tessa's stricken expression, she said, "A hot bath and food, miss, that's what you need. It won't make your brother any better for you to starve and let yourself get filthy."

Tessa looked down at herself. Camille's dress was ruined, that was evident—torn and stained with blood and ash in a dozen places. Her silk stockings were ripped, her feet filthy, her hands and arms streaked with grime. She hesitated to think about the state of her hair. "I suppose you're right."

The bathtub was an oval claw-footed affair hidden behind a Japanese screen in a corner of the room. Sophie had filled it with hot water that was already beginning to cool. Tessa slid behind the screen, undressed, and lowered herself into the bath. The hot water came up to her shoulders, warming her. For a moment she sat motionless, letting the heat soak into her chilled bones. Slowly she began to relax, and closed her eyes—

Memories of Will flooded in on her. Will, the attic, the way he had touched her hand. The way he had kissed her, then ordered her away.

She ducked under the surface of the water as if she could hide from the humiliating memory. It didn't work. *Drowning yourself won't help,* she told herself sternly. *Now, drowning Will, on the other hand . . .* She sat up, reached for the cake of lavender soap on the edge of the bath, and scrubbed her skin and hair with it until the water turned black with ash and dirt. Perhaps it wasn't actually possible to scrub away your thoughts of someone, but she could try.

Sophie was waiting for Tessa when she emerged from behind the screen. There was a tray of sandwiches and tea at the ready. In front of the mirror, she helped Tessa dress in her yellow gown trimmed with dark braid; it was fussier than Tessa would have preferred, but Jessamine had liked the design very much in the shop and had insisted that Tessa have it made for her. *I can't wear yellow, but it's ever so suitable for girls with dull brown hair like yours*, she'd said.

The feeling of the brush going through her hair was very pleasant; it reminded Tessa of when she had been a small girl and Aunt Harriet had brushed her hair for her. It was soothing enough that when Sophie spoke next, it jolted her slightly.

"Did you manage to get Mr. Herondale to take his medicine last night, miss?"

"Oh, I—" Tessa scrambled to collect herself, but it was too late; scarlet color had flooded up her neck into her face. "He didn't want to," she finished lamely. "But I convinced him in the end."

"I see." Sophie's expression didn't change, but the rhythmic strokes of the brush through Tessa's hair began to come faster. "I know it's not my place, but—"

"Sophie, you can say anything you want to me, truly."

"It's just—Master Will." Sophie's words came out in a rush. "He isn't someone you should care for, Miss Tessa. Not like that. He isn't to be trusted, or relied on. He—he isn't what you think he is."

Tessa clasped her hands in her lap. She felt a vague sense of unreality. Had things really gone so far that she needed to be warned off Will? And yet it was good to have someone to talk to about him. She felt a bit like a starving person being offered food. "I don't know what I think he is, Sophie. He's like one thing sometimes, and then he can change completely, like the wind changing, and I don't know why, or what's happened—"

"Nothing. Nothing's happened. He just doesn't care about anyone but himself."

"He cares about Jem," Tessa said quietly.

The brush went still; Sophie had paused, frozen. There was something she wanted to say, Tessa thought, something she was holding herself back from saying. But what was it?

The brush began to move again. "That's not enough, though."

"You mean that I shouldn't wring my heart out over some boy who will never care for me—"

"No!" Sophie said. "There are worse things than that. It's all right to love someone who doesn't love you back, as long as they're worth you loving them. As long as they *deserve* it."

The passion in Sophie's voice surprised Tessa. She twisted around to look at the other girl. "Sophie, is there someone you care for? Is it Thomas?"

Sophie looked astonished. "*Thomas?* No. What ever gave you that idea?"

"Well, because I think he cares for you," Tessa said. "I've seen him looking at you. He watches you when you're in the room. I suppose I thought . . ."

Her voice trailed off at Sophie's flabbergasted look.

"Thomas?" Sophie said again. "No, that couldn't be. I'm sure he hasn't any such thoughts about me."

Tessa didn't move to contradict her; clearly, whatever

feelings Thomas might have had, Sophie didn't return them. Which left . . .

"Will?" Tessa said. "Do you mean you cared for Will once?" *Which would explain the bitterness and the dislike,* she thought, considering how Will treated girls who fancied him.

"*Will?*" Sophie sounded absolutely horrified—horrified enough to forget to call Will Mr. Herondale. "Are you asking me if I was ever in love with *him?*"

"Well, I thought— I mean, he's awfully handsome." Tessa realized she sounded rather feeble.

"There's more to someone being lovable than the way they *look.* My last employer," Sophie said, her careful accent slipping with her excitement as she spoke, so that "last" sounded more like "larst," "he was always off on safari in Africa and India, shooting tigers and things. And he told me that the way you can tell if a bug or a snake is poisonous, like, is if it's got really lovely, bright markings. The more beautiful its skin is, the more deadly it is. That's what Will's like. All that pretty face and whatnot just hides how twisted up and rotten he is on the inside."

"Sophie, I don't know—"

"There's something dark in him," Sophie said. "Something black and dark that he's hiding. He's got some sort of secret, the kind that eats you up inside." She set the silver-haired brush down on the vanity, and Tessa saw with surprise that her hand was shaking. "You mark my words."

After Sophie left, Tessa took the clockwork angel from her bedside table and strung it around her neck. As it settled against her chest, she felt immediately reassured. She had missed it while she'd been disguised as Camille. Its presence was a comfort, and—though it was foolish, she knew—she thought perhaps that if she visited Nate while wearing it, he might feel its presence and be reassured as well.

She kept her hand on it as she shut the bedroom door behind her, made her way down the corridor, and knocked on his door softly. When there was no answer, she took hold of the knob and pushed the door open. The curtains in the room were drawn back, the room half-filled with light, and she could see Nate asleep on his back against a mound of pillows. He had one arm flung across his forehead, and his cheeks were bright with fever.

He wasn't alone, either. In the armchair by the head of the bed sat Jessamine, a book open on her lap. She met Tessa's surprised look with a cool and level stare.

"I—," Tessa began, and collected herself. "What are you doing here?"

"I thought I would read to your brother for a while," Jessamine said. "Everyone's been asleep half the day, and he was being cruelly neglected. Just Sophie checking in on him, and you can't count on *her* for decent conversation."

"Nate's unconscious, Jessamine; he doesn't *want* conversation."

"You can't be sure," Jessamine said. "I've heard that people can hear what you say to them even if they're quite unconscious, or even dead."

"He's not *dead*, either."

"Certainly not." Jessamine gave him a lingering look. "He's far too handsome to die. Is he married, Tessa? Or is there a girl back in New York who has a claim on him?"

"On *Nate*?" Tessa stared. There had always been girls, all sorts of girls, who'd been interested in Nate, but he had the attention span of a butterfly. "Jessamine, he isn't even conscious. Now is hardly the time—"

"He'll get better," Jessamine announced. "And when he does, he'll know I'm the one who nursed him back to health. Men always fall in love with the woman who nurses them back to health. 'When pain and anguish wring the brow, / A ministering angel thou!'" she finished, with a self-satisfied smirk. Seeing Tessa's horrified look, she scowled. "What's wrong? Am I not good enough for your precious brother?"

"He doesn't have any money, Jessie—"

"I have enough money for both of us. I just need someone to take me away from this place. I told you that."

"In fact, you asked me if I'd be the one to do it."

"Is *that* what's putting you out of countenance?" Jessamine asked. "Really, Tessa, we can still be the best of friends once we're sisters-in-law, but a man is always better than a woman for this sort of thing, don't you think?"

Tessa could think of nothing to say in reply.

Jessamine shrugged. "Charlotte wishes to see you, by the way. In the drawing room. She wanted me to tell you. You don't need to worry about Nathaniel. I've been checking his temperature every quarter hour and putting cold compresses on his forehead besides."

Tessa wasn't sure she believed any of this, but as Jessamine was patently uninterested in giving up her place by Nathaniel's side, and it hardly seemed worth a battle, she turned with a disgusted sigh and left the room.

The door to the drawing room, when she reached it, was

slightly ajar; she could hear raised voices from the other side. She hesitated, her hand half-lifted to knock—then she heard the sound of her own name and she froze.

"This isn't the London Hospital. Tessa's brother shouldn't be here!" It was Will's voice, raised to a shout. "He's not a Downworlder, just a stupid, venal mundane who found himself mixed up in something he couldn't manage—"

Charlotte replied, "He can't be treated by mundane doctors. Not for what's wrong with him. Be reasonable, Will."

"He already knows about Downworld." The voice was Jem's: calm, logical. "In fact, he may know quite a bit of important information that *we* don't know. Mortmain claimed Nathaniel was working for de Quincey; he might have information about de Quincey's plans, the automatons, the whole Magister business—all of it. De Quincey wanted him dead, after all. Perhaps it was because he knew something he shouldn't."

There was a long silence. Then, "We can call in the Silent Brothers again, then," said Will. "They can claw through his mind, see what they find. We needn't wait for him to wake up."

"You know that sort of process is delicate with mundanes," protested Charlotte. "Brother Enoch has already said that the fever has driven Mr. Gray into hallucinations. It's impossible for him to sort through what in the boy's mind is the truth and what is feverish delirium. Not without damaging his mind, possibly permanently."

"I doubt it was that much of a mind to begin with." Tessa heard Will's tone of disgust even through the door and felt her stomach tighten with rage.

"You know nothing about the man." Jem spoke more coldly than Tessa had ever heard him speak before. "I can't imagine what's driving this mood of yours, Will, but it does you no credit."

"I know what it is," Charlotte said.

"You do?" Will sounded appalled.

"You're as upset as I am about how last night went. We had only two fatalities, true, but de Quincey's escape doesn't reflect well on us. It was my plan. I pushed it on the Enclave, and now they will blame me for anything that went wrong. Not to mention that Camille has had to go into hiding since we've no idea where de Quincey is, and by now he probably has a blood price on her head. And Magnus Bane, of course, is furious with us that Camille has vanished. So our best informant and our best warlock are lost to us at the moment."

"But we did stop de Quincey from murdering Tessa's brother and who knows how many more mundanes," Jem said. "That should count for something. Benedict Lightwood didn't want to believe in de Quincey's betrayal at first; now he has no choice. He knows you were right."

"That," said Charlotte, "is likely only going to make him angrier."

"Perhaps," said Will. "And perhaps if you hadn't insisted on tying the success of *my* plan to the functionality of one of Henry's ridiculous inventions, we wouldn't be having this conversation now. You can dance around it all you like, but the reason everything went wrong last night is because the Phosphor didn't work. Nothing Henry invents ever works. If you'd just admit your husband's a useless fool, we'd all be a lot better off."

"*Will.*" Jem's voice held cold fury.

"No. James, don't." Charlotte's voice shook; there was a sort of thump, as if she'd sat herself down very suddenly in a chair. "Will," she said, "Henry is a good, kind man and he loves you."

"Don't be maudlin, Charlotte." Will's voice held only scorn.

"He's known you since you were a boy. He cares for you like you were his own younger brother. As do I. All I've ever done is love you, Will—"

"Yes," said Will, "and I wish you wouldn't."

Charlotte made a pained noise, like a kicked puppy. "I know you don't mean that."

"I mean everything I say," said Will. "Especially when I tell you that we're better off sifting through Nathaniel Gray's mind now rather than later. If you're too sentimental to do it—"

Charlotte began to interrupt, but it didn't matter. This was too much for Tessa. She hurled the door open and stalked inside. The inside of the room was lit by a roaring fire, in contrast to the squares of dark gray glass that let in what there was of the cloudy twilight. Charlotte sat behind the large desk, Jem in a chair beside her. Will, on the other hand, was leaning against the fireplace mantel; he was flushed with obvious anger, his eyes blazing, his shirt collar askew. His eyes met Tessa's for a moment of pure astonishment. Any hope she had entertained that he might have magically forgotten what had happened in the attic the night before vanished. He flushed at the sight of her, his fathomless blue eyes darkening—and looked away, as if he couldn't stand to hold her gaze.

"I suppose you've been eavesdropping, then?" he asked. "And now you're here to give me a piece of your mind about your precious brother?"

"At least I have a mind to give you a piece of, which Nathaniel won't, if you have your way." Tessa turned to

Charlotte. "I won't let Brother Enoch go pawing through Nate's mind. He's sick enough already; it would probably kill him."

Charlotte shook her head. She looked exhausted, her face gray, her eyelids drooping. Tessa wondered if she'd slept at all. "Most assuredly, we will allow him to heal before we think about questioning him."

"What if he's ill for weeks? Or months?" Will said. "We might not have that much time."

"Why not? What's so urgent you want to risk my brother's life on it?" Tessa snapped.

Will's eyes were slivers of blue glass. "All you've ever cared about is finding your brother. And now you've found him. Good for you. But that was never *our* goal. You do realize that, don't you? We don't usually go quite this far out of our way for the sake of one delinquent mundane."

"What Will is trying to say," Jem interjected, "though failing at civility, is—" He broke off, and sighed. "De Quincey said that your brother was someone he had trusted. And now de Quincey is gone, and we have no idea where he's hiding. The notes we found in his office hint that de Quincey believed there would soon be a war between Downworlders and Shadowhunters, a war those clockwork creatures he was working on doubtless figured into prominently. You can see why we want to know where he is, and what else your brother might know."

"Maybe *you* want to know those things," Tessa said, "but it's not my fight. I'm not a Shadowhunter."

"Indeed," said Will. "Don't think we don't know that."

"Be quiet, Will." Charlotte's tone held more than its usual asperity. She turned from him to Tessa, her brown eyes beseeching. "We trust you, Tessa. You need to trust us, too."

"No," Tessa said. "No, I don't." She could feel Will's gaze on her and was suddenly filled with a startling rage. How *dare* he be cold to her, angry at her? What had she done to deserve it? She'd let him kiss her. That was all. Somehow, it was as if that alone had erased everything else she had done that evening—as if now that she'd kissed Will, it no longer mattered that she had also been brave. "You wanted to use me—just like the Dark Sisters did—and the moment you had a chance to, the moment Lady Belcourt came along and you needed what I could do, you wanted me to do it. Never mind how dangerous it was! You behave as if I have some responsibility to your world, your laws and your Accords, but it's your world, and you're the ones meant to govern it. It's not my fault if you're doing a rotten job!"

Tessa saw Charlotte whiten and sit back. She felt a sharp twinge in her chest. It wasn't Charlotte she had meant to hurt. Still, she went on. She couldn't help herself, the words coming out in a flood, "All your talk about Downworlders and how you don't hate them. That's all nothing, isn't it? Just words. You don't mean them. And as for mundanes, have you ever thought maybe you'd be better at protecting them if you didn't despise them all so much?" She looked at Will. He was pale, his eyes blazing. He looked—she wasn't sure she could describe his expression. Horrified, she thought, but not at her; the horror ran deeper than that.

"Tessa," Charlotte protested, but Tessa was already fumbling for the door. She turned at the last moment, on the threshold, to see them all staring at her.

"Stay away from my brother," she snapped. "And *don't* follow me."

***

Anger, Tessa thought, was satisfying in its own way, when you gave in to it. There was something peculiarly gratifying about shouting in a blind rage until your words ran out.

Of course, the aftermath was less pleasant. Once you'd told everyone you hated them and not to come after you, where exactly did you *go*? If she went back to her own room, it was as much as saying she was just having a tantrum that would wear off. She couldn't go to Nate and bring her black mood into his sickroom, and lurking anywhere else meant risking being found sulking by Sophie or Agatha.

In the end she took the narrow, winding stairs that led down through the Institute. She made her way through the witch-lit nave and came out onto the broad front steps of the church, where she sank down on the top stair and wrapped her arms around herself, shivering in the unexpectedly cold breeze. It must have rained sometime during the day, for the steps were damp, and the black stone of the courtyard shone like a mirror. The moon was out, darting in between racing scuds of cloud, and the huge iron gate gleamed blackly in the fitful light. *We are dust and shadows.*

"I know what you're thinking." The voice that came from the doorway behind Tessa was soft enough that it could almost have been part of the wind that rattled the leaves on the tree branches.

Tessa turned. Jem stood in the arch of the doorway, the white witchlight behind him lighting his hair so that it shone like metal. His face, though, was hidden in shadow. He held his cane in his right hand; the dragon's eyes gleamed watchfully at Tessa.

"I don't think you do."

"You're thinking, *If they call this damp nastiness summer, what must winter be like?* You'd be surprised. Winter's actually much the same." He moved away from the door and sat down on the step beside Tessa, though not too close. "It's spring that's really lovely."

"Is it?" Tessa said, without much real interest.

"No. It's actually quite foggy and wet as well." He looked sideways at her. "I know you said not to follow you. But I was rather hoping you just meant Will."

"I did." Tessa twisted round to look up at him. "I shouldn't have shouted like that."

"No, you were quite right to say what you did," said Jem. "We Shadowhunters have been what we are for so long, and are so insular, that we often forget to look at any situation from someone else's point of view. It is only ever about whether something is good for the Nephilim or bad for the Nephilim. Sometimes I think we forget to ask whether it is good or bad for the world."

"I never meant to hurt Charlotte."

"Charlotte is very sensitive about the way the Institute is run. As a woman, she must fight to be heard, and even then her decisions are second-guessed. You heard Benedict Lightwood at the Enclave meeting. She feels she has no freedom to make a mistake."

"Do any of us? Do any of *you*? Everything is life and death to you." Tessa took a long breath of the foggy air. It tasted of city, metal and ashes and horses and river water. "I just—I feel sometimes as if I can't bear it. Any of it. I wish I'd never learned what I was. I wish Nate had stayed home and none of this had ever happened!"

"Sometimes," Jem said, "our lives can change so fast that the change outpaces our minds and hearts. It's those times, I think, when our lives have altered but we still long for the time before everything was altered—that is when we feel the greatest pain. I can tell you, though, from experience, you grow accustomed to it. You learn to live your new life, and you can't imagine, or even really remember, how things were before."

"You're saying I'll get used to being a warlock, or whatever it is that I am."

"You've always been what you are. That's not new. What you'll get used to is knowing it."

Tessa took a deep breath, and let it out slowly. "I didn't mean what I said upstairs," she said. "I don't think the Nephilim are as dreadful as all that."

"I know you didn't mean it. If you had, you wouldn't be here. You'd be at your brother's side, guarding him against our dire intentions."

"Will didn't really mean what he said, either, did he," Tessa said after a moment. "He wouldn't hurt Nate."

"Ah." Jem looked out toward the gate, his gray eyes thoughtful. "You're correct. But I'm surprised you know it. *I* know it. But I have had years to understand Will. To know when he means what he says and when he doesn't."

"So you don't ever get angry at him?"

Jem laughed out loud. "I would hardly say *that*. Sometimes I want to strangle him."

"How on earth do you prevent yourself?"

"I go to my favorite place in London," said Jem, "and I stand and look at the water, and I think about the continuity of life, and how the river rolls on, oblivious of the petty upsets in our lives."

Tessa was fascinated. "Does that work?"

"Not really, but after that I think about how I could kill him while he slept if I really wanted to, and then I feel better."

Tessa giggled. "So where is it, then? This favorite place of yours?"

For a moment Jem looked pensive. Then he bounded to his feet, and held out the hand that did not clasp the cane. "Come along, and I'll show you."

"Is it far?"

"Not at all." He smiled. He had a lovely smile, Tessa thought—and a contagious one. She couldn't help smiling back, for what felt like the first time in ages.

Tessa let herself be pulled to her feet. Jem's hand was warm and strong, surprisingly reassuring. She glanced back at the Institute once, hesitated, and let him draw her through the iron gate and out into the shadows of the city.

14

Blackfriars Bridge

Twenty bridges from Tower to Kew
Wanted to know what the River knew,
For they were young and the Thames was old,
And this is the tale that the River told.
–Rudyard Kipling, "The River's Tale"

Stepping through the Institute's iron gate, Tessa felt a bit like Sleeping Beauty leaving her castle behind its wall of thorns. The Institute was in the center of a square, and streets left the square in each cardinal direction, plunging into narrow labyrinths between houses. Still with his hand courteously on her elbow, Jem led Tessa down a narrow passage. The sky overhead was like steel. The ground was still damp from the rain earlier in the day, and the sides of the buildings that seemed to press in on either side were streaked with damp and stained with black residues of dust.

Jem talked as they went, not saying much of import but keeping up a soothing chatter, telling her what he had thought of London when he had first come here, how everything had seemed to him a uniform shade of gray—even the people! He had been unable to believe it could rain so much in one place, and so unceasingly. The damp had seemed to come up from the floors and into his bones, so that he'd thought he would eventually sprout mold, in the manner of a tree. "You *do* get used to it," he said as they came out from the narrow passage and into the broadness of Fleet Street. "Even if sometimes you feel as if you ought to be able to be wrung out like a washrag."

Remembering the chaos of the street during the day, Tessa was comforted to see how much quieter it was in the evening, the thronging crowds reduced to the occasional figure striding along the pavement, head down, keeping to the shadows. There were still carriages and even single riders in the road, though none seemed to notice Tessa and Jem. A glamour at work? Tessa wondered, but didn't ask. She was enjoying just listening to Jem talk. This was the oldest part of the city, he told her, where London had been born. The shops that lined the street were closed, their blinds drawn, but advertisements still blared from every surface, advertisements for everything from Pears soap to hair tonic to announcements urging people to attend a lecture on spiritualism. As Tessa walked, she caught glimpses of the spires of the Institute between the buildings, and couldn't help but wonder if anyone else could see them. She remembered the parrot woman with the green skin and feathers. Was the Institute really hidden in plain sight? Curiosity getting the better of her, she asked Jem as much.

"Let me show you something," he said. "Stop here." He took Tessa by the elbow and turned her so that she was facing across the street. He pointed. "What do you see there?"

She squinted across the street; they were near the intersection of Fleet Street and Chancery Lane. There seemed nothing remarkable about where they stood. "The front of a bank. What else is there to see?"

"Now let your mind wander a bit," he said, still in the same soft voice. "Look at something else, the way you might avoid looking directly at a cat so as not to frighten it. Glance at the bank again, out of the corner of your eye. Now look at it, directly, and very fast!"

Tessa did as directed—and stared. The bank was gone; in its place was a half-timbered tavern, with great diamond-paned windows. The light within the windows was tinted with a reddish glow, and through the open front door more red light poured out onto the pavement. Through the glass dark shadows moved—not the familiar shadows of men and women, but shapes too tall and thin, too oddly elongated or many-limbed to be human. Bursts of laughter interrupted a high, sweet, thin music, haunting and seductive. A sign hanging over the door showed a man reaching to tweak the nose of a horned demon. Lettered below the image were the words THE DEVIL TAVERN.

This is where Will was the other night. Tessa looked toward Jem. He was staring at the tavern, his hand light on her arm, his breathing slow and soft. She could see the red light of the pub reflected in his silvery eyes like sunset on water. "Is *this* your favorite place?" she asked.

The intensity went out of his gaze; he looked at her, and

laughed. "Lord, no," he said. "Just something I wanted you to see."

Someone came out the tavern door then, a man in a long black overcoat, an elegant watered silk hat placed firmly on his head. As he glanced up the street, Tessa saw that his skin was an inky dark blue, his hair and beard as white as ice. He moved east toward the Strand as Tessa watched, wondering if he would garner curious stares, but his passage was no more noted by passersby than that of a ghost would be. In fact, the mundanes who passed in front of the Devil Tavern seemed barely to notice it at all, even when several spindly, chittering figures exited and nearly knocked over a tired-looking man wheeling an empty cart. He paused to look around for a moment, puzzled, then shrugged and went on.

"There was a very ordinary tavern there once," said Jem. "As it grew more and more infested with Downworlders, the Nephilim became concerned about the intertwining of the Shadow World with the mundane world. They barred mundanes from the place by the simple expedient of using a glamour to convince them that the tavern had been knocked down and a bank erected in its place. The Devil is a nearly exclusively Downworlder haunt now." Jem glanced up at the moon, a frown crossing his face. "It's growing late. We'd better move on."

After a single glance back at the Devil, Tessa moved after Jem, who continued to chat easily as they went, pointing out things of interest—the Temple Church, where the law courts were now, and where once the Knights Templar had sustained pilgrims on their route to the Holy Land. "They were friends of the Nephilim, the knights. Mundanes, but not without their own knowledge of the Shadow World. And of course," he added, as they came out from the network of streets and onto Blackfriars Bridge itself, "many think that the Silent Brothers are the original Black Friars, though no one can prove it. This is it," he added, gesturing before him. "My favorite place in London."

Looking out over the bridge, Tessa couldn't help but wonder what Jem liked so much about the place. It stretched from one bank of the Thames to the other, a low granite bridge with multiple arches, the parapets painted dark red and gilded with gold and scarlet paint that gleamed in the moonlight. It would have been pretty if it hadn't been for the railway bridge that ran along the east side of it, silent in the shadows but still an ugly latticework of iron railings stretching away to the river's opposite bank.

"I know what you're thinking," Jem said again, just as he had outside the Institute. "The railway bridge, it's hideous. But it means people rarely come here to admire the view. I enjoy the solitude, and just the look of the river, silent under the moon."

They walked to the center of the bridge, where Tessa leaned against a granite parapet and looked down. The Thames was black in the moonlight. The expanse of London stretched away on either bank, the great dome of St. Paul's looming up behind them like a white ghost, and everything shrouded in the softening fog that laid a gently blurring veil over the harsh lines of the city.

Tessa glanced down at the river. The smell of salt and dirt and rot came off the water, mixing with the fog. Still there was something portentous about London's river, as if it carried the weight of the past in its currents. A bit of old poetry came into her head. "'*Sweet Thames, run softly till I end my song,*'" she said, half under her breath. Normally she would never have quoted poetry aloud in front of anyone, but there was something about Jem that made her feel that whatever she did, he wouldn't pass judgment on her.

"I've heard that bit of rhyme before," was all he said. "Will's quoted it at me. What is it?"

"Spenser. 'Prothalamion.'" Tessa frowned. "Will does seem to have an odd affinity for poetry for someone so . . . so . . ."

"Will reads constantly, and has an excellent memory," said Jem. "There is very little he does not remember." There was something in his voice that lent weight to his assertion beyond the mere statement of fact.

"You like Will, don't you?" said Tessa. "I mean, you're fond of him."

"I love him as if he were my brother," said Jem matter-of-factly.

"You can say that," Tessa said. "However horrid he is to everyone else, he loves *you*. He's kind to you. What did you ever do, to make him treat you so differently from all the rest?"

Jem leaned sideways against the parapet, his gaze on her but still faraway. He tapped his fingers thoughtfully against the jade top of his cane. Taking advantage of his clear distraction, Tessa let herself stare at him, marveling a little at his strange beauty in the moonlight. He was all silver and ashes, not like Will's strong colors of blue and black and gold.

Finally he said, "I don't know, really. I used to think it was because we were both without parents, and therefore he felt we were the same—"

"I'm an orphan," Tessa pointed out. "So is Jessamine. He doesn't think he is like us."

"No. He doesn't." Jem's eyes were guarded, as if there were something he wasn't saying.

"I don't understand him," Tessa said. "He can be kind one moment and absolutely awful the next. I cannot decide if he is kind or cruel, loving or hateful—"

"Does it matter?" Jem said. "Is it required that you make such a decision?"

"The other night," she went on, "in your room, when Will came in. He said he had been drinking all night, but then, later, when you—later he seemed to become instantly sober. I've seen my brother drunk. I know it doesn't vanish like that in an instant; even my aunt throwing a pail of cold water in Nate's face wouldn't have roused him from stupor, not if he were truly intoxicated. And Will didn't smell of alcohol, or seem ill the next morning. But why would he lie and say he was drunk if he wasn't?"

Jem looked resigned. "And there you have the essential mystery of Will Herondale. I used to wonder the same thing myself. How anyone could drink as much as he claimed and survive, much less fight as well as he does. So one night I followed him."

"You *followed* him?"

Jem grinned crookedly. "Yes. He went out, claiming an assignation or some such, and I followed him. If I'd known what to expect, I would have worn sturdier shoes. All night he walked through the city, from St. Paul's to Spitalfields Market to Whitechapel High Street. He went down to the river and wandered about the docks. Never did he stop to speak to a single soul. It was like following a ghost. The next morning he was ready with some ribald tale of false adventures, and I never demanded the truth. If he wishes to lie to me, then he must have a reason."

"He lies to you, and yet you trust him?"

"Yes," Jem said. "I trust him."

"But—"

"He lies consistently. He always invents the story that will make him look the worst."

"Then, has he told you what happened to his parents? Either the truth or lies?"

"Not entirely. Bits and pieces," Jem said after a long pause. "I know that his father left the Nephilim. Before Will was ever born. He fell in love with a mundane girl, and when the Council refused to make her a Shadowhunter, he left the Clave and moved with her to a very remote part of Wales, where they thought they wouldn't be interfered with. The Clave was furious."

"Will's mother was a mundane? You mean he is only half a Shadowhunter?"

"Nephilim blood is dominant," said Jem. "That's why there are three rules for those who leave the Clave. First, you must sever contact with any and all Shadowhunters you have ever known, even your own family. They can never speak to you again, nor can you speak to them. Second, you cannot call upon the Clave for help, no matter what your danger. And the third . . ."

"What's the third?"

"Even should you leave the Clave," said Jem, "they can still lay claim to your children."

A little shiver went through Tessa. Jem was still staring out at the river, as if he could see Will in its silvered surface. "Every six years," he said, "until the child is eighteen, a representative of the Clave comes to your family and asks the child if they would like to leave their family and join the Nephilim."

"I can't imagine anyone would," Tessa said, appalled. "I mean, you'd never be able to speak to your family again, would you?"

Jem shook his head.

"And Will agreed to that? He joined the Shadowhunters regardless?"

"He refused. Twice, he refused. Then, one day—Will was twelve or so—there was a knock on the Institute door and Charlotte answered it. She would have been eighteen then, I think. Will was standing there on the steps. She told me he was covered in road dust and dirt as if he'd been sleeping in hedgerows. He said, 'I am a Shadowhunter. One of you. You have to let me in. I have nowhere else to go.'"

"He said that? Will? 'I have nowhere else to go'?"

He hesitated. "You understand, all this is information I heard from Charlotte. Will's never mentioned a word of any of it to me. But that's what she claims he said."

"I don't understand. His parents—they're dead, aren't they? Or they would have come looking for him."

"They did," Jem said quietly. "A few weeks after Will arrived, Charlotte told me, his parents followed. They came to the front door of the Institute and banged on it, calling for him. Charlotte went into Will's room to ask him if he wanted to see them. He had crawled under the bed and had his hands over his ears. He wouldn't come out, no matter what she did, and he wouldn't see them. I think Charlotte finally went down and sent them away, or they left of their own accord, I'm not sure—"

"Sent them away? But their child was inside the Institute. They had a right—"

"They had no right." Jem spoke gently enough, Tessa thought, but there was something in his tone that put him as far away from her as the moon. "Will chose to join the Shadowhunters. Once he made that choice, they had no more claim on him. It was the right and responsibility of the Clave to turn them away."

"And you've never asked him why?"

"If he wanted me to know, he'd tell me," Jem said. "You asked why I think he tolerates me better than other people. I'd imagine it's precisely *because* I've never asked him why." He smiled at her, wryly. The cold air had whipped color into his cheeks, and his eyes were bright. Their hands were close to each other's on the parapet. For a brief, half-confused moment Tessa thought that he might be about to put his hand over hers, but his gaze slid past her and he frowned. "Bit late for a walk, isn't it?"

Following his gaze, she saw the shadowy figures of a man and a woman coming toward them across the bridge. The man wore a workman's felt hat and a dark woolen coat; the woman had her hand on his arm, her face inclined toward his. "They probably think the same thing about us," Tessa said. She looked up into Jem's eyes. "And you, did you come to the Institute because you had nowhere else to go? Why didn't you stay in Shanghai?"

"My parents ran the Institute there," said Jem, "but they were murdered by a demon. He—it—was called Yanluo." His voice was very calm. "After they died, everyone thought that the safest thing for me would be to leave the country, in case the demon or its cohorts came after me as well."

"But why here, why England?"

"My father was British. I spoke English. It seemed reasonable." Jem's tone was as calm as ever, but Tessa sensed there was something he wasn't telling her. "I thought I would feel more at home here than I would in Idris, where neither of my parents had ever been."

Across the bridge from them the strolling couple had paused at a parapet; the man seemed to be pointing out features of the railway bridge, the woman nodding as he spoke. "And did you—feel more at home, that is?"

"Not precisely," Jem said. "Almost the first thing I realized when I came here was that my father never thought of himself as British, not the way an Englishman would. Real Englishmen are British first, and gentlemen second. Whatever else it is they might be—a doctor, a magistrate or landowner—comes third. For Shadowhunters it's different. We are Nephilim, first and foremost, and only after that do we make a nod to whatever country we might have been born and bred in. And as for third, there is no third. We are only ever Shadowhunters. When other Nephilim look at me, they see only a Shadowhunter. Not like mundanes, who look at me and see a boy who is not entirely foreign but not quite like them either."

"Half one thing and half another," Tessa said. "Like me. But *you* know you're human."

Jem's expression softened. "As are you. In all the ways that matter."

Tessa felt the backs of her eyes sting. She glanced up and saw that the moon had passed behind a cloud, giving it a pearlescent luster. "I suppose we should go back. The others must be worried."

Jem moved to offer her his arm—and paused. The strolling

couple Jem had noted before were suddenly in front of them, blocking their way. Though they must have moved very swiftly to reach the far side of the bridge so fast, they stood eerily still now, their arms linked. The woman's face was concealed in the shadow of a plain bonnet, the man's hidden beneath the brim of his felt hat.

Jem's hand tightened on Tessa's arm, but his voice was neutral when he spoke. "Good evening. Is there something we can help you with?"

Neither of them spoke, but they moved a step closer, the woman's skirt rustling in the wind. Tessa looked around, but there was no one else on the bridge, no one visible at either embankment. London seemed utterly deserted under the blurring moon.

"Pardon me," Jem said. "I'd appreciate it if you'd let me and my companion go by." He took a step forward, and Tessa followed. They were close enough now to the silent couple that when the moon came out from behind its cloud, flooding the bridge with silvery light and illuminating the face of the man in the felt hat, Tessa recognized him instantly.

The tangled hair; the wide once-broken nose and scarred chin; and most of all the protruding, popping eyes, the same eyes as the woman who stood beside him, her blank stare fixed on Tessa in a manner terribly reminiscent of Miranda's.

But you're dead. Will killed you. I saw your body. Tessa whispered, "It's him, the coachman. He belongs to the Dark Sisters."

The coachman chuckled. "I *belong*," he said, "to the Magister. While the Dark Sisters served him, I served them. Now I serve him alone."

The coachman's voice sounded different from how Tessa

remembered—less thick, more articulate, with an almost sinister smoothness. Beside Tessa, Jem had gone very still. "Who are you?" he demanded. "Why are you following us?"

"The Magister has directed us to follow you," the coachman said. "You are Nephilim. You are responsible for the destruction of his home, the destruction of his people, the Children of the Night. We are here to deliver a declaration of war. And we are here for the girl." He turned his eyes to Tessa. "She is the property of the Magister, and he will have her."

"The Magister," said Jem, his eyes very silver in the moonlight. "Do you mean de Quincey?"

"The name you give him does not matter. He is the Magister. He has told us to deliver a message. That message is war."

Jem's hand tightened on the head of his cane. "You serve de Quincey but are not vampires. What are you?"

The woman standing beside the coachman made a strange sighing noise, like the high whistle of a train. "Beware, Nephilim. As you slay others, so shall you be slain. Your angel cannot protect you against that which neither God nor the Devil has made."

Tessa began to turn toward Jem, but he was already in motion. His hand swung up, the jade-headed cane in it. There was a flash. A wickedly sharp and shimmering blade shot from the end of the cane. With a swift turn of his body, Jem plunged the blade forward and slashed it into the coachman's chest. The man staggered back, a high whirring sound of surprise issuing from his throat.

Tessa drew in her breath. A long slash across the coachman's shirt gaped open, and beneath it was visible neither flesh nor blood but shining metal, raggedly scored by Jem's blade.

Jem drew his blade back, letting out a breath, satisfaction mixed with relief. "I knew it—"

The coachman snarled. His hand darted into his coat and withdrew a long serrated knife, the kind butchers used to cut through bone, while the woman, snapping into action, moved toward Tessa, her ungloved hands outstretched. Their movements were jerky, uneven—but very, very fast, much faster than Tessa would have guessed they could move. The coachman's companion advanced on Tessa, her face expressionless, her mouth half-open. Something metallic gleamed inside it—metal, or copper. *She has no gullet, and I would guess, no stomach. Her mouth ends in a sheet of metal behind her teeth.*

Tessa retreated until her back hit the parapet. She looked for Jem, but the coachman was advancing on him again. Jem slashed away at him with the blade, but it seemed only to slow the man down. The coachman's coat and shirt hung away from his body now in ragged strips, clearly showing the metal carapace beneath.

The woman grabbed for Tessa, who darted aside. The woman lumbered forward and crashed into the parapet. She seemed to feel no more pain than the coachman did; she drew herself stiffly upright and turned to move toward Tessa again. The impact seemed to have damaged her left arm, though, for it hung bent at her side. She swung toward Tessa with her right arm, fingers grasping, and seized her by the wrist. Her grip was tight enough to make Tessa scream as the small bones in her wrist flared with pain. She clawed at the hand that held her, her fingers sinking deep into slick, soft skin. It peeled away like the skin of a fruit, Tessa's nails scraping against the metal beneath with a harshness that sent shivers up her spine.

She tried to jerk her hand back, but she only succeeded in pulling the woman toward her; she was making a whirring, clicking noise in her throat that sounded unpleasantly insectile, and up close her eyes were pupil-less and black. Tessa pulled her foot back to kick out—

And there was the sudden clang of metal on metal; Jem's blade flashed down with a clean slice, cutting the woman's arm in half at the elbow. Tessa, released, fell back, the bodiless hand falling from her wrist, striking the ground at her feet; the woman was jerking around toward Jem, *whir-click*, *whir-click*. He moved forward, striking at the woman hard with the flat of the cane, knocking her back a step, and then another and another until she hit the railing of the bridge so hard that she overbalanced. Without a cry she fell, plunging toward the water below; Tessa raced to the railing just in time to see her slip beneath the surface. No bubbles rose to show where she had vanished.

Tessa spun back around. Jem was clutching his cane, breathing hard. Blood ran down the side of his face from a cut, but he seemed otherwise unharmed. He held his weapon loosely in one hand as he gazed at a dark humped shape on the ground at his feet, a shape that moved and jerked, flashes of metal showing between the ribbons of its torn clothing. When Tessa moved closer she saw that it was the body of the coachman, writhing and jerking. His head had been sliced cleanly away, and a dark oily substance pumped from the stump of his neck, staining the ground.

Jem reached up to push his sweat-dampened hair back, smearing the blood across his cheek. His hand shook. Hesitantly Tessa touched his arm. "Are you all right?"

His smile was faint. "I should be asking *you* that." He shuddered slightly. "Those mechanical *things*, they unnerve me. They—" He broke off, staring past her.

At the south end of the bridge, moving toward them with sharp staccato motions, were at least a half dozen more of the clockwork creatures. Despite the jerkiness of their movements, they were approaching swiftly, almost hurtling forward. They were already a third of the way across the bridge.

With a sharp *click* the blade vanished back into Jem's cane. He seized Tessa's hand, his voice breathless. "*Run.*"

They ran, Tessa clutching his hand, glancing behind only once, in terror. The creatures had made it to the center of the bridge and were moving toward them, gathering speed. They were male, Tessa saw, dressed in the same kind of dark woolen coats and felt hats as the coachman had been. Their faces gleamed in the moonlight.

Jem and Tessa reached the steps at the end of the bridge, and Jem kept a tight grip on Tessa's hand as they hurtled down the stairs. Her boots slipped on the damp stone, and he caught her, his cane clattering awkwardly against her back; she felt his chest rise and fall against hers, hard, as if he were gasping. But he couldn't be out of breath, could he? He was a Shadowhunter. The *Codex* said they could run for miles. Jem pulled away, and she saw that his face was tight, as if he were in pain. She wanted to ask him if he'd been hurt, but there was no time. They could hear clattering footsteps on the stairs above them. Without a word Jem took hold of her wrist again and pulled her after him.

They passed the Embankment, lit by the glow of its dolphin lamps, before Jem turned aside and plunged between two buildings into a narrow alley. The alley sloped up, away from the river. The air between the buildings was dank and close, the cobblestones slick with filth. Washing flapped like ghosts from windows overhead. Tessa's feet were screaming in their fashionable boots, her heart slamming against her chest, but there was no slowing down. She could *hear* the creatures behind them, hear the *whir-click* of their movements, closer and closer.

The alley opened out into a wide street, and there, rising up before them, was the looming edifice of the Institute. They dashed through the entrance, Jem releasing her as he whirled to slam and lock the gates behind them. The creatures reached them just as the bolts slid home; they crashed against the gate like windup toys unable to stop themselves, rattling the iron with a tremendous crash.

Tessa backed up, staring. The clockwork creatures were pressed up against the gates, their hands reaching through the gaps in the iron. She looked around wildly. Jem stood beside her. He was as white as paper, one hand pressed to his side. She reached for his hand, but he stepped back, out of her reach. "Tessa." His voice was uneven. "Get into the Institute. You need to get inside."

"Are you hurt? Jem, are you injured?"

"No." His voice was muffled.

A rattle from the gate made Tessa look up. One of the clockwork men had his hand through a gap in the gate and was pulling at the iron chain that held it closed. As she stared in fascinated horror, she saw that he was dragging at the loops of metal with such force that the skin was peeling away from his fingers, showing the jointed metal hands beneath. There was obviously tremendous strength in those hands. The metal was warping and twisting in his grip; it was clearly a matter of minutes before the chain split and broke.

Tessa seized hold of Jem's arm. His skin was burning hot to the touch; she could feel it through his clothes. "Come *on*."

With a groan he let her pull him toward the front door of the church; he was staggering, and leaning on her heavily, his breath rattling in his chest. They lurched up the stairs, Jem sliding out of her grip almost the moment they reached the top step. He hit the ground on his knees, choking coughs ripping through him, his whole body spasming.

The gate burst open. The clockwork creatures spilled through into the drive, led by the one who had torn the chain apart, his skin-stripped hands gleaming in the moonlight.

Remembering what Will had said, that one had to have Shadowhunter blood to open the door, Tessa reached for the bellpull that hung beside it and yanked it, hard, but heard no sound. Desperate, she whirled back to Jem, still crouched on the ground. "Jem! Jem, please, you have to open the door—"

He raised his head. His eyes were open, but there was no color to them. They were all white, like marbles. She could see the moon reflected in them.

"Jem!"

He tried to rise to his feet, but his knees gave out; he slumped to the ground, blood running from the corners of his mouth. The cane had rolled from his hand, almost to Tessa's feet.

The creatures had reached the foot of the steps; they began to surge upward, lurching a little, the one with the skinned hands in the lead. Tessa flung herself against the doors of the Institute, pounding her fists against the oak. She could hear the hollow reverberations of her blows echoing on the other side, and despaired. The Institute was so huge, and there was no *time.*

At last she gave up. Turning away from the door, she was horrified to see that the leader of the creatures had reached Jem; it was bending over him, its skinned metal hands on his chest.

With a cry she seized up Jem's cane and brandished it. "Get away from him!" she cried.

The creature straightened up, and in the moonlight, for the first time, she saw its face clearly. It was smooth, almost featureless, only indentations where the eyes and mouth should have been, and no nose. It raised its skinned hands; they were stained dark with Jem's blood. Jem himself lay very still, his shirt torn, blood pooling blackly around him. As Tessa stared in horror, the clockwork man wiggled his bloody fingers at her, in a sort of grotesque parody of a wave—then turned and sprang away down the steps, almost scuttling, like a spider. He dashed through the gates and was lost to view.

Tessa moved toward Jem, but the other automatons moved swiftly to block her way. They were *all* as blank-faced as their leader, a matching set of faceless warriors, as if there had not quite been time to *finish* them.

With a *whir-click* a pair of metal hands reached for her, and she swung the cane, almost blindly. It connected with the side of a clockwork man's head. She felt the impact of wood against metal ringing up her arm, and he staggered to the side, but only for a moment. His head whipped back around with incredible speed. She swung again, the cane slamming against his shoulder this time; he lurched, but other hands flashed out, seizing the cane, yanking it from her grasp with such force that the skin of her hand burned. She remembered the painful strength of Miranda's grip on her, as the automaton who had snatched the cane from her brought it down across his knee with stunning force.

It snapped in half with an awful sound. Tessa whirled to run, but metal hands clamped down on her shoulders, yanking her back. She struggled to pull free—

And the doors of the Institute burst open. The light that poured from them blinded her momentarily, and she could see nothing but the outline of dark figures, ringed in light, spilling from the church's interior. Something whistled by her head, grazing her cheek. There was the grinding sound of metal on metal, and then the clockwork creature's arms relaxed and she fell forward onto the steps, choking.

Tessa looked up. Charlotte stood above her, her face pale and set, a sharp metal disc in one hand. Another, matching, disc was buried in the chest of the mechanical man who had held her. He was twisting and spasming in a circle, like a malfunctioning toy. Blue sparks flew from the gash in his neck.

Around him the rest of the creatures were spinning and lurching as the Shadowhunters converged on them, Henry bringing his seraph blade down in an arc, slicing open the chest of one of the automatons, sending it reeling and jerking into the shadows. Beside him was Will, swinging what looked like a sort of scythe, over and over, chopping another of the creatures to bits with such fury that it sent up a fountain of blue sparks. Charlotte, darting down the steps, threw the second of her disks; it sheared through the head of a metal monster with a sickening noise. He crumpled to the ground, leaking more sparks and black oil.

The remaining two creatures, seeming to think better

of the situation, turned and sprang toward the gates. Henry darted after them with Charlotte on his heels, but Will, dropping his weapon, turned and raced back toward the steps. "What happened?" he shouted at Tessa. She stared, too dazed to answer. His voice rose, tinged with furious panic. "Are you hurt? Where's Jem?"

"I'm not hurt," she whispered. "But Jem, he collapsed. There." She pointed to where Jem lay, crumpled in the shadows beside the door.

Will's face went blank, like a slate wiped clean of chalk. Without looking at her again he raced up the stairs and dropped down by Jem, saying something in a low voice. When there was no reply, Will raised his head, shouting for Thomas to come help him carry Jem, and shouting something else, something Tessa couldn't make out through her dizziness. Perhaps he was shouting at her. Perhaps he thought this was all her fault? If she hadn't grown so angry, if she hadn't run away and made Jem follow her—

A dark shadow loomed in the lit doorway. It was Thomas, tousle-haired and serious, who went without a word to kneel down by Will. Together they lifted Jem to his feet, an arm slung around each of their shoulders. They hurried inside without a backward glance.

Dazed, Tessa looked out over the courtyard. Something was strange, different. It was the sudden silence after all the clamor and noise. The destroyed clockwork creatures lay in shattered pieces about the courtyard, the ground was slick with viscous fluid, the gates hung open, and the moon shone blankly down on everything just as it had shone down on her and Jem on the bridge, when he had told her that she was human.

15
Foreign Mud

Ah God, that love were as a flower or flame,
That life were as the naming of a name,
That death were not more pitiful than desire,
That these things were not one thing and the same!
–Algernon Charles Swinburne, "Laus Veneris"

"Miss Tessa." The voice was Sophie's. Tessa turned and saw her framed in the doorway, a lantern swinging from her hand. "Are you all right?"

Tessa felt pitifully grateful to see the other girl. She had been feeling so alone. "I'm not hurt. Henry has gone after the creatures, though, and Charlotte—"

"They'll be just fine." Sophie put a hand on Tessa's elbow. "Come, let's get you inside, miss. You're bleeding."

"I am?" Puzzled, Tessa put her fingers up to touch her

forehead; they came away stained red. "I must have struck my head when I fell against the steps. I didn't even feel it."

"Shock," Sophie said calmly, and Tessa thought how many times in her employment here Sophie must have done these things—bandaged up cuts, wiped away blood. "Come along, and I'll get a compress for your head."

Tessa nodded. With a last glance over her shoulder at the destruction in the courtyard, she let Sophie guide her back inside the Institute. The next short while was something of a blur. After Sophie helped her upstairs and into an armchair in the drawing room, she bustled off and returned moments later with Agatha, who pressed a cup of something hot into Tessa's hand.

Tessa knew what it was the moment she smelled it—brandy and water. She thought of Nate and hesitated, but once she'd had a few mouthfuls, things began to swim back into focus. Charlotte and Henry returned, bringing with them the smell of metal and fighting. Tight-lipped, Charlotte set her weapons down on a table and called for Will. He didn't respond, but Thomas did, hurrying down the corridor, his coat stained with blood, to tell her that Will was with Jem, and that Jem was going to be all right.

"The creatures injured him, and he lost some blood," Thomas said, running a hand through his tangled brown hair. He looked at Sophie as he said it. "But Will gave him an *iratze*—"

"And his medicine?" Sophie asked quickly. "Has he had some of that?"

Thomas nodded, and the tight set of Sophie's shoulders relaxed just a bit. Charlotte's gaze softened as well. "Thank you, Thomas," she said. "Perhaps you can see if he requires anything else?"

Thomas nodded, and set off back down the corridor with a last glance over his shoulder at Sophie, who did not seem to notice. Charlotte sank down onto the ottoman opposite Tessa. "Tessa, can you tell us what happened?"

Clutching the cup, her fingers cold despite its heat, Tessa shuddered. "Did you catch the ones that escaped? The—whatever they are. The metal monsters?"

Charlotte shook her head gravely. "We pursued them through the streets, but they disappeared once we reached Hungerford Bridge. Henry thinks there was some magic involved."

"Or a secret tunnel," Henry said. "I did also suggest a secret tunnel, my dear." He looked at Tessa. His friendly face was streaked with blood and oil, his brightly striped waistcoat slashed and torn. He looked like a schoolboy who'd been in a bad scrape of some sort. "Did you see them coming out of a tunnel, perhaps, Miss Gray?"

"No," Tessa said, her voice half a whisper. To clear her throat, she took another sip of the drink Agatha had given her, and set the cup down before running through it all—the bridge, the coachman, the chase, the words the creature had spoken, the way they had burst through the Institute gates. Charlotte listened with a pinched white face; even Henry looked grim. Sophie, sitting quietly on a chair, attended to the story with the grave intensity of a schoolgirl.

"They said it was a declaration of war," Tessa finished. "That they were coming to wreak revenge on us—on you, I suppose—for what happened to de Quincey."

"And the creature referred to him as the Magister?" Charlotte asked.

Tessa pressed her lips together firmly to keep them from trembling. "Yes. He said the Magister wanted me and that he had been sent to retrieve me. Charlotte, this is my fault. If it weren't for me, de Quincey wouldn't have sent those creatures tonight, and Jem—" She looked down at her hands. "Maybe you should just let him have me."

Charlotte was shaking her head. "Tessa, you heard de Quincey last night. He hates Shadowhunters. He would strike at the Clave regardless of you. And if we gave you to him, all we would be doing is placing a potentially valuable weapon in his hands." She looked at Henry. "I wonder why he waited this long. Why not come for Tessa when she was out with Jessie? Unlike demons, these clockwork creatures can go out during the day."

"They *can*," said Henry, "but not without alarming the populace—not yet. They don't look enough like ordinary human beings to pass without exciting comment." He took a shining gear from his pocket and held it up. "I examined the remains of the automatons down in the courtyard. These ones de Quincey sent after Tessa on the bridge are not like the one in the crypt. They're more sophisticated, made of tougher metals, and with a more advanced jointure. Someone's been working on the design in those blueprints Will found, refining it. The creatures are faster now, and deadlier."

But how refined? "There was a spell," Tessa said quickly. "On the blueprint. Magnus deciphered it. . . ."

"The binding spell. Meant to tie a demon energy to an automaton." Charlotte looked at Henry. "Did de Quincey—?"

"Succeed in performing it?" Henry shook his head. "No. Those creatures are simply configured to follow a pattern, like music boxes. But they are not animate. They do not have intelligence or will or life. And there is nothing demonic about them."

Charlotte exhaled in relief. "We *must* find de Quincey before he succeeds in his goal. Those creatures are difficult enough to kill as it is. The Angel knows how many of them he's made, or how difficult they'd be to kill if they had the cunning of demons."

"An army born neither of Heaven nor Hell," said Tessa softly.

"Exactly," said Henry. "De Quincey must be found and stopped. And in the meantime, Tessa, you must stay in the Institute. Not that we want to keep you a prisoner here, but it would be safer if you remained inside."

"But for how long—?" Tessa began—and broke off, as Sophie's expression changed. She was looking at something over Tessa's shoulder, her hazel eyes suddenly wide. Tessa followed her gaze.

It was Will. He stood in the doorway of the drawing room. There was a streak of blood across his white shirt; it looked like paint. His face was still, almost masklike, his gaze fixed on Tessa. As their eyes met across the room, she felt the pulse jump in her throat.

"He wants to talk to you," Will said.

There was a moment of silence as everyone in the drawing room looked at him. There was something forbidding about the intensity of Will's gaze, the tension of his stillness. Sophie had her hand at her throat, her fingers nervously fluttering at her collar.

"Will," Charlotte said finally. "Do you mean Jem? Is he all right?"

"He's awake and talking," Will said. His gaze slid momentarily to Sophie, who had glanced down, as if to hide her expression. "And now he wants to speak to Tessa."

"But . . ." Tessa looked toward Charlotte, who seemed troubled. "Is he all right? Is he well enough?"

Will's expression didn't change. "He wants to talk to you," he said, enunciating each word very clearly. "So you will get up, and you will come with me, and you will talk to him. Do you understand?"

"Will," Charlotte began sharply, but Tessa was already rising, smoothing down her rumpled skirts with the flat of her hands. Charlotte looked worriedly at her, but said nothing more.

Will was utterly silent as they made their way down the corridor, witchlight sconces throwing their shadows against the far walls in spindly patterns. There was blackish oil as well as blood splattered on his white shirt, smudging his cheek; his hair was tangled, his jaw set. She wondered if he had slept at all since dawn, when she had left him in the attic. She wanted to ask him, but everything about him—his posture, his silence, the set of his shoulders—said that no questions would be welcome.

He pushed open the door of Jem's room and ushered her in ahead of him. The only light in the room came from the window and from a taper of witchlight on the bedside table. Jem lay half-under the covers of the high carved bed. He was as white as his nightshirt, the lids of his closed eyes dark blue. Leaning against the side of the bed was his jade-headed cane.

Somehow it had been repaired and was whole again, gleaming as if new.

Jem turned his face toward the sound of the door, not opening his eyes. "Will?"

Will did something then that amazed Tessa. He forced his face into a smile, and said, in a passably cheerful tone, "I brought her, like you asked."

Jem's eyes flicked open; Tessa was relieved to see that they had returned to their usual color. Still, they had the look of shadowed holes in his pale face.

"Tessa," he said, "I'm so sorry."

Tessa looked at Will—for permission or guidance, she wasn't sure, but he was staring straight ahead. Clearly he would be no help. Without another glance at him she hurried across the room and sank down in the chair by the side of Jem's bed. "Jem," she said in a low voice, "you shouldn't be sorry, or be apologizing to me. I should be the one apologizing. You didn't do anything wrong. I was the target of those clockwork things, not you." She patted the coverlet gently; wanting to touch his hand but not daring to. "If it wasn't for me, you never would have been hurt."

"Hurt." Jem spoke the word on an exhale of breath, almost with disgust. "I wasn't hurt."

"James." Will's tone held a warning note.

"She should know, William. Otherwise she'll think this was all her fault."

"You were ill," Will said, not looking at Tessa as he spoke. "It's nobody's fault." He paused. "I just think you should be careful. You're not well still. Talking will just tire you out."

"There are more important things than being careful." Jem

struggled to sit up, the cords in his neck straining as he lifted himself, propping his back against the pillows. When he spoke again, he was slightly breathless. "If you don't like it, Will, you don't have to stay."

Tessa heard the door open and close behind her with a soft click. She knew without looking that Will had gone. She couldn't help it—a slight pang went through her, the way it always seemed to do when he left a room.

Jem sighed. "He's so stubborn."

"He was right," Tessa said. "At least, he was right that you don't need to tell me anything you don't want to. I know none of it was your fault."

"Fault has nothing to do with it," Jem said. "I just think you might as well have the truth. Concealing it rarely helps anything." He looked toward the door for a moment, as if his words were half-meant for the absent Will. Then he sighed again, raking his hands through his hair. "You know," he said, "that for most of my life I lived in Shanghai with my parents? That I was raised in the Institute there?"

"Yes," Tessa said, wondering if he was still a little dazed. "You told me, on the bridge. And you told me that a demon had killed your parents."

"*Yanluo,*" said Jem. There was hatred in his voice. "The demon had a grudge against my mother. She'd been responsible for the death of a number of its demon offspring. They'd had a nest in a small town called Lijiang, where they'd been feeding on local children. She burned the nest out and escaped before the demon found her. Yanluo bided its time for years—Greater Demons live forever—but it never forgot. When I was eleven, Yanluo found a weak spot in the ward that protected the Institute, and tunneled inside. The demon killed the guards and took my family prisoner, binding us all to chairs in the great room of the house. Then it went to work.

"Yanluo tortured me in front of my parents," Jem went on, his voice empty. "Over and over it injected me with a burning demon poison that scorched my veins and tore at my mind. For two days I went in and out of hallucinations and dreams. I saw the world drowned in rivers of blood, and I heard the screams of all the dead and dying throughout history. I saw London burning, and great metal creatures striding here and there like huge spiders—" He caught his breath. He was very pale, his nightshirt stuck to his chest with sweat, but he waved away Tessa's expression of concern. "Every few hours I would come back to reality long enough to hear my parents screaming for me. Then on the second day, I came back and heard only my mother. My father had been silenced. My mother's voice was raw and cracked, but she was still saying my name. Not my name in English, but the name she had given me when I was born: Jian. I can still hear her sometimes, calling out for me."

His hands were tight on the pillow he held, tight enough that the fabric had begun to tear.

"Jem," Tessa said softly. "You can stop. You needn't tell me all of it now."

"You remember when I said that Mortmain had probably made his money smuggling opium?" he asked. "The British bring opium into China by the ton. They have made a nation of addicts out of us. In Chinese we call it 'foreign mud' or 'black smoke.' In some ways Shanghai, my city, is built on opium. It wouldn't exist as it does without it. The city is full of dens where hollow-eyed men starve to death because all they want is the drug, more of the drug. They'll give anything for it. I used to despise men like that. I couldn't understand how they were so weak."

He took a deep breath.

"By the time the Shanghai Enclave became worried at the silence from the Institute and broke in to save us, both my parents were already dead. I don't remember any of it. I was screaming and delirious. They took me to the Silent Brothers, who healed my body as well as they could. There was one thing they couldn't fix, though. I had become addicted to the substance the demon had poisoned me with. My body was dependent on it the way an opium addict's body is dependent on the drug. They tried to wean me off it, but going without it caused terrible pain. Even when they were able to block the pain with warlock spells, the lack of the drug pushed my body to the brink of death. After weeks of experimentation they decided that there was nothing to be done: I could not live without the drug. The drug itself meant a slow death, but to take me off it would mean a very quick one."

"Weeks of experimentation?" Tessa echoed. "When you were only eleven years old? That seems cruel."

"Goodness—real goodness—has its own sort of cruelty to it," said Jem, looking past her. "There, beside you on the bedside table, is a box. Can you give it to me?"

Tessa lifted the box. It was made of silver, its lid inlaid with an enamel scene that depicted a slim woman in white robes, barefoot, pouring water out of a vase into a stream. "Who is she?" she asked, handing the box to Jem.

"Kwan Yin. The goddess of mercy and compassion. They say she hears every prayer and every cry of suffering and does what she can to answer it. I thought perhaps if I kept the cause of my suffering in a box with her image on it, it might make that suffering a little less." He flicked open the clasp on the box, and the lid slid back. Inside was a thick layer of what Tessa thought at first was ash, but the color was too bright. It was a layer of thick silvery powder almost the same bright silver color as Jem's eyes.

"This is the drug," he said. "It comes from a warlock dealer we know in Limehouse. I take some of it every day. It's why I look so—so ghostly; it's what drains the color from my eyes and hair, even my skin. I wonder sometimes if my parents would even recognize me. . . ." His voice trailed off. "If I have to fight, I take more. Taking less weakens me. I had taken none today before we went out to the bridge. That's why I collapsed. Not because of the clockwork creatures. Because of the drug. Without any in my system, the fighting, the running, was too much for me. My body started feeding on itself, and I collapsed." He shut the box with a snap, and handed it back to Tessa. "Here. Put it back where it was."

"You don't need any?"

"No. I've had enough tonight."

"You said that the drug meant a slow death," Tessa said. "So do you mean the drug is killing you?"

Jem nodded, strands of bright hair falling across his forehead.

Tessa felt her heart skip a painful beat. "And when you fight, you take more of it? So, why don't you stop fighting? Will and the others—"

"Would understand," Jem finished for her. "I know they would. But there is more to life than not dying. I am a

Shadowhunter. It is what I am, not just what I do. I can't live without it."

"You mean you don't want to."

Will, Tessa thought, would have been angry if she'd said that to him, but Jem just looked at her intently. "I mean I don't want to. For a long time I searched for a cure, but eventually I stopped, and asked Will and the rest to stop as well. I am not this drug, or its hold on me. I believe that I am better than that. That my life is about more than that, however and whenever it might end."

"Well, I don't want you to die," Tessa said. "I don't know why I feel it so strongly—I've just met you—but I don't want you to die."

"And I trust you," he said. "I don't know why—I've just met you—but I do." His hands were no longer clutching the pillow, but lying flat and still on the tasseled surface. They were thin hands, the knuckles just slightly too big for the rest of them, the fingers tapering and slender, a thick white scar running across the back of his right thumb. Tessa wanted to slide her own hand over his, wanted to hold his tightly and comfort him—

"Well, this is all very touching." It was Will, of course, having come soundlessly into the room. He had changed his bloody shirt, and he seemed to have washed up hastily. His hair looked damp, his face scrubbed, though the crescents of his nails were still black with dirt and oil. He looked from Jem to Tessa, his face carefully blank. "I see that you told her."

"I did." There was nothing challenging in Jem's tone; he never looked at Will with anything but affection, Tessa thought, no matter how provoking Will was. "It's done. There's no more need for you to fret about it."

"I disagree," said Will. He gave Tessa a pointed look. She remembered what he had said about not tiring Jem out, and rose from her chair.

Jem gave her a wistful look. "Must you go? I was rather hoping you'd stay and be a ministering angel, but if you must go, you must."

"I'll stay," Will said a bit crossly, and threw himself down in the armchair Tessa had just vacated. "I can minister angelically."

"None too convincingly. And you're not as pretty to look at as Tessa is," Jem said, closing his eyes as he leaned back against the pillow.

"How rude. Many who have gazed upon me have compared the experience to gazing at the radiance of the sun."

Jem still had his eyes closed. "If they mean it gives you a headache, they aren't wrong."

"Besides," Will said, his eyes on Tessa, "it's hardly fair to keep Tessa from her brother. She hasn't had a chance to look in on him since this morning."

"That's true." Jem's eyes fluttered open for a moment; they were silvery black, dark with sleep. "My apologies, Tessa. I nearly forgot."

Tessa said nothing. She was too busy being horrified that Jem wasn't the only one who had nearly forgotten about her brother. *It's all right*, she wanted to say, but Jem's eyes were shut again, and she thought he might be asleep. As she watched, Will leaned forward and drew up the blankets, covering Jem's chest.

Tessa turned around and let herself out as quietly as she could.

The light in the corridors was burning low, or perhaps it had simply been brighter in Jem's room. Tessa stood for a moment, blinking, before her eyes adjusted. She gave a start. "Sophie?"

The other girl was a series of pale smudges in the dimness—her pale face, and the white cap dangling from her hand by one of its ties.

"Sophie?" Tessa said. "Is something wrong?"

"Is he all right?" Sophie demanded, a strange small hitch in her voice. "Is he going to be all right?"

Too startled to make sense of her question, Tessa said, "Who?"

Sophie stared at her, her eyes mutely tragic. "Jem."

Not Master Jem, or Mr. Carstairs. Jem. Tessa looked at her in utter astonishment, suddenly remembering. *It's all right to love someone who doesn't love you back, as long as they're worth you loving them. As long as they deserve it.*

Of course, Tessa thought. *I'm so stupid. It's Jem she's in love with.*

"He's fine," she said as gently as she could. "He's resting, but he was sitting up and talking. He'll be quite recovered soon, I'm sure. Perhaps if you wanted to see him—"

"No!" Sophie exclaimed at once. "No, that wouldn't be right or proper." Her eyes were shining. "I'm much obliged to you, miss. I—"

She turned then, and hurried away down the corridor. Tessa looked after her, troubled and perplexed. How could she not have seen it earlier? How could she have been so blind? How strange to have the power to literally transform yourself into other people, and yet be so unable to put yourself in their place.

***

The door to Nate's room was slightly ajar; Tessa pushed it open the rest of the way as quietly as she could, and peered inside.

Her brother was a heaped mound of blankets. The light from the guttering candle on the bedside table illuminated the fair hair spread across his pillow. His eyes were closed, his chest rising and falling regularly.

In the armchair beside the bed sat Jessamine. She, too, was asleep. Her blond hair was coming out of its carefully arranged chignon, the curls tumbling down onto her shoulders. Someone had thrown a heavy woolen blanket over her, and her hands clutched it, drawing it up against her chest. She looked younger than Tessa had ever seen her look, and vulnerable. There was nothing about her of the girl who had slaughtered the faerie in the park.

It was so odd, Tessa thought, what brought out tenderness in people. It was never what you would have expected. As quietly as she could, she turned away, shutting the door behind her.

Tessa slept fitfully that night, waking often amid dreams of clockwork creatures coming for her, reaching out their spindly metal-jointed hands to catch and tear at her skin. Eventually that dissolved into a dream of Jem, who lay asleep in a bed while silver powder rained down on him, burning where it struck the coverlet he lay under, until eventually the whole bed burned, and Jem slept peacefully on, oblivious to Tessa's warning cries.

Finally she dreamed of Will, standing at the apex of the dome of St. Paul's, alone under the light of a white, white moon. He wore a black frock coat, and the Marks on his skin were plain to be seen on his neck and hands under the glow of the sky. He looked down on London like a bad angel pledged to save the city from its own worst dreams, while below him London slept on, indifferent and unknowing.

Tessa was torn from her dream by a voice in her ear, and a hand vigorously shaking her shoulder. “Miss!” It was Sophie, her voice sharp. “Miss Gray, you simply *must* wake. It’s your brother.”

Tessa shot upright, scattering pillows. Afternoon light poured through the bedroom windows, illuminating the room—and Sophie’s anxious face. “Nate’s awake? He’s all right?”

“Yes—I mean, no. I mean, I don’t know, miss.” There was a little catch in Sophie’s voice. “You see, he’s gone missing.”

16

The Binding Spell

And once, or twice, to throw the dice
Is a gentlemanly game,
But he does not win who plays with Sin
In the secret House of Shame.
—Oscar Wilde, "The Ballad of Reading Gaol"

"Jessamine! Jessamine, what's going on? Where's Nate?"

Jessamine, who was standing just outside Nate's room, whirled to face Tessa as she hurried up the corridor. Jessamine's eyes were red-rimmed, her expression angry. Loose curls of blond hair were coming out of the usually neatly arranged knot at the back of her head. "I don't *know*," she snapped. "I fell asleep in the chair beside the bed, and when I woke up, he was gone—just gone!" She narrowed her eyes. "Gracious, you look ghastly."

Tessa glanced down at herself. She hadn't bothered with

a crinoline, or even shoes. She'd just thrown on a dress and slid her bare feet into slippers. Her hair was straggling down around her shoulders, and she imagined she likely resembled the madwoman Mr. Rochester kept in his attic in *Jane Eyre*.

"Well, Nate can't have gone very far, not as ill as he is," Tessa said. "Isn't anyone *looking* for him?"

Jessamine threw up her hands. "Everyone's looking for him. Will, Charlotte, Henry, Thomas, even Agatha. I don't suppose you want us to roust poor Jem out of bed and make him part of the search party too?"

Tessa shook her head. "Honestly, Jessamine—" She broke off, turning away. "Well, I'm going to look as well. You can stay here if you like."

"I do like." Jessamine tossed her head as Tessa spun away and stalked off down the corridor, her mind whirling. Where on earth could Nate have gone? Had he been feverish, delirious? Had he gotten out of bed not knowing where he was and staggered off to look for her? The thought made her heart clench. The Institute was a baffling maze, she thought as she turned yet another blind corner into yet another tapestry-lined corridor. If she could barely find her way around it even now, how could Nate possibly—

"Miss Gray?"

Tessa turned and saw Thomas emerging from one of the doors along the hall. He was in shirtsleeves, his hair tousled as usual, his brown eyes very serious. She felt herself go very still. *Oh, God, it's bad news.* "Yes?"

"I've found your brother," Thomas said, to Tessa's astonishment.

"You *have*? But where was he?"

"In the drawing room. Got himself a bit of a hiding place, behind the curtains, he had." Thomas spoke hastily, looking sheepish. "Minute he saw me, he went right off his chump. Started screamin' and yellin'. Tried to bolt right past me, an' I nearly had to give him one over the gash to keep him quiet—" At Tessa's look of incomprehension, Thomas paused, and cleared his throat. "That is to say, I'm afraid I may have frightened him, miss."

Tessa put her hand over her mouth. "Oh, dear. But he's all right?"

It seemed that Thomas did not know quite where to look. He was embarrassed to have found Nate cowering behind Charlotte's curtains, Tessa thought, and she felt a wave of indignation on Nate's behalf. Her brother wasn't a Shadowhunter; he hadn't grown up killing things and risking his life. Of course he was terrified. And he was probably delirious with fever, on top of that. "I had better go in and see him. Just me, you understand? I think he needs to see a familiar face."

Thomas looked relieved. "Yes, miss. And I'll wait out here, just for now. You just let me know when you want me to summon the others."

Tessa nodded and moved past Thomas to push the door open. The drawing room was dim, the only illumination the gray afternoon light that spilled through the tall windows. In the shadows the sofas and armchairs scattered about the room looked like crouched beasts. In one of the larger armchairs by the fire sat Nate. He had found the bloodstained shirt and trousers he had been wearing at de Quincey's, and had put them on. His feet were bare. He sat with his elbows on his knees, his face in his hands. He looked wretched.

"Nate?" Tessa said softly.

At that he looked up—and sprang to his feet, a look of incredulous happiness on his face. "Tessie!"

With a little cry Tessa rushed across the room and threw her arms around her brother, hugging him fiercely. She heard him give a little whimper of pain, but his arms went around her too, and for a moment, embracing him, Tessa was back in her aunt's little kitchen in New York, with the smell of cooking all around her and her aunt's soft laughter as she scolded them for making so much noise.

Nate pulled away first, and looked down at her. "God, Tessie, you look so different. . . ."

A shudder went through her. "What do you mean?"

He patted her cheek, almost absently. "Older," he said. "Thinner. You were a round-faced little girl when I left New York, weren't you? Or is that just the way I remember you?"

Tessa reassured her brother that she was still the same little sister he'd always known, but her mind was only partly engaged with his question. She couldn't help staring at him worriedly; he no longer looked as gray as he had, but he was still pale, and bruises stood out in blue, black, and yellow patches on his face and neck. "Nate . . ."

"It's not as bad as it looks," he said, reading the anxiety on her face.

"Yes, it is. You should be in bed, resting. What are you doing in here?"

"I was trying to find *you*. I knew you were here. I saw you, before that bald bastard with the missing eyes got at me. I figured they'd imprisoned you, too. I was going to try to get us out."

"Imprisoned? Nate, no, it's not like that." She shook her head. "We're safe here."

He narrowed his eyes at her. "This is the Institute, isn't it? I was warned about this place. De Quincey said it was run by madmen, monsters who called themselves Nephilim. He said they keep the damned souls of men penned up in some kind of box of theirs, screaming—"

"What, the Pyxis? It holds bits of demon energy, Nate, not men's souls! It's perfectly harmless. I'll show it to you later, in the weapons room, if you don't believe me."

Nate looked no less grim. "He said that if the Nephilim got their hands on me, they'd take me apart, piece by piece, for breaking their Laws."

A cold shiver went up Tessa's spine; she drew away from her brother, and saw that one of the drawing room windows was open, the curtains fluttering in the breeze. So her shiver had been more than just nerves. "Did you open the window? It's so cold in here, Nate."

Nate shook his head. "It was open when I came in."

Shaking her head, Tessa went across the room and drew the window down. "You'll catch your death—"

"Never mind my death," Nate said irritably. "What about the Shadowhunters? Are you saying they haven't kept you imprisoned here?"

"No." Tessa turned away from the window. "They haven't. They're strange people, but the Shadowhunters have been kind to me. I *wanted* to stay here. They've been generous enough to let me."

Nate shook his head. "I don't understand."

Tessa felt a spark of anger, which surprised her; she pushed it back. It wasn't Nate's fault. There was so much he didn't know. "Where else was I going to go, Nate?" she asked, crossing the room to him and taking his arm. She led him back over to the armchair. "Sit down. You're exhausting yourself."

Nate sat obediently, and looked up at her. There was a distant look in his eyes. Tessa knew that look. It meant he was plotting, hatching some mad plan, dreaming a ridiculous dream. "We can still get away from this place," he said. "Get to Liverpool, get on a steamer. Go back to New York."

"And do what?" Tessa said as gently as she could. "There's nothing there for us. Not with Aunt dead. I had to sell all our things to pay for the funeral. The apartment's gone. There was no rent money. There's no place for us in New York, Nate."

"We'll make a place. A new life."

Tessa looked at her brother sadly. There was pain in seeing him like this, his face full of hopeless pleading, bruises blossoming on his cheekbones like ugly flowers, his fair hair still matted in places with blood. Nate was not like other people, Aunt Harriet had always said. He had a beautiful innocence about him that had to be protected at all costs.

And Tessa had tried. She and her aunt had hidden Nate's own weaknesses from him, the consequences of his own flaws and failings. Never telling him of the work Aunt Harriet had had to do to make up the money he had lost gambling, of the taunts Tessa had endured from other children, calling her brother a drunk, a wastrel. They had hidden these things from him to keep him from being hurt. But he had been hurt anyway, Tessa thought. Maybe Jem was right. Maybe the truth was always best.

Sitting down on the ottoman opposite her brother, she

looked at him steadily. "It can't be like that, Nate. Not yet. This mess we're both in now, it will follow us even if we run. And if we run, we'll be alone when it does find us. There will be no one to help or protect us. We need the Institute, Nate. We need the Nephilim."

Nate's blue eyes were dazed. "I guess so," he said, and the phrase struck Tessa, who had heard nothing but British voices for nearly two months, as so American that she felt homesick. "It's because of me that you're here. De Quincey tortured me. Made me write those letters, send you that ticket. He told me he wouldn't hurt you once he had you, but then he never let me see you, and I thought—I thought—" He raised his head and looked at her dully. "You ought to hate me."

Tessa's voice was firm. "I could never hate you. You're my brother. You're my blood."

"Do you think when all this is over, we can go back home?" Nate asked. "Forget all this ever happened? Live normal lives?"

Live normal lives. The words conjured up an image of herself and Nate in some small, sunny apartment. Nate could get another job, and in the evening she could cook and clean for him, while on weekends they could walk in the park or take the train to Coney Island and ride the carousel, or go to the top of the Iron Tower and watch the fireworks explode at night over the Manhattan Beach Hotel. There would be real sunshine, not like this gray watery version of summer, and Tessa could be an ordinary girl, with her head in a book and her feet planted firmly on the familiar pavement of New York City.

But when she tried to hold this mental picture in her head, the vision seemed to crumble and fall away from her, like a cobweb when you tried to lift it whole in your hands. She saw Will's face, and Jem's, and Charlotte's, and even Magnus's as he said, *Poor thing. Now that you know the truth, you can never go back.*

"But we are not normal," said Tessa. "I am not normal. And you know that, Nate."

He looked down at the floor. "I know." He gave a helpless little wave of his hand. "So it's true. You are what de Quincey said you were. Magical. He said you had the power to change shape, Tessie, to become anything you wanted to be."

"Did you even believe him? It's true—well, almost true—but I barely believed it myself at first. It's so strange—"

"I've seen stranger things." His voice was hollow. "God, it ought to have been me."

Tessa frowned. "What do you mean?"

But before he could answer, the door swung open. "Miss Gray." It was Thomas, looking apologetic. "Miss Gray, Master Will is—"

"Master Will is right here." It was Will, ducking nimbly around Thomas, despite the other boy's bulk. He was still in the clothes he'd changed into the night before, and they looked rumpled. Tessa wondered if he'd slept in the chair in Jem's room. There were blue-gray shadows under his eyes, and he looked tired, though his eyes brightened—with relief? amusement? Tessa couldn't tell—as his gaze fell on Nate.

"Our wanderer, found at last," he said. "Thomas tells me you were hiding behind the curtains?"

Nate looked at Will dully. "Who are you?"

Quickly Tessa made the introductions, though neither boy seemed all that happy to meet the other. Nate still looked as if he were dying, and Will was regarding Nate as if he were a new scientific discovery, and not a very attractive one at that.

"So you're a Shadowhunter," Nate said. "De Quincey told me that you lot were monsters."

"Was that before or after he tried to eat you?" Will inquired.

Tessa rose quickly to her feet. "Will. Might I speak to you in the corridor for a moment, please?"

If she had expected resistance, she didn't get it. After a last hostile look at Nate, Will nodded and went with her silently out into the hall, closing the drawing room door behind him.

The illumination in the windowless corridor was variable, the witchlight casting discrete bright pools of light that didn't quite touch one another. Will and Tessa stood in the shadows between two of the pools, looking at each other—warily, Tessa thought, like angry cats circling in an alley.

It was Will who broke the silence. "Very well. You have me alone in the corridor—"

"Yes, yes," said Tessa impatiently, "and thousands of women all over England would pay handsomely for the privilege of such an opportunity. Can we put aside the display of your wit for a moment? This is important."

"You want me to apologize, do you?" Will said. "For what happened in the attic?"

Tessa, caught off guard, blinked. "The *attic*?"

"You want me to say I'm sorry that I kissed you."

At the words, the memory rose up again in Tessa with an unexpected clarity—Will's fingers in her hair, the touch of his hand on her glove, his mouth on hers. She felt herself flush and hoped furiously that it wouldn't be visible in the dimness. "What—no. No!"

"So you don't want me to be sorry," Will said. He was smiling very slightly now, the sort of smile a small child might bend upon the castle he has just built out of toy blocks, before he destroys it with a wave of his arm.

"I don't care whether you're sorry or not," Tessa said. "That's not what I wanted to talk to you about. I wanted to tell you to be kind to my brother. He's been through an awful ordeal. He doesn't need to be interrogated like some sort of criminal."

Will replied more quietly than Tessa would have thought. "I understand that. But if he's hiding anything—"

"Everyone hides things!" Tessa burst out, surprising herself. "There are things I know he's ashamed of, but that doesn't mean they need to matter to you. It's not as if you tell everyone everything, do you?"

Will looked wary. "What are you on about?"

What about your parents, Will? Why did you refuse to see them? Why do you have nowhere to go but here? And why, in the attic, did you send me away? But Tessa said none of those things. Instead she said, "What about Jem? Why didn't you tell me he was ill the way he is?"

"*Jem?*" Will's surprise seemed genuine. "He didn't want me to. He considers it his business. Which it is. You might recall, I wasn't even in favor of him telling you himself. He thought he owed you an explanation, but he didn't. Jem owes nothing to anyone. What happened to him wasn't his fault, and yet he carries the burden of it and is ashamed—"

"He has nothing to be ashamed of."

"*You* might think so. Others see no difference between his illness and an addiction, and they despise him for being weak. As if he could just stop taking the drug if he had enough willpower." Will sounded surprisingly bitter. "They've said as much, sometimes to his face. I didn't want him to have to hear you say it too."

"I would never have said that."

"How would I have guessed what you might say?" Will said. "I don't really know you, Tessa, do I? Any more than you know me."

"You don't want anyone to know you," Tessa snapped. "And very well, I won't try. But don't pretend that Jem is just like you. Perhaps he'd rather people knew the truth of who he is."

"Don't," Will said, his blue eyes darkening. "Don't think you know Jem better than I do."

"If you care about him so much, why aren't you doing anything to help him? Why not look for a cure?"

"Do you think we *haven't*? Do you think Charlotte hasn't looked, Henry hasn't looked, that we haven't hired warlocks, paid for information, called in favors? Do you imagine Jem's death is just something we have all accepted without ever fighting against it?"

"Jem told me that he had asked you all to stop looking," Tessa said, calm in the face of his anger, "and that you had. Haven't you?"

"He told you that, did he?"

"*Have* you stopped?"

"There is nothing to find, Tessa. There is no cure."

"You don't know that. You could keep looking and not ever tell him you were looking. There might be something. Even the littlest chance—"

Will raised his eyebrows. The flickering corridor light deepened the shadows under his eyes, the angular bones of his cheeks. "You think we should disregard his wishes?"

"I think that you should do whatever you can, even if it means you must lie to him. I think I don't understand your acceptance of his death."

"And I think that *you* do not understand that sometimes the only choice is between acceptance and madness."

Behind them in the corridor someone cleared their throat. "What's going on here, then?" asked a familiar voice. Both Tessa and Will had been so caught up in their conversation that they had not heard Jem approaching. Will gave a guilty start before turning to look at his friend, who was regarding them both with calm interest. Jem was fully dressed but looked as if he had just woken from a feverish sleep, his hair mussed and his cheeks burning with color.

Will looked surprised, and not entirely pleased, to see him. "What are you doing out of bed?"

"I ran into Charlotte in the hall. She said we were all meeting in the drawing room to talk with Tessa's brother." Jem's tone was mild, and it was impossible to tell from his expression how much of Tessa and Will's conversation he had overheard. "I'm well enough to listen, at least."

"Oh, good, you're all here." It was Charlotte, hurrying up the corridor. Behind her strode Henry, and on either side of him, Jessamine and Sophie. Jessie had changed into one of her nicest dresses, Tessa observed, a sheer blue muslin, and she was carrying a folded blanket. Sophie, beside her, held a tray with tea and sandwiches on it.

"Are those for Nate?" Tessa asked, surprised. "The tea, and the blankets?"

Sophie nodded. "Mrs. Branwell thought he'd likely be hungry—"

"And *I* thought he might be cold. He was shivering so last night," Jessamine put in eagerly. "Should we bring these things in to him, then?"

Charlotte looked to Tessa for her approval, which disarmed her. Charlotte would be kind to Nate; she couldn't help it. "Yes. He's waiting for you."

"Thank you, Tessa," Charlotte said softly, and then she pushed the drawing room door open and went in, followed by the others. As Tessa moved to go after them, she felt a hand on her arm, a touch so light she almost might not have noticed it.

It was Jem. "Wait," he said. "Just a moment."

She turned to look at him. Through the open doorway she could hear a murmur of voices—Henry's friendly baritone, Jessamine's eager falsetto rising as she said Nate's name. "What is it?"

He hesitated. His hand on her arm was cool; his fingers felt like thin stems of glass against her skin. She wondered if the skin over the bones of his cheeks, where he was flushed and feverish, would be warmer to the touch.

"But my sister—" Nate's voice floated into the hallway, sounding anxious. "Is she joining us? Where is she?"

"Never mind. It's nothing." With a reassuring smile Jem dropped his hand. Tessa wondered, but turned and went into the drawing room, Jem behind her.

Sophie was kneeling by the grate, building up the fire; Nate was still in the armchair, where he sat with Jessamine's blanket thrown over his lap. Jessamine, upright on a stool nearby, was beaming proudly. Henry and Charlotte sat on the sofa opposite Nate—Charlotte clearly bursting with curiosity—and Will, as usual, was holding up the nearest wall by leaning against it and looking both irritable and amused at the same time.

As Jem went to join Will, Tessa fixed her attention on her brother. Some of the tension had gone out of him when she'd come back into the room, but he still looked miserable. He was plucking at Jessamine's blanket with his fingertips. She crossed the room and sank down onto the ottoman at his feet, resisting the urge to ruffle his hair or pat his shoulder. She could feel all the eyes in the room on her. Everyone was watching her and her brother, and she could have heard a pin drop.

"Nate," she said softly. "I assume everyone has introduced themselves?"

Nate, still picking at the blanket, nodded.

"Mr. Gray," said Charlotte, "we have spoken to Mr. Mortmain already. He has told us a great deal about you. About your fondness for Downworld. And gambling."

"Charlotte," Tessa protested.

Nate spoke heavily. "It's true, Tessie."

"No one blames your brother for what happened, Tessa." Charlotte made her voice very gentle as she turned back to Nate. "Mortmain says you already knew he was involved in occult practices when you arrived in London. How did you know that he was a member of the Pandemonium Club?"

Nate hesitated.

"Mr. Gray, we simply need to understand what happened to you. De Quincey's interest in you—I know you aren't well, and we have no wish to cruelly interrogate you, but if you could offer us even a little information, it might be of the most invaluable assistance—"

"It was Aunt Harriet's sewing notions," Nate said in a low voice.

Tessa blinked. "It was what?"

Nate continued, in a low voice. "Our aunt Harriet always kept mother's old jewelry box on the nightstand by her bed. She said she kept sewing notions in it, but I—" Nate took a deep breath, looking at Tessa as he spoke. "I was in debt. I'd made a few rash bets, had lost some money, and I was in a bad way. I didn't want you or Aunt to know. I remembered there was a gold bracelet Mother used to wear when she was alive. I got it into my head that it was still in that jewelry box and that Aunt Harriet was just too stubborn to sell it. You know how she is—how she *was*. Anyway, I couldn't let the idea go. I knew that if I could pawn the bracelet, I could get the money to pay off my debts. So one day when you and Aunt were out, I got hold of the box and searched it.

"Of course the bracelet wasn't in it. But I did find a false bottom to the case. There was nothing in it of any worth, just a wadded-up bunch of old papers. I snatched them when I heard you coming up the stairs, and took them back to my room."

Nate paused. All eyes were on him. After a moment Tessa, no longer able to hold her questions in, said, "*And?*"

"They were Mother's diary pages," Nate said. "Torn out of their original binding, with quite a few missing, but it was enough for me to put together a strange story.

"It began when our parents were living in London. Father was gone often, working in Mortmain's offices down at the docks, but mother had Aunt Harriet to keep her company, and me to keep her occupied. I had just been born. That was, until Father began to come home night after night increasingly distressed. He reported odd doings on the factory floor, bits of machinery malfunctioning in strange ways, noises heard at all hours, and even the night watchman gone missing one night. There were rumors, too, that Mortmain was involved in occult practices." Nate sounded as if he were remembering as much as reciting the tale. "Father shrugged the rumors off at first but eventually repeated them to Mortmain, who admitted everything. I gather he managed to make it sound rather harmless, as if he were just having a bit of a lark with spells and pentagrams and things. He called the organization he belonged to the Pandemonium Club. He suggested that Father come to one of their meetings, and bring Mother."

"Bring Mother? But he couldn't possibly have wanted to do that—"

"Probably not, but with a new wife and a new baby, Father would have been eager to please his employer. He agreed to go, and to bring Mother with him."

"Father should have gone to the police—"

"A rich man like Mortmain would have had the police in his pocket," interrupted Will. "Had your father gone to the police, they would have laughed at him."

Nathaniel pushed the hair back off his forehead; he was sweating now, strands of hair sticking to his skin. "Mortmain arranged a carriage to come for both of them late at night, when no one would be watching. The carriage brought them to Mortmain's town house. After that there were many missing pages, and no details about what happened that night. It was the first time they went, but not, I learned, the last. They met with the Pandemonium Club several times over the course of the next few months. Mother, at least, hated going, but they continued to attend the meetings until something changed abruptly. I don't know what it was; there were few pages after that. I was able to discern that when they left London, they did it under cover of night, that they told no one where they were going, and they left no forwarding address. They might as well have vanished. Nothing in the diary, though, said anything about why—"

Nathaniel broke off his story with a fit of dry coughing. Jessamine scrambled for the tea that Sophie had left on the side table, and a moment later was pressing a cup into Nate's hand. She gave Tessa a superior expression as she did so, as if to point out that Tessa really ought to have thought of it first.

Nate, having quieted his coughing with tea, continued. "Having found the diary pages, I felt as if I'd stumbled across a gold mine. I'd heard of Mortmain. I knew the man was as rich as Croesus, even if he was evidently a bit mad. I wrote to him and told him I was Nathaniel Gray, the son of Richard and Elizabeth Gray, that my father was dead, and so was my mother, and in among her papers I had found evidence of his occult activities. I intimated that I was eager to meet him and discuss possible employment, and that if he proved less eager to meet me, there were several newspapers that I imagined would be interested in my mother's diary."

"That was enterprising." Will sounded nearly impressed.

Nate smiled. Tessa shot him a furious look. "Don't look pleased with yourself. When Will says 'enterprising,' he means 'morally deficient.'"

"No, I mean enterprising," said Will. "When I mean morally deficient, I say, 'Now, that's something *I* would have done.'"

"That's enough, Will," Charlotte interrupted. "Let Mr. Gray finish his story."

"I thought perhaps he'd send me a bribe, some money to

shut me up," Nate went on. "Instead I got a first-class steamer ticket to London and the official offer of a job once I arrived. I figured I was onto a good thing, and for the first time in my life, I didn't plan on messing it up.

"When I got to London, I went straight to Mortmain's house, where I was ushered into the study to meet him. He greeted me with great warmth, telling me how glad he was to see me and how I looked just like my dear dead mother. Then he grew serious. He sat me down and told me he had always liked my parents and had been saddened when they had left England. He had not known they were dead until he received my letter. Even if I were to go public with what I knew about him, he claimed he would happily give me a job and do whatever he could for me, for my parents' sake.

"I told Mortmain that I would keep his secret—*if* he brought me with him to attend a meeting of the Pandemonium Club, that he owed it to me to show me what it was he had shown my parents. The truth was, the mentioning of gambling in my mother's diary had sparked my interest. I imagined a meeting of a group of men silly enough to believe in magic and devils. Surely it wouldn't be difficult to win a bit of money off such fools." Nate closed his eyes.

"Mortmain agreed, reluctantly, to take me. I suppose he had no choice. That night the meeting was at de Quincey's town house. The moment the door opened, I knew I was the fool. This was no group of amateurs dabbling in spiritualism. This was the real thing, the Shadow World my mother had made only glancing reference to in her diary. It was *real*. I can barely describe my sense of shock as I stared around me—creatures of indescribable grotesqueness filled the room. The

Dark Sisters were there, leering at me from behind their whist cards, their nails like talons. Women with their faces and shoulders powdered white smiled at me with blood running out the corners of their mouths. Little creatures whose eyes changed color scuttled across the floor. I had never imagined such things were real, and I said as much to Mortmain.

"'There are more things in Heaven and earth, Nathaniel, than are dreamt of in your philosophy,' he said.

"Well, I knew the quote because of you, Tessa. You were always reading Shakespeare at me, and I even paid attention some of the time. I was about to tell Mortmain not to make fun of me, when a man came up to us. I saw Mortmain go stiff as a board, as if this were someone he was frightened of. He introduced me as Nathaniel, a new employee, and told me the man's name. De Quincey.

"De Quincey smiled. I knew immediately he wasn't human. I'd never seen a vampire before, with that death white skin of theirs, and of course when he smiled, I saw his teeth. I think I just stared. 'Mortmain, you're keeping things from me again,' he said. 'This is more than just a new employee. This is Nathaniel Gray. Elizabeth and Richard Gray's son.'

"Mortmain stammered something, looking baffled. De Quincey chuckled. 'I do hear things, Axel,' he said. Then he turned to me. 'I knew your father,' he told me. 'I liked him quite a bit. Perhaps you'd join me for a game of cards?'

"Mortmain shook his head at me, but I'd seen the card room when I'd come into the house, of course. I was drawn to the gaming tables like a moth to light. I sat playing faro all night with a vampire, two werewolves, and a wild-haired warlock. I made my jack that night—won a great deal of money, and drank a great deal of the colorful sparkling drinks that were passed around the room on silver trays. At some point Mortmain left, but I didn't care. I emerged in the dawn light feeling exultant, on top of the world—and with an invitation from de Quincey to return to the club whenever I liked.

"I was a fool, of course. I was having such a high old time of it because the drinks were mixed with warlock potions, addictive ones. And I had been *allowed* to win that evening. I went back of course, without Mortmain, night after night. At first I won—won steadily, which was how I was able to send money back to you and Aunt Harriet, Tessie. It certainly wasn't from working at Mortmain's. I went into the office irregularly, but I could barely concentrate even on the simple tasks I was assigned. All I thought about was getting back to the club, drinking more of those drinks, winning more money.

"Then I started to lose. The more I lost, the more obsessed I became with winning it back. De Quincey suggested I start playing on tick, so I borrowed money; I stopped coming into the office at all. I slept all day, and gambled all night. I lost everything." His voice was remote. "When I got your letter that Aunt had died, Tessa, I thought it was a judgment on me. A punishment for my behavior. I wanted to rush out and buy a ticket to return to New York that day—but I had no money. Desperate, I went to the club—I was unshaved, miserable, red-eyed. I must have looked like a man at his lowest ebb, because it was then that de Quincey approached me with a proposition. He drew me into a back room and pointed out that I had lost more money to the club than any one man could ever pay back. He seemed amused by it all, the devil, flicking invisible dust off his cuffs, grinning at me with those needle teeth. He asked me what I'd be willing to give to pay off my debts. I said, 'Anything.' And he said, 'What about your sister?'"

Tessa felt the hairs on her arms rise, and was uncomfortably aware of the eyes of everyone in the room on her. "What—what did he say about me?"

"I was utterly taken off guard," said Nate. "I didn't recall having discussed you with him, ever, but I had been drunk so many times at the club, and we had spoken very freely. . . ." The teacup in his hand rattled in its saucer; he set them both down, hard. "I asked him what he could possibly want with my sister. He told me that he had reason to know that one of my mother's children was . . . special. He had thought it might be me, but having had leisure to observe me, the only thing unusual about me was my foolishness." Nate's tone was bitter. "'But your sister, your sister is something else again,' he told me. 'She has all the power you do not. I have no intention of harming her. She is far too important.'

"I spluttered and begged for more information, but he was unyielding. Either I procured Tessa for him, or I would die. He even told me what it was I had to do."

Tessa exhaled slowly. "De Quincey told you to write me that letter," she said. "He had you send me the tickets for the *Main*. He had you bring me here."

Nate's eyes pleaded with her to understand. "He swore he wouldn't hurt you. He told me all he wanted was to teach you to use your power. He told me you'd be honored and wealthy beyond imagining—"

"Well, that's just fine, then," interrupted Will. "It's not as if there are more important things than money." His eyes were blazing with indignation; Jem looked no less disgusted.

"It's not Nate's fault!" Jessamine snapped. "Didn't you hear him? De Quincey would have killed him. And he knew who Nate was, where he came from; he would have found Tessa eventually anyway, and Nate would have died for no reason."

"So that's your objective ethical opinion, is it, Jess?" Will said. "And I suppose it has nothing to do with the fact that you've been drooling over Tessa's brother since he arrived. Any mundane will do, I suppose, no matter how useless—"

Jessamine let out an indignant squawk, and rose to her feet. Charlotte, her voice rising, tried to quiet them both as they shouted at each other, but Tessa had stopped listening; she was looking at Nate.

She had known for some time her brother was weak, that what her aunt had called innocence was really spoiled pettish childishness; that being a boy, the firstborn, and beautiful, Nate had always been the prince of his own tiny kingdom. She had understood that, while it had been his job as older brother to protect her, really it had always been she, and her aunt, who had protected him.

But he was her brother; she loved him; and the old protectiveness rose in her, as it always did where Nate was concerned, and probably always would. "Jessamine's right," she said, raising her voice to cut through the angry voices in the room. "It wouldn't have done him any good to refuse de Quincey, and there's no point arguing about it now. We still need to know what de Quincey's plans are. Do you know, Nate? Did he tell you what he wanted with me?"

Nate shook his head. "Once I agreed to send for you, he kept me trapped in his town house. He had me send a letter to Mortmain, of course, resigning from his employment; the poor man must have thought I was throwing his generosity back in his face. De Quincey wasn't planning on taking his eyes off me until he had you in hand, Tessie; I was his insurance. He gave the Dark Sisters my ring to prove to you that I was in their power. He promised me over and over that he wouldn't hurt you, that he was simply having the Sisters teach you to use your power. The Dark Sisters reported on your progress every day, so I knew you were still alive.

"Since I was there in the house anyway, I found myself observing the workings of the Pandemonium Club. I saw that there was an organization to the ranks. There were those who were very low down, clinging to the fringes, like Mortmain and his ilk. De Quincey and the higher-ups mostly kept them around because they had money, and they teased them with little glimpses of magic and the Shadow World to keep them coming back for more. Then there were those such as the Dark Sisters and others, those who had more power and responsibility in the club. They were all supernatural creatures, no humans. And then, at the top, was de Quincey. The others called him the Magister.

"They often held meetings to which the humans and those lower down weren't invited. That was where I first heard about Shadowhunters. De Quincey despises Shadowhunters," Nate said, turning to Henry and Charlotte. "He has a grudge against them—against you. He kept talking about how much better things would be when Shadowhunters were destroyed and Downworlders could live and trade in peace—"

"What tosh." Henry looked genuinely offended. "Don't know what kind of peace he thinks there'd be, without Shadowhunters."

"He talked about how there'd never been a way to defeat Shadowhunters before because their weapons were so superior. He said the legend was that God had meant the Nephilim to be superior warriors, so no living creature could destroy them. So, apparently he thought, 'Why not a creature who *wasn't* living at all?'"

"The automatons," said Charlotte. "His machine army."

Nate looked puzzled. "You've seen them?"

"A few of them attacked your sister last night," said Will. "Fortunately, we Shadowhunter monsters were around to save her."

"Not that she was doing too badly by herself," Jem murmured.

"Do you know anything about the machines?" Charlotte demanded, leaning forward eagerly. "Anything at all? Did de Quincey ever talk about them in front of you?"

Nate shrank back in his chair. "He did, but I didn't understand most of it. I don't have a mechanical mind, really—"

"It's simple." It was Henry, using the tone of someone trying to calm a frightened cat. "Right now these machines of de Quincey's just run on mechanisms. They have to be wound up, like clocks. But we found a copy of a spell in his library that indicates that he's trying to find a way to make them *live*, a way to bind demon energy to the clockwork shell and bring it to life."

"Oh, that! Yes, he talked about *that*," Nathaniel replied, like a child pleased to be able to give the right answer in a schoolroom. Tessa could practically see the ears of the Shadowhunters pricking up with excitement. This was what they really wanted to know. "That's what he hired the Dark Sisters for—not just for training Tessa. They're warlocks, you know, and they were meant to be figuring out how it could be done. And they did. It wasn't long ago—a few weeks—but they did."

"They did?" Charlotte looked shocked. "But, then why hasn't de Quincey done it yet? What's he waiting for?"

Nate looked from her anxious face to Tessa's, and all around the room. "I—I thought you knew. He said the binding charm could only be generated at the full moon. When that happens, the Dark Sisters will get to work, and then—he's got dozens of the things stored in his hideaway, and I know he plans to make many more—hundreds, thousands, perhaps. I suppose he'll animate them, and . . ."

"The full moon?" Charlotte, glancing toward the window, bit her lip. "That will be very soon—tomorrow night, I think."

Jem straightened up like a shot. "I can check the lunar tables in the library. I'll be right back." He vanished through the door.

Charlotte turned to Nate. "You're quite sure about this?"

Nate nodded, swallowing hard. "When Tessa escaped from the Dark Sisters, de Quincey blamed me, even though I hadn't known anything about it. He told me he was going to let the Night Children drain my blood as a punishment. He kept me imprisoned for days before the party. He didn't care what he said in front of me then. He knew I was going to die. I heard him talking about how the Sisters had mastered the binding spell. That it wasn't going to be long before the Nephilim were destroyed, and all the members of the Pandemonium Club could rule London in their stead."

Will spoke, his voice harsh. "Have you any idea where de Quincey might be hiding now that his house has burned?"

Nate looked exhausted. "He has a hideaway in Chelsea. He would have gone to ground there with those who are loyal to him—there are still probably a hundred vampires of his clan who weren't at the town house that night. I know exactly where the place is. I can show you on a map—" He broke off as Jem burst into the room, his eyes very wide.

"It's not tomorrow," Jem said. "The full moon. It's tonight."

17

Call the Darkness Down

The old church tower and garden wall
Are black with autumn rain,
And dreary winds foreboding call
The darkness down again.
–Emily Brontë, "The Old Church Tower"

While Charlotte dashed to the library to notify the Enclave that emergency action would need to be taken that evening, Henry remained in the drawing room with Nathaniel and the others. He was surprisingly patient as Nate painstakingly indicated on a map of London the spot where he believed de Quincey's hideaway to be—a house in Chelsea, near the Thames. "I don't know which one it is exactly," Nate said, "so you'll have to be careful."

"We are always careful," Henry said, ignoring Will's wry

look in his direction. Not long after that, however, he sent Will and Jem to the weapons room with Thomas to ready a stock of seraph blades and other armaments. Tessa remained in the drawing room with Jessamine and Nate while Henry hurried off to the crypt to retrieve some of his more recent inventions.

As soon as the others had gone, Jessamine commenced fluttering around Nate—building up the fire for him, going to fetch another blanket to wrap around his shoulders, and offering to find a book to read aloud to him, which he declined. If Jessamine was hoping to win Nate's heart by fussing over him, Tessa thought, she would be in for a disappointment. Nate expected to be fussed over and would hardly notice her special attentions.

"So what's going to happen now?" he asked finally, half-buried under a mound of blankets. "Mr. and Mrs. Branwell—"

"Oh, call them Henry and Charlotte. Everyone does," Jessamine said.

"They'll be notifying the Enclave—that's all the rest of London's Shadowhunters—of the location of de Quincey's hideaway, so they can plan an attack," said Tessa. "But really, Nate, you shouldn't be worrying about these things. You should be resting."

"So it'll just be us." Nate's eyes were closed. "In this big old place. Seems strange."

"Oh, Will and Jem won't be going with them," said Jessamine. "I heard her talking to them in the weapons room when I went to get the blanket."

Nate's eyes opened. "They *won't?*" He sounded astonished. "Why not?"

"They're too young," said Jessamine. "Shadowhunters are

considered adults at eighteen, and for this kind of undertaking—something dangerous that the whole Enclave is participating in—they tend to leave the younger ones at home."

Tessa felt a strange little pang of relief, which she covered by asking hurriedly, "But that's so odd. They let Will and Jem go to de Quincey's—"

"And that's why they can't go now. Apparently, Benedict Lightwood is arguing that the raid on de Quincey's turned out as badly as it did because Will and Jem are insufficiently trained, though how any of it was meant to be Jem's fault, I'm not sure. If you ask me, he wants an excuse to make Gabriel stay at home, even though he's already eighteen. He babies him horribly. Charlotte said he told her that there have been whole Enclaves wiped out in a single night before, and the Nephilim have an obligation to leave the younger generation standing, to carry on, as it were."

Tessa's stomach twisted. Before she could say anything, the door opened and Thomas came in. He was carrying a stack of folded clothes. "These are old things of Master Jem's," he said to Nate, looking slightly embarrassed. "It looks like you might be about the same size, and, well, you ought to have something to wear. If you'll accompany me back to your room, we can see if they fit."

Jessamine rolled her eyes. Tessa wasn't sure why. Perhaps she thought castoffs weren't good enough for Nate.

"Thank you, Thomas," Nate said, rising to his feet. "And I must tender my apologies for my earlier behavior, when I, ah, hid from you. I must have been feverish. That's the only explanation."

Thomas flushed. "Just doing my job, sir."

"Perhaps you should get some sleep," Tessa said, noting the dark rings of exhaustion around her brother's eyes. "There won't be much for us to do now, not until they return."

"Actually," Nate said, looking from Jessamine to Tessa, "I think I've had enough of rest. A fellow ought to get back on his feet eventually, oughtn't he? I could stand to eat a bite of something, and I wouldn't mind some company. If you wouldn't mind my joining you here once I'm dressed?"

"Of course not!" Jessamine looked delighted. "I'll ask Agatha to prepare something light. And perhaps a game of cards to keep us occupied after we eat. Sandwiches and tea, I think." She clapped her hands together as Thomas and Nate left the room, and turned to Tessa, her eyes bright. "Won't that be fun?"

"Cards?" Tessa, who had been shocked nearly speechless by Jessamine's suggestion, found her voice. "You think we ought to play *cards*? While Henry and Charlotte are off fighting de Quincey?"

Jessamine tossed her head. "As if our moping around would help them! I'm sure they'd rather we were cheerful and active in their absence rather than idle and morose."

Tessa frowned. "I really don't think," she said, "that suggesting cards to Nate was a kind idea, Jessamine. You know perfectly well he has . . . trouble . . . with gambling."

"We're not going to *gamble*," Jessamine said airily. "Just a friendly game of cards. Really, Tessa, must you be such a wet blanket?"

"A *what*? Jessamine, I know you're only trying to keep Nate happy. But this isn't the way—"

"And I suppose *you've* mastered the art of winning men's affections?" Jessamine snapped, her brown eyes sparking with anger. "You think I haven't seen you looking at Will with puppy-dog eyes? As if he were even— Oh!" She threw up her hands. "Never mind. You make me sick. I'm going to talk to Agatha without you." With that, she rose to her feet and flounced out of the room, pausing in the doorway only to say "And I know you don't care how you look, but you ought to at least fix your hair, Tessa. It looks like birds are living in it!" before the door slammed shut behind her.

Silly as Tessa knew it was, Jessamine's words stung. She hastened back to her room to splash water on her face and run a hairbrush through her tangled hair. Looking at her own white face in the mirror, she tried not to wonder if she still looked like the sister Nate remembered. Tried not to imagine how she might have changed.

Finished, she hurried out into the corridor—and nearly walked directly into Will, who was leaning against the corridor wall opposite her door, examining his nails. With his usual disregard for manners, he was in shirtsleeves, and over the shirt was a series of leather straps crisscrossing his chest. Across his back hung a long, thin blade; she could see the hilt of it just over his shoulder. Thrust through his belt were several long, thin white seraph blades.

"I—" Jessamine's voice echoed in Tessa's head: *You think I haven't seen you looking at Will with puppy-dog eyes?* The witchlight was burning low. Tessa hoped it was too dim in the corridor for him to see her blush. "I thought you weren't going with the Enclave tonight," she said finally, more to have something to say than anything else.

"I'm not. I'm bringing these down to Charlotte and Henry

in the courtyard. Benedict Lightwood is sending his carriage for them. It's faster. It should be here shortly." It was dark in the corridor, dark enough that though Tessa thought that Will was smiling, she wasn't sure. "Concerned about my safety, are you? Or had you planned to gift me with a favor so I could wear it into battle like Wilfred of *Ivanhoe*?"

"I never liked that book," Tessa said. "Rowena was such a ninny. Ivanhoe should have chosen Rebecca."

"The dark-haired girl, not the blonde? Really?" Now she was almost sure he was smiling.

"Will—?"

"Yes?"

"Do you think the Enclave will actually manage to kill him? De Quincey, that is?"

"Yes." He spoke without hesitation. "The time for negotiation has passed. If you've ever seen terriers in a rat-baiting pit—well, I don't suppose you would have. But that's what it will be like tonight. The Clave will dispatch the vampires one by one until they are wiped out utterly."

"You mean there will be no more vampires in London?"

Will shrugged. "There are always vampires. But de Quincey's clan will be gone."

"And once it's over—once the Magister is gone—I suppose there will be no more reason for Nate and me to stay in the Institute, will there?"

"I—" Will seemed genuinely taken aback. "I suppose— Yes, well, that's true. I imagine that you would prefer to stay in a less . . . violent locale. Perhaps you could even see some of the nicer parts of London. Westminster Abbey—"

"I would prefer to go home," Tessa said. "To New York."

Will said nothing. The witchlight in the corridor had faded; in the shadows she couldn't clearly see his face.

"Unless there were a reason for me to stay," she went on, half-wondering what she herself even meant by that. It was easier to talk to Will like this, when she couldn't see his face, and could only sense his presence near hers in the dark corridor.

She didn't see him move, but she felt his fingers touch the back of her hand lightly. "Tessa," he said. "Please don't worry. Soon it will all be settled."

Her heart thumped painfully against her ribs. Soon *what* would be settled? He couldn't mean what she thought he did. He had to mean something else. "Don't *you* wish to go home?"

He didn't move, his fingers still brushing her hand. "I can't ever go home."

"But why not?" she whispered, but it was too late. She felt him retreating from her. His hand drew back from hers. "I know your parents came to the Institute when you were twelve and you refused to see them. Why? What did they do to you that was so dreadful?"

"They did nothing." He shook his head. "I must go. Henry and Charlotte are waiting."

"Will," she said, but he was already walking away, a slim dark shadow moving toward the stairs. "Will," she called after him. "Will, who is Cecily?"

But he was already gone.

By the time Tessa returned to the drawing room, Nate and Jessamine were there, and the sun had begun to set. She went immediately to the window and looked out. In the courtyard below, Jem, Henry, Will, and Charlotte were gathered, their shadows cast long and dark across the Institute's steps. Henry was putting a last *iratze* rune on his arm while Charlotte seemed to be giving Jem and Will instructions. Jem was nodding, but Tessa could tell even at this distance that Will, whose arms were crossed over his chest, was being recalcitrant. *He wants to go with them,* she thought. *He doesn't want to stay here.* Jem probably wanted to go as well, but he wouldn't complain about it. That was the difference between the two boys. One of the differences, at any rate.

"Tessie, are you sure you don't want to play?" Nate turned to look at his sister. He was back in his armchair, a rug over his legs, cards laid out on a small table between him and Jessamine beside a silver tea service and a small plate of sandwiches. His hair looked slightly damp, as if he had washed it, and he was wearing Jem's clothes. Nathaniel had lost weight, Tessa could tell, but Jem was slender enough that his shirt was still a little tight on Nate at the collar and cuffs—though Jem's shoulders were still broader, and Nate looked a little slighter of frame in Jem's jacket.

Tessa was still looking out the window. A great black carriage had drawn up, with a design on the door of two burning torches, and Henry and Charlotte were getting into it. Will and Jem had vanished from view.

"She's sure." Jessamine sniffed when Tessa didn't answer. "Just look at her. She looks so disapproving."

Tessa tore her gaze from the window. "I'm not disapproving. It just seems wrong to play games while Henry and Charlotte and others are out risking their lives."

"Yes, I know, you said that before." Jessamine set her cards down. "Really, Tessa. This happens all the time. They go off to battle; they come back. There's nothing worth getting worked up over."

Tessa bit her lip. "I feel I ought to have said good-bye or good luck, but with all the rushing about—"

"You needn't worry," Jem said, coming into the drawing room, Will just behind him. "Shadowhunters don't say good-bye, not before a battle. Or good luck. You must behave as if return is certain, not a matter of chance."

"We don't require luck," said Will, throwing himself into a chair beside Jessamine, who shot him an angry look. "We have a heavenly mandate, after all. With God on your side, what does luck matter?" He sounded surprisingly bitter.

"Oh, stop being so depressing, Will," said Jessamine. "We're playing cards. You can either join the game or be quiet."

Will raised an eyebrow. "What are you playing?"

"Pope Joan," said Jessamine coolly, dealing out cards. "I was just explaining the rules to Mr. Gray."

"Miss Lovelace says you win by ridding yourself of all your cards. That seems backward to me." Nate grinned across the table at Jessamine, who dimpled annoyingly.

Will poked at the steaming cup that sat beside Nathaniel's elbow. "Is there any tea in this," he inquired, "or is it simply *pure* brandy?"

Nate flushed. "Brandy is restorative."

"Yes," said Jem, a little edge to his voice. "It often restores men right to the poorhouse."

"Really! The two of you! Such hypocrites. It isn't as if Will doesn't drink, and Jem—" Jessamine broke off, biting her lip. "You two are just fussing because Henry and Charlotte wouldn't take you along with them," she said finally. "Because you're too *young*." She smiled at Nate across the table. "I prefer the company of a more mature gentleman, myself."

Nate, Tessa thought disgustedly, *is exactly two years older than Will. Hardly a century. Nor is he by any stretch of the imagination "mature."* But before she could say anything, a great, echoing boom sounded through the Institute.

Nate raised his eyebrows. "I thought this wasn't a real church. I thought there were no bells."

"There aren't. That sound isn't church bells ringing." Will rose to his feet. "That's the summoning bell. It means someone is downstairs and demands conference with the Shadowhunters. And since James and I are the only ones here . . ."

He looked at Jessamine, and Tessa realized he was waiting for Jessamine to contradict him, to say that she was a Shadowhunter too. But Jessamine was smiling at Nate, and he was leaning in to say something in her ear; neither of them was paying attention to what else was going on in the room.

Jem looked at Will and shook his head. They both turned toward the door; as they went out, Jem looked at Tessa and gave her a little shrug. *I wish you were a Shadowhunter,* she thought his eyes were saying, but maybe it was simply what she hoped they were saying. Perhaps he was merely smiling at her kindly and there was no meaning in it.

Nate poured himself another hot water and brandy. He and Jessamine had abandoned the pretense that they were playing cards and were leaning close to each other, murmuring in low voices. Tessa felt a dull thump of disappointment. Somehow she had expected that Nate's ordeal would have made him more thoughtful—more inclined to understand that there were larger things at work in the world, more important things than his own immediate pleasures. She expected nothing better of Jessamine, but what had once seemed charming in Nate now grated on her nerves in a way that surprised her.

She leaned toward the window again. There was a carriage in the courtyard. Will and Jem were on the front steps. With them was a man in evening dress—elegant black tailcoat, high silk hat, a white waistcoat that shone under the witchlight torches. He looked like a mundane to Tessa, though at this distance it was difficult to tell. As she watched, he raised his arms and made a broad gesture. She saw Will look at Jem, and Jem nod, and wondered what on earth they were talking about.

She looked past the man to the coach behind him—and froze. Instead of a coat of arms, the name of a business enterprise was painted across one of the doors: MORTMAIN AND COMPANY.

Mortmain. The man her father had worked for, whom Nathaniel had blackmailed, who had introduced her brother to the Shadow World. What was he doing here?

She looked at Nate again, her feeling of annoyance washed away by a wave of protectiveness. If he knew Mortmain was here, he would doubtless be upset. It would be better if she found out what was going on before he did. She slid off the windowsill and made her way quietly to the door; deep in conversation with Jessamine, Nate hardly seemed to notice as she left the room.

It was surprisingly easy for Tessa to find her way to the huge stone-bound spiral stairway that speared through the center of the Institute. She must have been learning her way around the place at last, she decided as she made her way down the steps to the ground floor, and found Thomas standing in the entryway.

He was holding a massive sword, point down, his face very serious. Behind him the massive double doors of the Institute were open on a rectangle of blue-black London twilight, lit by the blaze of the courtyard's witchlight torches. He looked taken aback at the sight of Tessa. "Miss Gray?"

She pitched her voice low. "What's going on out there, Thomas?"

He shrugged. "Mr. Mortmain," he said. "He wanted to speak with Mr. and Mrs. Branwell, but since they're not here—"

Tessa started toward the door.

Thomas, startled, moved to prevent her. "Miss Gray, I don't think—"

"You'll have to use that sword on me to stop me, Thomas," Tessa said in a cold voice, and Thomas, after a moment's hesitation, moved aside. Tessa, with a twinge, hoped she hadn't hurt his feelings, but he looked more astonished than anything else.

She moved past him, onto the steps outside the Institute, where Will and Jem were standing. A hard breeze was coming up, ruffling her hair and making her shiver. At the foot of the stairs stood the man she had seen from the window. He was shorter than she would have imagined: small and wiry-looking, with a tanned, friendly face beneath the brim of his tall hat. Despite the elegance of his clothes, he had the bluff, natural bearing of a sailor or tradesman.

"Yes," he was saying, "Mr. and Mrs. Branwell were kind enough to call on me last week. And were even kinder, I understand, in keeping our meeting something of a secret."

"They didn't tell the Enclave about your occult experimentations, if that is what you mean," Will said a bit shortly.

Mortmain reddened. "Yes. It was a favor. And I had thought to return the favor in kind—" He broke off, looking past Will at Tessa. "And who is this? Another Shadowhunter?"

Will and Jem both turned at the same time and saw Tessa. Jem looked pleased to see her; Will, of course, looked exasperated, and perhaps a touch amused. "Tessa," he said. "Couldn't keep your nose out, could you?" He turned back to Mortmain. "This is Miss Gray, of course. Nathaniel Gray's sister."

Mortmain looked appalled. "Oh, good God. I should have realized. You look like him. Miss Gray—"

"I don't think she does, actually," Will said, but rather quietly, so Tessa doubted Mortmain could hear him.

"You can't see Nate," Tessa said. "I don't know if that's why you've come here, Mr. Mortmain, but he isn't well enough. He needs to recover from his ordeal, not be reminded of it."

The lines deepened at the corners of Mortmain's mouth. "I'm not here to see the boy," he said. "I recognize that I failed him, failed him abominably. Mrs. Branwell made that clear—"

"You should have looked for him," Tessa said. "My brother. You let him sink into the Shadow World without a trace." Some small part of Tessa's mind was amazed she was being so bold, but she went on, regardless. "When he told you he'd gone to work for de Quincey, you should have done something. You knew what kind of man de Quincey was—if you can even call him a man."

"I know." Mortmain looked gray beneath his hat. "That is why I am here. To try to make up for what I've done."

"And how do you propose to do that?" asked Jem, in his clear, strong voice. "And why *now*?"

Mortmain looked at Tessa. "Your parents," he said, "were good, kind people. I have always regretted introducing them to the Shadow World. At the time, I thought it all a delightful game and a bit of a joke. I have learned otherwise since. To assuage that guilt, I will tell you what I know. Even if it means I must flee England to escape de Quincey's wrath." He sighed. "Some time ago, de Quincey ordered from me a number of mechanical parts—cogs, cams, gears, and the like. I never asked what he needed them for. One does not inquire such things of the Magister. Only when you Nephilim came to see me did it occur to me that his need for them might be connected to a nefarious purpose. I investigated, and an informant within the club told me that de Quincey intended to build an army of mechanical monsters meant to destroy the ranks of Shadowhunters." He shook his head. "De Quincey and his ilk may despise Shadowhunters, but I do not. I am only a human man. I know they are all that stand between me and a world in which I and my kind are the playthings of demons. I cannot stand behind what de Quincey is doing."

"That is all very well," Will said, a hint of impatience in his voice, "but you are not telling us anything we do not already know."

"Did you also know," Mortmain said, "that he paid a pair of warlocks called the Dark Sisters to create a binding spell that would animate these creatures not with mechanics but with demonic energies?"

"We did," said Jem. "Though I believe there is only one Dark Sister remaining. Will destroyed the other one."

"But her sister brought her back via a necromantic charm," said Mortmain, a hint of triumph in his tone, as if he were relieved to at last have a piece of information that they did not. "Even now the two of them are ensconced in a mansion in Highgate—it used to belong to a warlock, until de Quincey had him killed—working on the binding spell. If my sources are correct, the Dark Sisters will attempt to implement the spell tonight."

Will's blue eyes were dark and thoughtful. "Thank you for the information," he said, "but de Quincey will soon be no more of a threat to us, or his mechanical monsters, either."

Mortmain's eyes widened. "Is the Clave to move against the Magister? Tonight?"

"Goodness," said Will. "You really do know all the terms, don't you. It's very disconcerting in a mundane." He smiled pleasantly.

"You mean you're not going to tell me," said Mortmain ruefully. "I suppose you wouldn't. But you should know that de Quincey has at his disposal hundreds of those clockwork creatures. An army. The moment the Dark Sisters work their spell, the army will rise and join with de Quincey. If the Enclave is to defeat him, it would be wise to ensure that that army does not rise, or they will be nearly impossible to defeat."

"Are you aware of the Dark Sisters' location, beyond the fact that it is in Highgate?" asked Jem.

Mortmain nodded. "Most certainly," he said, and rattled off a street name and house number.

Will nodded. "Well, we'll certainly take all this under advisement. Thank you."

"Indeed," said Jem. "Good evening, Mr. Mortmain."

"But—" Mortmain looked taken aback. "Are you going to do something about what I've told you, or not?"

"I said we'd take it under advisement," Will told him. "As for you, Mr. Mortmain, you look like a man with somewhere to be."

"What?" Mortmain glanced down at his evening dress, and chuckled. "I suppose so. It's just—if the Magister finds out that I've told you all this, my life could be in danger."

"Then perhaps it is time for a holiday," Jem suggested. "I've heard Italy is very pleasant this time of year."

Mortmain looked from Will to Jem and back again, and then seemed to give up. His shoulders sagged. He raised his eyes to Tessa. "If you could pass along my apologies to your brother . . ."

"I don't think so," Tessa said, "but thank you, Mr. Mortmain."

After a long pause he nodded, then turned away. The three of them watched as he climbed back into his carriage. The sound of the horses' hooves was loud in the courtyard as the carriage pulled away and rattled through the Institute gates.

"What are you going to do?" Tessa asked the moment the carriage was out of sight. "About the Dark Sisters?"

"Go after them, of course." Will's color was high, his eyes glittering. "Your brother said de Quincey had dozens of those creatures at his disposal; Mortmain says there are hundreds. If Mortmain's correct, we must get to the Dark Sisters before they work their spell, or the Enclave may well be walking into a slaughter."

"But—perhaps it would be better to warn Henry and Charlotte and the others—"

"How?" Will managed to make the one word sound cutting. "I suppose we could send Thomas to warn the Enclave, but there is no guarantee he will get there in time, and if the Dark Sisters manage to raise the army, he could simply be killed with the rest. No, we must manage the Dark Sisters on our own. I killed one of them before; Jem and I ought to be able to manage two."

"But perhaps Mortmain is wrong," Tessa said. "You have only his word; he might have faulty information."

"He might," Jem acknowledged, "but can you imagine if he doesn't? And we ignored him? The consequence to the Enclave could be utter destruction."

Tessa, knowing he was right, felt her heart sink. "Maybe I could help. I fought the Dark Sisters with you once before. If I could accompany you—"

"No," Will said. "It's out of the question. We have so little time to prepare that we must rely on our fighting experience. And you have none."

"I fought off de Quincey at the party—"

"I said no." Will's tone was final. Tessa looked at Jem, but he gave only an apologetic shrug as if to say that he was sorry but Will was right.

She turned her gaze back to Will. "But what about Boadicea?"

For a moment she thought he'd forgotten what he'd said to her in the library. Then the glimmer of a smile tugged at the corner of his mouth, as if he'd tried to fight it and couldn't. "You will be Boadicea someday, Tessa," he said, "but not tonight." He turned to Jem. "We ought to get Thomas and tell him to ready the carriage. Highgate's not close; we'd best get started."

Full night had descended on the city by the time Will and Jem stood out by the carriage, preparing to depart. Thomas was checking the fastenings on the horses while Will, his stele a white flash in the dimness, scrawled a Mark on Jem's bare forearm. Tessa, having registered her disapproval, stood on the steps and watched them, a hollow feeling in her stomach.

After satisfying himself that the harnesses were secure, Thomas turned and ran lightly up the steps, stopping when Tessa raised a hand to halt him. "Are they going now?" she asked. "Is that all?"

He nodded. "All ready to go, miss." He had tried to get Jem and Will to take him along, but Will was concerned that Charlotte would be angry at Thomas for participating in their exploit and had told him not to come.

"Besides," Will had said, "we ought to have a man in the house—someone to protect the Institute while we're gone. Nathaniel doesn't count," he'd added, with a sideways glance at Tessa, who had ignored him.

Will slid Jem's sleeve down, covering the Marks he had made. As he returned his stele to his pocket, Jem stood looking up at him; their faces were pale smudges in the torchlight. Tessa raised her hand, then lowered it slowly. What was it he had said? *Shadowhunters don't say good-bye, not before a battle. Or good luck. You must behave as if return is certain, not a matter of chance.*

The boys, as if alerted by her gesture, looked up toward her. She thought she could see the blue of Will's eyes, even from where she stood. He wore a strange look as their eyes locked, the look of someone who has just woken up and wonders if what they are looking at is real or a dream.

It was Jem who broke away and ran up the stairs to her. As he reached her, she saw that he had high color in his face, and his eyes were bright and hot. She wondered how much of the drug Will had let him take, so that he would be ready to fight.

"Tessa—," he said.

"I didn't mean to say good-bye," she said quickly. "But—it seems odd to let you leave without saying anything at all."

He looked at her curiously. He did something that surprised her then, and took her hand, turning it over. She looked down at it, at her bitten fingernails, the still-healing scratches along the backs of her fingers.

He kissed the back of it, just a light touch of his mouth, and his hair—as soft and light as silk—brushed her wrist as he lowered his head. She felt a shock go through her, strong enough to startle her, and she stood speechless as he straightened, his mouth curving into a smile.

"*Mizpah,*" he said.

She blinked at him, a little dazed. "What?"

"A sort of good-bye without saying good-bye," he said. "It is a reference to a passage in the Bible. '*And Mizpah, for he said, the Lord watch between me and thee when we are absent one from another.*'"

There was no chance for Tessa to say anything in response, for he had turned and run down the steps to join Will, who was as motionless as a statue, his face upturned, at the foot of the steps. His hands, sheathed in black gloves, were in fists at his sides, Tessa thought. But perhaps it was a trick of the light, for when Jem reached him and touched him on the shoulder, he turned with a laugh, and without another look at Tessa, he swung himself up into the driver's seat, Jem following him. He cracked the whip, and the carriage rattled through the gate, which slammed shut behind it as if pushed by invisible hands. Tessa heard the lock catch, a hard click in the silence, and then the sound of church bells ringing somewhere in the city.

Sophie and Agatha were waiting in the entryway for Tessa when she came back inside; Agatha was saying something to Sophie, but Sophie didn't appear to be listening. She looked over at Tessa as she came in, and something about the way she looked, for a moment, reminded Tessa of the way Will had looked at her in the courtyard. But that was ridiculous; there were no two people in the world more unalike than Sophie and Will.

Tessa stepped aside as Agatha went to close the great, heavy double doors. She had just pushed them shut, panting slightly, when the knob of the leftmost door, untouched, began to turn.

Sophie frowned. "They can't be back so soon, can they?"

Agatha gazed down, perplexed, at the turning knob, her hands still braced against the door—then stood back as the doors swung wide before her.

A figure stood on the doorstep, backlit by the light outside. For a moment all Tessa could tell was that he was tall and clad in a frayed jacket. Agatha, her head tipping back as she gazed upward, said in a startled voice, "Oh, my Lor'—"

The figure moved. Light flashed on metal; Agatha screamed and staggered. She seemed to be trying to back away from the stranger, but something was preventing her.

"Dear God in Heaven," Sophie whispered. "*What is that?*"

For a moment Tessa saw the whole scene frozen, as if it were a painting—the open door, the clockwork automaton, the one with the stripped bare hands, still in the same worn gray jacket. And still, dear God, with Jem's blood on its hands, dried red-black on the dull gray flesh, and the strips of copper showing through where the skin had been scraped or pulled away.

One bloodstained hand gripped Agatha's wrist; clamped in the other was a long, thin knife. Tessa moved forward, but it was already too late. The creature swung the blade with blinding speed, and buried it in Agatha's chest.

Agatha choked, her hands going to the blade. The creature stood, ragged and terrifying and unmoving as she clawed at the knife hilt; then, with appalling swiftness, it yanked the blade back, letting her crumple to the ground. Nor did the automaton remain to watch her fall, but turned and walked back out the door through which it had come.

Galvanized, Sophie screamed "Agatha!" and ran to her side. Tessa dashed to the door. The clockwork creature was walking down the steps, into the empty courtyard. She stared after it. What on earth had it come for, and why was it leaving now? But there was no time to dwell on that. She reached for the rope of the summoning bell and pulled it, hard. As the sound clanged through the building, she slammed the door shut, dropping the lock bar into place, then turned to help Sophie.

Together they managed to lift Agatha and half-carry, half-drag her across the room, where they fell to their knees beside her. Sophie, ripping strips of fabric from her white apron and pressing them over Agatha's wound, said in a tone of wild panic, "I don't understand, miss. Nothing should be able to touch that door—none but one with Shadowhunter blood should be able to turn the doorknob."

But he had Shadowhunter blood, Tessa thought with a sudden horror. Jem's blood, staining its metal hands like paint. Could that be why it had bent over Jem that night after the bridge? Could that be why it had fled, once it had gotten what it wanted—his blood? And didn't that mean it could come back whenever it wanted?

She began to rise to her feet, but it was already too late. The bar that held the door closed cracked with a noise like a gunshot, and tumbled to the ground in two pieces. Sophie looked up and screamed again, though she didn't move away from Agatha as the door burst open, a window onto the night.

The steps of the Institute were no longer empty; they were teeming, but not with people. Clockwork monsters swarmed up them, their movements jerky, their faces blank and staring. They were not quite like the ones Tessa had seen before. Some looked as though they had been put together so hastily that they had no faces at all, just smooth ovals of metal patched here and there with uneven bits of human skin. Even more horrible, quite a few of them had bits of machinery in place of arms or legs. One automaton had a scythe where his arm ought to have been; another sported a saw that stuck out of the hanging sleeve of his shirt like a parody of a real arm.

Tessa rose and flung herself against the open door, trying to heave it shut. It was heavy, and seemed to move agonizingly slowly. Behind her, Sophie was screaming, helplessly, over and over; Agatha was horribly silent. With a ragged gasp Tessa pushed at the door one more time—

And jerked her hands back as the door was torn out of her grasp, ripped from its hinges like a handful of weeds ripped out of the earth. She fell back as the automaton who had seized the door flung it aside and heaved itself forward, its metal feet clanking against the stone as it lurched over the threshold—followed by another and then another of its mechanical brethren, at least a dozen of them, advancing toward Tessa with their monstrous arms outstretched.

By the time Will and Jem reached the mansion in Highgate, the moon had begun to rise. Highgate was on a hill in the north part of London, commanding an excellent view of the city below, pale under the moon's light, which turned the fog and coal smoke that hung over the city into a silvery cloud. *A dream city,* Will thought, *floating in the air.* A bit of poetry hung at the edges of his mind, something about the terrible wonder of London, but his nerves were tight with the jangling tension of impending battle, and he could not remember the words.

The house was a great Georgian pile, set in abundant parkland. A high brick wall ran around it, the slanting dark mansard roof just visible above it from the street. A shiver of cold passed over Will as they drew near it, but he was unsurprised to feel such a thing in Highgate. They were near what Londoners called the Gravel Pit Woods at the city's edge, where thousands of bodies had been dumped during the Great Plague. Lacking a proper burial, their angry shades haunted the neighborhood even now, and Will had been sent up here more than once, thanks to their activities.

A black metal gate set into the mansion's wall kept out intruders, but Jem's Open rune made short work of the lock. After leaving the carriage just inside the gate, the two Shadowhunters found themselves on the curving drive that led up to the house's front entrance. The path was weed-ridden and overgrown, and the gardens stretched out around it, dotted with crumbling outbuildings and the blackened stumps of dead trees.

Jem turned to Will, eyes feverish. "Shall we get on with it?"

Will drew a seraph blade from his belt. "*Israfel*," he whispered, and the weapon blazed up like a fork of contained lightning. Seraph blades burned so brightly that Will always expected them to give off heat, but their blades were ice cold to the touch. He remembered Tessa telling him that Hell was cold, and he fought back the odd urge to smile at the memory. They'd been running for their lives, she ought to have been terrified, and there she had been, telling him about the *Inferno* in precise American tones.

"Indeed," he said to Jem. "It's time."

They ascended the front steps and tried the doors. Though Will had expected them to be locked, they were open, and gave way at the touch with a resonant creaking. He and Jem edged inside the house, the light of their seraph blades illuminating the way.

They found themselves in a grand foyer. The arched windows behind them had probably once been magnificent. Now they alternated whole panes with broken ones. Through the spiderwebbing cracks in the glass, a view of the tangled and overgrown parkland beyond was visible. The marble underfoot was cracked and broken, weeds growing up through it as they had been growing through the stones of the drive. Before Will and Jem, a great curving staircase swept upward, toward the shadowy first floor.

"This can't be right," Jem whispered. "It's as if no one's been here in fifty years."

Barely had he finished speaking when a sound rose on the night air, a sound that lifted the hairs on Will's neck and made the Marks on his shoulders burn. It was singing—but not pleasant singing. It was a voice capable of reaching notes no human voice could reach. Overhead, the chandelier's crystal pendants rattled like wineglasses set to vibrating at the touch of a finger.

"*Someone's* here," Will muttered back. Without another word he and Jem turned so that their backs were to each other. Jem faced the open front doorway; Will, the vast curving stairs.

Something appeared at the head of the stairs. At first Will saw only an alternating pattern of black and white, a shadow that moved. As it drifted downward, the singing sound grew louder, and the hairs on Will's neck prickled more. Sweat dampened the hair at his temples and ran down the small of his back, despite the chill air.

She was halfway down the stairs before he recognized her—Mrs. Dark, her long, bony body clad in a sort of nun's habit, a shapeless dark robe that fell from her neck to her feet. A lightless lantern swung from one clawed hand. She was alone—though not quite, Will realized as she paused on the landing, for the thing she was clutching in her hand was not a lantern after all. It was her sister's severed head.

"By the Angel," Will whispered. "Jem, look."

Jem looked, and swore too. Mrs. Black's head dangled from a plait of gray hair, which Mrs. Dark clutched as if it were a priceless artifact. The head's eyes were open, and perfectly white, like boiled eggs. Its mouth hung open too, a line of dried black blood threading from one corner of the lips.

Mrs. Dark stopped her song and giggled, like a schoolgirl. "Naughty, naughty," she said. "Breaking into my house like this. Bad little Shadowhunters."

"I thought," Jem said under his breath, "that the other sister was alive."

"Maybe this one brought her sister back to life and then chopped her head off again?" Will muttered. "Seems a lot of work for no real gain, but then . . ."

"Murdering Nephilim," Mrs. Dark snarled, fixing her gaze on Will. "Not content with killing my sister once, are you? You must return and prevent me even from giving her a second life. Do you know—have you any idea—what it's like to be entirely *alone?*"

"More than you can ever imagine," Will said tightly, and saw Jem glance at him sideways, puzzled. *Stupid*, Will thought. *I shouldn't say such things.*

Mrs. Dark swayed on her feet. "You are mortal. You are alone for a moment of time, a single breath of the universe. I am alone forever." She clutched the head to her tightly. "What difference does it make to you? Surely there are darker crimes in London that more urgently require the attention of the Shadowhunters than my poor attempts to bring back my sister."

Will's gaze met Jem's. The other boy shrugged. Clearly he was as confused as Will was. "It's true that necromancy is against the Law," Jem said, "but so is binding demon energies. And that does require our attention, quite urgently."

Mrs. Dark stared at them. "Binding demon energies?"

"There is no point in pretending. We know your plans exactly," said Will. "We know of the automatons, the binding spell, your service to the Magister—whom the rest of our Enclave is, right now, tracking to his hiding place. By tonight's end he will be utterly erased. There is no one for you to call on, nowhere for you to hide."

At that, Mrs. Dark paled markedly. "The Magister?" she whispered. "You have found the Magister? But how . . ."

"That's right," Will said. "De Quincey escaped us once, but not this time. We know where he is, and—"

But his words were drowned out—by laughter. Mrs. Dark was bent over the staircase railing, howling with mirth. Will and Jem stared in confusion as she straightened up. Blackish tears of hilarity streaked her face. "De Quincey, the Magister!" she cried. "That poncing, preening vampire! Oh, what a joke! You fools, you stupid little fools!"

18

Thirty Pieces of Silver

Blot out his name, then, record one lost soul more,
One task more declin'd, one more foot-path untrod,
One more devil's-triumph and sorrow for angels,
One wrong more to man, one more insult to God!
—Robert Browning, "The Lost Leader"

Tessa staggered back from the door. Behind her, Sophie was frozen, kneeling over Agatha, her hands pressed to the older woman's chest. Blood soaked through the pitiful cloth bandage under her fingers; Agatha had gone a horrible putty color and was making a noise like a teakettle boiling. When she saw the clockwork automatons, her eyes widened and she tried to push Sophie away with her bloody hands, but Sophie, still screaming, clung tenaciously to the older woman, refusing to move.

"Sophie!" There was a clatter of footsteps on the stairs, and Thomas burst into the entryway, his face very white. In his hand he gripped the massive sword Tessa had seen him holding earlier. With him was Jessamine, parasol in hand. Behind her was Nathaniel, looking absolutely terrified. "What on earth—?"

Thomas broke off, staring from Sophie, Tessa, and Agatha to the door and back again. The automatons had come to a halt. They stood in a line just inside the doorway, as still as puppets whose strings were no longer being pulled. Their blank faces stared straight ahead.

"Agatha!" Sophie's voice rose to a wail. The older woman was still, her eyes wide open but unfocused. Her hands hung limply at her sides.

Though it made her skin prickle to turn her back on the machines, Tessa bent and put her hand on Sophie's shoulder. The other girl shook her off; she was making little whimpering noises, like a kicked dog. Tessa darted a glance behind her toward the automatons. They were still as motionless as chess pieces, but how long could that last? "Sophie, please!"

Nate was breathing in pants, his eyes fixed on the door, his face as white as chalk. He looked as if he wanted nothing more than to turn and run. Jessamine glanced at him once, a look of surprise and disdain, before turning to Thomas. "Get her on her feet," she said. "She'll listen to you."

After a single startled glance at Jessamine, Thomas bent down and, gently but firmly, pried Sophie's hands from Agatha, raising her to her feet. She clung to him. Her hands and arms were as red as if she had come from a slaughterhouse, and her apron was nearly ripped in half and was printed with bloodied handprints. "Miss Lovelace," he said in a low voice, keeping Sophie close against him with the hand not holding the sword. "Take Sophie and Miss Gray to the Sanctuary—"

"No," said a drawling voice from behind Tessa, "I don't think so. Or rather, certainly, take the servant girl and go where you like with her. But Miss Gray will be remaining here. As will her brother."

The voice was familiar—shockingly so. Very slowly Tessa turned.

Standing among the frozen machines as if he had simply appeared there by magic was a man. Just as ordinary-looking as Tessa had thought he was before, though his hat was gone now, and his graying head was bare under the witchlight.

Mortmain.

He was smiling. Not as he had been smiling earlier, with affable cheerfulness. His smile now was almost sickening in its glee. "Nathaniel Gray," he said. "Excellently done. I admit that my faith in you was tested—tested sorely—but you have recovered admirably from your past missteps. I'm proud of you."

Tessa whirled to look at her brother, but Nate seemed to have forgotten she was there—that anyone else was there. He was staring past her at Mortmain, the oddest expression—a mix of fear and worship—stamped on his face. He moved forward, pushing past Tessa; she reached to hold him back, but he shook off her reaching hand with a flick of annoyance. At last he was standing directly in front of Mortmain.

With a cry he went to his knees and clasped his hands in front of him, almost as if he were praying.

"It was only ever my desire," he said, "to serve you, Magister."

***

Mrs. Dark was still laughing.

"But what is it?" Jem said in bewilderment, raising his voice to be heard over her peals of laughter. "What do you mean?"

Despite her ragged appearance Mrs. Dark managed an air of triumph. "De Quincey isn't the Magister," she sneered. "He's just a stupid bloodsucker, no better than the others. That you were so easily fooled proves you have no idea who the Magister is—or what you're facing. You're dead, little Shadowhunters. Little walking dead men."

That was too much for Will's temper. With a snarl he lunged toward the steps, his seraph blade outstretched. Jem called for him to stop, but it was too late. Mrs. Dark, her lips drawn back from her teeth like a hissing cobra's, swung her arm forward and flung her sister's severed head toward Will. With a yell of disgust he ducked aside, and she took the opportunity to charge down the steps, past Will, and through the arched doorway at the west side of the foyer, into the shadows beyond.

Mrs. Black's head, meanwhile, bumped down several stairs and came to rest gently against the toe of Will's boot. He looked down, and winced. One of her eyelids had drooped closed, and her tongue hung, gray and leathery, out of her mouth, for all the world as if she were leering at him.

"I may be sick," he announced.

"There's no time for you to be sick," said Jem. "Come on—"

And he dashed through the archway after Mrs. Dark. Nudging the warlock's severed head out of the way with the toe of his boot, Will followed after his friend at a run.

***

"Magister?" Tessa repeated blankly. *But that's impossible. De Quincey is the Magister. Those creatures on the bridge, they said they served him. Nate said . . .* She stared at her brother. "Nate?"

Speaking aloud was a mistake. Mortmain's gaze fell on Tessa, and he grinned. "Seize the shape-changer," he said to the clockwork creatures. "Don't let her go."

"Nate!" Tessa cried, but her brother did not so much as turn to look at her, as the creatures, brought back to sudden life, lurched forward, whirring and clicking, moving toward Tessa. One of them seized her, its metal arms like a vise as they encircled her chest, crushing the breath out of her.

Mortmain grinned at Tessa. "Don't be too hard on your brother, Miss Gray. He really is cleverer than I gave him credit for. It was his idea that I lure young Carstairs and Herondale out of the place with a far-fetched tale, that I might enter unmolested."

"What's going on?" Jessamine's voice trembled as she looked from Nate, to Tessa, to Mortmain, and back again. "I don't understand. Who is this, Nate? Why are you kneeling to him?"

"He is the Magister," said Nate. "If you were wise, you would kneel too."

Jessamine looked incredulous. "This is de Quincey?"

Nate's eyes flashed. "De Quincey is a peon, a serf. He *answers* to the Magister. Few even know the Magister's true identity; I am one of the chosen. The favored."

Jessamine made a rude noise. "Chosen to kneel on the ground, are you?"

Nate's eyes flashed, and he scrambled to his feet. He shouted something at Jessamine, but Tessa could not hear it.

The metal mannequin had tightened its grip on her to the point where she could barely breathe, and dark spots were beginning to float in front of her eyes. She was dimly aware of Mortmain shouting at the creature to loosen its grip on her, but it did not obey. She clawed at its metal arms with weakening fingers, barely aware of something fluttering at her throat, a fluttering that felt as if a bird or a butterfly were trapped beneath the collar of her dress. The chain around her neck was vibrating and twitching. She managed to look down, her vision blurred, and saw to her amazement that the little metal angel had emerged from beneath the collar of her dress; it soared upward, lifting the chain over her head. Its eyes seemed to glow as it flew upward. For the first time its metallic wings were spread, and Tessa saw that each wing was edged with something shimmering and razor-sharp. As she watched in amazement, the angel dived like a hornet, slashing with the edges of its wings at the head of the creature holding her—slicing through copper and metal, sending up a shower of red sparks.

The sparks stung Tessa's neck like a shower of hot cinders, but she barely noticed; the creature's arms loosened around her, and she wrenched herself away as it spun and staggered, its arms jerking blindly in front of it. She couldn't help but be reminded somehow of a sketch she'd seen of an angry gentleman at a garden party waving off bees. Mortmain, noticing a beat too late what was going on, shouted, and the other creatures lurched into motion, surging toward Tessa. She looked around wildly, but could no longer see the tiny angel. It seemed to have vanished.

"Tessa! Get out of the way!" A cold little hand caught at her wrist. It was Jessamine, yanking her backward as Thomas, having released Sophie, dived in front of her. Jessamine thrust Tessa behind her, toward the stairs at the back of the entryway, and moved forward with her parasol whirling. Her face was set with determination. It was Thomas who struck the first blow. Lunging forward with his sword, he sheared through the chest of a creature who was lurching toward him, hands outstretched. The machine man staggered backward, whirring loudly, red sparks spraying from its chest like blood. Jessamine laughed at the sight and laid about her with her parasol. The whirling edge of it sliced through the legs of two of the creatures, sending them toppling forward to flop on the ground like landed fish.

Mortmain looked vexed. "Oh, for goodness' sake. You—" He snapped his fingers, pointing at an automaton, one that had something that looked like a metal tube welded to its right wrist. "Get rid of her. The Shadowhunter."

The creature raised its arm jerkily. A bolt of streaky red fire shot from the metal tube. It hit Jessamine square in the chest, knocking her backward. Her parasol skittered from her hand as she struck the ground, her body twitching, her eyes open and glassy.

Nathaniel, who had moved to stand beside Mortmain on the sidelines of the melee, laughed.

A sizzling bolt of hatred went through Tessa, shocking her with its intensity. She wanted to throw herself at Nate and rip her nails down his cheek, kick him until he screamed. It wouldn't take much, she knew. He'd always been a coward where pain was concerned. She started forward, but the creatures, having dealt with Jessamine, had already swung back around toward her. Thomas, his hair plastered to his face with sweat and a long bloody rent slashed across the front of his shirt, moved to place himself in front of her. He was laying about himself magnificently with the sword, with great, sweeping strokes. It was hard to believe he wasn't slashing the creatures to ribbons—and yet they proved surprisingly dexterous. Ducking out of his way, they kept coming, their eyes fixed on Tessa. Thomas spun to look at her, his gaze wild. "Miss Gray! Now! Take Sophie!"

Tessa hesitated. She did not want to run. She wanted to stand her ground. But Sophie was huddling, transfixed behind her, her eyes full of terror.

"Sophie!" Thomas cried, and Tessa could hear what was in his voice, and knew she had been right about his feelings for Sophie. "The Sanctuary! *Go!*"

"No!" Mortmain shouted, turning to the clockwork creature that had attacked Jessamine. As it raised its arm, Tessa caught hold of Sophie's wrist and began to drag her toward the stairs. A bolt of red fire hit the wall beside them, scorching the stone. Tessa shrieked but didn't slow, yanking Sophie up the spiral staircase, the smell of smoke and death following them as they ran.

Will dashed through the archway that separated the foyer from the room beyond—and came up short. Jem was already there, staring around him in bewilderment. Though there were no exits from the room other than the one they had just come through, Mrs. Dark was nowhere to be seen.

The room, though, was far from empty. It had most likely been a dining room once, and huge portraits adorned the walls, though they had been ripped and slashed to unrecognizability.

A great crystal chandelier hung overhead, fronded with strings of gray cobweb that drifted in the disturbed air like ancient lace curtains. It had probably once hung over a grand table. Now it swung over a bare marble floor that had been painted with a series of necromantic patterns—a five-pointed star inside a circle inside a square. Inside the pentagram stood a repulsive stone statue, the figure of some hideous demon, with twisted limbs and clawed hands. Horns rose from its head.

All around the room were scattered the remains of dark magic—bones and feathers and strips of skin, pools of blood that seemed to bubble like black champagne. There were empty cages lying on their sides, and a low table on which was spread an array of bloody knives and stone bowls filled with unpleasant dark liquids.

In all the gaps between the pentagram's five points were runes and squiggles that hurt Will's eyes when he looked at them. They were the opposite of the runes in the Gray Book, which seemed to speak of glory and peace. These were necromantic symbols that spoke of ruin and death.

"Jem," Will said, "these are not the preparations for a binding spell. This is the work of necromancy."

"She was trying to bring back her sister, isn't that what she said?"

"Yes, but she was doing nothing else." A dreadful dark suspicion had begun to blossom in the back of Will's mind.

Jem did not reply; his attention seemed to be fixed on something across the room. "There's a cat," he said in a low whisper, pointing. "In one of those cages over there."

Will glanced where his friend pointed. Indeed, a bristling

gray cat was huddled in one of the locked animal cages along the wall. "And?"

"It's still alive."

"It's a cat, James. We have bigger things to worry about—"

But Jem was already walking away. He reached the animal's cage and scooped it up, holding the cage at eye level. The cat looked to be a gray Persian, with a squashed-in face and yellow eyes that regarded Jem malevolently. Suddenly it arched its back and hissed loudly, its eyes fixed on the pentagram. Jem looked up—and stared.

"*Will,*" he said in a warning tone. "Look."

The statue in the middle of the pentagram had moved. Instead of crouching, it had straightened until it was standing upright. Its eyes burned with a sulfuric glow. It was only when its triple row of mouths smiled that Will realized it was not stone after all, just a creature of hard gray stonelike skin. A demon.

Will ducked back and flung Israfel reflexively, not really expecting the gesture to do much good. It didn't. As it sailed near the pentagram, the blade bounced off an invisible wall and clattered to the marble floor. The demon in the pentagram cackled. "You attack me here?" it demanded in a high, thin voice. "You could bring the host of Heaven against me and they could do nothing! No angelic power can breach this circle!"

"Mrs. Dark," Will said between his teeth.

"So you recognize me now, do you? No one ever claimed you Shadowhunters were clever." The demon bared its greenish fangs. "This is my true form. An ugly surprise for you, I suppose."

"I daresay it's an improvement," said Will. "You weren't much to look at before, and at least the horns are dramatic."

"What are you, then?" Jem demanded, setting the cage, the cat still in it, down on the floor at his feet. "I thought you and your sister were warlocks."

"My sister was a warlock," hissed the creature that had been Mrs. Dark. "I am a full-blood demon—*Eidolon*. A shape-changer. Like your precious Tessa. But unlike her I cannot *become* what I transform into. I cannot touch the minds of the living or the dead. So the Magister did not want me." Thin hurt was in the creature's voice. "He enlisted me to train her. His precious little protégée. My sister as well. We know the ways of the Change. We were able to force it on her. But she was never grateful."

"That must have hurt you," Jem said in his most soothing voice. Will opened his mouth, but seeing Jem's warning look, closed it again. "Seeing Tessa get what you wanted, and not appreciating it."

"She never understood. The honor that was being done her. The glory that would be hers." The yellow eyes burned. "When she fled, the Magister's rage fell on me—I had disappointed him. He swore out a bounty on me."

That jolted Jem, or seemed to. "You mean de Quincey wanted you dead?"

"How many times must I tell you that de Quincey is not the Magister? The Magister is—" The demon broke off with a growl. "You try to trick me, little Shadowhunter, but your trick will not work."

Jem shrugged. "You cannot remain in that pentagram forever, Mrs. Dark. Eventually the rest of the Enclave will come. We will starve you out. And then you will be ours, and you know how the Clave deals with those who break the Law."

Mrs. Dark hissed. "Perhaps he has forsaken me," she said, "but I still fear the Magister more than I fear you, or your Enclave."

More than I fear the Enclave. She should have been afraid, Will thought. What Jem had said to her was true. She ought to be afraid, but she wasn't. In Will's experience, when someone who ought to be afraid wasn't, the reason was rarely bravery. Usually it meant that they knew something you didn't.

"If you will not tell us who the Magister is," said Will, his voice edged with steel, "perhaps you can answer a simple question instead. Is Axel Mortmain the Magister?"

The demon let out a wail, then clapped its bony hands over its mouth and sank, burning-eyed, to the ground. "The Magister. He will think I told you. I will never earn his forgiveness now—"

"Mortmain?" echoed Jem. "But he is the one who warned us— Ah." He paused. "I see." He had gone very white; Will knew his thoughts were chasing down the same winding road Will's just had. He would probably have gotten there first—Will suspected Jem was in fact cleverer than he was himself—but he lacked Will's tendency to assume the absolute worst about people and proceed from there. "Mortmain lied to us about the Dark Sisters and the binding spell," he added, thinking out loud. "In fact, it was Mortmain who put the idea in Charlotte's head in the first place that de Quincey was the Magister. If it were not for him, we would never have suspected the vampire. But why?"

"De Quincey is a loathsome beast," wailed Mrs. Dark, still crouched inside her pentagram. She seemed to have decided there was no more point in concealment. "He disobeyed

Mortmain at every turn, wishing to be the Magister himself. Such insubordination must be punished."

Will's gaze met Jem's. He could tell they were both thinking the same thing. "Mortmain saw an opportunity to throw suspicion on a rival," Jem said. "That is why he chose de Quincey."

"He could have hidden those plans for automatons in de Quincey's library," agreed Will. "It is not as if de Quincey ever admitted they were his, or even seemed to recognize them when Charlotte showed them to him. And Mortmain could have told those automatons on the bridge to claim they were working for the vampire. In fact, he could have etched de Quincey's seal into that clockwork girl's chest and left her in the Dark House for us to find, as well—all to divert suspicion from himself."

"But Mortmain is not the only one who ever pointed the finger at de Quincey," said Jem, and his voice was heavy. "Nathaniel Gray, Will. Tessa's brother. When two people tell the same lie . . ."

"They are working together," Will finished. He felt, for a moment, something almost like satisfaction, which quickly faded. He had disliked Nate Gray, had hated the way Tessa had treated him as if he could do no wrong, and then he'd despised himself for his own jealousy. To know that he had been correct about Nate's character was one thing, but at what price?

Mrs. Dark laughed, a high, whining sound. "Nate Gray," she spat. "The Magister's little human lapdog. He sold his sister to Mortmain, you know. Just for a handful of silver, he did it. Just for a few sops to his vanity. I would never have treated my own sister so. And you say it is demons who are evil, and the humans who need protecting from us!" Her voice rose to a cackle.

Will ignored her; his mind was whirling. Dear God, that whole story of Nathaniel's about de Quincey had been a trick, a lie to set the Clave off on a false track. Then why have Mortmain appear as soon as they had gone? *To get rid of us, Jem and I,* Will thought grimly. *Nate couldn't have known we two wouldn't be going with Charlotte and Henry. He had to improvise something quickly when we stayed behind.* Thus Mortmain and this extra trickery. Nate had been in it with Mortmain since the beginning.

And now Tessa is in the Institute with him. Will felt sick to his stomach. He wanted to turn and run out the door, race back to the Institute, and beat Nathaniel's head against a wall. Only years of training, and fear for Henry and Charlotte, kept him where he was.

Will whirled on Mrs. Dark. "What is his plan? What will the Enclave find when they reach Carleton Square? Certain slaughter? *Answer me!*" he shouted. Fear made his voice crack. "Or by the Angel, I will make sure that the Clave tortures you before you die. What is his plan for them?"

Mrs. Dark's yellow eyes flashed. "What does the Magister care about?" she hissed. "What has he ever cared about? He despises the Nephilim, but what is it that he wants?"

"Tessa," said Jem immediately. "But she is safe in the Institute, and even his blasted clockwork army can't break inside. Even without us there—"

In a wheedling voice Mrs. Dark said, "Once, when I was in the Magister's confidence, he spoke to me of a plan he had to invade the Institute. He planned to paint the hands of his mechanical creatures with the blood of a Shadowhunter, thus allowing him to open the doors."

"The blood of a Shadowhunter?" Will echoed. "But—"

"Will." Jem had his hand at his chest, where the clockwork creature had torn the skin that night on the steps of the Institute. "*My* blood."

For a moment Will stood perfectly still, staring at his friend. Then, without a word, he turned and raced for the dining room doors; Jem, pausing only to seize the cat's cage, followed. As they reached them, the doors slammed shut as if pushed, and Will came to a skidding halt. He spun to see Jem behind him, looking baffled.

In her pentagram Mrs. Dark was howling with laughter. "Nephilim," she gasped between peals. "Stupid, stupid Nephilim. Where is your angel now?"

As they stared, enormous flames leaped up around the walls, licking up the curtains covering the windows, shimmering along the edges of the floor. The flames burned with a weird blue-green color, and the smell was thick and ugly—a demon smell. Inside its cage the cat was going wild, throwing itself against the bars again and again and howling.

Will drew a second seraph blade from his belt and cried, "*Anael!*" Light burst from the blade, but Mrs. Dark only laughed.

"When the Magister sees your charred corpses," she cried, "then he will forgive me! Then he will welcome me back!"

Her laughter rose, high and horrible. Already the room was dim with smoke. Jem, raising his sleeve to cover his mouth, said to Will in a choking voice, "Kill her. Kill her, and the fire will die."

Will, his grip tight on the hilt of Anael, growled, "Don't you think I would if I could? She's in the pentagram."

"I *know.*" Jem's eyes were full of meaning. "Will, cut it *down.*"

Because it was Jem, Will knew what he meant immediately,

without being told explicitly. Spinning to face the pentagram, he raised the shining Anael, took aim, and flung the blade—not toward the demon but up toward the thick metal chain that supported the massive chandelier. The blade sheared through the chain like a knife through paper, there was a rending sound, and the demon had time only to scream once before the massive chandelier descended, a crashing comet of twisting metal and shattering glass. Will threw his arm across his eyes as debris rained over them all—smashed bits of stone, fragments of crystal, and chunks of rust. The floor shook underneath him as if the earth were quaking.

When all was quiet at last, he opened his eyes. The chandelier lay like the wreck of some immense ship twisted and destroyed at the bottom of the sea. Dust rose like smoke from the wreckage, and from one corner of the pile of smashed glass and metal a trickle of greenish black blood threaded across the marble. . . .

Jem had been right. The flames were gone. Jem himself, still gripping the handle of the cat's cage, was gazing at the wreckage. His already pale hair had whitened further with plaster dust, and his cheeks were streaked with ash. "Nicely done, William," he said.

Will did not reply; there was no time for it. Throwing the doors—which opened easily under his hands now—wide, he raced out of the room.

Tessa and Sophie flew up the Institute's steps together until Sophie gasped, "Here! This door!" and Tessa flung it open and burst into the corridor beyond. Sophie pulled her wrist out of Tessa's grasp and spun to slam the door shut behind them and slide the bolt closed. She leaned against it for a moment, breathing hard, her face streaked with tears.

"Miss Jessamine," she whispered. "Do you think—"

"I don't know," Tessa said. "But you heard Thomas. We must get to the Sanctuary, Sophie. It's where we'll be safe." *And Thomas wants me to make sure you stay safe*. "You're going to have to show me where it is. I can't find my way there by myself."

Slowly Sophie nodded and drew herself upright. In silence she led Tessa through a winding mass of corridors until they reached the one corridor she remembered from the night when she had met Camille. After taking a lamp from a holder on the wall, Sophie lit it, and they hurried on, until they finally reached the great iron doors with their pattern of *C*s. Brought up sharply in front of the doors, Sophie put a hand to her mouth. "The key!" she whispered. "I've forgotten the bloody—pardon me, miss—key!"

Tessa felt a wave of frustrated anger, but pushed it back. Sophie had just had a friend die in her arms; she could hardly be blamed for forgetting a key. "But you know where Charlotte keeps it?"

Sophie nodded. "I'll run and fetch it. You wait here, miss."

She hurried off down the corridor. Tessa watched her go until her white cap and sleeves faded into the shadows, leaving Tessa alone in the darkness. The only light in the corridor came from the illumination that seeped beneath the doors to the Sanctuary. She pressed herself back against the wall as the shadows gathered thickly around her, as if she could disappear into the wall. She kept seeing the blood pouring out of Agatha's chest, staining Sophie's hands; kept hearing the brittle sound of Nate's laugher as Jessamine collapsed—

It came again, harsh and as brittle as glass, echoing out of the darkness behind her.

Sure she was imagining things, Tessa whirled, her back toward the Sanctuary doors. Before her in the hallway, where a moment before there had been empty air, someone was standing. Someone with fair hair and a grin plastered across his face. Someone carrying a long, thin knife in his right hand.

Nate.

"My Tessie," he said. "That was very impressive. I wouldn't have thought either you or the servant could run that fast." He twirled the knife between his fingers. "Unfortunately for you, my master has gifted me with certain . . . powers. I can move faster than you can think." He smirked. "Probably much faster, to judge by how long it took you to catch on to what was going on downstairs."

"Nate." Tessa's voice shook. "It's not too late. You can stop this."

"Stop *what?*" Nate looked directly at her, for the first time since he had knelt to Mortmain. "Stop acquiring incredible power and immense knowledge? Stop being the favored acolyte of the most powerful man in London? I'd be a fool to stop all this, little sister."

"Favored acolyte? Where was he when de Quincey was about to drain your blood?"

"I had disappointed him," Nate said. "*You* disappointed him. You ran from the Dark Sisters, knowing what it would cost me. Your sisterly affection leaves something to be desired, Tessie."

"I let the Dark Sisters torture me for your sake, Nate. I did *everything* for you. And you—you let me believe de Quincey was the Magister. All the things you claimed de Quincey did were done by Mortmain, weren't they? He's the one who wanted me brought here. He's the one who employed the Dark Sisters. All that rubbish about de Quincey was just to lure the Enclave away from the Institute."

Nate smirked. "What was it Aunt Harriet used to say, that cleverness that comes too late is hardly cleverness at all?"

"And what will the Enclave find when they go to the address you claimed was de Quincey's nest? Nothing? An empty house, a burned-out ruin?" She began to retreat from him, until her back struck the cold iron doors.

Nate followed, his eyes gleaming like the blade in his hand. "Oh, dear me, no. That bit was true. It wouldn't do to have the Enclave realize so soon that they'd been made fools of, would it? Better to keep them busy, and cleaning out de Quincey's little hiding place will keep them quite busy indeed." He shrugged. "You're the one who gave me the idea to let the blame for everything fall on the vampire, you know. After what happened the other night, he was a dead man, anyway. The Nephilim had their sights set on him, which made him useless to Mortmain. Sending the Enclave off to get rid of him and Will and Jem off to rid my master of that pestiferous Mrs. Dark—well, it's three birds with one stone, really, isn't it? And quite a clever plan of mine, if I do say so myself."

He was preening, Tessa thought in disgust. Proud of himself. Most of her wanted to spit in his face, but she knew she should keep him talking, give herself a chance to think of a way out of the situation. "You certainly fooled us," she said, hating herself. "How much of that story you told was the truth? How much was lies?"

"Quite a bit was the truth, if you really want to know. The

best lies are based on the truth, at least in part," he bragged. "I came to London thinking I was going to blackmail Mortmain with my knowledge of his occult activities. The fact was, he couldn't have cared less about that. He wanted to get a look at me because he wasn't sure, you see. Wasn't sure if I was our parents' first child or their second. He thought I might be *you*." He grinned. "He was as pleased as punch when he realized I wasn't the child he was looking for. He wanted a girl, you see."

"But why? What does he want with me?"

Nate shrugged. "I don't know. Nor do I care. He told me that if I procured you for him, and you turned out to be all he hoped you would be, he would make me his disciple. After you fled, he gave me to de Quincey in revenge. When you brought me here, to the heart of the Nephilim, it was a second chance to offer the Magister what I'd lost for him before."

"You contacted him?" Tessa felt sick. She thought of the open window in the drawing room, Nate's flushed face, his claim that he hadn't opened it. Somehow, she knew, he had sent Mortmain a message. "You let him know you were here? That you were willing to betray us? But you could have stayed! You would have been safe!"

"Safe, and powerless. Here I'm an ordinary human, weak and contemptible. But as Mortmain's disciple, I will stand at his right hand when he rules the British Empire."

"You're mad," Tessa said. "The whole thing's ridiculous."

"I assure you it isn't. By this time next year Mortmain will be ensconced in Buckingham Palace. The Empire will bow before his rule."

"But you won't be beside him. I see how he looks at you. You're not a disciple; you're a tool to be used. When he gets what he wants, he will throw you aside like rubbish."

Nate's grip tightened on the knife. "Not true."

"It is true," Tessa said. "Aunt always said you were too trusting. It's why you're such an awful gambler, Nate. You're such a liar yourself, but you never can tell when you're being lied to. Aunt said—"

"Aunt Harriet." Nate laughed softly. "So unfortunate the way she died." He grinned. "Didn't you think it was a bit odd that I'd sent you a box of chocolates? Something I knew *you* wouldn't eat? Something I knew she would?"

Nausea gripped Tessa, a pain in her stomach as if Nate's knife were twisting there. "Nate—you wouldn't—Aunt Harriet loved you!"

"You have no idea what I would do, Tessie. No idea at all." He spoke rapidly, almost fevered in his intensity. "You think of me as a fool. Your foolish brother who needs to be protected from the world. So easily duped and taken advantage of. I heard you and Aunt discussing me. I know neither of you ever thought I'd make anything of myself, ever do anything you could be proud of me for. But now I have. *Now I have*," he snarled, as if completely unaware of the irony in his words.

"You've made a murderer of yourself. And you think I ought to be proud? I'm ashamed to be related to you."

"Related to me? You're not even human. You are some *thing*. You are no part of me. From the moment Mortmain told me what you really are, you were dead to me. I have no sister."

"Then why," said Tessa in a voice so quiet she could barely hear it herself, "do you keep calling me Tessie?"

He looked at her for a moment in stark confusion. And as she looked back at her brother—the brother she had thought was all she had left in the world—something moved beyond Nate's shoulder, and Tessa wondered if she was seeing things, if perhaps she was going to faint.

"I wasn't calling you Tessie," he said. He sounded baffled, almost lost.

A feeling of unbearable sadness gripped her. "You're my brother, Nate. You'll always be my brother."

His eyes narrowed. For a moment Tessa thought perhaps he had *heard* her. Perhaps he would reconsider. "When you belong to Mortmain," he said, "I shall be bound to him forever. For I am the one who made it possible for him to have you."

Her heart sank. The thing beyond Nate's shoulder moved again, a disturbance of the shadows. It was real, Tessa thought. Not her imagination. There was something behind Nate. Something moving toward them both. She opened her mouth, then closed it again. *Sophie,* she thought. She hoped the other girl would have the sense to run away before Nate came for her with the knife.

"Come along, then," he said to Tessa. "There's no reason to make a fuss. The Magister isn't going to hurt you—"

"You cannot be sure of that," Tessa said. The figure behind Nate was almost upon him. There was something pale and glimmering in its hand. Tessa fought to keep her eyes locked on Nate's face.

"I am sure." He sounded impatient. "I am not a fool, Tessa—"

The figure exploded into movement. The pale and glimmering object rose above Nate's head and came down with a heavy crash. Nate pitched forward, crumpling to the ground. The blade rolled from his hand as he struck the carpet and lay still, blood staining his pale blond hair.

Tessa looked up. In the dim light she could see Jessamine standing over Nate, a furious expression on her face. The remains of a shattered lamp were still clutched in her left hand.

"Not a fool, perhaps." She prodded Nate's recumbent form with a disdainful toe. "But not your most shining moment, either."

Tessa could only stare. "*Jessamine?*"

Jessamine looked up. The neckline of her dress was torn, her hair had come down out of its pins, and there was a purpling bruise on her right cheek. She dropped the lamp, which narrowly missed hitting Nate once again in the head, and said, "I'm quite all right, if that's what you're so pop-eyed about. It wasn't me they wanted, after all."

"Miss Gray! Miss Lovelace!" It was Sophie, out of breath from running up and down stairs. In one hand she held the slender iron Sanctuary key. She looked down at Nate as she reached the end of the corridor, her mouth opening in surprise. "Is he all right?"

"Oh, who cares if he's all right?" Jessamine said, bending to pick up the knife that Nate had dropped. "After all the lies he told! He lied to *me*! I really thought—" She flushed dark red. "Well, it doesn't matter now." She straightened and whirled on Sophie, her chin held high. "Now, don't just stand there staring, Sophie, do let us into the Sanctuary before God knows what comes after us all and tries to kill us again."

Will burst out of the mansion and onto the front steps, Jem just behind him. The lawn ahead of them was stark in the moonlight; their carriage was where they had left it in the center of the drive. Jem was relieved to see that the horses hadn't spooked despite all the noise, though he supposed that Balios and Xanthos, belonging to Shadowhunters as they did, had probably seen much worse.

"Will." Jem came to a stop beside his friend, trying to conceal the fact that he needed to catch his breath. "We must get back to the Institute as soon as possible."

"You will get no disagreement from me on that front." Will gave Jem a keen look; Jem wondered if his face was as flushed and feverish-looking as he feared. The drug, which he had taken in a great quantity before they'd left the Institute, was wearing off faster than it should have been; at another time the realization would have prickled Jem with anxiety. Now he put it aside.

"Do you think Mortmain expected us to kill Mrs. Dark?" he asked, less because he felt the question was an urgent one than because he needed a few more moments to catch his breath before he climbed into the carriage.

Will had his jacket open and was rummaging in one of the pockets. "I imagine so," he said, almost absently, "or probably he hoped we'd all kill one another, which would have been ideal for him. Clearly he wants de Quincey dead as well and has decided to use the Nephilim as his own band of personal assassins." Will drew a folding knife from his inner pocket and looked at it with satisfaction. "A single horse," he observed, "is much faster than a carriage."

Jem gripped the cage he was holding tighter. The gray cat, behind its bars, was looking around with wide yellow interested eyes. "Please tell me you aren't going to do what I suspect you're going to do, Will."

Will flipped the knife open and started up the drive.

"There's no time to lose, James. And Xanthos can pull the carriage perfectly well by himself, if you're the only one in it."

Jem went after him, but the heavy cage, as well as his own fevered exhaustion, slowed his progress. "What are you doing with that knife? You're not going to murder the horses, are you?"

"Of course not." Will raised the blade and began to slash at the harness fastening Balios, his favored of the two animals, to the carriage.

"Ah," said Jem. "I see. You're going to ride off on that horse like Dick Turpin and leave me here. Have you gone mad?"

"Someone's got to look after that cat." The girth and traces fell away, and Will swung himself up onto Balios.

"But—" Really alarmed now, Jem set the cage down. "Will, you can't—"

It was too late. Will dug his heels into the horse's sides. Balios reared and neighed, Will clinging on resolutely—Jem could have sworn he was *grinning*—and then the horse wheeled and pounded toward the gates. Inside of a moment, horse and rider were out of sight.

19

Boadicea

Seal'd her mine from her first sweet breath.
Mine, mine by a right, from birth till death
Mine, mine—our fathers have sworn.
—Alfred, Lord Tennyson, "Maud"

As the doors of the Sanctuary closed behind them, Tessa looked around apprehensively. The room was darker than it had been when she had come here to meet Camille. There were no candles burning in the great candelabras, only flickering witchlight that emanated from sconces on the walls. The angel statue continued to weep its endless tears into the fountain. The air in the room was bone-chillingly cold, and she shivered.

Sophie, having slipped the key back into her pocket, looked as nervous as Tessa felt. "Here we are, then," she said. "It's awful cold in this place."

"Well, we won't be here long, I'm sure," said Jessamine. She was still holding Nate's knife, which glittered in her hand. "*Someone* will come back to rescue us. Will, or Charlotte—"

"And find the Institute full of clockwork monsters," Tessa reminded her. "And Mortmain." She shuddered. "I'm not sure it'll be quite so simple as you make it out to be."

Jessamine looked at Tessa with cold dark eyes. "Well, you needn't sound as if it's my fault. If it weren't for you, we wouldn't be in this mess."

Sophie had moved to stand among the massive pillars, and was looking very small. Her voice echoed off the stone walls. "That's not very kind, miss."

Jessamine perched herself on the edge of the fountain, then rose to her feet again, frowning. She brushed at the back of her dress, now stained with damp, in an exasperated manner. "Perhaps not, but it's true. The only reason the Magister is here is because of Tessa."

"I told Charlotte all this was my fault." Tessa spoke quietly. "I told her to send me away. She wouldn't."

Jessamine tossed her head. "Charlotte's softhearted, and so is Henry. And Will—Will thinks he's Galahad. Wants to save everyone. Jem, too. None of them are practical."

"I suppose," Tessa said, "if it had been your decision to make . . ."

"You'd have been out the door with nothing but the key of the street to your name," Jessamine said, and sniffed. Seeing the way Sophie was looking at her, she added, "Oh, really! Don't be such a mush-mouth, Sophie. Agatha and Thomas would still be alive if I'd been in charge, wouldn't they?"

Sophie went pale, her scar standing out along her cheek like the mark of a slap. "Thomas is dead?"

Jessamine looked as if she knew she'd made a mistake. "I didn't mean that."

Tessa looked at her, hard. "What happened, Jessamine? We saw you injured—"

"And precious little any of you did about it either," Jessamine said, and sat down with a flounce on the fountain wall, apparently forgetting to worry about the state of her dress. "I was unconscious . . . and when I awoke, I saw that all of you had gone but Thomas. Mortmain was gone too, but those creatures were still there. One of them began to come after me, and I looked for my parasol, but it had been trampled to shreds. Thomas was surrounded by those creatures. I went toward him, but he told me to run, so . . . I ran." She tilted her chin up defiantly.

Sophie's eyes flashed. "You left him there? Alone?"

Jessamine set the knife down on the wall with an angry clatter. "I'm a lady, Sophie. It is expected that a man sacrifice himself for a lady's safety."

"That's *rubbish*!" Sophie's hands were tight little fists at her sides. "You're a *Shadowhunter*! And Thomas is just a mundane! You could have helped him. You just wouldn't—because you're selfish! And—and awful!"

Jessamine gaped at Sophie, her mouth wide open. "How dare you speak to me like—"

She broke off as the door of the Sanctuary resounded with the noise of the heavy knocker falling. It sounded again, and then a familiar voice, raised, called out to them, "Tessa! Sophie! It's Will."

"Oh, thank God," Jessamine said—clearly just as relieved to be free of her conversation with Sophie as she was to be rescued—and hurried toward the door. "Will! It's Jessamine. I'm in here too!"

"And you're all three all right?" Will sounded anxious in a way that tightened Tessa's chest. "What happened? We raced here from Highgate. I saw the door of the Institute open. How in the Angel's name did Mortmain get in?"

"He evaded the wards somehow," Jessamine said bitterly, reaching for the door handle. "I've no idea how."

"It hardly matters now. He's dead. The clockwork creatures are destroyed."

Will's tone was reassuring—so why, Tessa thought, did she not feel reassured? She turned to look at Sophie, who was staring at the door, a sharp vertical frown line between her eyes, her lips moving very slightly as if she were whispering something under her breath. Sophie had the Sight, Tessa remembered—Charlotte had said so. Tessa's sense of unease rose and crested like a wave.

"Jessamine," she called. "Jessamine, don't open the door—"

But it was too late. The door had swung wide. And there on the threshold stood Mortmain, flanked by clockwork monsters.

Thank the Angel for glamours, Will thought. The sight of a boy riding bareback on a charging black horse down Farringdon Road would normally be enough to raise eyebrows even in a metropolis as jaded as London. But as Will went by—the horse kicking up great puffs of London dust as it reared and snorted its way through the streets—no one turned a hair or batted the lash of an eye. Yet even as they seemed not to see him, they found reasons to move out of his way—a dropped pair of eyeglasses, a step to the side to avoid a puddle in the road—and avoid being trampled.

It was almost five miles from Highgate to the Institute; it had taken them three-quarters of an hour to cover the distance in the carriage. It took Will and Balios only twenty minutes to make the return trip, though the horse was panting and lathered with sweat by the time Will pounded through the Institute gates and drew up in front of the steps.

His heart sank immediately. The doors were open. Wide open, as if inviting in the night. It was strictly against Covenant Law to leave the doors of an Institute standing ajar. He had been correct; something was terribly wrong.

He slid from the horse's back, boots clattering loudly against the cobblestones. He looked for a way to secure the animal, but as he'd cut its harness, there was none, and besides, Balios looked inclined to bite him. He shrugged and made for the steps.

Jessamine gasped and leaped back as Mortmain stepped into the room. Sophie screamed and ducked behind a pillar. Tessa was too shocked to move. The four automatons, two on either side of Mortmain, stared straight ahead with their shining faces like metal masks.

Behind Mortmain was Nate. A makeshift bandage, stained with blood, was tied around his head. The bottom of his shirt—Jem's shirt—had a ragged strip torn from it. His baleful gaze fell on Jessamine.

"You stupid whore," he snarled, and started forward.

"Nathaniel." Mortmain's voice cracked like a whip; Nate

froze. "This is not an arena in which to enact your petty revenges. There is one more thing I need from you; you know what it is. Retrieve it for me."

Nate hesitated. He was looking at Jessamine like a cat with its gaze fixed on a mouse.

"Nathaniel. To the weapons room. Now."

Nate dragged his gaze from Jessie. For a moment he looked at Tessa, the rage in his expression softening into a sneer. Then he turned on his heel and stalked from the room; two of the clockwork creatures peeled themselves from Mortmain's side and followed him.

The door closed behind him, and Mortmain smiled pleasantly. "The two of you," he said, looking from Jessamine to Sophie, "get out."

"No." The voice was Sophie's, small but stubborn, though to Tessa's surprise, Jessamine showed no inclination to leave either. "Not without Tessa."

Mortmain shrugged. "Very well." He turned to the clockwork creatures. "The two girls," he said. "The Shadowhunter and the servant. Kill them both."

He snapped his fingers and the clockwork creatures sprang forward. They had the grotesque speed of skittering rats. Jessamine turned to run, but she had gone only a few steps when one of them seized her, lifting her off the ground. Sophie darted among the pillars like Snow White fleeing into the woods, but it did her little good. The second creature caught up to her swiftly and bore her to the ground as she screamed. In contrast Jessamine was utterly silent; the creature holding her had one metal hand clamped across her mouth and the other around her waist, fingers digging in cruelly. Her feet kicked uselessly in the air like the feet of a criminal dangling at the end of a hangman's rope.

Tessa heard her own voice as it emerged from her throat as if it were a stranger's. "Stop it. Please, please, stop it!"

Sophie had broken away from the creature holding her and was scrambling across the floor on her hands and knees. Reaching out, it caught her by the ankle and jerked her backward across the floor, her apron tearing as she sobbed.

"*Please,*" Tessa said again, fixing her eyes on Mortmain.

"*You* can stop it, Miss Gray," he said. "Promise me you won't try to run." His eyes burned as he looked at her. "Then I'll let them go."

Jessamine's eyes, visible above the metal arm clamping her mouth, pleaded with Tessa. The other creature was on its feet, holding Sophie, who dangled limply in its grip.

"I'll stay," Tessa said. "You have my word. Of course I will. Just let them go."

There was a long pause. Then, "You heard her," Mortmain said to his mechanical monsters. "Take the girls out of this room. Bring them downstairs. Don't harm them." He smiled then, a thin, crafty smile. "Leave Miss Gray alone with me."

Even before he passed through the front doors, Will felt it—the jangling sense that something dreadful was happening here. The first time he'd ever felt this sensation, he'd been twelve years old, holding that blasted box—but he'd never imagined feeling it in the fastness of the Institute.

He saw Agatha's body first, the moment he stepped over the threshold. She lay on her back, her glassy eyes staring up at the ceiling, the front of her plain gray dress soaked with blood.

A wave of almost overwhelming rage washed over Will, leaving him light-headed. Biting his lip hard, he bent to close her eyes before he rose and looked around.

The signs of a melee were everywhere—torn scraps of metal, bent and broken gears, splashes of blood mixing with pools of oil. As Will moved toward the stairs, his foot came down on the shredded remains of Jessamine's parasol. He gritted his teeth and moved on to the staircase.

And there, slumped across the lowest steps, lay Thomas, eyes closed, motionless in a widening pool of scarlet. A sword rested on the ground beside him, a little ways away from his hand; its edge was chipped and dented as if he had been using it to hack apart rocks. A great jagged piece of metal protruded from his chest. It looked a little like the torn blade of a saw, Will thought as he crouched down by Thomas's side, or like a sharp bit of some larger metal contraption.

There was a dry burning in the back of Will's throat. His mouth tasted of metal and rage. He rarely grieved during a battle; he saved his emotions for afterward—those he had not already learned to bury so deeply that he barely felt them at all. He had been burying them since he was twelve years old. His chest knotted with pain now, but his voice was steady when he spoke. "Hail and farewell, Thomas," he said, reaching to close the other boy's eyes. "*Ave—*"

A hand flew up and gripped his wrist. Will stared down, dumbfounded, as Thomas's glassy eyes slid toward him, pale brown under the whitish film of death. "Not," he said, with a clear effort to get the words out, "a Shadowhunter."

"You defended the Institute," Will said. "You did as well as any of us would have done."

"No." Thomas closed his eyes, as if exhausted. His chest rose, barely; his shirt was soaked almost black with blood. "You'd've fought 'em off, Master Will. You know you would."

"Thomas," Will whispered. He wanted to say, *Be quiet, and you'll be all right when the others get here.* But Thomas manifestly would not be all right. He was human; no healing rune could help him. Will wished that Jem were here, instead of himself. Jem was the one you wanted with you when you were dying. Jem could make anyone feel that things were going to be all right, whereas Will privately suspected that there were few situations that his presence did not make worse.

"She's alive," Thomas said, not opening his eyes.

"What?" Will was caught off guard.

"The one you come back for. Her. Tessa. She's with Sophie." Thomas spoke as if it were a fact obvious to anyone that Will would have come back for Tessa's sake. He coughed, and a great mass of blood poured out of his mouth and down his chin. He didn't seem to notice. "Take care of Sophie, Will. Sophie is—"

But Will never found out what Sophie was, because Thomas's grip went suddenly slack, and his hand fell away and struck the stone floor with an ugly thump. Will drew back. He had seen death enough times, and knew when it had come. There was no need to close Thomas's eyes; they were closed already. "Sleep, then," he said, not quite knowing where the words came from, "good and faithful servant of the Nephilim. And thank you."

It wasn't enough, not nearly enough, but it was all there was. Will scrambled to his feet and dashed up the staircase.

***

The doors had closed behind the clockwork creatures; the Sanctuary was very silent. Tessa could hear the water splashing in the fountain behind her.

Mortmain stood regarding her calmly. He still wasn't frightening to look at, Tessa thought. A small, ordinary man, with dark hair going gray at his temples, and those odd light eyes. "Miss Gray," he said, "I had hoped our first time alone together would be a more pleasant experience for us both."

Tessa's eyes burned. She said, "What are you? A warlock?"

His smile was swift, and without feeling. "Merely a human being, Miss Gray."

"But you did magic," she said. "You spoke in Will's voice—"

"Anyone can learn to imitate voices, with the proper training," he said. "A simple trick, like sleight of hand. No one ever expects them. Certainly not Shadowhunters. They believe humans are good at nothing, as well as being good for nothing."

"No," Tessa whispered. "They don't think that."

His mouth twisted. "How quickly you have grown to love them, your natural enemies. We will soon train you out of that." He moved forward, and Tessa shrank back. "I will not hurt you," he said. "I merely want to show you something." He reached into the pocket of his coat and drew out a gold watch, very fine-looking, on a thick gold chain.

Is he wondering what *time* it is? The mad urge to giggle rose up in the back of Tessa's throat. She forced it down.

He held the watch out to her. "Miss Gray," he said, "please take this."

She stared at him. "I don't want it."

He moved toward her again. Tessa retreated until the back

of her skirts brushed the low wall of the fountain. "Take the watch, Miss Gray."

Tessa shook her head.

"Take it," he said. "Or I will recall my clockwork servants and have them crush the throats of your two friends until they are dead. I need only go to the door and call to them. It is your choice."

Bile rose in the back of Tessa's throat. She stared at the watch he held out to her, dangling on its gold chain. It was clearly unwound. The hands had long ago stopped spinning, the time seemingly frozen at midnight. The initials J. T. S. were carved on the back in elegant script.

"Why?" she whispered. "Why do you want me to take it?"

"Because I want you to Change," Mortmain said.

Tessa's head jerked up. She stared at him incredulously. *"What?"*

"This watch used to belong to someone," he said. "Someone I very much want to meet again." His voice was even, but there was a sort of undercurrent beneath it, an eager hunger that terrified Tessa more than any rage might have. "I know the Dark Sisters taught you. I know you know your power. You are the only one in the world who can do what you do. I know this because *I made you.*"

"You *made* me?" Tessa stared. "You're not saying—you can't be my father—"

"Your father?" Mortmain laughed shortly. "I am a human, not a Downworlder. There is no demon in me, nor do I consort with demons. There is no blood shared between the two of us, Miss Gray. And yet if it were not for me, you would not exist."

"I don't understand," Tessa whispered.

"You don't need to understand." Mortmain's temper was visibly fraying. "You need to do as I tell you. And I am telling you to Change. *Now.*"

It was like standing in front of the Dark Sisters again, frightened and alert, her heart pounding, being told to access a part of herself that terrified her. Being told to lose herself in that darkness, that nothingness between self and other. Perhaps it would be easy to do as he told her—to reach out and take the watch as commanded, to abandon herself in someone else's skin as she had done before, with no will or choice of her own.

She looked down, away from Mortmain's searing gaze, and saw something glittering on the fountain wall just behind her. A splash of water, she thought for a moment—but no. It was something else. She spoke then, almost without meaning to.

"No," she said.

Mortmain's eyes narrowed. "What was that?"

"I said no." Tessa felt as if she were outside herself somehow, watching herself face down Mortmain as if she were watching a stranger. "I won't do it. Not unless you tell me what you mean when you say you made me. Why am I like this? Why is it that you need my power so badly? What do you plan to force me to do for you? You are doing more than just building an army of monsters. I can see that. I'm not a fool like my brother."

Mortmain slid the watch back into his pocket. His face was an ugly mask of rage. "No," he said. "You are not a fool like your brother. He is a fool and a coward. You are a fool who has some courage. Though it will do you little good. And it is your friends who will suffer for it. While you watch." He turned on his heel then and strode toward the door.

Tessa bent down and seized up the object that had glittered behind her. It was the knife Jessamine had put there, the blade gleaming in the Sanctuary witchlight. "Stop," she cried. "Mr. Mortmain. *Stop.*"

He turned then, and saw her holding the knife. A look of disgusted amusement spread across his face. "Really, Miss Gray," he said. "Do you honestly think you can harm me with that? Did you think I came entirely unarmed?" He moved his jacket aside slightly, and she saw the butt of a pistol, gleaming at his belt.

"No," she said. "No, I don't think I can hurt you." She turned the knife around then, so that the hilt was away from her, the blade pointing directly at her own chest. "But if you take one more step toward that door, I promise you, I'll put this knife through my heart."

Repairing the mess Will had made of the carriage harnesses took Jem longer than he would have liked, and the moon was worryingly high in the sky by the time he rattled through the gates of the Institute and pulled Xanthos up at the foot of the steps.

Balios, untethered, was standing by the newel post at the foot of the stairs, looking exhausted. Will must have ridden like the devil, Jem thought, but at least he had arrived safely. It was a small bit of reassurance, considering that the doors of the Institute stood wide, sending a dart of horror through him. It was a sight that seemed so wrong that it was like looking at a face missing eyes or a sky with no stars. It was something that simply should not be.

Jem raised his voice. "Will?" he called. "Will, can you hear me?" When there was no answer, he leaped down from the driver's seat of the carriage and reached up to pull his jade-headed cane down after him. He held it lightly, balancing the weight. His wrists had begun to ache, which concerned him. Usually withdrawal from the demon powder began as pain in his joints, a dull ache that spread slowly until his whole body burned like fire. But he could not afford that pain now. There was Will to think about, and Tessa. He could not rid himself of the image of her on the steps, looking down at him as he spoke the ancient words. She had looked so worried, and the thought that she might have been worried about him had given him an unexpected pleasure.

He turned to start up the steps, and paused. Someone was already coming down them. More than one person—a crowd. They were backlit by the light of the Institute, and for a moment he blinked at them, seeing only silhouettes. A few seemed strangely misshapen.

"Jem!" The voice was high, desperate. Familiar.

Jessamine.

Galvanized, Jem darted up the stairs, and then paused. In front of him stood Nathaniel Gray, his clothes torn and spotted with blood. A makeshift bandage was wound around his head and was soaked with blood by his right temple. His expression was grim.

On either side of him moved clockwork automatons, like obedient servants. One flanked his right side, one his left. Behind were two more. One held a struggling Jessamine; the other a limp, half-insensible Sophie.

"Jem!" Jessamine shrieked. "Nate's a liar. He was helping

Mortmain all this time—Mortmain's the Magister, not de Quincey—"

Nathaniel whirled. "Silence her," he barked at the clockwork creature behind him. Its metal arms tightened around Jessamine, who choked and fell silent, her face white with pain. Her eyes darted toward the automaton on Nathaniel's right. Following her gaze, Jem saw that the creature held the familiar golden square of the Pyxis in its hands.

At the look on his face, Nate smiled. "None but a Shadowhunter can touch it," he said. "No *living creature*, that is. But an automaton is not alive."

"That is what all this was about?" Jem demanded, astounded. "The Pyxis? What possible use could it be to you?"

"My master wants demon energies, and demon energies he shall have," said Nate pompously. "Nor will he forget that I am the one who provided them for him."

Jem shook his head. "And what will he give you then? What did he give you to betray your sister? Thirty pieces of silver?"

Nate's face twisted, and for a moment Jem thought he could see through the blandly handsome mask to what was really underneath—something malignant and repellent that made Jem want to turn away and retch. "That thing," he said, "is not my sister."

"It is hard to believe, isn't it," said Jem, making no effort to hide his loathing, "that you and Tessa share anything at all, even a single drop of blood. She is so much finer than you."

Nathaniel's eyes narrowed. "She is not my concern. She belongs to Mortmain."

"I don't know what Mortmain has promised you," Jem said, "but I can promise you that if you hurt Jessamine or Sophie—

and if you take the Pyxis from these premises—the Clave will hunt you. And find you. And kill you."

Nathaniel shook his head slowly. "You don't understand," he said. "None of the Nephilim understand. The most you can offer is to let me live. But the Magister can promise me that *I won't ever die.*" He turned to the clockwork creature on his left, the one not holding the Pyxis. "Kill him," he said.

The automaton sprang toward Jem. It was faster by far than the creatures Jem had faced on Blackfriars Bridge. He barely had time to flip the catch that released the blade at the end of his cane and raise it, before the thing was on him. The creature squealed like a braking train when Jem drove the blade directly into its chest and sawed it from side to side, tearing the metal wide open. The creature spun away, spraying a Catherine wheel of red sparks.

Nate, caught by the spray of fire, yelled and jumped back, beating at the sparks burning holes into his clothes. Jem took the opportunity to leap up two of the steps and slam Nate across the back with the flat of his blade, knocking him to his knees. Nate twisted around to look for his clockwork protector, but it was staggering from side to side across the steps, sparks fountaining from its chest; it seemed evident that Jem had severed one of its central mechanisms. The automaton holding the Pyxis stood stock-still; clearly Nate was not its first priority.

"Drop them!" Nate cried to the clockwork creatures holding Sophie and Jessamine. "Kill the Shadowhunter! Kill him, do you hear?"

Jessamine and Sophie, released, tumbled to the ground, both gasping but clearly still alive. Jem's relief was short-lived, though, as the second pair of automatons lurched toward him, moving with incredible speed. He slashed out at one with his cane. It leaped back, out of range, and the other raised a hand—not a hand, really, more a square block of metal, its side edged with ragged teeth like a saw—

A yell came from behind Jem, and Henry charged past him, wielding a massive broadsword. He swung it hard, slashing through the automaton's raised arm and sending its hand flying. It skidded across the cobblestones, sparking and hissing, before bursting into flames.

"Jem!" It was Charlotte's voice, raised in warning. Jem spun, and saw the other automaton reaching for him from behind. He drove his blade into the creature's throat, sawing at the copper tubes inside, while Charlotte slashed at its knees with her whip. With a high whine, it collapsed to the ground, legs severed. Charlotte, her pale face set, brought the whip down again, while Jem turned to see that Henry, his ginger hair pasted to his forehead with sweat, was lowering his broadsword. The automaton he had attacked was now a heap of scrap metal on the ground.

In fact, bits of clockwork were scattered across the courtyard, some of it still burning, like a field of fallen stars. Jessamine and Sophie were clinging to each other; Jessamine supporting the other girl, whose throat was necklaced with dark bruises. Jessamine met Jem's eyes across the steps. He thought it might have been the first time she'd really ever looked like she was glad to see him.

"He's gone," she said. "Nathaniel. He vanished with that creature—and the Pyxis."

"I don't understand." Charlotte's bloodied face was a mask of shock. "Tessa's brother . . ."

"Everything he said to us was a lie," said Jessamine. "The whole business with sending you off after the vampires was a diversion."

"Dear God," said Charlotte. "So de Quincey wasn't lying—" She shook her head, as if to clear it of cobwebs. "When we reached his house in Chelsea, we found him there with just a few vampires, no more than six or seven—certainly not the hundred Nathaniel had warned about, and no clockwork creatures that anyone could find. Benedict slew de Quincey, but not before the vampire laughed at us for calling him the Magister—said we had let Mortmain make fools of us. *Mortmain.* And I'd thought he was just—just a mundane."

Henry sank down on the top step, his broad sword clanking. "This is a disaster."

"Will," Charlotte said dazedly, as if in a dream. "And Tessa. Where are they?"

"Tessa's in the Sanctuary. With Mortmain. Will—" Jessamine shook her head. "I didn't realize he was here."

"He's inside," Jem said, raising his gaze to the Institute. He remembered his poison-racked dream—the Institute in flames, a haze of smoke over London, and great clockwork creatures striding to and fro among the buildings like monstrous spiders. "He would have gone after Tessa."

Mortmain's face had drained of blood. "What are you doing?" he demanded, striding toward her.

Tessa set the tip of the blade to her chest and pushed. The pain was sharp, sudden. Blood bloomed on the bosom of her dress. "Don't come any closer."

Mortmain stopped, his face contorted with fury. "What

makes you think I care if you live or die, Miss Gray?"

"As you said, you made me," said Tessa. "For whatever reason, you desired that I exist. You valued me enough that you would not have wanted the Dark Sisters to harm me in any permanent way. Somehow, I am significant to you. Oh, not my *self*, of course. My power. That is what matters to you." She could feel blood, warm and wet, trickling down her skin, but the pain was nothing compared to her satisfaction at seeing the look of fear on Mortmain's face.

He spoke through gritted teeth. "What is it you want from me?"

"No. What is it you want from *me*? Tell me. Tell me why you created me. Tell me who my true parents are. Was my mother really my mother? My father, my father?"

Mortmain's smile was twisted. "You are asking the wrong questions, Miss Gray."

"Why am I . . . what I am, and Nate is only human? Why is he not like me?"

"Nathaniel is only your half brother. He is nothing more than a human being, and not a very good example of that. Do not mourn that you are not more like him."

"Then . . ." Tessa paused. Her heart was racing. "My mother could not have been a demon," she said quietly. "Or anything supernatural, because Aunt Harriet was her sister, and she was only human. So it must have been my father. My father was a demon?"

Mortmain grinned, a sudden ugly grin. "Put down the knife and I will give you your answers. Perhaps we can even summon up the thing that fathered you, if you are so desperate to meet him—or should I say 'it'?"

"Then I am a warlock," Tessa said. Her throat felt tight. "That is what you are saying."

Mortmain's pale eyes were full of scorn. "If you insist," he said, "I suppose that is the best word for what you are."

Tessa heard Magnus Bane's clear voice in her head: *Oh, you're a warlock. Depend on it.* And yet—

"I don't believe any of this," Tessa said. "My mother, she would never have—not with a demon."

"She had no idea." Mortmain sounded almost pitying. "No idea that she was being unfaithful to your father."

Tessa's stomach lurched. This was nothing she hadn't thought might be possible, nothing she hadn't wondered about. Still, to hear it spoken aloud was something else. "If the man I thought was my father, was not my father, and my true father was a demon," she said, "then why am I not marked like a warlock is marked?"

Mortmain's eyes sparkled with malevolence. "Indeed, why are you not? Perhaps because your mother had no idea what she was, any more than you do."

"What do you mean? My mother was human!"

Mortmain shook his head. "Miss Gray, you continue to ask the wrong questions. What you must understand is that much was planned so that you would someday come to be. The planning began even before me—and I carried it forward, knowing I was overseeing the creation of something unique in the world. Something unique that would belong to me. I knew that I would one day marry you, and you would be mine forever."

Tessa looked at him in horror. "But why? You don't *love* me. You don't know me. You didn't even know what I looked like! I could have been hideous!"

"It would not have mattered. You can appear as hideous or as beautiful as you like. The face you wear now is only one of a thousand possible faces. When will you learn that there is no *real* Tessa Gray?"

"Get out," Tessa said.

Mortmain looked at her with his pale eyes. "What did you say to me?"

"Get out. Leave the Institute. Take your monsters with you. Or I will stab myself in the heart."

For a moment he hesitated, his hands clenching and unclenching at his sides. This must have been what he was like when forced to make a lightning-swift business decision—to buy or to sell? To invest or to expand? He was a man used to sizing up the situation in an instant, Tessa thought. And she was only a girl. What chance did she have to outmaneuver him?

Slowly he shook his head. "I don't believe you'll do it. You may be a warlock, but you're still a young girl. A delicate female." He took a step toward her. "Violence is not in your nature."

Tessa gripped the handle of the knife tightly. She could feel everything—the hard slick surface under her fingers, the pain where it pierced her skin, the beat of her own heart. "Don't come a step closer," she said in a shaking voice, "or I'll do it. I'll drive the knife in."

The tremble in her voice seemed to give him conviction; his jaw firmed, and he moved toward her with a confident stride. "No, you won't."

Tessa heard Will's voice in her head. *She took poison rather than let herself be captured by the Romans. She was braver than any man.*

"Yes," she said. "I will."

Something in her face must have changed, for the confidence went from his expression and he lunged toward her, his arrogance gone, reaching desperately for the knife. Tessa spun away from Mortmain, turning to face the fountain. The last thing she saw was the silvery water splashing high above her as she drove the knife toward her chest.

Will was breathless as he approached the doors of the Sanctuary. He had fought two of the clockwork automatons in the stairwell and had thought he was done for, until the first one—having been run through several times with Thomas's sword—began to malfunction and pushed the second creature out a window before collapsing and crashing down the stairs in a whirlwind of crumpling metal and shooting sparks.

Will had cuts on his hands and arms from the creatures' jagged metal hides, but he had not slowed down for an *iratze.* He drew out his stele as he ran, and hit the Sanctuary doors at a dead run. He slashed the stele across the doors' surface, creating the fastest Open rune of his life.

The doors' lock slid back. Will took a split second of time to switch his stele for one of the seraph blades on his belt. "*Jerahmeel,*" he whispered, and as the blade blazed up with white fire, he kicked the Sanctuary doors open.

And froze in horror. Tessa lay crumpled by the fountain, whose water was stained with red. The front of her blue and white dress was a sheet of scarlet, and blood spread from beneath her body in a widening pool. A knife lay by her limp right hand, its hilt smeared with blood. Her eyes were closed.

Mortmain knelt by her side, his hand on her shoulder. He

glanced up as the doors burst open, and then staggered to his feet, backing away from Tessa's body. His hands were red with blood, and his shirt and jacket were stained with it.

"I . . . ," he began.

"You killed her," Will said. His voice sounded stupid to his own ears, and very far away. He saw again in his mind's eye the library of the house he had lived in with his family as a child. His own hands on the box, curious fingers unclasping the catch that held it closed. The library filled with the sound of screaming. The road to London, silver in the moonlight. The words that had gone through his head, over and over, as he'd walked away from everything he had ever known, forever. *I have lost everything. Lost everything.*

Everything.

"No." Mortmain shook his head. He was fiddling with something—a ring on his right hand, made of silver. "I didn't touch her. She did this to herself."

"You lie." Will moved forward, the shape of the seraph blade beneath his fingers comforting and familiar in a world that seemed to shift and change around him like the landscape of a dream. "Do you know what happens when I drive one of these into human flesh?" he rasped, raising Jerahmeel. "It will burn as it cuts you. You will die in agony, burning from the inside out."

"You think you grieve her loss, Will Herondale?" Mortmain's voice was full of torment. "Your grief is nothing to mine. Years of work—dreams—more than you could ever imagine, wasted."

"Then be comforted, for your pain will be of short duration," said Will, and he lunged forward, blade outstretched.

He felt it graze the cloth of Mortmain's jacket—and meet no further resistance. He stumbled forward, righted himself, and stared. Something clinked to the floor at his feet, a brass button. His blade must have severed it from Mortmain's jacket. It winked at him from the ground like a mocking eye.

Shocked, Will dropped the seraph blade. Jerahmeel fell to the floor, still burning. Mortmain was gone—entirely gone. He had vanished like a warlock might vanish, a warlock who had trained in the practice of magic for years. For a human, even a human with occult knowledge, to accomplish such a thing . . .

But that didn't matter; not now. Will could think of only one thing. *Tessa.* Half in dread, half in hope, he crossed the room to where she lay. The fountain made its wretched soothing noises as he knelt down and lifted her into his arms.

He had held her like this only once before, in the attic, the night they had burned de Quincey's town house. The memory of it had come to him, unbidden, often enough since. Now it was torture. Her dress was soaked in blood; so was her hair, and her face was streaked with it. Will had seen enough injuries to know that no one could lose blood like this and live.

"Tessa," he whispered. He crushed her against him; it didn't matter now what he did. He buried his face in the crook of her neck, where her throat met her shoulder. Her hair, already beginning to stiffen with blood, scratched his cheek. He could feel the beat of her pulse through her skin.

He froze. Her *pulse?* His heart leaped; he drew away, meaning to lower her to the ground, and found her looking at him with wide gray eyes.

"Will," she said. "Is it really you, Will?"

Relief crashed over him first, followed instantly by a boiling terror. To have Thomas die before his eyes, and now this, too. Or perhaps she could be saved? Though not with Marks. How were Downworlders healed? It was knowledge only the Silent Brothers had. "Bandages," Will said, half to himself. "I must get bandages."

He began to loosen his grip on her, but Tessa caught at his wrist with her hand. "Will, you must be careful. Mortmain—he's the Magister. He was here—"

Will felt as if he were choking. "Hush. Save your strength. Mortmain's gone. I must get help—"

"No." She tightened her grip on him. "No, you needn't do that, Will. *It's not my blood.*"

"What?" he said, staring. Perhaps she was delirious, he thought, but her grip and her voice were surprisingly strong for someone who should have been dead. "Whatever he did to you, Tessa—"

"*I* did it," she said in the same firm little voice. "I did it to myself, Will. It was the only way I knew to make him go away. He would never have left me here. Not if he'd thought I was alive."

"But—"

"I *Changed.* When the knife touched me, I Changed, just in that moment. It was something that Mortmain had said that gave me the idea—that sleight of hand is a simple trick and that no one ever expects it."

"I don't understand. The blood?"

She nodded, her small face alight with relief, with her pleasure in telling him what she had done. "There was a woman, once, that the Dark Sisters made me Change into, who had died of a gunshot wound, and when I Changed her blood poured all over me. Did I tell you that? I thought perhaps I had, but it doesn't matter—I remembered it, and I Changed into her, just for that moment, and the blood came, as it had before. I turned away from Mortmain so he couldn't see me change, and crumpled forward as if the knife had truly gone in—and indeed, the force of the Change, doing it so quickly, made me quite sincerely faint. The world went dark, and then I heard Mortmain calling my name. I knew I must have come back to myself, and I knew I must pretend to be dead. I fear he would have certainly found me out had you not arrived." She looked down at herself, and Will could have sworn there was a faintly smug tone to her voice as she said, "I tricked the Magister, Will! I would not have thought it possible—he was so confident of his superiority over me. But I recalled what you had said about Boadicea. If it had not been for your words, Will . . ."

She looked up at him with a smile. The smile broke what was left of his resistance—shattered it. He had let the walls down when he'd thought she was gone, and there was no time to build them back up. Helplessly he pulled her against him. For a moment she clung to him tightly, warm and alive in his arms. Her hair brushed his cheek. The color had come back into the world; he could breathe again, and for that moment he breathed her in—she smelled of salt, blood, tears, and Tessa.

When she drew back from his embrace, her eyes were shining. "I thought when I heard your voice that it was a dream," she said. "But you are real." Her eyes searched his face, and, as if satisfied at what they found there, she smiled. "You are real."

He opened his mouth. The words were there. He was about to say them when a jolt of terror went through him, the terror of someone who, wandering in a mist, pauses only to realize that they have stopped inches from the edge of a gaping abyss. The way she was looking at him—she could read what was in his eyes, he realized. It must have been written plainly there, like words on the page of a book. There had been no time, no chance, to hide it.

"Will," she whispered. "Say something, Will."

But there was nothing to say. There was only the emptiness, as there had been before her. As there always would be.

I have lost everything, Will thought. *Everything.*

20
Awful Wonder

Yet each man kills the thing he loves,
By each let this be heard,
Some do it with a bitter look,
Some with a flattering word,
The coward does it with a kiss,
The brave man with a sword!
—Oscar Wilde, "The Ballad of Reading Gaol"

The Marks that denoted mourning were red for Shadowhunters. The color of death was white.

Tessa had not known that, had not read it in the *Codex*, and so had been startled to see the five Shadowhunters of the Institute going out to the carriage dressed all in white like a wedding party as she and Sophie had watched from the windows of the library. Several members of the Enclave had been killed cleaning out de Quincey's vampire nest. In name the funeral was for them, though they were also burying Thomas and Agatha. Charlotte had explained that Nephilim burials were generally for Nephilim only, but an exception could be made for those who had died in the service of the Clave.

Sophie and Tessa, though, had been forbidden to go. The ceremony itself was still closed to them. Sophie had told Tessa it was better anyway, that she did not want to see Thomas burn and his ashes scattered in the Silent City. "I would rather remember him as he was," she'd said, "and Agatha, too."

The Enclave had left a guard behind them, several Shadowhunters who had volunteered to stay and watch over the Institute. It would be a long time, Tessa thought, before they ever left it unguarded again.

She had passed the time while they were gone reading in the window alcove—nothing to do with Nephilim or demons or Downworlders, but a copy of *A Tale of Two Cities* that she'd found on Charlotte's shelf of Dickens books. She had resolutely tried to force herself not to think about Mortmain, about Thomas and Agatha, about the things Mortmain had said to her in the Sanctuary—and most especially, not about Nathaniel or where he might be now. Any thought of her brother made her stomach tighten and the backs of her eyes prickle.

Nor was that all that was on her mind. Two days before, she had been forced to appear before the Clave in the library of the Institute. A man the others called the Inquisitor had questioned her about her time with Mortmain, over and over, alert for any changes in her story, until she was exhausted. They had questioned her about the watch he had wanted to give her, and whether she knew who it had belonged to, or what the initials

J. T. S. might stand for. She did not, and as he had taken it with him when he'd vanished, she pointed out, that was unlikely to change. They had questioned Will, too, about what Mortmain had said to him before he'd disappeared. Will had borne the inquest with surly impatience, to no one's surprise, and had eventually been dismissed with sanctions, for rudeness and insubordination.

The Inquisitor had even demanded that Tessa strip off her clothes, that she might be searched for a warlock's mark, but Charlotte had put a quick stop to that. When Tessa had at last been allowed to go, she had hurried out into the corridor after Will, but he had gone. It had been two days since then, and in that time she had hardly seen him, nor had they spoken beyond the occasional polite exchange of words in front of others. When she had looked at him, he had looked away. When she had left the room, hoping he would follow, he hadn't. It had been maddening.

She couldn't help but wonder if she was alone in thinking that something significant had passed between them there on the floor of the Sanctuary. She had woken out of a darkness more profound than any she had encountered during a Change before, to find Will holding her, the most plainly distraught look she could have envisioned on his face. And surely she couldn't have imagined the way he'd said her name, or looked at her?

No. She could not have imagined that. Will cared for her, she was sure of it. Yes, he had been rude to her almost since he had met her, but then, that happened in novels all the time. Look how rude Darcy had been to Elizabeth Bennet before he'd proposed, and really, quite rude during as well. And

Heathcliff was never anything but rude to Cathy. Though she had to admit that in *A Tale of Two Cities*, both Sydney Carton and Charles Darnay had been very kind to Lucie Manette. *And yet I have had the weakness, and have still the weakness, to wish you to know with what a sudden mastery you kindled me, heap of ashes that I am, into fire. . . .*

The troubling fact was that since that night in the Sanctuary, Will had neither looked at her nor said her name again. She thought she knew the reason for it—had guessed at it in the way Charlotte had looked at her, the way everyone was being so quiet around her. It was evident. The Shadowhunters were going to send her away.

And why shouldn't they? The Institute was for Nephilim, not Downworlders. She had brought death and destruction down on the place in the short time she'd been here; God only knew what would happen if she remained. Of course, she had nowhere to go, and no one to go *to*, but why should that matter to them? Covenant Law was Covenant Law; it could not be changed or broken. Maybe she would wind up living with Jessamine after all, in some town house in Belgravia. There were worse fates.

The rattle of carriage wheels on the cobblestones outside, signaling the return of the others from the Silent City, brought her out of her glum reverie. Sophie hurried down the stairs to greet them while Tessa watched through the window as they left the carriage, one by one.

Henry had his arm around Charlotte, who was leaning against him. Then came Jessamine, with pale flowers wound through her fair hair. Tessa would have admired how she looked, had she not held the sneaking suspicion that Jessamine probably enjoyed funerals because she knew she appeared especially pretty in white. Then came Jem, and then Will, looking like two chess pieces from some odd game, both Jem's silver hair and Will's tangled black locks set off by the pallor of their clothes. White Knight and Black Knight, Tessa thought as they went up the steps and vanished into the Institute.

She had only just set her book down on the seat beside her when the library door opened and Charlotte came in, still pulling off her gloves. Her hat was gone, and her brown hair stood out around her face in humidity-frizzed curls.

"I rather thought I'd find you in here," she said, crossing the room to sink into a chair opposite Tessa's window seat. She dropped the white kid gloves on the nearby table and sighed.

"Was it . . . ?" Tessa began.

"Awful? Yes. I hate funerals, though the Angel knows I've been to dozens." Charlotte paused and bit her lip. "I sound like Jessamine. Forget that I said that, Tessa. Sacrifice and death are part of the Shadowhunting life, and I have always accepted that."

"I know." It was very quiet. Tessa imagined she could feel her heart beating hollowly, like the tick of a grandfather clock in a great empty room.

"Tessa . . . ," Charlotte began.

"I already know what you are going to say, Charlotte, and it is quite all right."

Charlotte blinked. "You do? It . . . is?"

"You want me to go," Tessa said. "I know that you met with the Clave before the funeral. Jem told me. I can't imagine they would think you should allow me to remain. After all the trouble and the dreadfulness I've brought down on you. Nate. Thomas and Agatha—"

"The Clave does not care about Thomas and Agatha."

"The Pyxis, then."

"Yes," Charlotte said slowly. "Tessa, I think you have entirely the wrong idea. I didn't come to ask you to leave; I came to ask you to stay."

"To stay?" The words seemed disconnected from any meaning. Surely Charlotte could not have meant what she'd said. "But the Clave . . . They must be angry. . . ."

"They *are* angry," said Charlotte. "With Henry and me. We were utterly taken in by Mortmain. He used us as his instruments, and we allowed it. I was so proud of the clever and handy way I had taken charge of him that I never stopped to think that perhaps he was the one taking charge. I never stopped to think that not a single living creature other than Mortmain and your brother had ever confirmed that de Quincey was the Magister. All the other evidence was circumstantial, and yet I let myself be convinced."

"It was very convincing." Tessa hastened to reassure Charlotte. "The seal we found on Miranda's body. The creatures on the bridge."

Charlotte made a bitter sound. "All characters in a play that Mortmain put on for our benefit. Do you know that, search as we have, we have not been able to find a scrap of evidence as to what other Downworlders controlled the Pandemonium Club? None of the mundane members have a clue, and since we destroyed de Quincey's clan, the Downworlders are more distrustful of us than ever."

"But it's only been a few days. It took Will six weeks to find the Dark Sisters. If you keep looking . . ."

"We don't have that much time. If what Nathaniel said

to Jem was true, and Mortmain plans to use the demon energies inside the Pyxis to animate his clockwork mannequins, we have only the time it will take him to learn to open the box." She shrugged a little. "Of course, the Clave believes that is impossible. The Pyxis can be opened only with runes, and only a Shadowhunter can draw them. But then again, only a Shadowhunter ought to have been able to gain access to the Institute."

"Mortmain is very clever."

"Yes." Charlotte's hands were tightly knotted in her lap. "Did you know that Henry is the one who told Mortmain about the Pyxis? What it was called, and what it did?"

"No . . ." Tessa's reassuring words had deserted her.

"You couldn't. No one knows that. Only I do, and Henry. He wants me to tell the Clave, but I won't. They already treat him so badly, and I . . ." Charlotte's voice shook, but her small face was set. "The Clave is convening a tribunal. My conduct, and Henry's, will be examined and voted upon. It is possible that we will lose the Institute."

Tessa was appalled. "But you're wonderful at running the Institute! The way you keep everything organized and in place, the way you manage it all."

Charlotte's eyes were wet. "Thank you, Tessa. The fact is that Benedict Lightwood has always wanted the place of head of the Institute for himself, or for his son. The Lightwoods have a great deal of family pride and despise taking orders. If not for the fact that Consul Wayland himself named my husband and me as the successors to my father, I am sure Benedict *would* be in charge. All I have ever wanted is to run the Institute, Tessa. I will do anything to keep it. If you would only help me—"

"Me? But what can I do? I know nothing of Shadowhunter politics."

"The alliances we forge with Downworlders are some of our most priceless assets, Tessa. Part of the reason I am still where I am is my affiliation with warlocks such as Magnus Bane and vampires such as Camille Belcourt. And you, you are a precious commodity. What you can do has already helped the Enclave once; the aid you could offer us in future could be incalculable. And if you are known to be a firm ally of mine, it will only help me."

Tessa held her breath. In her mind she saw Will—Will as he had looked in the Sanctuary—but, almost to her surprise, he was not all that her thoughts contained. There was Jem, with his kindness and gentle hands; and Henry making her laugh with his odd clothes and funny inventions; and even Jessamine, with her peculiar fierceness and occasional surprising bravery.

"But the Law," she said in a small voice.

"There is no Law against you remaining here as our guest," said Charlotte. "I have searched the archives and have found nothing that would prevent you from staying, if you consented. So do you consent, Tessa? Will you stay?"

Tessa dashed up the steps to the attic; for the first time in what felt like forever, her heart was almost light. The attic itself was much as she remembered, the high small windows letting in a little sunset light, for it was almost twilight now. There was a tipped-over pail on the floor; she maneuvered around it on her way to the narrow steps that led up to the roof.

He is often to be found there when he is troubled, Charlotte had said. *And I have rarely seen Will so troubled. The loss of*

Thomas and Agatha has been more difficult for him than I foresaw.

The steps ended in a square overhead door, hinged on one side. Tessa pushed the trapdoor open, and climbed out onto the Institute's roof.

Straightening, she looked around. She stood in the wide, flat center of the roof, which was surrounded by a waist-high wrought iron railing. The bars of the railing ended in finials shaped like sharpened fleur-de-lis. At the far end of the roof stood Will, leaning against the railing. He did not turn, even as the trapdoor swung shut behind her and she took a step forward, rubbing her scratched palms against the fabric of her dress.

"Will," she said.

He did not move. The sun had begun to set in a torrent of fire. Across the Thames, factory smokestacks belched smoke that trailed dark fingers across the red sky. Will was leaning on the railing as if he were exhausted, as if he intended to fall forward across the javelin-sharp finials and end it all. He gave no sign of hearing Tessa as she approached and moved to stand beside him. From here the steeply pitched roof fell away to a dizzying view of the cobblestones below.

"Will," she said again. "What are you doing?"

He did not look at her. He was staring out at the city, a black outline against the reddened sky. The dome of St. Paul's shone through the mucky air, and the Thames ran like dark strong tea below it, bracketed here and there with the black lines of bridges. Dark shapes moved by the river's edge—mudlarks, searching through the filth thrown up by the water, hoping to find something valuable to sell.

"I remember now," Will said without looking at her, "what it was I was trying to remember the other day. It was Blake. '*And I behold London, a Human awful wonder of God.*'" He stared out over the landscape. "Milton thought Hell was a city, you know. I think maybe he had it half-right. Perhaps London is just Hell's entrance, and we are the damned souls refusing to pass through, fearing that what we will find on the other side will be worse than the horror we already know."

"Will." Tessa was bewildered. "Will, what is it, what's wrong?"

He gripped the railing with both hands, his fingers whitening. His hands were covered with cuts and scratches, his knuckles scraped red and black. There were bruises on his face, too, darkening the line of his jaw, purpling the skin under his eye. His lower lip was split and swollen, and he had done nothing to heal any of it. She could not imagine why.

"I should have known," he said. "That it was a trick. That Mortmain was lying when he came here. Charlotte so often vaunts my skill at tactics, but a good tactician is not blindly trusting. I was a fool."

"Charlotte believes it's her fault. Henry believes it's his fault. I believe it's *my* fault," Tessa said impatiently. "We can't all have the luxury of blaming ourselves, now, can we?"

"Your fault?" Will sounded puzzled. "Because Mortmain is obsessed with you? That hardly seems—"

"For bringing Nathaniel here," Tessa said. Just saying it out loud made her feel as if her chest were being squeezed. "For urging you to trust him."

"You loved him," said Will. "He was your brother."

"He still is," Tessa said. "And I still love him. But I know what he is. I always did know what he was. I just didn't want to believe it. I suppose we all lie to ourselves sometimes."

"Yes." Will sounded tight and distant. "I suppose we do."

Quickly Tessa said, "I came up here because I have good news, Will. Won't you let me tell you what it is?"

"Tell me." His voice was dead.

"Charlotte says I can stay here," Tessa said. "At the Institute."

Will said nothing.

"She said there's no Law against it," Tessa went on, a little bewildered now. "So I won't need to leave."

"Charlotte would never have made you leave, Tessa. She cannot bear to abandon even a fly caught in a spider's web. She would not have abandoned you." There was no life in Will's voice and no feeling. He was simply stating a fact.

"I thought . . ." Tessa's elation was fading quickly. "That you would be at least a little pleased. I thought we were becoming friends." She saw the line of his throat move as he swallowed, hard, his hands tensing again on the rail. "As a friend," she went on, her voice dropping, "I have come to admire you, Will. To care for you." She reached out, meaning to touch his hand, but she drew back, startled by the tension in his posture, the whiteness of the knuckles that gripped the metal railing. The red mourning Marks stood out, scarlet against the whitened skin, as if they had been cut there with knives. "I thought perhaps . . ."

At last Will turned to look directly at her. Tessa was shocked at the expression on his face. The shadows under his eyes were so dark, they looked hollow.

She stood and stared at him, willing him to say what the hero in a book would say now, at this moment. *Tessa, my feel-*

ings for you have grown beyond mere feelings of friendship. They are so much more rare and precious than that. . . .

"Come here," he said instead. There was nothing welcoming in his voice, or in the way he stood. Tessa fought back her instinct to shy away, and moved toward him, close enough for him to touch her. He reached out his hands and touched her hair lightly, brushing back the stray curls around her face. "Tess."

She looked up at him. His eyes were the same color as the smoke-stained sky; even bruised, his face was beautiful. She wanted to be touching him, wanted it in some inchoate, instinctive way she could neither explain nor control. When he bent to kiss her, it was all she could do to hold herself back until his lips met hers. His mouth brushed hers and she tasted salt on him, the tang of bruised and tender skin where his lip was cut. He took her by the shoulders and pulled her closer to him, his fingers knotting in the fabric of her dress. Even more than in the attic, she felt caught in the eddy of a powerful wave that threatened to pull her over and under, to crush and break her, to wear her down to softness as the sea might wear down a piece of glass.

She reached to lay her hands on his shoulders, and he drew back, looking down at her, breathing very hard. His eyes were bright, his lips red and swollen now from kissing as well as injuries.

"Perhaps," he said, "we should discuss our arrangements, then."

Tessa, still feeling as if she were drowning, whispered, "Arrangements?"

"If you are going to be staying," he said, "it would be to our advantage to be discreet. It might perhaps be better to use your room. Jem tends to come in and out of mine as if he lives in the place, and he might be puzzled to find the door locked. Your quarters, on the other hand—"

"Use my room?" she echoed. "Use it for what?"

Will's mouth quirked up at the corner; Tessa, who had been thinking about how beautifully shaped his lips were, took a moment to realize with a sense of distant surprise that the smile was a very cold one. "You cannot pretend you don't know. . . . You are not entirely ignorant of the world, I think, Tessa. Not with that brother of yours."

"Will." The warmth was going out of Tessa like the sea drawing back from the land; she felt cold, despite the summer air. "I am not like my brother."

"You care for me," Will said. His voice was cool and sure. "And you know that I admire you, the way that all women know when a man admires them. Now you have come to tell me you will be here, available to me, for as long as I might wish it. I am offering you what I thought you wanted."

"You cannot mean that."

"And you cannot have imagined I meant anything more," Will said. "There is no future for a Shadowhunter who dallies with warlocks. One might befriend them, employ them, but not . . ."

"Marry them?" Tessa said. There was a clear picture in her head of the sea. It had drawn back entirely from the shore, and she could see the small creatures it had left gasping in its wake, flapping and dying on the bare sand.

"How forward." Will smirked; she wanted to slap the expression off his face. "What did you really expect, Tessa?"

"I did not expect you to insult me." Tessa's voice threatened to shake; somehow, she kept it firm.

"It cannot be the unwanted consequences of a dalliance that concern you," Will mused. "Since warlocks are unable to have children—"

"What?" Tessa stepped back as if he had pushed her. The ground felt unsteady under her feet.

Will looked at her. The sun was nearly completely gone from the sky. In the near darkness the bones of his face looked prominent and the lines at the corners of his mouth were as harsh as if he were racked by physical pain. But his voice when he spoke was even. "You didn't know that? I thought someone would have told you."

"No," Tessa said softly. "No one told me."

His gaze was steady. "If you are not interested in my offer . . ."

"Stop," she said. This moment, she thought, was like the edge of a broken bit of glass, clear and sharp and painful. "Jem says you lie to make yourself look bad," she said. "And perhaps that is true, or perhaps he simply wishes to believe that about you. But there is no reason or excuse for cruelty like this."

For a moment he looked actually unnerved, as if she had truly startled him. The expression was gone in an instant, like the shifting shape of a cloud. "Then there is nothing more for me to say, is there?"

Without another word she spun on her heel and walked away from him, toward the steps that led back down into the Institute. She did not turn to see him looking after her, a still black silhouette against the last embers of the burning sky.

* * *

Lilith's Children, known also by the name warlocks, are, in the manner of mules and other crossbreeds, sterile. They cannot produce offspring. No exceptions to this rule have been noted. . . .

Tessa looked up from the *Codex* and stared, unseeing, out the window of the music room, though it was too dark outside for much of a view. She had taken refuge here, not wanting to return to her own room, where she would eventually be discovered moping by Sophie or, worse, Charlotte. The thin layer of dust over everything in this room reassured her that she was much less likely to be found here.

She wondered how she had missed this fact about warlocks before. To be fair, it was not in the *Codex*'s section on warlocks, but rather in the later section on Downworld crossbreeds such as half faeries and half werewolves. There were no half warlocks, apparently. Warlocks could not have children. Will hadn't been lying to hurt her; he'd been telling the truth. Which seemed worse, in a way. He would have known that his words weren't a light blow, easily resolved.

Perhaps he had been correct. What else had she really thought would happen? Will was Will, and she should not have expected him to be anything else. Sophie had warned her, and still she hadn't listened. She knew what Aunt Harriet would have said about girls who didn't listen to good advice.

A faint rustling sound broke into her brown study. She turned, and at first saw nothing. The only light in the room came from a single witchlight sconce. Its flickering light played over the shape of the piano, the curving dark mass of the harp covered with a heavy drop cloth. As she stared, two bright points of light resolved themselves, close to the floor, an odd green-yellow color. They were moving toward her, both at the same pace, like twin will-o'-the-wisps.

Tessa expelled her held breath suddenly. *Of course.* She leaned forward. "Here, kitty." She made a coaxing noise. "Here, kitty, kitty!"

The cat's answering meow was lost in the noise of the door opening. Light streamed into the room, and for a moment the figure in the doorway was just a shadow. "Tessa? Tessa, is that you?"

Tessa knew the voice immediately—it was so near to the first thing he had ever said to her, the night she had walked into his room: *Will? Will, is that you?*

"Jem," she said resignedly. "Yes, it's me. Your cat seems to have wandered in here."

"I can't say that I'm surprised." Jem sounded amused. She could see him clearly now as he came into the room; witchlight from the corridor flooded in, and even the cat was clearly visible, sitting on the floor and washing its face with a paw. It looked angry, the way Persian cats always did. "He seems to be a bit of a gadabout. It's as if he demands to be introduced to everyone—" Jem broke off then, his eyes on Tessa's face. "What's wrong?"

Tessa was so taken off guard that she stammered. "W-why would you ask me that?"

"I can see it on your face. Something's happened." He sat down on the piano stool opposite her. "Charlotte told me the good news," he said as the cat rose to its feet and slunk across the room to him. "Or at least, I thought it was good news. Are you not pleased?"

"Of course I'm pleased."

"Hm." Jem looked unconvinced. Bending down, he held out his hand to the cat, who rubbed its head against the back of his fingers. "Good cat, Church."

"Church? Is that the cat's name?" Tessa was amused despite herself. "Goodness, didn't it used to be one of Mrs. Dark's familiars or some such thing? Perhaps Church isn't the best name for it!"

"*He*," Jem corrected with mock severity, "was not a familiar but a poor creature she planned to sacrifice as part of her necromantic spell casting. And Charlotte's been saying that we ought to keep him because it's good luck to have a cat in a church. So we started calling him "the church cat," and from that . . ." He shrugged. "Church. And if the name helps keep him out of trouble, so much the better."

"I do believe he's looking at me in a superior manner."

"Probably. Cats think they're superior to everyone." Jem scratched Church behind the ears. "What are you reading?"

Tessa showed him the *Codex*. "Will gave it to me. . . ."

Jem reached out and took it from her, with such deftness that Tessa had no time to draw her hand back. It was still open to the page she'd been studying. Jem glanced down at it, and then back up at her, his expression changing. "Did you not know this?"

She shook her head. "It is not so much that I dreamed of having children," she said. "I had not thought so far ahead in my life. It's more that this seems yet another thing that separates me from humanity. That makes me a monster. Something set apart."

Jem was silent for a long moment, his long fingers stroking the gray cat's fur. "Perhaps," he said, "it is not such a bad thing to be set apart." He leaned forward. "Tessa, you know that although it seems you are a warlock, you have an ability we have never seen before. You carry no warlock's mark. With so much about you uncertain, you cannot allow this one piece of information to drive you to despair."

"I am not despairing," Tessa said. "It's just— I have been lying awake these past few nights. Thinking about my parents. I barely remember them, you see. And yet I cannot help but wonder. Mortmain said my mother did not know that my father was a demon, but was he lying? He said she did not know what *she* was, but what does that mean? Did she ever know what I was, that I was not human? Is that why they left London as they did, so secretively, under cover of darkness? If I am the result of something—something hideous—that was done to my mother without her knowing, then how could she ever have loved me?"

"They hid you from Mortmain," said Jem. "They must have known he wanted you. All those years he searched for you, and they kept you safe—first your parents, then your aunt. That is not the act of an unloving family." His gaze was intent on her face. "Tessa, I do not want to make you promises I cannot keep, but if you truly wish to know the truth about your past, we can seek it out. After all you have done for us, we owe you that much. If there are secrets to be learned about how you came to be what you are, we can learn them, if that is what you desire."

"Yes. That is what I want."

"You may not," said Jem, "like what you discover."

"It is better to know the truth." Tessa was surprised by the conviction in her own voice. "I know the truth about Nate, now, and painful as it is, it is better than being lied to. It is better than going on loving someone who cannot love me back. Better than wasting all that feeling." Her voice shook.

"I think he did," said Jem, "and does love you, in his way, but you cannot concern yourself with that. It is as great a thing to love as it is to be loved. Love is not something that can be wasted."

"It is hard. That is all." Tessa knew she was being self-pitying, but she could not seem to shake it off. "To be so alone."

Jem leaned forward and looked at her. The red Marks stood out like fire on his pale skin, making her think of the patterns that traced the edges of the Silent Brothers' robes. "My parents, like yours, are dead. So are Will's, and Jessie's, and even Henry's and Charlotte's. I am not sure there is anyone in the Institute who is not an orphan. Otherwise we would not be here."

Tessa opened her mouth, and then closed it again. "I know," she said. "I am sorry. I was being perfectly selfish not to think—"

He held up a slender hand. "I am not blaming you," he said. "Perhaps you are here because you are otherwise alone, but so am I. So is Will. So is Jessamine. And even, to an extent, Charlotte and Henry. Where else could Henry have his laboratory? Where else would Charlotte be allowed to put her brilliant mind to work the way she can here? And though Jessamine pretends to hate everything, and Will would never admit to needing anything, they have both made homes for themselves here. In a way, we are not here just because we have nowhere else; we need nowhere else, because we have the Institute, and those who are in it are our family."

"But not *my* family."

"They could be," said Jem. "When I first came here, I was twelve years old. It most decidedly did not feel like home to me then. I saw only how London was not like Shanghai, and I was homesick. So Will went down to a shop in the East End and bought me this." He drew out the chain that hung around his neck, and Tessa saw that the flash of green she'd noticed before was a green stone pendant in the shape of a closed hand. "I think he liked it because it reminded him of a fist. But it was jade, and he knew jade came from China, so he brought it back to me and I hung it on a chain to wear it. I still wear it."

The mention of Will made Tessa's heart contract. "I suppose it is good to know he can be kind sometimes."

Jem looked at her with keen silver eyes. "When I came in—that look on your face—it wasn't just because of what you read in the *Codex*, was it? It was about Will. What did he say to you?"

Tessa hesitated. "He made it very clear that he didn't want me here," she said at last. "That my remaining at the Institute is not the happy chance I thought it was. Not in his view."

"And after I just finished telling you why you should consider him family," Jem said, a bit ruefully. "No wonder you looked as if I'd just told you something awful had happened."

"I'm sorry," Tessa whispered.

"Don't be. It's Will who ought to be sorry." Jem's eyes darkened. "We shall throw him out onto the streets," he proclaimed. "I promise you he'll be gone by morning."

Tessa started and sat upright. "Oh—no, you can't mean that—"

He grinned. "Of course I don't. But you felt better for a moment there, didn't you?"

"It was like a beautiful dream," Tessa said gravely, but she smiled when she said it, which surprised her.

"Will is . . . difficult," Jem said. "But family is difficult. If I didn't think the Institute was the best place for you, Tessa, I would not say that it was. And one can build one's own family. I know you feel inhuman, and as if you are set apart, away from life and love, but . . ." His voice cracked a little, the first time Tessa had heard him sound unsure. He cleared his throat. "I promise you, the right man won't care."

Before Tessa could reply, there was a sharp tapping against the glass of the window. She looked toward Jem, who shrugged. He heard it too. Crossing the room, she saw that indeed there was something outside—a dark winged shape, like a small bird struggling to get inside. She tried to lift the window sash, but it seemed stuck.

She turned, but Jem had already appeared at her side, and he pushed the window open. As the dark shape fluttered inside, it flew straight for Tessa. She raised her hands and caught it out of the air, feeling the sharp metal wings flutter against her palms. As she held it, they closed, and its eyes closed too. Once more it held its metal sword quietly, as if waiting to be wakened again. *Tick-tick* went its clockwork heart against her fingers.

Jem turned from the open window, the wind ruffling his hair. In the yellow light, it shone like white gold. "What is it?"

Tessa smiled. "My angel," she said.

Epilogue

It had grown late, and Magnus Bane's eyelids were drooping with exhaustion. He set Horace's *Odes* down upon the end table and gazed thoughtfully at the rain-streaked windows that looked out onto the square.

This was Camille's house, but tonight she was not in it; it seemed to Magnus unlikely that she would be home again for many more nights, if not for longer. She had left the city after that disastrous night at de Quincey's, and though he had sent her a message telling her it was safe to return, he doubted she would. He could not help but wonder if, now that she had exacted revenge on her vampire clan, she would still desire his company. Perhaps he had only ever been something to throw in de Quincey's face.

He could always depart—pack up and go, leave all this borrowed luxury behind him. This house, the servants, the books, even his clothes, were hers; he had come to London with nothing. It wasn't as if Magnus couldn't earn his own money. He had been quite wealthy in the past, on occasion, though having too much money usually bored him. But remaining here, however annoying, was still the most likely path to seeing Camille again.

A knock on the door broke him out of his reverie, and he turned to see Archer, the footman, standing in the doorway. Archer had been Camille's subjugate for years, and regarded Magnus with loathing, likely because he felt that a liaison with a warlock wasn't the right sort of attachment for his beloved mistress.

"There's someone to see you, sir." Archer lingered over the word "sir" just long enough for it to be insulting.

"At this hour? Who is it?"

"One of the Nephilim." A faint distaste colored Archer's words. "He says his business with you is urgent."

So it wasn't Charlotte, the only one of the London Nephilim that Magnus might have expected to see. For several days now he had been assisting the Enclave, watching while they questioned terrified mundanes who had been members of the Pandemonium Club, and using magic to remove the mundanes' memories of the ordeal when it was over. An unpleasant job, but the Clave always paid well, and it was wise to remain in their favor.

"He is," Archer added, with deepening distaste, "also very wet."

"Wet?"

"It is raining, sir, and the gentleman is not wearing a hat. I offered to dry his clothes, but he declined."

"Very well. Send him in."

Archer's lips thinned. "He is waiting for you in the parlor. I thought he might wish to warm himself by the fire."

Magnus sighed inwardly. He could, of course, demand that Archer show the guest into the library, a room he preferred. But it seemed like a great deal of effort for little return, and besides, if he did, the footman would sulk for the next three days. "Very well."

Gratified, Archer melted away, leaving Magnus to make his own way to the parlor. The door was closed, but he could see from the light that gleamed beneath the door that there was a fire, and light, inside the room. He pushed the door open.

The parlor had been Camille's favorite room and bore her decorating touches. The walls were painted a lush burgundy, the rosewood furniture imported from China. The windows that otherwise would have looked out onto the square were covered with velvet curtains that hung straight from floor to ceiling, blocking out any light. Someone was standing in front of the fireplace, his hands behind his back—a slender someone with dark hair. When he turned, Magnus recognized him immediately.

Will Herondale.

He was, as Archer had said, wet, in the manner of someone who did not care one way or another whether it rained on him or not. His clothes were drenched, his hair hanging in his eyes. Water streaked his face like tears.

"William," Magnus said, honestly surprised. "What on earth are you doing here? Has something happened at the Institute?"

"No." Will's voice sounded as if he were choking. "I'm here on my own account. I need your help. There is—there is absolutely no one else that I can ask."

"Really." Magnus looked at the boy more closely. Will was beautiful; Magnus had been in love many times throughout the years, and normally beauty of any sort moved him, but Will's never had. There was something dark about the boy, something hidden and strange that was hard to admire. He seemed to show nothing real to the world. Yet now, under his dripping black hair, he was as white as parchment, his hands clenched at his sides so tightly that they were shaking. It seemed clear that some terrible turmoil was ripping him apart from the inside out.

Magnus reached behind himself and locked the parlor door. "Very well," he said. "Why don't you tell me what the problem is?"

A NOTE ON TESSA'S LONDON

The London of *Clockwork Angel* is, as much as I could make it, an admixture of the real and the unreal, the famous and the forgotten. The geography of real Victorian London is preserved as much as possible, but there were times that wasn't possible. For those wondering about the Institute: There was indeed a church called All-Hallows-the-Less that burned in the Great Fire of London in 1666; it was located, however, in Upper Thames Street, not where I have placed it, just off Fleet Street. Those familiar with London will recognize the location of the Institute, and the shape of its spire, as that of the famous St. Bride's Church, beloved of newspapermen and journalists, which goes unmentioned in *Clockwork* as the Institute has taken its place. There is no Carleton Square in reality, though there is a Carlton Square; Blackfriars Bridge, Hyde Park, the Strand—even Gunther's ice cream shop—all existed and are presented to the best of my researching abilities. Sometimes I think all cities have a shadow self, where the memory of great events and great places lingers after those places themselves are gone. To that end, there *was* a Devil Tavern on Fleet Street and Chancery, where Samuel Pepys and Dr. Samuel Johnson drank, but though it was demolished in 1787, I like to think Will can visit its shadow self in 1878.

A NOTE ON THE POETRY

The poetry quotations at the beginning of each chapter are by and large taken from poetry Tessa would be familiar with, either of her era, or a staple from before it. The exceptions are the poems by Wilde and Kipling—still Victorian poets, but dating later than the 1870s—and the poem by Elka Cloke at the beginning of the volume, "Thames River Song," which was written specifically for this book. A longer version of the poem can be found at the author's website: ElkaCloke.com.

Acknowledgments

Much thanks for familial support from my mother and father, as well as Jim Hill and Kate Connor; Nao, Tim, David, and Ben; Melanie, Jonathan, and Helen Lewis; Florence and Joyce. To those who read and critiqued and pointed out anachronisms—Clary, Eve Sinaiko, Sarah Smith, Delia Sherman, Holly Black, Sarah Rees Brennan, Justine Larbalestier—tons of thanks. And thanks to those whose smiling faces and snarky remarks keep me going another day: Elka Cloke, Holly Black, Robin Wasserman, Maureen Johnson, Libba Bray, and Sarah Rees Brennan. Thanks to Margie Longoria for her support of Project Book Babe. Thanks to Lisa Gold: Research Maven (http://lisagoldresearch.wordpress.com) for her help in digging up hard-to-find primary sources. My always-gratitude to my agent, Barry Goldblatt; my editor, Karen Wojtyla; and the teams at Simon & Schuster and Walker Books for making it all happen. And lastly, my thanks to Josh, who did a lot of laundry while I was doing revisions on this book, and only complained some of the time.